THE LOST DRESSMAKER OF PARIS

W0008582

SUZANNE FORTIN

embla
books

First published in Great Britain in 2023 by

Bonnier Books UK Limited
4th Floor, Victoria House, Bloomsbury Square, London, WC1B 4DA
Owned by Bonnier Books
Sveavägen 56, Stockholm, Sweden

A CIP catalogue record for this book is available from the British Library.

ISBN: 9781471415647

This book is typeset using Atomik ePublisher

Embla Books is an imprint of Bonnier Books UK
www.bonnierbooks.co.uk

In memory of my nan, Emily Louise Morris.

Chapter 1

Nathalie, Paris, August 1942

I unfolded the thin brown tissue paper, spreading it out across the fabric, smoothing it with my hand to ensure the pattern piece lay flat on the silk, before pinning it in place, just as Papa had shown me. Théodule Leroux was one of the most sought-after tailors in Paris. His list of customers was a glossary of the most important, rich, and famous people who sought not just the skills Papa offered, but the prestige that came with wearing one of his pieces.

I eyed the red silk spread out on the workbench. It had once been a long, flowing evening gown I had worn to a party several years ago – before the Germans came. There was definitely no cause to celebrate these days and, as with many of my other dresses, I was preparing to repurpose the garment into several small items suitable for a young child. I would donate the repurposed clothes to those in need. Two years on from when Paris fell, times were difficult. The ordinary Frenchwoman couldn't afford to buy new clothes, and more and more housewives were turning their hand to making their own garments or repurposing their existing ones. My dressmaking skills had been called upon numerous times as word spread that Théodule Leroux's daughter, Nathalie, was happy to help and to advise on any alterations.

I loved the freedom that dress designing gave me. It was an antidote to the lack of physical freedom imposed by the war. One day, I hoped to open my own fashion house, where my many paper designs would be brought to life in silks, velvets, cottons, organza.

I hummed to myself as I spread another pattern piece over the silk. Here in the cutting room of Papa's shop, I could pretend the war raging in Europe and the German occupation of my beloved city weren't happening. Here I could indulge myself in dreams of fashion shows and lavish parties – Paris, London, Milan, and even America, where the stars of Hollywood would clamour to wear my gowns.

The scissors made a satisfying crunch against the wooden workbench as they sliced through the fabric. Papa's instructions to let the scissors do the work filtered through my mind as I followed the edge of the paper pattern and glided the blade up the long side seam.

'*Bonjour*, Nathalie.'

I looked up as Papa came into the room. He smiled and kissed me twice on each cheek. 'I didn't see you at breakfast this morning.'

'I wanted to come here early and finish cutting out these pieces.'

'*Très bien*. Very good.' Papa picked up the drawing I had done of what I intended the children's dresses to look like. 'You have made good use of the fabric.' I couldn't help the small swell of pride that rose in my heart at his praise.

'Ah, there you are.' Edgar, my brother, appeared in the doorway. 'We should open the shop,' he added, turning to Papa.

Papa checked his pocket watch. 'Indeed, we should.' He headed through to the shop, the keys jangling in his hand as he went.

I began gathering up the pattern pieces. During the day, I worked for Papa, repairing shirts, fastening buttons, and hand finishing some of the more delicate and expensive items the Germans were so fond of. Much as I hated the thought of assisting the officers, many of our regular French clientele had disappeared.

Edgar came into the room and began to help me to clear the workbench.

'Where have you been this morning?' I asked in a whisper.

'I don't know what you mean,' he replied, trying to look innocent but failing.

'When I came down here this morning, you weren't in your room,' I said. 'I take it you sneaked back just in time for breakfast?'

I had long suspected my brother had connections with the French Resistance and was possibly even an active member. As a child, he had suffered from TB and this instantly ruled him out of joining the French army. So far, he had been allowed to stay in Paris and work in the family tailoring business, mostly because of connections Papa had with people in authority. What that meant in real terms was Théodule Leroux had associates who were officially collaborating with the Germans under the rule of Pétain.

'I met some friends,' said Edgar.

'Why don't you just admit to me your friends are part of the Resistance,' I whispered, leaning over the workbench to him.

'Why would I admit that for you to repeat it to your boyfriend?' He gave a raise of his eyebrows.

'You think Alphonse can't be trusted? I don't know whether to be offended,' I said, surprised at the suggestion. I had been friends with Alphonse since we were at school together, although at twenty-three, he was two years older than me and we had slipped into becoming boyfriend and girlfriend just before the war broke out. Yes, Alphonse was a police officer, but I didn't feel he was sympathetic towards the German regime, not enough to betray any secrets, anyway.

'You shouldn't be offended but you shouldn't be blind either,' said Edgar, folding a piece of fabric and dropping it onto the pile along with the others.

'Are you suggesting Alphonse is involved?' I frowned, finding it hard to take the accusation seriously.

'I have not heard his name mentioned. Not yet anyway,' replied Edgar. 'But you cannot be too careful. You cannot deny the police help the Germans.'

'But they have to help.'

'Do they?' Edgar held my gaze. 'There are two ways of helping. One benefits the Germans and the other benefits Paris. They could use their position to pass on information to help fight against the regime, but they choose not to.'

The sound of Papa calling from the shop brought the conversation to a halt. 'You could get yourself arrested for talking like that,' I warned.

Edgar stood in front of the doorway. 'I need to tell you something.'

He frowned and glanced down at the ground. 'What is it?' I could tell, whatever it was, it was troubling him greatly. I hated that at just twenty years old, he had the worry and weight on his shoulders of someone twice his age.

'I may not be here for much longer,' he said.

'What are you talking about?' I knew Papa was waiting for us, but I was very confused by Edgar's statement.

'I'm thinking of going underground.'

'Underground? The Resistance?' I whispered the words, not daring to say them any louder, not least because I didn't want Papa to hear.

Edgar nodded. 'I want to do more. Passing on bits of information, gossip from the officers in the shop. It's not doing much. You could do that anyway. You speak German better than I do.'

It was true. I was proficient in both English and German, but I kept it quiet. In fact, Papa had insisted neither of us ever let it be known that we spoke German. The thought of Edgar leaving and joining the underground network filled me with dread. 'You'd be in so much danger. What would Maman think?'

'She would think I was stupid and brave. Just as you and

4

Papa would.' He said it with such confidence, and I couldn't argue. It was true.

'But she would also be scared. We all would.'

'I know, but I don't want to sit around doing nothing, when I know I can do so much more.' His eyes lit up with excitement.

'This is serious, Edgar,' I said. 'It's not a game. It's life or death. If they catch you, you will be killed. Obviously, before that, you will be tortured for days or weeks.'

He stood a little straighter. Already taller than me by several inches. 'I know. I am prepared to die for my country.'

The pride I felt for my brother was immense. I could tell from the look in his eyes and the set of his jaw that he meant it. He would do this with or without his family's blessing. 'Are you going to tell Papa?'

He shook his head. 'No. He will try to talk me out of it. It will cause too much tension and I don't want to argue with Maman.'

'So telling me is the easy option. I have to break the news to them?' I didn't relish the thought in the slightest, but I understood what Edgar meant.

'If you don't mind?'

'I don't have a choice. When will you leave?'

'Probably by the end of the week. I will go in the night.'

'I will miss you,' I whispered. I stepped forward and hugged him. 'Please be careful.'

'I will miss you too. I'll be in contact once the dust settles.' He returned the embrace. 'If you need me before then, leave a hat on the mannequin in the window. That will be our signal that you need to speak to me.'

As we went to join Papa in the shop, I mused at how it seemed I had inadvertently become involved in the Resistance movement by taking my brother's place as resident eavesdropper. I wasn't sure how I felt about it, but I think pride was the main emotion.

* * *

That evening at dinner, the conversation turned to the news that Monsieur Willet from across the road had been arrested. Apparently, someone had reported him for anti-German speech.

'But who would have reported him?' I asked. 'Monsieur Willet is an old man; he barely leaves his apartment.'

'Someone with a grudge against him,' said Maman. 'Someone who wants his apartment. I don't know. These days not only do we live in fear of the Germans, but we also live in fear of our neighbours reporting us to gain favour with *les Boches*.'

'Times are difficult,' said Papa. 'We must always be on our guard. We will get through this war if we comply and don't draw attention to ourselves. Peace will come and I want my family intact at the end.'

'Sitting back and allowing these atrocities against our fellow Parisians makes us complicit,' said Edgar.

I knew he was thinking of the Cohen family – Edgar had gone to school with the son. They were rounded up with hundreds of other Jewish families. None of them had come back. There was an accusation in his tone, and although Edgar's anger wasn't directed at Papa, it reflected the injustice and helplessness we all felt.

'Edgar, mind your manners,' warned Maman, passing a bowl of soup down the table.

'But don't you see?' continued Edgar. 'Our silence means we are simply condoning the actions of the Germans.'

'Edgar,' warned Maman again, this time fixing him with a look. 'I do not want an argument. Everyone knows how awful it is. Your father was merely—'

'It's all right, Therese,' said Papa. 'It is good that Edgar questions.' He turned to Edgar. 'An ideal world does not exist. We must take considered and measured actions. Subtle ones that do not get us noticed. Always exercise caution and care.'

And there the conversation ended as Maman declared

there must be no more talk of the occupation. She changed the subject to her sister, Clarice, who lived in Southern Brittany, and how Maman was hoping to visit soon as Clarice had a supply of vegetables for us. 'In fact,' said Maman, 'Nathalie, you can come with me to the countryside. Can't she, Théodule? I'm going for a week and two pairs of hands means we can bring more supplies back with us.'

'Yes, that's a good idea,' agreed Papa.

I didn't mind. I hadn't seen my cousins for over a year and it would be nice to escape Paris for a while. Gaston was the eldest at twenty-eight. Rachelle was twenty-one like me and the youngest was Odile at just fifteen. We used to visit several times a year before the war. 'I'd love to go,' I said.

'Good. I shall arrange a travel pass for you,' said Maman. 'Now eat up, everyone, before the soup goes cold.'

When I went to bed that night, the prospect of seeing my cousins again excited me. I had many happy memories of weeks spent in the Breton countryside with the Grandis family. I missed those carefree days.

Eventually, I could feel my eyes growing heavy and sleep beckoning me. The background noise of the city wasn't as noticeable as it used to be before the war. Now, with a nine o'clock curfew, the only sounds were German patrols either on foot or in their vehicles crawling along the streets, on the lookout for anyone who had defied the rules. Occasionally, there were shouts and the sound of running feet, and I always hoped whoever was being chased down got away. Tonight, though, the noise that jolted me from my semi-consciousness was the unmistakable creak of Edgar's door and the squeak of the floorboards outside my room.

I threw back the covers and jumped out of bed, trying to be as quiet as possible so as not to disturb Maman and Papa. I wrapped my cardigan around me and crept out just as Edgar reached the top of the stairs. He looked around at me and placed one finger to his lips before beckoning me to follow him downstairs. Edgar was carrying a green canvas knapsack on his shoulder. He stopped at the bottom of the stairs to grab his coat, hat, and boots, before tiptoeing through to the kitchen. I followed, closing the door behind me.

'You're really going?' I asked.

He nodded. 'Yes. I can't sit back and do nothing. I have to take action.'

I nodded, fully understanding his feelings. 'I wish I could come too.'

'You need to be the eyes and ears here,' he said seriously as he tied the laces on his boots. 'Just keep listening. Write nothing down.'

'How will I pass the information to you?'

'I'll let you know. I'll be in touch in the next week.' He stood up and pulled his cap down. 'I need to go.'

I looked at my little brother, who now looked like a man. His expression, his stance, his demeanour had changed in those few minutes and I was proud of him. I stepped forward and hugged him. 'Be careful. I will miss you, but always know I am proud of you.'

'I will miss you, too. Tell Maman and Papa not to worry.'

We moved apart, and I laughed. 'Not to worry? I think Maman is going to string me up alive for letting you go.'

We hugged once more, and I stood in the doorway as I watched my brave brother go to fight for our country. I tamped down the fear, replacing it with the pride I felt for him and his decision.

Chapter 2

Darcie, West Sussex, September 2022

No matter how many times she did this, the nerves were always the same. It was the anticipation of the unknown. The excitement that she might be on the brink of an amazing discovery juxtaposed with the thought that it might be nothing of any value or significance.

Darcie slid into the seat at the back of the auction room, nodding and smiling at some of the regular bidders she encountered at the monthly auction. The thrill of entering the bidding arena, coupled with the prospect of some extraordinary finds, filled the room with an undercurrent of suspense that only fuelled Darcie's adrenaline-soaked veins.

She sourced a great deal of the stock here for her Vintaged and Loved shop in the nearby Sussex market town of Petworth.

The lady from Pre-Loved By You smiled as Darcie sat down in the seats behind her.

Darcie glanced around the room and spotted the man from Magpies Collectables. She'd been bidding against Magpies for the past six years, since she'd first started visiting auctions. He was a couple of decades her senior, but they both had an eye for the same type of collectables in everything vintage.

The auction got off to a prompt start at 2.30 p.m. and Darcie followed with interest as the lots were auctioned off. From her seat at the back of the room, she had a good view of the other regular bidders and, in particular, Magpies.

Finally, the auctioneer called out Lot 176. This was the left-luggage lockers removed recently from a disused waiting room of a West Sussex train station.

Her heart was thumping as the bidding opened. Magpies went straight in with a high opening offer. Darcie waited as two other bidders joined in. She wanted to see how high it would go and if at least two of them would back off before she waded in. They quickly moved through the prices, levelling out at £230.

'So, I have two-thirty at the side of the room. Any latecomers?' The auctioneer called out as he looked around the hall, his gaze pausing momentarily on Darcie before moving on. 'Going once! Going twice!'

His gaze came back to Darcie. Her heart was beating hard. She had been holding her nerve for this. She raised her paddle and mouthed 'two-forty' to the auctioneer.

'Latecomer at the back of the room with two-forty.' He looked to Magpies who gave a brief nod. 'And two-fifty.' Back to Darcie. 'Two-sixty.' The auctioneer pinged back and forth. The bidding soon reached £320. Then £350, £390.

It was Darcie's turn to come back with a higher bid.

'Four hundred,' she confirmed to the auctioneer before she had time to talk herself out of it.

The bidding was gathering quite a bit of attention from the rest of the room as it now became a spectator sport. The next thing she knew, they had reached £450. She was at her limit, but something inside her was not letting her lose out. She had to buy the lockers. She raised her paddle another time.

'Four-sixty!'

'Four-sixty,' repeated the auctioneer. 'That's, four-sixty. Any advances on four-sixty? Going once. Going twice.' The auctioneer paused dramatically. 'Sold.' He whacked the gavel down on the desk and then, in a well-practised signature movement, he spun the gavel around and pointed the handle at Darcie. 'Thank you. And well done.'

As she walked around to the cashier's office, the adrenaline and euphoria ebbed away, leaving her with the cold reality that she had spent £460 that afternoon and the worst part was, the lockers were a complete gamble. She was such an idiot getting carried away like that, but still she couldn't quite override the feeling of excitement that came with the purchase.

The warehouse staff at the auction house helped put the luggage lockers into the back of her 1960s Morris Minor Traveller. Darcie had already removed the contents of the lockers, which comprised an old brown leather suitcase, a plastic drawstring bag, and an old coat, together with a tennis racket. She would wait until she got home before having a proper look at everything.

When she arrived back at Petworth, she pulled into the parking space behind her shop, Vintaged and Loved.

Her mother, Lena, and her younger sister, Chloe, came out to greet her. 'How did you get on?' asked Lena.

Darcie opened the double doors to the boot and patted the set of four metal lockers. 'I won.' She beamed, hoping they wouldn't ask her about the price.

'Here, I'll give you a hand to get them out,' said Chloe.

With Chloe on one end of the lockers and Darcie on the other, they manoeuvred them past the annexe where Lena lived, through the back door and down the hallway into the shop. 'Just put them over here by the till for now,' instructed Darcie. 'I'm not sure where I'll put them yet.'

She cast her gaze around the shop at the wonderful and beautiful clothing she had acquired over the years. There were dresses from the 1920s through to the 2000s hung around the space, with different sections for the different eras. Each section was styled appropriately, predominately with clothing, but also with era-specific props.

The Sixties section had Andy Warhol-esque pop art, and a record player on a small coffee table; while the Seventies section was all about flower power; and the Eighties was rara skirts, leg warmers, block colours, and shoulder pads. Each decade clearly identified. Out of the nine different areas, her favourite was the 1940s with the setting of a dance hall and a mannequin she'd recovered from a skip, now dressed up like Vera Lynn, complete with an old-fashioned microphone. Darcie loved to play big-band swing music in the shop and sometimes sported some of the clothing as a walking advert for her business. 'I think I might add the lockers to the 1940s scene and make it bigger,' she mused.

'It's always a popular era, especially when Goodwood Revival weekend is on,' said Chloe.

Vintaged and Loved looked over the main square of Petworth, surrounded by the Petworth Arms pub, a café, a church, a convenience store on one side and an antique shop on the other. The market town was renowned for its antique shops, closely followed in second place by its tea rooms and coffee shops. Darcie's business was a good fit for the town, especially when, as Chloe had pointed out, Goodwood Revival was on and people came from all over the world to relive the nostalgia of yesteryear. The week leading up to the local festival saw the footfall through her shop increase tenfold.

'Have you looked inside the lockers yet?' asked Lena.

'I did. There's a suitcase, a bag, and a couple of bits. I'll just get them now,' said Darcie. 'We can have a quick look.'

'Do you want me to close the shop up?' asked Lena.

'Good idea. It's nearly five o'clock anyway,' said Darcie. She watched her mum from the corner of her eye, reaching up to slide the bolts across at the top of the door and then bending down to the bottom bolt. Darcie was conscious that the bending and stretching weren't always easy for her mother. Lena had lived with chronic back pain for the past fifteen years, following a car accident when Darcie was eleven. With her maternal grandmother living in Cornwall and an absent father, Darcie had become prime carer, not just for Lena, but for her younger sister, Chloe, as well. The three-year age gap had, seemingly overnight, stretched to what felt like a chasm when Darcie's role as big sister switched into a mothering role. It was only in more recent years that the balance had shifted to a more sisterly equilibrium.

There was always something exciting about opening a left-luggage case and Darcie had been lucky with a few of them in the past, yielding contents she could either sell in her shop or donate to a clothing bank. It was a gamble, but it was also addictive.

'Open it up, then,' encouraged Lena, taking the seat behind the counter.

'Drum roll,' said Chloe theatrically, and she rapped the countertop accordingly.

Darcie picked up the drawstring bag and placed it on the countertop. Pausing for dramatic effect, she looked at her sister and mum before loosening the neck of the bag and peeking inside. There was a bundle of clothing, and Darcie tipped it out onto the wooden surface. There was a distinct smell of mustiness and an old, very old, sweaty type of stench.

'Oh God, it stinks!' said Chloe, covering her nose and mouth with her hand.

'It looks like a PE kit,' said Lena, who was leaning away with her face screwed up at the smell.

'Great,' said Darcie, having a quick look to make sure it really wasn't anything exciting. 'No. Definitely looks like a smelly PE kit or even a football kit.' She scooped it up and stuffed it back into the bag and tightened the cord. 'I'll throw that straight in the outside bin.'

'I'll do it now,' said Chloe. She hooked the drawstring on her index finger and, holding it at arm's length, strode through the back of the shop and out into the yard.

Darcie could hear the lid of the wheelie bin open and clatter shut again. Chloe came back into the shop. 'There, job done.' She eyed the suitcase Darcie was now heaving onto the counter. 'Let's hope that's not the rest of the class's

PE kits. The whole bloody football team's kit or something equally disgusting.'

'Well, we're about to find out,' said Darcie, her thumbs poised to flick the catches. 'You ready?'

Chloe stood back. 'Quick then.'

Darcie released the locks and lifted the lid. With a degree of care, she took a breath. 'It's OK. No stinky PE kits here,' she announced. 'Just a bit musty, that's all.' There was a hardback A4-sized book on top of what looked like a large sheet of brown paper. Darcie picked up the book and opened it to the first page.

She looked in amazement at the artwork before her. It was a sketch of a woman in a 1940s-style evening gown and notes written alongside, indicating the colour and the fabric. She turned the page and another equally beautiful sketch greeted her.

'Oh, wow!' exclaimed Chloe, peering closer. 'It's like an art project.'

Darcie continued turning the pages. Each design was unique and, with the exception of one page where the designs looked less proficient, they all appeared to be drawn by the same hand and all in the 1940s style. 'I don't think it's an art project,' she said at last. 'I think this is an actual designer's book. A fashion designer.'

'What's in the case under that paper?' asked Lena.

Darcie put the book to one side for a moment. Her hands trembled as she rested them on top of the paper. 'I don't know what I've found, but I have goosebumps and a funny butterfly sensation in my stomach.'

'Just take the paper off and let us look,' urged Chloe, the excitement clear in her voice. 'If you don't, then I will.'

Darcie took a deep breath and then removed the paper. There was some neatly folded blue satin fabric.

Darcie lifted it out and carefully unfolded the material, before holding it up. It was a dark blue satin, figure-hugging dress, cut on the bias with a deep cowl back. It oozed a sophisticated Hollywood glamour. 'This is beautiful,' she said, admiring the dress.

Lena was already flicking through the pages. 'There,' she declared triumphantly. 'There's the blue evening dress. It's tiny though. Whoever this was for must have been very small. I mean, look at that waist. I'm sure I couldn't even get that around my leg, let alone my body.'

Darcie laid the dress out on top of the suitcase. 'To think no one has seen or touched this dress in all these years. It's at least forty years, but maybe even longer.'

'Are the designs signed by anyone?' asked Lena. 'What's that squiggle in the bottom right-hand corner?'

'It's on all the pages,' said Chloe. 'I can't make out what it says, though. It doesn't look like a signature, more like a mark of some kind, but it's the same on every page, so it must be the same person.'

Darcie inspected the mark. 'It's hard to say; it's like a figure of eight joined into a number four, but all in one movement. Whoever designed these certainly had an eye for detail and fashion,' said Darcie after studying the page for a few moments. She looked back at the garment. 'And the dress hasn't been thrown together, either. It's a very professional job. I just don't understand why there isn't a label, though.'

'I'd say there's a lot of love gone into this piece,' remarked Lena.

'I'll do some research tonight,' said Darcie. 'Maybe I can find something online that might give me a clue to who the designer is.'

'They're probably English,' said Chloe. 'And possibly local to the south of England. I'm not sure how they would have ended up in a left-luggage locker in a little station in West Sussex otherwise.'

'It's all very intriguing,' said Lena. 'Who would leave something so wonderful in a locker and forget all about it?'

'Unless they meant to come back for it and for some reason

couldn't,' said Darcie. 'Maybe something happened to them, and no one knew it was even there. I'd be mortified if I lost something like this.' She gazed at the dress and sketchbook. She had a deep sense of wanting to find out who these had once belonged to. She wanted to know the story behind the garment and the design book. It felt significant, and yet she did not know why.

Chapter 3

Nathalie

'What do you mean, he left last night?' demanded Maman from across the breakfast table.

'What I said: he left to join the Resistance last night,' I repeated. I hated the fact Maman was so angry with me, but I had known she would be and I was prepared. I could also tell that she was upset. The anger was coming from a place of fear. 'He was determined to go, and by leaving in the night, he didn't have to face either of you. He didn't want his parting words to be cross ones.'

Papa put down his coffee cup. So far he had said nothing as Maman had questioned me about where Edgar was, having found his bedroom empty that morning. Now he spoke. 'It sounds like Edgar had this planned for some time.'

'He did,' I replied.

'And why didn't you tell us before?' It was Maman again.

'Come now, Therese, we can't blame Nathalie for this,' said Papa. 'It was Edgar's decision and his alone. I doubt very much that Nathalie would have been able to talk him out of it.'

'No, but if she'd told us, then we could have made him see sense.' Maman dabbed her face with the edge of her apron. 'We could have forbidden him to go.'

Papa shook his head and let out a sigh. 'I don't believe we would have been able to change his mind, and arguing with him could have driven him away sooner, maybe when his plan wasn't fully in place or when the people he was going to weren't ready for him. That could have put him in more danger.'

'No. You're wrong,' said Maman. 'If I'd spoken to him, he would have stayed for me. Besides, you talk like you agree with what he's done.'

'It's not so much that, but I admire him for having principles and wanting to do something for his country,' said Papa.

'What use to his country is he when he is arrested by the Gestapo . . . or worse.' With that, Maman rushed from the room.

I went to follow her, but Papa put a hand on my arm. 'Leave your mother for now. In time she will come to terms with what he's done.'

'I asked him not to go,' I said. 'But you know what Edgar is like. He's stubborn. He made me promise not to tell a soul.'

'Then you have done the right thing by your brother and kept your promise. That isn't as easy as it sounds.'

'No, it wasn't. I knew Maman would take it badly.'

'We had better open up the shop,' said Papa.

From down the hallway, I could hear Maman crying and I felt desperately sorry for her, but I knew she was a strong woman, and she wouldn't go to pieces.

It was quiet in the shop that morning. As usual now, most of the trade was from the Germans. I spent the morning repairing clothing other women, who weren't so handy with the needle, had brought in. The tinkle of the bell above the shop door was a welcome relief from the boredom. I looked up from the shirt I was sewing buttons onto, and through the doorway to the shop.

'*Bonjour*, Hauptmann Kranz,' my father said as a German officer walked in. Kranz was a frequent visitor to the shop and often bought gifts to send back to his family in Germany.

'*Bonjour*, Monsieur Leroux.'

'How can I help you?'

'I'm actually here on official business,' said Kranz.

Immediately I heard that, my heart missed a beat and my stomach turned in fright. I listened intently from the back room.

'Where is the boy? Your son?'

'My son? He's on an errand for me,' said Papa without faltering.

'Hmm. I was hoping to speak to him.' Kranz tapped his thigh with the palm of his hand in irritation. 'How long will he be?'

Before Papa could answer, I pressed the foot pedal on the sewing machine and then let out a loud screech, followed up with a hearty groan.

'What was that?' demanded Kranz.

'Excuse me,' I heard Papa say. I looked up as he rushed into the cutting room. 'What have you done?'

Unfortunately, Kranz had followed Papa through and was standing next to him, both men peering down at me.

I wrapped one hand over the other hand and sucked air in through my teeth. 'I caught my finger in the sewing machine,' I said.

'Is it bleeding?' Kranz frowned.

'Maybe you should run it under the tap,' suggested Papa. I could see the look of confusion in his eyes, and I let out another wail before rocking myself back and forth.

'Nathalie, let me see,' said Papa. He turned to Kranz. 'I'm sorry, I need to attend to my daughter.'

Kranz took another look at me before giving a curt nod. 'I'll come back another time to see your son.' He marched out of the room and then the shop.

'Are you all right?' asked Papa, rushing to my side.

I held my hands up to him, with an exaggerated sorrowful look on my face, and then I flung my hands open. 'Ta-da! All better now.'

Papa let out a breath. 'Nathalie!' he scolded. 'That was a very stupid thing to do.'

I shrugged. 'It made him stop asking about Edgar.'

'Don't do that again. What if he had insisted on looking at your finger?'

I hadn't actually thought that far ahead, but I didn't want to admit it to Papa. '*Alors*, he didn't, so no harm done.'

Papa shook his head in exasperation. 'You are going to get yourself in trouble one day.' Despite the admonishment, he put his arm around my shoulders and kissed the top of my head. 'Now, you'd better get on with whatever it is you're supposed to be doing.' He gestured to the pile of clothing at the end of the workbench, awaiting my attention.

I felt happier as I set about working my way through the garments. It seemed Papa had forgiven me already about Edgar and that meant Maman would too. Although I was worried about Edgar, I knew he had plenty of connections and he wouldn't have done anything without preparing properly first. The fact that he'd said he'd contact me in a few days' time, was also reassuring. I felt a little guilty withholding that nugget of information from my parents, but if Maman knew I was meeting Edgar, she'd want to come or insist Papa meet him and drag him back home. None of that was going to happen. I was proud of Edgar and, not for the first time, a little envious.

I spent the rest of the morning working on the clothes and was pleased with the progress I was making with them. Lunch was another twenty minutes away, so I tidied up the workshop. I kept as many scraps of fabric as possible to save for patching clothing and patchwork blankets, which I would pass on to whoever needed them. What couldn't be reused, I gathered into a paper bag and took to the outside bin.

Our shop was on the corner of a busy crossroads, with several cafés and restaurants, which proved very popular with the Germans. A high stone wall enclosed the courtyard of the shop and a gate led out onto the street. Before the war, we often would sit outside in the courtyard to have our lunch on sunny days. I had been a keen gardener, and although the space was small, it had become a little piece of paradise in the city. The flowers and shrubs in the pots attracted insects and bees. I often wondered what bees were doing in the middle of the city and liked to think they appreciated the garden I'd created.

But we didn't sit out in the courtyard anymore. There was a different atmosphere in the city. On the face of it, Paris continued much as it had before the occupation with theatres, cafés, and restaurants open, but instead of French and European tourists, these were now full of German soldiers who treated the city as a holiday destination.

To sit here and listen to German voices laughing and joking in the nearby cafés stuck in our throats, especially when food was becoming more difficult to find and the queues at the bakers and butchers were becoming longer and longer. I could hear the light-hearted conversations going on now in the café as the Germans enjoyed the hospitality of the owners.

I had just put the bag of scrap fabric in the bin and had paused to inspect the flowers that had survived the past couple of years when I heard the distinct voice of Kranz on the other side of the garden wall. He had stopped to greet another German, who I assumed was of equal rank by the easy way they were talking to each other.

I froze on the spot as indecision gripped me. Should I just carry on with what I was doing, or should I quietly sneak back inside? It was when I heard the other German mention propaganda leaflets that I made my decision to stay and listen. Adrenaline coursed through me as I crouched down at a disused flower tub and actively listened, tuning in to the German language and what they were saying.

'Yes, they were distributed early this morning. They were shoved through people's doors and nailed up on trees. They were everywhere.' He went on to say how the Gestapo had demanded the source of the leaflets be found immediately and that those guilty of printing and distributing be arrested for interrogation.

The second German officer didn't sound very happy about

it. There was a note of irritation in his voice. He muttered something that I didn't quite catch, but it left me with the distinct impression that the pressure he was coming under to find the culprits did not impress him.

'We've had a tip-off about a bookshop in the area,' he said to Kranz. 'It's the one on the corner near the bridge. We're going to pay them a visit.'

'Tonight?' asked Kranz.

'No. In a day or two. Once the dust has settled and they think they are safe.' The officer gave a chuckle. 'Lure them into a false sense of security and catch them when they are not expecting us.'

Kranz laughed. 'That sounds like an excellent plan.'

'Get those fucking Gestapo off my back anyway,' came the reply.

With that, they said their goodbyes and I heard their footsteps depart. I blew out a long breath. I knew exactly which bookshop they meant. It belonged to Monsieur Cadue, an elderly gentleman who Papa knew by sight. I couldn't believe that he would be involved with the Resistance. He seemed a very unassuming man. He had been old forever, or so it seemed. I would have to warn him about what was happening. I hesitated. Would Monsieur Cadue take me seriously? Would he think it was a trap? People were so wary of each other these days. Neighbours would report one another for the slightest infringement of the rules. If the warning came from the Resistance, he might take it more seriously. I needed to get a message to Edgar and would put the hat on the mannequin in the shop window before we closed for lunch. Hopefully, he would see it or someone who knew the secret sign would tell him I had important information.

Chapter 4

Nathalie

I don't know if Papa noticed the hat on the mannequin in the shop window or not. If he did, he didn't mention it. I tried not to give anything away for the rest of the afternoon and evening, even though I felt guilty not telling my parents. I had to keep it that way for everyone's safety, especially my brother's. My parents went to bed ahead of me, which wasn't unusual. I was a night owl and liked the stillness and calm the darkness brought. There was something reassuring and soothing about a silent house, knowing everyone was safely in bed. Of course, that tranquillity had been tarnished somewhat since the arrival of the Germans, but still I found comfort in the darkness.

'I'm going to read my book for a while,' I had said to Maman.

'Don't strain your eyes,' she replied, before dropping a kiss on my head.

'When you come to bed, make sure the downstairs door is locked,' Papa had said. He had given me a look that I hadn't been able to decipher and I wondered whether he suspected I might have a plan of some sort.

I didn't know when Edgar would come or indeed how I would know. We hadn't discussed that part of the plan. He'd just said I would know when it was him. Again, the less information the better for everyone's safety. It was difficult to concentrate on my book while I waited, and by the time

23

it got to midnight, I was convinced Edgar wasn't coming. Maybe he didn't see the hat or he couldn't come tonight. The clock on the mantelpiece ticked its way into the next day, and I was just about to go to bed when I heard a noise. It was coming from the kitchen, which overlooked the back of the property.

I sat still. Waiting. Listening.

There it was again.

It was definitely coming from the kitchen. It sounded like tapping on the window.

As light-footed as possible, I made my way downstairs and out into the courtyard. It was so dark, I could barely see. The chatter and noise from the late-night drinkers at the bar across the road could still be heard. It would only be the soldiers, as the rest of us had to abide by the nine o'clock curfew. I stepped out further into the courtyard. I resisted the urge to whisper Edgar's name into the night, just in case it was a trap.

'Who's there?' I opted for instead, keeping my voice low and quiet.

A hand suddenly went around my mouth from behind. I grabbed at the hand and then I heard a voice in my ear. 'Shh. It's me, Edgar.'

Immediately, I relaxed, and the hand lifted from my mouth. I turned around, coming face to face with my brother. 'What did you do that for?' I demanded.

'I didn't want to make you jump and scream out loud.'

'You nearly gave me a heart attack.'

'Sorry, my dear sister.' There was amusement in his voice and my anger evaporated.

'I'm glad you got my message,' I replied, the tension dropping from my shoulders. I hugged Edgar, as a wave of relief he was there washed over me. 'Are you well?'

'*Oui. Pas trop mal.* Not too bad,' he replied. 'How are Papa and Maman?'

'Maman is very cross with me for not telling her you were leaving.'

'And Papa?'

'He pretended to be cross but I think secretly he's very proud of you,' I replied. 'That's not to say they aren't both worried about you.'

'You can tell them I'm fine.'

'I'll do nothing of the sort. They would never forgive me if they found out I've met with you and not told them.'

'I will be in touch with them soon. When it's safe to do so.'

'I know.'

'So, what is it you wanted me for?' asked Edgar, moving back into the shadows of the garden wall. 'I'm sure it wasn't to tell me you missed me.'

I flicked his arm with the back of my hand. 'No, it wasn't. You haven't been gone long enough for me to miss you.'

Edgar chuckled. 'So, what is it?'

I quickly relayed to him the conversation I'd overheard between Kranz and another officer. 'You have to warn Monsieur Cadue. If he has a printing press, then the Germans mustn't find it.' I paused as a thought struck me. 'Let me see your hands.'

'What?'

I snatched up Edgar's hands and peered at them in the dim light of the moon. 'What's all that?' I asked, pointing to black smudge marks. 'If it's ink, you need to be more careful.'

Edgar pulled his hands away. 'The less you know, the better.'

'Please don't tell me you've been hiding out at the bookshop, just a few hundred metres away, all this time?'

'As I said, the less you know, the better.'

I took that as a yes, but knew he was right. If I knew nothing, then I couldn't accidentally tell anyone or worse still, break under an interrogation. 'I won't ask any more questions,' I said. Even suspecting something and not speaking up was an arrestable offence these days. 'Do you need anything? Food? Money?' I delved into my pocket where I had a few francs

I had made from repairing some garments for the Germans last week.

'Keep your money,' said Edgar. 'I don't want to take it.'

I pushed it into his hands. 'Take it as my way of helping. What do I need it for? I can't spend it on anything.'

'Very well. Thank you.' He pushed the folded and now somewhat crumpled notes into the pocket of his trousers. 'I do need you to do something for me, though.'

'Of course. What is it?'

'The grey woollen fabric block in the storeroom. I need it.'

'You need it? What for?'

Edgar sighed. 'You're not supposed to ask questions, remember? Can you get it for me?'

'What, now?'

'Yes.'

'What about Papa when he notices it's gone?' I asked. I didn't have a problem helping Edgar, but I wasn't sure whether Papa would be thrilled. 'You can't take it all. How much do you need?'

'Enough to make a jacket with. I also need matching thread.'

'A jacket, you say?' There was only one sort of jacket Edgar would need to make using that fabric, and it wasn't for him to swan around Paris in. The grey wool was an exact match for a German officer's uniform. It was why we had it in stock for any repairs they asked us to make.

'Please, just two metres.'

'Wait there.' I hurried back into the storeroom and, making sure the curtains were drawn, I switched on a small lamp in the corner and took the block of fabric from the shelf. Spreading it out on the workbench, I measured and cut two metres, before replacing the block on the shelf. Edgar stepped out from the shadows as I went back into the garden.

He took the fabric and thread and stuffed it inside his own coat under his arm. 'Thank you. I must go. I've been here too long already.'

We looked at each other in the darkness and I had an overwhelming sense of love and fear for him. I hugged him again, and he held me tightly before kissing me on each side of my face. We didn't speak. We didn't need to. Our thoughts were as one. With one last look at the gate, he slipped out into the night.

Tears sprang to my eyes and, as I went back indoors and lay in my bed that night, I couldn't shake off the anxiety that had pitched up inside of me. I had this awful feeling that something bad was going to happen to Edgar, and I knew I would not see him again.

The feeling stayed with me until I went to sleep and was there the moment I woke up.

When I went down to the shop with Papa to open up, he even asked me if I was feeling all right. 'You look very pale,' he said. 'Is something wrong?'

'No. I'm fine,' I reassured him. I kept myself busy in the workroom that morning.

Just as we were about to close for lunch, it surprised me to see Alphonse appear in the shop.

'Alphonse. I wasn't expecting to see you,' I said. He was wearing his police uniform, and I forced myself to smile – I much preferred to see him in civilian clothes. I hated everything the blue uniform stood for. Collaborating with the Germans – it repulsed me.

'Nathalie. I wondered if you would like to join me for lunch,' said Alphonse, removing his hat and running a hand through his blond hair.

I looked at Papa, hoping he'd say I was needed in the shop. I really didn't want to be seen out with a police officer. It always made me feel uncomfortable. Papa, however, didn't read the unspoken message I was trying to convey. 'What a splendid idea. Take as long as you like.'

Before I could protest, I was bustled out of the door. I knew Papa thought that at least this way I'd have something decent to eat, especially as the lack of food was becoming an issue in the city.

'How are you today?' asked Alphonse. 'I haven't seen you for nearly a week.'

'I'm very well, but I've been busy in the shop, that's all.'

We went into a small but popular café, which overlooked a small square. German soldiers who treated the city more like a holiday resort with every passing week occupied most of the tables.

We ordered a coffee each and some food.

'What have you been so busy with in the shop?' asked Alphonse.

'Making garments for those in need,' I replied. 'Reusing some old clothing and making it into something else. Something practical.'

'You're very clever with the needle. I shall look forward to the day when you will sew buttons onto my shirts and darn my socks.' Alphonse smiled at me, but I couldn't return the expression. 'What's wrong?' he asked, a frown now settling on his face.

'I don't envisage myself sewing buttons and darning socks for anyone,' I said. 'I'll have my own business when the war is over. My own fashion house. You'll have to find someone else to do that for you.' It was possibly an unwarranted display of petulance, but I hated the way everyone had me married and at home before I had even experienced anything of what life had to offer.

'A fashion house?' repeated Alphonse, as if the words were alien to his mouth. 'Why would you want that?' He made a huffing noise. 'No wife of mine will work and she certainly won't have a fashion house.'

'*Alors*, just as well I will not be your wife, isn't it?' I heard myself saying out loud.

If I'd surprised myself, then I had certainly surprised Alphonse. He looked at me, aghast. 'I don't know what's got into you today, Nathalie, but you're behaving very . . .' he waved his hand in the air as if searching for the appropriate word '. . . very disagreeably,' he concluded.

'You mean, I'm not agreeing with you? That I'm not behaving like a young woman should? That I'm not grateful that you might want to marry me? Is that what you mean?'

'Nathalie, keep your voice down. You're drawing attention,' said Alphonse, clearly annoyed now.

'And that wouldn't do, would it? That's not very subservient,' I snapped back.

'Nathalie! Where is all this coming from?' asked Alphonse. His voice was calmer now. 'This is not like you. Is something wrong?'

I let out a sigh. 'I'm sorry. I just don't like being told what I can and can't do with my life,' I said, and then lowering my voice so the Germans in the restaurant couldn't hear me: 'It's bad enough that we can't live our lives properly under occupation, but then to have my dreams torn away, it's unbearable. My dreams are the only things that keep me going. They give me hope to carry on and believe that one day all this will be over.'

'I think maybe you should manage the expectations of your dreams. It's good to have dreams, but they need to be realistic.' He smiled and patted my hand. 'Now, tell me, where is your brother today? I didn't see him in the shop.'

'He . . . err . . . He was running an errand for Papa,' I said, ensuring I kept to Papa's story in case anyone was eavesdropping.

'An errand? Doing what?' asked Alphonse.

I shrugged. 'I don't know. I've been in the workroom. I haven't been paying attention.'

Alphonse put his cutlery down and took a sip of his coffee, eyeing me over the rim of the cup. He slowly placed it down on the saucer. 'Does Edgar often pop out?'

I frowned. 'I don't keep track of him. Like I said, I'm usually in the workroom.'

'He should be careful he doesn't draw attention to himself.'

29

'What do you mean?'

'Come, Nathalie, you know,' said Alphonse. 'I wouldn't want to see him be taken in for questioning, especially if he's involved in anything untoward.'

I tried to quell the bubble of alarm rising from my stomach. 'Of course he's not.'

'But you said yourself, you don't know what he does, where he goes or even when. Can you be sure?'

'I trust my brother completely.' Now it was my turn to pat Alphonse's hand in the same patronising way he'd done to me. 'And you have no need to worry.'

Alphonse looked down at my hand and then up at me. 'I'm just saying this because I care about you,' he said. 'If Edgar is doing something he shouldn't . . .'

He let the end of the sentence hang in the air.

'He's not,' I said, withdrawing my hand.

'If you have any doubts or worries, you can tell me. Perhaps I could speak to Edgar, as a friend, and warn him.'

'I have no doubts at all,' I replied, my voice tense and my tone firm.

Edgar sat back in his chair and appraised me for several moments. When he replied there was a brittleness to his voice. 'I hope you're right; otherwise he could bring a lot of trouble to you and your family. You do know that, don't you?'

'Of course I know that,' I said, feigning indignation. 'And I would thank you to take that tone from your voice. I'm your girlfriend, not a suspect.' I said the words with far more conviction than I felt. I knew at that moment, now wasn't the time to make an enemy of Alphonse.

My fear was turned to reality the following morning. I was woken by the sound of hammering on the front door to the shop and shouting voices ordering us to open up.

Fear churned my stomach and my throat tightened. It could only mean one thing. It was the German authorities. I threw my bedcovers back and jumped out of bed, hurriedly finding my clothes to put on. If they were coming into the house, I didn't want to be caught in my nightdress.

My bedroom door flew open and Maman rushed in. 'Hurry. Get dressed,' she urged, as she fastened her housecoat around her. Beyond her, I saw Papa rush along the hallway, and then his hurried feet on the stairs.

'*J'arrive. J'arrive tout de suite*. I'm coming. I'm coming now,' he called out.

The banging had paused for a moment and then started up again.

'*Viens*. Come. *Dépêche-toi*. Hurry up.' Maman urged me out of the bedroom and down the stairs to the dining room on the middle floor of the building. She pulled out a chair from the dining table and indicated for me to sit down. 'When they come up, you're not to say anything unless they speak to you. Do you understand?'

I nodded vigorously. The nerves were a jumble in my stomach and tingling to my fingertips. 'Why do you think they are here?'

Maman looked at me. 'I would have thought that was obvious. Edgar.'

Before I could ask anything else, I could hear more raised voices and the sound of booted feet trampling at speed up the wooden staircase. Two soldiers burst into the dining room, rifles in their hands. Maman let out a small cry of alarm. I stifled mine and refused to let myself flinch as the soldiers stormed across the room. One of them grabbed Maman's arm and shoved her into the chair next to me.

Papa came into the room, flanked by a French police officer and a German officer. Unsurprisingly, it was Hauptmann Kranz.

It was the police officer accompanying him who made me gasp. It was Alphonse! His eyes didn't meet mine but remained fixed straight ahead. What a coward that he couldn't look me in the eye.

'Please, Monsieur Leroux. Take a seat,' said the officer.

He gave a small nod toward Maman. 'Madame Leroux.' Then he turned his attention to me. '*Fräulein.*'

Unlike Alphonse, Kranz met my gaze. I don't know why he insisted on referring to me with the German equivalent to mademoiselle, but for whatever reason, he addressed me that way. '*Bonsoir, monsieur,*' I replied, noticing the tremble in my voice, which I hated myself for.

'I am sorry to call on you so early in the morning,' said Kranz, without a trace of regret. 'But I was hoping I would find Edgar here. Alas, I don't see him.'

I kept my gaze on Kranz, not wishing to blink or to avert my eyes for fear of giving anything away.

Papa spoke. 'Edgar didn't come home last night,' he said. 'We don't know where he is.'

'Why do you not know where he is? Did he not say?' Kranz slowly circled the table, and I saw Maman tense even further as he walked behind her.

'*Non.* He just went without saying goodbye,' said Papa.

'Where did he go?' There was a sharpness to Kranz's tone. His heels dug into the floorboards with every precise step he took, before coming to a halt at a space at the table.

'We don't know,' replied Papa.

'Not good enough!' shouted Kranz, making us all jump. 'I will ask again: where is your son?'

'I do not know. That is the truth,' repeated Papa.

With that, Kranz grabbed my hair and yanked my head backwards, nearly pulling me off my chair. I cried out in pain, gripping the roots of my hair.

Maman went to leap to her feet, but she was roughly pushed back down and held there by one soldier. From the corner of my eye I could see Alphonse, and yet he still wouldn't look at me.

Kranz yanked harder and then, still holding me by the hair, dragged me to my feet. 'I will ask you again, Monsieur Leroux: where is your son?'

Papa got to his feet, and the other soldier trained his

rifle on him. 'We don't know,' he said in a calm voice that countered the look in his eyes.

Kranz turned to Alphonse. 'Why don't you ask your girlfriend where her brother is?'

Alphonse looked up at the German, who was several inches taller and broader than he was. There was uncertainty on Alphonse's face and this time he threw a glance my way. He stuttered initially. 'Na . . . Nathalie . . . t-t-tell them . . . t-t-tell them where Edgar is.'

'I don't know,' I insisted.

Kranz let out an exaggerated sigh. 'This is getting us nowhere.' He threw me to the floor. 'Get on your knees,' he ordered, jabbing me between the shoulder blades with the toe of his boot.

I did as I was told. The only relief was that they had not asked me to stand. My legs were shaking with fear and I didn't think they would hold me.

'Ask her again. If she says she doesn't know, shoot her,' Kranz said to Alphonse.

'NO!' screamed Maman, only to receive a slap from the soldier. She clasped her hand to her face.

'W-what?' There was genuine fear in Alphonse's voice.

'Are you defying an order?' snapped Kranz. 'I can have you arrested for that. Now take out your gun. That's it. Point it at the back of her head. Get her to tell you.'

The hard metal of the gun muzzle wavered against the back of my skull and I knew Alphonse must be shaking. Tears came to my eyes, but I refused to let them fall. I blinked them back. I would not allow this bastard to see how he was making me feel.

'Nathalie . . . please,' began Alphonse. 'Please don't make me do this. Just tell them.'

'Oh, stop wasting time,' said Kranz. 'If you don't get it out of her, I shall.'

'Nathalie,' said Alphonse. This time there was anger in his voice. 'Where is Edgar? TELL ME!'

'I don't know,' I replied, amazed that I sounded so calm when inside I thought I was going to vomit.

It was Papa who spoke. 'He's left to join the Resistance, but we don't know where he's gone. Please, let my daughter go.'

There was a silence that felt like it went on for minutes when, in reality, it was just seconds.

'Put the gun away,' said Kranz. 'You, Monsieur Leroux, could have made that a lot easier for everyone if you'd just said that in the first place.'

Kranz continued to question us for over twenty minutes, after which he seemed satisfied we weren't withholding any more secrets.

'Next time,' he said, 'don't make me drag the information from you. I won't be so patient.'

He marched out of the room, followed closely by the soldiers.

'I'm sorry,' muttered Alphonse before scurrying away after Kranz.

I didn't reply. I couldn't even bring myself to look at him. Instead, I fixed my gaze on the mantelpiece. It was only when I heard him leave and the door close that I allowed the fear to wash over me. I rushed to the bathroom, vomiting up an empty stomach. The acidic bile burned my throat. After that, I collapsed into Maman's arms, and we both cried for a long time.

Chapter 5

Darcie

After the discovery of the patterns and sketchbook, Darcie spent the rest of the evening and any spare time she had the following day trying to find some reference to them on the internet. It was frustrating work, as she had little to go on, not even a name.

On the second day, she pushed her laptop away and sighed. 'I just can't find anything,' she said to Lena, who she was sharing a cup of tea with in the annexe while the shop was quiet.

'Maybe there's nothing to find,' said Lena, wincing as she moved in her chair to find a more comfortable position.

'Do you need another cushion?' asked Darcie, poised to grab one from the sofa if necessary.

'No. I'll be fine. Just a bit stiff today.'

Darcie checked the date on her watch. Lena wore a morphine patch 24/7 that was changed once a week. Usually, towards the end of the week, the effects of the morphine began to wear off and Lena felt the pain in her back more acutely. 'It's patch day tomorrow,' Darcie said, offering some encouragement. 'I can change it tonight before you go to bed, if you want?'

'I'll see how I get on,' said Lena.

As her mother lifted her cup to her mouth, Darcie noticed the shake in her hands. It happened when Lena was experiencing a lot of pain, something to do with the nerve endings having too much pain to control. 'Do you want a hot water bottle for your back?'

'That'd be nice.'

'You only have to ask, Mum,' said Darcie, getting up from the table and going over to the kettle. 'Don't suffer in silence just because you'd sooner not bother me.' She looked back over her shoulder at Lena. 'Because it's not a bother at all.'

'I know, it's just—'

'It's just you being too proud,' said Darcie. She switched on the kettle and waited for it to boil, before filling up the hot water bottle, wrapping it in a towel and placing it behind Lena's back. 'There.'

'Thank you, darling. I wish you didn't have to do all this for me. Maybe I should just go and live with Granny in her warden-assisted place.'

'Mum, stop. You'll do no such thing,' said Darcie. Lena said this from time to time. Regardless of whether she was serious or not, Darcie had no intention of packing her mother off to the end of the country. 'Anyway, I don't want you stuck down in Cornwall. Not exactly convenient to pop in for a cup of tea.' She gave Lena a reassuring hug and sat down in front of the laptop again.

'Are you going to put the book and dress on the website?' asked Lena. 'Or even take them back to auction? I'm sure someone would be very keen to have those.'

The idea had already crossed Darcie's mind, but something was stopping her. 'I'm going to keep them for now,' she said. 'I want a little more time to research them.' She wasn't ready to surrender them just yet.

'Well, I suppose you know best,' said Lena in a way that clearly implied she didn't think Darcie was making the best decision.

'I just don't want to rush into a decision and regret it,' explained Darcie. 'I don't know what it is about the sketchbook and dress, but they feel important. Special.' She

36

rubbed her eyes. She'd been looking at a screen of one sort or another for far too long the past couple of days.

'You look tired,' said Lena. 'I wish you'd take a break. I mean a proper break, like a holiday. You could do something fun for a change. I'll be able to manage, and I'll have Chloe on hand if I need her. You can afford to close the shop for a week.'

Darcie turned to look at her mum. 'A holiday? It's a lovely idea but I *can't* afford to close the shop for an entire week; besides, where would I go and who would I go with?'

'You could go on one of those singles holidays,' said Lena. 'You might even meet someone.' Lena emphasised the last word for effect.

'Honestly, Mum, I've no interest in meeting anyone right now,' said Darcie. 'After the last blind date Chloe set me up on, I'm giving men a wide berth for the time being.'

'But that was a year ago,' protested Lena. 'Look, darling, I don't want you to miss out on any more of life than you already have. Stuck here caring for me when you should be out having fun.'

'What's brought all this on?' asked Darcie.

Lena put her cup down. 'I know you've given up a lot for me over the years and I am truly grateful, but I do worry that it's at the expense of your happiness.'

'I'm happy as I am,' said Darcie. It might not have been strictly true, right at this moment in her life, but generally speaking, she was happy, if a little lonely, but she was used to that. It came with being the oddball at school who was a history geek and never being able either to afford to join in with the outings of her peers or not having the time because she was caring for her mum. She gave Lena what she hoped was a reassuring smile and kissed her on the cheek. 'Stop worrying.'

'Mother's prerogative,' replied Lena, but she let the matter drop, for which Darcie was grateful.

It was another quiet day in the shop and after making Lena her lunch and then settling her in her chair, where she would likely sleep for a few hours, Darcie went back to the shop and resumed her internet search for the source of the dress and sketchbook. Once again, it was a fruitless endeavour.

Frustrated at the lack of forward motion in her search, Darcie decided to do something constructive. She could begin with cleaning the dress. She felt a strong sense of connection to the original dressmaker and believed, for some reason, that the suitcase had been destined to fall into her hands.

In her work area, she placed the suitcase on the cutting table and took out the dress, placing it on a coat hanger. It was then she noticed the suitcase had an inside pocket with an elasticated top. In their excitement the other day, none of them had noticed or, if they did, hadn't thought to check in the pocket. Darcie pulled the elastic top open and was surprised to see there was, indeed, something in there. A piece of paper, maybe? She pulled it out and was amazed to see it was a train ticket and a small brown envelope folded in half.

The ticket was a muted blue, and she could make out the writing on it.

London to Pulborough
20 September 1942
1 Adult

She unfolded the envelope. The name Nathalie Leroux with a date September 1942 was written in faded blue ink. The envelope reminded Darcie of the type used for weekly or monthly pay, when people were paid in cash, which, of course, would tie in with the date.

Darcie turned the envelope over and on the seal was a black stamp mark, almost like a coat of arms with a tree in the centre, a crown above it and a banner underneath. She let out a gasp as she read the cursive styled words on the banner: *Ritz Paris*.

Darcie looked at the ticket and envelope, trying to work out where the connection was. How was a train station in Pulborough connected to a Nathalie Leroux and the Ritz in Paris?

Darcie grabbed the sketchbook and looked at the signature. At a stretch, she supposed the figure of eight could represent the letter 'N' and the other mark could be a fancy 'L'. Was this a type of shorthand signature?

Darcie typed the name Nathalie Leroux into her laptop and was met with several results, which she was sure weren't the Nathalie she was looking for. In all fairness, Nathalie Leroux was probably no longer alive. Even if she'd been twenty in 1942, that would make her one hundred years old now. What a shame Darcie wouldn't be able to reunite the drawings with who she assumed was the rightful owner. But how exactly did they end up in West Sussex? She'd probably never know.

She looked up as the door opened and in came Hannah, with her art folder in her hand. She and Darcie had struck up a friendship over their love for fashion when Hannah had come into the shop while researching for her GSCE Textiles course. Hannah was now in her last year of A levels, studying Fashion and Textiles, and Darcie had become something of a mentor to her.

'Hi, Darcie. You said to call in when I got a moment. Sorry I didn't come yesterday.'

'That's OK, don't worry. It's just lovely to see you. And you've brought your folder.'

Hannah's red-streaked hair was tied back in some sort of messy ponytail arrangement that Darcie suspected took rather longer to arrange than the appearance would have you believe. Hannah was wearing a tie-dye purple skirt with an oversized sweatshirt and hand-decorated canvas ankle boots. The blue glass nose stud matched her sky-blue eyes. Darcie loved the eclectic, hippy look Hannah went for.

'Oh, what have you got there?' Hannah asked, coming

over to the workbench and looking at the dress hanging up. 'It's amazing. Oh, and this? Wow! Did you draw that?' Hannah was looking at the sketchbook now. 'Can I see?'

'Sure. It's not mine though,' said Darcie. 'I got it at the auction the other day. The left-luggage one.'

'These are beautiful,' said Hannah. 'Oh, wow. Gorgeous. I wish I was this good. Who is the designer? Do you know?'

'Possibly someone called Nathalie Leroux, but I can't find anything about her. I think she might be French by the spelling of her name with an "h" in it. Typically, that's the French spelling. I think she had some connection with the Ritz during the war.'

'The Ritz?' Hannah looked at Darcie. 'You know who was there during the war, don't you?'

'In terms of someone famous, well, yes, it was where Coco Chanel lived.'

'Perhaps Nathalie Leroux knew her? Or maybe look up Coco Chanel and see if there's any connection,' said Hannah, putting the book down and admiring the dress again.

'It's a possibility, I suppose, but Chanel closed down all their couture house boutiques during the war,' said Darcie. 'They only kept one open, the one opposite the Ritz as it happens – 21 rue Cambon. It sold perfume and accessories to the Germans. None of the Parisians could afford such luxuries.'

'I guess it's a long shot,' said Hannah.

'I'm sure it would be documented if she had another fashion designer working with her at the Ritz during the war,' said Darcie, closing the sketchbook. 'So, are you going to let me have a look at your stuff now?' She nodded towards Hannah's folder, and Hannah lifted it onto the workbench and unzipped it.

'These are the sketches I've done today,' said Hannah, pulling out several sheets of paper.

Darcie looked at the drawings and, not for the first time, admired Hannah's vision and sense of style. It was nothing like her own, but she could see the talent in the work. 'These are great,' she said.

By now, Hannah was busy tapping on her phone. No doubt Instagramming or Snapchatting or whatever it was the kids did these days. Darcie continued to look through Hannah's work. She remembered doing her own A levels, and it wasn't without a pang of sadness that she remembered how she had often fantasised about going to art college. It was then that Lena's health had taken a turn for the worse and Darcie had realised it was an impossible dream. Still, she loved the thought that Hannah was going to go. She could live vicariously through her friend's experience, if nothing else.

Hannah looked up abruptly from her phone. 'Oh. My. God.' She looked at Darcie with an open mouth. 'This is unreal.'

'What?' asked Darcie.

'This! Where's that sketchbook? No. Not mine. That one you got at auction.'

Darcie passed it over. 'What is it?'

'Wait. Let me check first.' Hannah flicked through the pages to the blue evening gown with the oversized bow at the shoulder and a fishtail skirt. She looked back at her phone and then gave the dress hanging up another long look before finally speaking. 'This is fucking unreal.'

Darcie let the swear word slide. She was too intrigued by whatever it was Hannah had found. 'Can you please tell me what is so . . . unreal?'

Hannah clasped her phone to her chest as she grinned madly at Darcie. 'You might want to sit down.'

'You might want to just tell me!'

'OK. Look at this.' Slowly, Hannah turned the phone around so Darcie could see the screen.

'Oh. My. God,' said Darcie, inadvertently repeating what Hannah had just said. 'It's the bloody dress!'

'It's not just the dress,' Hannah said excitedly. 'Look who's wearing it. Coco Chanel, no less.'

Chapter 6

Darcie

For what must be the one hundredth time, Darcie looked at the photograph Hannah had found of Chanel. She was still having trouble believing it was the same dress. To be fair, the photograph was black and white and a little grainy, so it was difficult to see the detail, but it looked exactly the same as the one in the suitcase.

'You don't think it's a replica?' asked Chloe that evening after Darcie had relayed the story to her.

'I know it could be, and my sensible head is telling me that's exactly what it is. That perhaps whoever Nathalie Leroux was, she was an art student, and she'd copied Chanel's designs for her studies.'

'I guess if it was during the war, then this Nathalie might not have been able to continue at art school or whatever is the equivalent over there and maybe just began copying other people's designs for fun. Can't you get an expert opinion?'

Darcie raised her eyebrows. 'Excuse me?' she said, not without humour. 'I am an expert.'

Chloe laughed. 'You know what I mean: a Chanel expert.'

'I did think about writing to them. If I can get the dress authenticated, then it could be worth a lot of money.'

'I guess there's nothing they can do, like demand you give them the dress back,' said Chloe.

'No, that's right. It's mine. I bought it fair and square. There was nothing dodgy about the sale at all.'

After Darcie had gone downstairs and made sure Lena was up, had taken her meds and was comfortable for the morning, she opened up the shop. Then she sat down to compose her email to the House of Chanel.

She kept it brief and to the point.

Hello

I recently purchased some items from a left-luggage auction in West Sussex, UK, which included a dress and a sketchbook.

After a little research, I believe the dress might have a connection with the House of Chanel and wondered if you could confirm this, please? There is a picture on the internet showing Coco Chanel wearing what looks like the same dress I purchased. I have attached the link for the said photograph and also a photo of the dress I have.

I believe the sketchbook belonged to a woman named Nathalie Leroux but, to date, I haven't been able to find any further information. Do you have any records showing Nathalie Leroux worked at the Ritz for Coco Chanel during the war?

Are you able to confirm if the dress I have here is, in fact, the same dress that Coco Chanel is wearing and whether it is part of the Chanel collection?

I look forward to hearing from you.

Kind regards

Darcie Marchant

Vintaged and Loved

Darcie wasn't convinced they would even bother replying, but if they did, she was sure it wouldn't just end with a confirmation email. They would have to see the garment in person for the dress to be authenticated. She wondered how much they would charge for an authentication certificate and whether they would try to price her out of obtaining one. She'd cross that bridge when she got to it.

* * *

The following week was spent relentlessly checking her emails. By the tenth day though Darcie was giving up hope of them ever replying to her.

'They probably think I'm either crazy or a chancer,' she said to Lena, as they sat down for their mid-morning cup of tea. Darcie had refrained from doing anything further with the dress until she heard from the fashion house. She wanted to be sure she knew what she was dealing with, and if it did belong to Chanel once upon a time, then preserving it in the state and condition in which she'd bought it would be a key component and add authenticity to the backstory if she wanted to sell it on. There were plenty of private collectors who would love this sort of thing. She still couldn't get any leads on Nathalie Leroux, which was frustrating.

'How long are you going to wait for a reply?' asked Lena.

Darcie shrugged. 'I might send them a chaser email at the end of the month.'

'You should put a time limit on it,' said Lena. 'You might need to get some legal advice.'

'Hmm, probably should, I guess.' Darcie didn't particularly want to go down that route because of the costs involved.

She pulled up her emails on her phone and nearly dropped it when the notifications popped up.

'What is it?' asked Lena as Darcie fumbled with her phone.

'There's a reply from the House of Chanel.' Darcie stared at the phone.

'Well, what does it say?'

She tapped the screen, and the email downloaded onto her phone. 'OK, it says . . . "Dear Miss Marchant, thank you for getting in touch with us about the dress. We have looked at the photograph you sent and agree there does appear to be a remarkable similarity. However, in view of the circumstances in which you came by the dress, we feel it is highly unlikely to be a Chanel dress. Furthermore, the name Nathalie Leroux has no connection with the House of Chanel, either past or present.

'"However, we would like the opportunity to have the garment viewed by one of our experts, so we can say with certainty whether this is, in fact, a genuine Chanel or not. Please could you contact us and arrange a convenient appointment at our Paris office to have the garment reviewed? Yours sincerely, Christophe Padgett, Senior Manager, Vintage Collections".' Darcie looked up at Lena. 'They want me to go to Paris! With the dress.'

'That's amazing. How exciting.' Lena smiled broadly at her daughter.

'Well, yes, it is. I think,' said Darcie.

'Of course it is. Why would you think otherwise?'

Darcie fiddled with the heart pendant around her neck. 'I love the dress. Really love it, so, in a way, I don't want to part with it. But I've started worrying, what if they make a claim against the dress and demand I give it back to them? What if there's some kind of loophole I don't know about? I can't fight the mighty power of the House of Chanel.'

Lena looked thoughtful for a moment before speaking. 'What do you want to do with the dress? Notwithstanding all this Chanel business. Just think of the dress itself. What do you want to do with it?'

'I wouldn't mind keeping it but, to be honest, it's tiny. I don't think I'd fit into it.'

'So, what's the plan with it?'

'To sell it really,' confessed Darcie, even though she didn't like the idea. 'It would be a waste to keep it just because I like the look of it.'

'And if this dress is a Chanel number, then it's going to be worth soooo much money,' said Lena. 'They're going to have to pay you for it if they want it.'

'Or charge me for the authentication certificate, which could be significantly more than I could ever afford.'

'Don't be so pessimistic. Go to the meeting. Show them the

dress and see what happens from there. If you can't afford the certificate, you can get them to put it in writing that it's a genuine Chanel and that should be worth something when you come to sell it. I'm sure a private collector would love to get their hands on this.'

Everything Lena said was right. Darcie knew that, but she didn't want to trouble her mum with the problem of logistics. Getting to Paris, paying for flights, taxis, hotels, not to mention someone opening up the shop and manning it while she was away, all came at a cost – one she couldn't afford.

Before she had time to think of an excuse other than money, someone came into the shop.

'It's only me!' came Hannah's voice.

'We're in the back here,' called out Lena. 'Come on through.'

Darcie liked the fact that Lena was always so welcoming with Hannah. 'Hi-ya,' she greeted the eighteen-year-old.

'Hey, I was just wondering if you'd heard anything from Chanel yet?' she asked. So far, Hannah had been in nearly every day for an update. 'Please tell me they've replied. The suspense is killing me.'

'Actually, they have,' said Darcie, waving her phone at her friend. 'Just this minute.' She opened the email and passed it over to Hannah.

'Oh. My. God! This is amazing,' gushed Hannah. 'When are you going? They want to see it. They must think there's something in it, even though they're playing it down.'

'Darcie is dithering,' said Lena.

Hannah gave Darcie an old-fashioned look of disapproval. 'Dithering. Come on, Darcie, you can't be Dithering Darcie; you've got to be Decisive Darcie and go.'

Darcie laughed at the nickname. 'Hey, less of your cheek. You're supposed to respect your elders.'

Hannah gave her a hug. 'You know I love you really. Now, come on, you are going, aren't you?'

'It's not as easy as that,' said Darcie. 'I can't just nip off to Paris for a couple of days and leave the shop.'

'Of course you can,' said Hannah. 'Look, if you go at the beginning of July, I'll have finished sixth form by then and I can look after the shop.' She looked at Lena and then back at Darcie. 'That's if it's OK with you both.'

'Perfectly OK with me,' replied Lena quickly.

'That's really sweet, but I can't afford to pay you,' said Darcie, knowing she would have to be honest about it.

'I don't want paying,' said Hannah. 'I love your shop and it would be a brilliant experience to work here for a couple of days. You've helped me plenty with my coursework. Call it payback.'

'I didn't do it for payback,' protested Darcie.

'I know, but it's my way of saying thank you.' Hannah gave a satisfied grin. 'There, problem solved.'

'But there's also the cost of travelling,' said Darcie. 'Sorry, I don't want to sound like a party pooper but it's not cheap.'

'Ah, that's where I can help too,' said Hannah. 'My aunty works for Eurostar and can get a staff discount on travel. I can get you a really good deal, might even be able to get it for free.'

'Oh, I couldn't do that,' said Darcie.

'Yes, you could,' replied Hannah. 'You could even do it in a day, but if you had to stay, there are plenty of cheap Airbnbs. My sister got a really good deal when she went last year. Look, I'll show you.' With that, Hannah tapped at her phone and a minute later brought up several Parisian apartments. All at very reasonable prices.

'Wow, I just assumed it would be out of my price range,' said Darcie. She studied the website and a little flutter of excitement breezed around her stomach. She could actually afford to go.

'That all sounds perfect,' said Lena. 'What are you waiting for?'

Darcie looked at the website, then at the email, and then at her mum and friend. What was she waiting for, indeed?

Chapter 7

Nathalie

The day after the visit from Kranz, Alphonse had come into the shop and offered his sincere apologies to both my parents and me. Papa was more understanding than I expected him to be. I wished I could be so reasonable but something in my heart had died that night and I just didn't feel the same about Alphonse anymore. He assured me he would never have pulled the trigger, and I believed him. He wasn't brave enough. He was a coward. And that just made me dislike him even more.

It was, therefore, a relief when the travel passes came through, and Maman said we would go to Brittany the next day. I couldn't wait to be away from Paris and put as much distance between myself and Alphonse as possible.

Two days later, we were in Malestroit making the short walk to the farm on the outskirts of the town, where Maman's sister lived with her husband, Philippe, and their children. I had fond memories of times before the war when we would visit the Morbihan countryside and spend countless hours playing out in the fields, swimming in the lakes and exploring the surrounding areas, making friends with the locals and, of course, helping my uncle during harvest time. That was, of course, the real reason we went to visit, but we enjoyed being there. Edgar and Gaston would work out in the fields, harvesting the crops, while Rachelle, Odile, and I would go fruit picking. I remember well the gluttonous feeling of eating too many strawberries one particular year and Uncle Philippe telling us off. We had to pick potatoes the next day as a punishment.

News of our arrival in Malestroit must have reached Clarice's farm before we did, as my aunt was standing at the gate waiting for us. She waved wildly and ran down the road to greet Maman. The two sisters embraced fiercely, and then it was my turn to be enveloped in a big, warm hug. Almost immediately, I was swallowed up in the arms of Rachelle and Odile.

'We are so pleased to see you,' cried Rachelle.

As I hugged my cousins, I felt a wave of love, happiness, and relief. It had been two long years since we'd been together.

I linked my arms through my cousins', and we practically skipped our way back up to the farmhouse. I could smell vegetables cooking on the stove and coffee brewing in a pot on top of the range. 'Where is Gaston?' I asked as we sat down at the kitchen table.

Clarice glanced at Maman before she spoke. 'He's not here. It's just me, Philippe, and the girls.'

'Will he be here later?' I looked between my aunt and my cousins. And then it dawned on me. 'You mean he's not here at all?'

Clarice nodded. '*Oui. C'est ça.*'

'Is he—'

Clarice held up her hand. 'We don't know where he is.'

'The same way we don't know where Edgar is, I expect,' said Maman.

Now it was Clarice's turn to be surprised. She raised an eyebrow and then let out a sigh. 'We should both be proud of our sons, even if we aren't happy about the situation.'

'Indeed,' agreed Maman.

The door opened, and we all looked around to see my uncle Philippe standing in the doorway. 'Now there is a beautiful sight,' he declared. He hugged us all in turn. 'It's good to see you, Therese. How is Théodule?'

As the adults discussed the latest events of the war, Rachelle tapped my arm and beckoned me to follow her. 'We'll take the bags upstairs,' she said to her mother, picking up Maman's rather battered brown suitcase. 'Come on, Nathalie.'

I followed on, with Odile behind me.

'You're going to be sharing with me,' said Rachelle. 'But it does mean sharing a bed – just like we used to when we were younger.'

I smiled at the memories of us giggling at night-time, trying to be as quiet as possible so as not to wake anyone. We used to have midnight feasts and hold imaginary dances where we would twirl around the bedroom, humming tunes like Tchaikovsky's 'Waltz of the Flowers'.

Rachelle's bedroom hadn't changed over the years. The wrought-iron double-bed frame occupied most of the room, pushed up against the wall, which was papered with a large floral design. Opposite the bed was an open fireplace with a shelf and a mirror above. A white armoire took up most of the wall immediately to the left, with its arched head and ornately carved flowers. A dressing table stood in the alcove next to the fireplace and a chest of drawers on the opposite side. All the furniture was painted white, and a white muslin hung at the window. It was so much bigger than my room back in Paris and I loved the sense of space.

The windows were open, and the muslin billowed now and again on the breeze. I placed my suitcase on the floor and went over to the window, closing my eyes and breathing in the earthy smell of the fields and the fragrance of the jasmine that covered the front of the property. I could hear birds singing in the hedgerow and I revelled in the absence of noisy military vehicles trundling up and down the streets, the lack of German boots clipping along the path and the non-existence of German voices. Here, the farm was a sanctuary and an antidote to everything I had experienced of the war so far.

'I'm so glad to be here,' I sighed, flopping down onto the

bed. I ran my hand across the familiar patchwork quilt that Rachelle and I had spent many weeks making one summer, using up the old clothes and fabric we had collected.

'I wish you were staying in my room,' said Odile, perching on the end of the bed.

'Maybe I can sleep in your room one night,' I said. Odile had been just coming up to her fourteenth birthday when I last saw her, with her hair in plaits and an innocence about her. Now she was on the brink of womanhood and her hair was fashioned in a more grown-up style to match her age, but it wasn't her age or her hair that made her look older. It was her eyes. The innocent spark had gone, to be replaced by a sadness that only war could bring. 'Or maybe Rachelle will let you sleep in here one night. We could have one of our midnight feasts.'

Odile smiled. 'Yes, I'd like that.' She hopped up from the bed. 'I've got to help Maman with the dishes.' She kissed me on each side of the face before leaving.

'How is she?' I asked Rachelle, who was lying next to me on the bed. 'She seems subdued.'

Rachelle was silent for a long moment before she spoke. 'She had a bad experience. With a soldier.'

I sat upright. 'What?'

Rachelle closed her eyes and then opened them. 'He was a rogue soldier. He was drunk and Odile had gone to take some eggs to one of the neighbours and had the misfortune of encountering him alone on the road.'

'Oh, please don't say he . . .' I couldn't form the words that made me feel sick to even consider.

'He tried,' said Rachelle. 'But someone saw what was happening. They stopped him.'

'Stopped him?'

'Hit him over the head. Knocked him unconscious.'

'Who was it?'

'We don't know. Odile didn't recognise him. He just pulled Odile to her feet and told her to go.'

'Thank goodness someone was there to help. Were there any repercussions?'

'No. I suspect the soldier didn't report it, otherwise he would have had to explain what he was doing in the woods. Drunk.'

'But it's obviously affected Odile.'

'Yes. She won't leave the farm. Prefers to stay in the house if possible. If she leaves, she won't go out alone.' Rachelle let out a long breath. 'I'm worried she won't ever feel safe.'

'Give her time. I want to say when the war is over it will be better, but I can't make empty promises.'

'Promises are for fools,' said Rachelle.

We didn't speak any more about Odile that evening and I made an extra effort to include her without making it obvious Rachelle had told me what happened. Poor dear Odile. My heart raged at the absolute abuse of power by not just a German soldier but by a man against a defenceless teenager. I wished whoever had saved Odile had done a better job on the soldier. He didn't deserve any mercy.

Later that evening, I went along with Philippe and Rachelle to put the chickens away for the night and to check on the one pig they were allowed to keep.

'We have a permit for just the one pig and five chickens,' explained Philippe. 'If we want any more, then we have to get permission and we have to hand over six eggs to the Germans each day.'

'I didn't realise that,' I said.

'And it's not as if they need it,' complained Philippe. 'They never go hungry. They would sooner leave us with no food and waste it than let us have any more than necessary. It's another way to control us.'

'We aren't even allowed to collect firewood from the forest now,' said Rachelle. 'It is seen as theft.'

'That's outrageous!' I declared. 'I had no idea.'

'*Alors*, that's everything done,' said Philippe after we

had shooed all the hens into the coop for the night. 'Need to protect them from humans more than the foxes these days.'

We went to bed shortly after that and I remembered the early nights from staying here before. Philippe had to get up at dawn and it meant the rest of the house went to bed as well. Rachelle and I snuggled under the blankets and talked about anything other than the war. I felt we were both trying to recapture our younger days when we didn't have any cares in the world other than what we were going to do the following day. We used to talk about the local boys who we liked and we laughed now as we relived those nights, talking and giggling.

'We should go to sleep,' said Rachelle eventually. 'You must be tired from all that travelling.'

In fact, I didn't feel that tired. I don't know if it was the excitement of being back in Morbihan with my cousins or what Rachelle had told me about Odile, but I found it difficult to sleep that night. I heard the clock downstairs chime one o'clock in the morning. Rachelle rolled over in what I assumed was her sleep, but then I heard her push back the covers and blankets and slowly sit up. The shutters were closed and a blackout blind was in place across the window. I could barely see her. She was just a black mass. She moved over to the chair by the window and I could hear, more than see, that she was putting on her clothes.

'Rachelle,' I whispered. 'Is everything all right?'

'I thought you were asleep,' came back the reply.

'What are you doing?'

'Nothing.'

I sat up now, fully awake. 'Yes, you are. You're getting dressed.'

'Don't ask questions, Nathalie.'

'Just tell me, then I won't have to.' I pushed back my side of the covers and hopped out of bed.

'What are you doing?' asked Rachelle.

'I'm coming with you.'

'Nathalie, please.'

'Too late, I've got my cardigan on already.'

Rachelle let out a sigh. 'You were always tenacious like this when you were younger. I see you've not outgrown it.'

I smiled to myself and, tiptoeing, followed my cousin out of the room, down the stairs and out through the back door. When she darted across the back garden, I did too. When she hopped over the low wall at the side, I did likewise. And when she ran across the field and dived under the cover of the trees, I followed her.

We had only run a few yards into the forest but the trees were dense and their foliage allowed only a few slivers of light to find their way through the branches. The scent of pine was heavy in the air, as was the unsettling silence. All I could hear was our feet on the ground and our ragged breathing as we darted deeper into the darkness.

Soon we were swallowed up by the woodland and it was only then Rachelle stopped and, puffing hard, she rested against a tree. I came to a halt alongside her. Putting my hands on my hips, I leaned forward slightly, as I took deep breaths. '*Alors*, are you going to tell me what we're doing?'

'My dear cousin,' said Rachelle, after she had caught her breath. 'We are going to meet someone. Well, more than one person, actually.' She took my hand and began striding off deeper into the forest.

'Who?' I asked.

'It will be a surprise – for everyone. You're not supposed to be here, but I know I can trust you.'

Despite me asking several more times what was going on, Rachelle wouldn't answer my questions and I gave up. After about five minutes, Rachelle slowed her pace and picked her way through some trees.

'Do you know where you're going?' I asked.

'Shh.' She put her finger to her lips. 'Now, when we get there, you let me do the talking.'

We had only taken a few more steps when suddenly, from the darkness of the trees, the shadowy figure of a man jumped out in front of us. Then two more from each side. I could see they were holding rifles.

'Stop right there,' the first one ordered.

Chapter 8

Darcie

'Now stop fussing,' said Lena, as for the fourth time Darcie checked that all Lena's medication was up to date, that the instruction booklet for Chloe to refer to if needed had everything written down. Not to mention all the instructions she had typed up for Hannah in the shop.

'I can't help it. I haven't been away for ages,' said Darcie, knowing she was completely flapping about this trip.

'I am quite capable of looking after Mum,' said Chloe, folding her arms across her chest. 'I am a responsible adult. I have a responsible job. I do have responsibilities.' She exchanged an eye-roll with Lena.

'Oh, I know, I know,' said Darcie. 'I just feel a bit anxious about it, that's all.'

'Control freak,' muttered Chloe, and then winked at her sister.

'Not really. Well, maybe a little,' admitted Darcie. 'I'm just used to organising everything.'

Chloe went over and gave her sister a hug. 'And you do a splendid job but, honestly, we can manage. I'm working from home all this week, so I'll be here for Mum. Aiden's coming over to stay at the weekend . . .'

'The weekend? But I'll be back by then,' interrupted Darcie. She watched as her mother and sister exchanged a look. 'What's going on?'

'Now, darling, don't be cross,' said Lena, adjusting her

position in her chair. 'I took the liberty of extending your stay in Paris from two days to two weeks.'

'TWO WEEKS?' Darcie shouted the words out before she could stop herself. 'Two weeks? What are you on about? I can't stay for two weeks! What about you? The shop? The cost?'

Lena held up her hand to silence her. 'You've not had a holiday in such a long time; you deserve a proper break from everyone and everything. We've already been in touch with the owners of the apartment and extended your stay there.'

'But what about the shop?' protested Darcie, still trying to grapple with the idea of two weeks away.

'Ah, that's where I come in,' said Chloe, looking very pleased with herself. 'Not only am I working from home this week, but I have the following week off. So, Hannah is looking after it for the first five days and after that, I get to be boss.'

'And before you say anything about costs,' said Lena, 'Granny sent the money.'

'So it's a team effort,' said Chloe. 'You can't say no. We all want you to have a holiday and we know how much you love Paris. You always tell me how much you would love to have lived there. I know it's not a lifetime, but you can at least pretend for two weeks.'

'I don't know what to say,' said Darcie. She felt tears spring to her eyes. She was going on holiday. Her family and friends had come together to make this possible for her. 'Thank you so much. You are all so lovely. I'll phone Granny later and thank her.'

'She said not to worry about that right now. Just phone her when you're back and tell her all about it,' said Lena. 'We can visit her.'

'Now, you're not to worry about anything here,' said Chloe. 'Don't, I repeat, don't be phoning Hannah every five minutes. I've told her she's to block your number. Any problems, which there won't be, and she can come to me. Now, we'd better get going, otherwise you'll miss your flight.'

'Flight? I thought I was going on the Eurostar?' said Darcie.

'Oh, yes, you have Granny to thank for that. She offered before we had bought the train tickets,' said Lena. She passed the printed e-ticket over.

Darcie took the ticket, knowing she was beyond the point of objecting. 'I love you all very much,' she said, picking up her backpack. 'I shall miss you, but I'm so excited.'

'You're not allowed to miss us,' said Lena. 'Now go on; Chloe's halfway out of the door with your case already.'

By the time the plane touched down at Charles de Gaulle Airport and Darcie had transferred to the drop-off point in the city centre, she had resisted the urge to call home several times to check everything was OK. Using the directions Chloe had handed her, she took the Métro to the Montmartre area and, after a short walk, found herself outside the apartment building on rue Ordener. The double oak doors filled the stone archway, which separated two retail shops. She took a moment to take in her surroundings. The street was lined with trees, their bright green leaves a contrast to the cream-coloured stone of the buildings, which were six or seven storeys high with slate grey rooftops and dormer windows. Black wrought-iron balcony railings uniformly braced each of the full-length windows that opened out onto small balconies, where many window boxes were host to an abundance of brightly coloured flowers. Shops, cafés, restaurants, and banks, together with boutiques and independent stores, lined either side of the road. It was a bustling and busy road with cars and buses streaming by and people going about their daily business. It was a community within the wider community of the city, giving the feeling of being in a small town.

She pushed open one of the large oak doors and found herself in a communal foyer with a flight of stairs spiralling up to her left, while nestled in the embrace of the stairs was an old-fashioned birdcage elevator. Her apartment was on the fifth floor, and so she didn't have to struggle with her case and backpack, she opted for the elevator. The old elevator was beautiful, and Darcie took a selfie to send to Lena and Chloe later that evening.

She felt very glamorous, as if she were in a 1960s black-and-white French film. As she slid the cage door closed and, after she pressed the button, the mechanics clanked into life, taking her upwards. Darcie had gone for a more conventional look with her clothing today, with her three-quarter-length black capri trousers and hadn't been able to resist a black-and-white stripy top with a red neckerchief in her nod to French fashion.

Now that she had two weeks in the city, Darcie intended to check out some of the flea markets and second-hand clothing shops she had researched online. She had also marked the Printemps Haussmann department store for a visit. It was a world-leading department store for fashion and had a dedicated floor for retro clothing, as it acknowledged the need for sustainable fashion. Darcie doubted whether she'd be able to afford anything, but it would be worth a look all the same.

The elevator shuddered to a halt on the fifth floor. Darcie stepped out into the hallway and located her apartment. As per the instructions, she knocked on the adjacent door where she was greeted by a man, roughly her own age, who had been given key-holding duties.

In broken English, which was far better than her French, he said he didn't need to show her around as it was only one room.

Darcie was quite happy with that, and it was indeed only one room. There was a small kitchenette space immediately to her right. Directly opposite the kitchen was a folding door into the shower room. A sofa was on the right-hand side with a high-rise bed above it and on the left-hand wall was a small square table and two chairs. The best feature was the full-length double window. Darcie pulled back the net curtain and was greeted with the rooftops of the city beyond. On the flight over, she'd checked out the location and found she was less than a fifteen-minute walk from Sacré-Cœur Basilica.

Not wanting to waste a moment of her time in Paris, because she had no idea when, if ever, she'd be back, Darcie left her suitcase by the door and threw her backpack on the sofa. With just her shoulder bag, she headed out in search of the famous Montmartre basilica. Her meeting with Chanel was scheduled for the next day at ten-thirty, so she wanted to spend as much time as she could being a tourist.

Sacré-Cœur was as beautiful as she'd imagined it would be. Set against the clear blue sky, the white stone building with its domed roof stood proudly on the hilltop. Darcie wondered if her mysterious Nathalie Leroux had ever been here. Had she sat on the steps just as Darcie was doing now? If she had, it was probably before war came to the city. Darcie couldn't imagine there was any free time for the everyday citizen to wander around sightseeing or meeting up with friends during the occupation. No, it was probably German soldiers who had been here. She pushed the image from her mind, not wanting to tarnish the spot with such thoughts.

Using her phone, Darcie took some pictures of the building and the steps leading up to it, together with a couple of selfies. She wanted to document her trip so she could look back on it and relive her time here as much as possible.

'Would you like me to take your photo?' came a voice from behind her.

Darcie turned and saw a man, probably in his early thirties, with a sophisticated and very expensive-looking camera in his hands. His fair hair was cut shorter at the sides, leaving it longer on the top. He had the most amazing pale blue eyes.

Darcie realised he was waiting for an answer. 'Oh, it's OK, but thank you.' It was then she realised he had spoken to her in English, although with an American accent. 'How did you know I was English?' she asked.

He cocked his head and gave a lazy grin. 'It was an educated guess.' He nodded towards the map in her hands.

'Ah, my Paris street map with English words all across the cover,' she said.

'OK, busted. It wasn't so much an educated guess,' he confessed. 'Are you sure you don't want me to take your picture? I'm a street photographer. If you like what you see, you can go online and order some prints.'

She looked at the selfies on her phone and while they weren't great and the idea of having someone take some half-decent photos of her was appealing, Darcie was certain she wouldn't be able to justify the cost. 'I'm sure. But thanks anyway.'

'You don't have to buy them. I don't charge. It's just to build up my portfolio, which I can show to paying customers,' he explained. 'I have a website and social media accounts. You can check me out. I'm not a fraud. I'm not going to do anything with your photos.' He fished in his pocket and produced a business card, which he handed to Darcie. 'Matt Langdon. Here, you can see some of the photos I've posted on my social media.'

Matt took out his mobile and showed his Instagram page to Darcie. She had to admit she was pretty impressed with some of the photos he'd taken. 'And these are all just random strangers you've approached in the street?'

'Yeah. I just walk around places and if I see someone who has a unique or interesting look, then I ask if I can take some pictures.'

'And most people agree?'

'Most people.'

There was that half-smile on his face again. Darcie was sure it was one he knew could charm people into agreeing to anything. In fact, she was sure she was already relenting. 'You take good pictures,' she said.

'I just wanted to assure you I'm no creep.'

'Consider me convinced,' said Darcie, handing back his phone.

'You have such an interesting look. How about I just shoot some pictures and show them to you on the camera? If you don't like them, I'll delete them straight away.'

'You're persistent.'

'I just love street photography and I love studying interesting people.'

Whether it was the joy of being in Paris, the hot weather or just his obvious enthusiasm for his art, Darcie wasn't sure, but she found herself agreeing. 'I can't afford to buy any,' she said, thinking she might as well tell him straight.

'You don't have to. Like I said, no obligation.'

'OK, just a few.'

He put his hands together and did a small bow of gratitude. 'Thank you!'

Initially Darcie felt very self-conscious in front of the camera, but Matt had a way about him that put her at ease. He chatted to her and made her forget he was even taking her photo.

'So, what are you doing in Paris?' he asked as he got her to sit on the steps with the basilica in the background.

'On holiday for a couple of weeks.' Darcie glanced around at the passers-by and tourists and was reassured that none of them appeared to have any interest in what she was doing. 'What about you?'

'I'm here kinda on vacation.' He fiddled with the dial on the camera, checking back through the lens every now and again.

'Kind of?'

'Yep. A working vacation, if you like. Right, just look straight into the lens. No, don't smile. Rest your arms across your knees. Like you're pretty bored.'

Darcie laughed and then straightened her face. She felt anything but bored. 'Like this?'

'Great. Hold it. That's so cool. Now put your elbows on your knees and cup your face.'

'Have you always liked photography?' asked Darcie after Matt had shot several photos and was checking the screen on the camera again.

'Yeah. My mom's creative, so I guess I inherited that gene from her.'

'And your dad?'

He looked up and for a moment the easy-going manner dropped from his face but was almost instantly replaced with a smile. 'Not so much. He's a white-collar worker. Likes his office and dealing with facts and figures.' He held the camera up. 'This time, look off to your left. I'm gonna come in close from an angle.' Matt snapped away for a few more minutes, giving instructions, which Darcie dutifully complied with. 'These are great. Take a look.' Matt sat beside her on the step and, tilting the camera so she could see, began going through the shots.

'Well, they're a lot better than my selfies,' said Darcie.

'I'll take that as a compliment,' said Matt. There was a touch of humour in his voice, and Darcie liked the fact he wasn't too uptight about himself or his art.

'No, seriously, they're really good. Almost doesn't look like me.'

'Now, see here. They automatically sync to my phone and I can make a few adjustments with the settings.' He fiddled around for a minute before showing Darcie the final result.

'Wow! That's brilliant!' she said. 'You've changed the whole look of the photo.'

'Yeah, I like to make the sky more dramatic and the colours richer, introducing more light and shade.'

'I know it's all digital, but I love how things can be transformed and made into a different version of themselves.'

Matt looked at her with interest. 'You do? A lot of people don't like digital manipulation.'

'I think it's great. I do something similar but with clothes,' she found herself saying. 'I upcycle clothing, repair stuff, restore it or bring it up to date with a new twist. I have a shop where I sell vintage clothing and accessories.'

'Ah, it's all beginning to make sense now,' said Matt. 'Your vibe.' He made a sweeping movement with his hand towards her clothing. 'You've got an individual style. That's what drew me to you.'

'Very perceptive. And this is me dressing down to fit in.'

'Are you on social media?'

'Yep – Vintaged and Loved. My name's Darcie by the way.'

Matt held out his hand. 'Pleased to meet you, Darcie Bytheway.'

Darcie laughed out loud as she shook his hand. 'Marchant. Darcie Marchant.'

'Look, would you like to grab a coffee? If you're not in any rush.'

'I . . . err . . .' Her automatic response was to decline but, for some reason, she hesitated. What would the harm be in going for a coffee with him? He seemed normal enough and in a public place with people all around, it was a pretty safe bet.

Matt held up his hand. 'Hey, don't sweat it. It's no big deal if you don't want to.' He started packing his camera back into his rucksack. 'The pictures will be up on my Instagram and TikTok account later this evening. You can just grab a screenshot or if you want a high-resolution copy, just message me on one of the apps and I'll send it over to you.' He got to his feet.

Darcie stood too. 'I tell you what, why don't we get a takeaway coffee from the stall down by the carousel?' She gestured towards the bottom of the hill where the double-decker merry-go-round was situated and where she'd spotted the crêpe and coffee stall on her way up.

'Sure. That would be nice.'

It wasn't so busy down by the carousel and after ordering a hot chocolate for herself and a black coffee for Matt, which she insisted on paying for seeing as she'd made the invite, they sat down on one of the nearby benches to people-watch. The old-time music from the carousel filled the air as the horses glided up and down as they went around. French voices, old and young, mingled in the background, together with the smell of coffee and the sweet sugary smell of the crêpes being served.

'How long are you in Paris for?' asked Darcie. 'I know you said it was a mix of work and holiday.'

'I'm here for a month, but I may stay longer.'

'Sounds like you have a flexible working contract.' She wasn't sure he was completely telling her the truth, but maybe he just didn't like talking about his work.

'I'm here to cover a fashion shoot, actually,' he replied.

She wasn't surprised at this. It made sense that he'd be here for that sort of thing. 'That sounds very glamorous,' said Darcie, taking a sip of her drink. 'You know it's Chanel's haute couture fashion show this week.'

'I know.'

Darcie looked at him. He had that cheeky grin again. He raised his eyebrows, and the grin broadened. Darcie slowly brought the hot chocolate down from her mouth. 'Wait, don't tell me . . .'

He nodded. 'A-ha.'

'No. You're not here for that?'

'One hundred per cent.'

'Oh my God!' She knew she probably sounded overly excited at this, but she didn't care. 'That's amazing. Have you done it before?'

'A couple of years ago.'

'Oh, you're so lucky. You get to see all those clothes up close and in the flesh, so to speak.' The closest Darcie had ever got to seeing a fashion show was watching YouTube clips. The Chanel shows spanned three days, exclusively showcasing House of Chanel collections and were, by far, Darcie's favourite.

'It's cool, but probably not as cool as everyone thinks,'

confessed Matt. 'It's a bit of a scramble and there is a serious hierarchy for the photographers and who gets the best spot and who gets to photograph any of the top models or designers. I'm pretty low down in that pecking order.'

'I know, but even so.' She wondered whether she should tell him about the dress and her appointment with Chanel the next day, but she held back. Chanel had expressly requested that she didn't discuss this matter with anyone else beforehand.

'How would you like to go to the show on Tuesday?' he asked.

'What? Yeah, because I can just magic a ticket out of thin air.' Darcie looked on as a couple huddled together to take a selfie, angling the phone to get the basilica in the background and then laughing with each other as they took several attempts to get it right.

'You might not be able to, but I can.'

Darcie gave him a sceptical look. 'You can?'

'Absolutely.'

'What's the catch?'

'There's no catch.'

The young couple, seemingly happy with their selfie, were now at the little gift shop next to the carousel. The woman was looking at the array of colourful scarfs hanging among the racks of postcards, baseball caps, and practically any sort of Sacré-Cœur souvenirs imaginable. Her partner seemed intent on buying her some sort of gift.

Darcie smiled at the couple, before turning her attention back to Matt. 'There's always a catch when something sounds too good to be true.'

'Definitely no catch. You have my word. Ivy League college promise.' He held his hand across his body over his heart as if he was about to pledge allegiance to the US flag.

'Ivy League college promise? What even is that? Is it a thing?' Darcie couldn't help laughing at his very serious face.

'OK. It's not a thing. I just made it up, but I promise you, there is no catch.'

'You sure?' This surely was some sort of dream.

'Yeah. I've got a spare complimentary ticket. I might even be able to get another one if you want to bring someone with you.'

'I love the way you say so casually you can get another ticket.'

Matt gave a shrug. 'Perks of the job.'

'I just need the one.'

'Then that's no problem,' he said. 'It does mean you have to come into the press pack with me. I can arrange a pass for you while I'm there tomorrow and we can meet up on Tuesday at the venue.'

'It sounds amazing.'

'Then say yes.'

'Yes!' Darcie squealed. And it was amazing. Never in her wildest dreams did she think she'd be going to the Chanel haute couture show.

Matt laughed. 'It's a deal.'

Darcie wanted to hug him but restrained herself. 'Wait until I tell my mum and sister. They won't believe it. Thank you so much. That's very generous of you.'

'It's no big deal.' He dropped his empty coffee cup into the bin beside the bench before checking the time on his watch. His very expensive-looking watch, Darcie noted. He gave her an apologetic look. 'Sorry, but I've got to head off now. Thank you for letting me take your picture.'

Darcie was undeniably disappointed Matt was leaving, but she thanked him again and stayed sitting on the bench as he headed off down the hill.

Chapter 9

Nathalie

My heart was thumping in my chest. Were these the people we were meeting or had we been caught by someone else? They wore peaked caps, pulled low and shielding their eyes. One had a moustache and the other two had varying degrees of stubble.

'It's all right, it's Rachelle Grandis,' said the man, standing to the left.

'Yes, it's me,' said Rachelle.

I noted a hint of annoyance in her voice, as if she was put out they were even questioning her being there.

'Who is that?' The first man waved his gun in my direction, and I felt my knees wobble for a moment.

'That's my cousin. Nathalie Leroux,' replied Rachelle. 'Now, are you going to let us through?'

'You can come, but she can't,' replied the man.

'Well, she can't stay here on her own,' said Rachelle. She reached back and took my hand. 'Besides, if my brother finds out you've left our cousin alone in the forest, then he won't be very happy.'

It was the mention of Rachelle's brother that made me realise what we were doing. We had come to the forest to see Gaston.

'Just let her through,' said the man who had spoken the second time.

'You're not supposed to turn up with uninvited guests,' said the first man.

'Then my brother will tell me so when he sees me.' Rachelle returned the glare of the man but eventually he relented, albeit with a huff, and set off further into the forest. Rachelle followed, with me in tow.

It wasn't long before we encountered another sentry. 'Who's that?'

'Don't ask. She's Gaston's cousin,' replied the first man, and he carried on walking, ducking down under a low-hanging branch.

We rounded the corner where the path opened out into a clearing. I was amazed at what I saw. It looked like a small village. There was a fire in the centre, with a kettle hanging over it by a tripod of three sticks. Several men were sitting around it, smoking and talking. On the other side were several huts made of sticks, moss, and leaves. Sacking hung at the openings.

The chattering among the men at the campfire stopped when they saw us, or should I say, when they saw me. A stranger to them. They got to their feet.

The first man – whose name I still didn't know – called out to them. 'It's all right. Gaston's cousin, apparently. Someone get him.'

A younger lad, probably about my age, jumped to his feet and jogged over to one cabin. I could hear him talking in low tones, although I couldn't make out what he was saying. The next moment, the cloth door was flung open and my dear cousin Gaston appeared in the opening.

He was pulling his shirt over his head and then smoothing down his hair. 'Nathalie!' He cried in surprise and delight.

He strode over, kissing a greeting to his sister, and then after kissing me, he pulled me into a big hug, just like he always did. He held me at arm's length and grinned at me. 'Well, this is a surprise.'

I could almost hear the audible sigh of relief from the men in the camp. It seemed Gaston had some sort of influence here, and his enthusiastic greeting to me had reassured them.

They went back to whatever they had been chatting about before.

'Is everything all right?' he asked Rachelle. 'I didn't know you were coming tonight.'

'I have a message,' replied Rachelle.

I looked at my cousin in surprise as I realised Rachelle, too, had a part in the Resistance. It wasn't just her brother. I wondered if Clarice knew. I waited for Rachelle to speak.

'I was in the village today and I saw Monsieur Abreo. There's a supply train leaving the Ploërmel station tomorrow at midnight.'

'Did he say what they were moving?' the voice of another man interrupted us. One I hadn't heard before. It had a faint accent to it, British or possibly American. I looked beyond Gaston as the man approached. He was wearing traditional French clothes, but even in the dim light of the lantern Gaston was holding, I could see they didn't fit him that well. The trousers were a little on the short side, and the man must be six feet tall at least.

'Ammunition and some vehicles,' replied Rachelle. 'Probably troops as well.'

'We need specifics,' said the man, who I decided was British. I could just detect that twang in his voice that differed from an American accent.

'He's trying, but he won't get the inventory until tomorrow,' replied Rachelle.

'We don't want to waste time and manpower on something that's not worth it,' said the British man.

'Any form of resistance is worth it,' said Rachelle. 'It's not just one big act, it's lots of little ones.'

'There's always a price to pay afterwards though,' said the British man who I now pinned down to being English.

'Marcel is right,' said Gaston. 'We need more detail.'

'I'll do my best,' said Rachelle. I could tell she wasn't particularly happy.

'So, who is this?' asked the Englishman as if noticing

me for the first time. His eyes quickly looked me up and down.

I was a bit fed up with this question, but it seemed everyone here was on edge and liked to know who was who, especially an unannounced stranger. I spoke first. 'Nathalie Leroux. Gaston and Rachelle are my cousins.'

'I've not seen you before,' said the man, clearly dispensing with any formalities or niceties.

'You wouldn't have done,' I replied. I don't know why, but his attitude annoyed me. 'I'm from Paris. I'm here visiting my cousins.'

He raised an eyebrow. 'Paris. Is that so?'

'Yes, it is.'

'What do you do in Paris?'

I wasn't sure what relevance this had, but I answered. 'I'm a seamstress. My father has a tailoring shop.' I couldn't help my gaze flicking down to the ill-fitting trousers. When I looked back up at him, there was an amused look on his face.

'As you can tell, I didn't go to a tailor for these,' he replied. 'So, you're the famous seamstress I've been hearing all about.'

I looked at my cousins in confusion, wondering if he'd lost something in translation. 'What does he mean?'

Gaston put his arm around me. 'We need your help to make a few adjustments to some clothing.'

Now I really was confused. 'You need me? But you didn't even know I was coming.'

'That's not strictly true,' said Gaston. 'By the way, this is Marcel.'

Marcel gave a nod of acknowledgement to me. 'Mademoiselle.'

I didn't reply as Gaston carried on talking.

'We knew you were coming. Rachelle had told me, but what we didn't know was that we'd need your help. You see, our official tailor here at the camp isn't available to us anymore, and he was in the middle of a project.'

'You're talking in riddles. What do you mean?' I asked.

'What he means,' said Marcel, lighting a cigarette, 'is that our old tailor got himself shot, and he hadn't finished making some adjustments.' He waggled his leg around. 'Just in case you were wondering. Plus, we need a uniform altered. Gaston tells me you're pretty good with a needle and thread.'

'Shot?' I repeated.

'Yes, not here. Back in the village,' said Marcel. He said it so matter-of-factly.

'Dead?'

'*Oui*. Dead.' Marcel blew a smoke ring out. 'So, as you were on your way, we thought you could finish what he was doing.'

'I'm sorry, you must forgive my comrade for his manners,' said Gaston. 'He's not your typical Englishman,' he added conspiratorially. 'What we mean is, would you mind helping us? We'd really appreciate it and, as Rachelle said, every little bit helps.'

I didn't need asking twice. 'Of course I'll help you. I'd be honoured to do so.' I felt a small swell of pride hit my chest.

'There, I told you she'd say yes,' said Rachelle. She turned to me. 'I was going to ask you myself in the next day or so and then Gaston was going to arrange to meet you.'

'Ah, I see. Oh well, at least you don't have to wait a few more days to ask. Is there much to do to the uniform?'

Gaston smiled at me. 'It is just the trousers.'

'And my trousers,' said Marcel.

'Yours are not so important,' said Rachelle.

'I would say his are very important,' I said with a laugh, feeling upbeat at being asked to help. If I was going for humour with Marcel, I was a little off the mark. Instead of joining in with the laughter, he scowled at me instead, before mumbling something about needing to get his sleep and striding off back to his tent – his trouser legs flapping around his ankles as he did so.

'Oh, now you've upset him,' said Rachelle.

'Take no notice of Marcel. He's a good man, underneath that ballsy English exterior.'

'We should get back,' said Rachelle.

'Yes, of course,' said Gaston. 'I'll escort you.'

'No, you don't have to do that.' Rachelle placed a hand on his arm. 'Marcel is right – you need your sleep. Besides, if we run into any Germans, we are more likely to convince them we're harmless if we are on our own.'

Gaston looked appraisingly at his sister. 'Very well. But do not get caught.' He kissed Rachelle on the cheek and then me. 'Take care, cousin.'

With one last goodbye, Rachelle and I headed back through the forest, passing the Resistance members who were on guard. Rachelle had obviously done this journey many times as she didn't falter in the route she took, weaving us in and out of the trees, on and off the beaten pathways. It wasn't long before we were on the edge of the forest and the farmland.

Rachelle took a quick look around and, once certain there was no one about, we scurried across the field and back into the farmhouse.

The next few days passed quietly, and I spent the time helping my cousins on the farm and, in the afternoons, I spent time with Odile. I showed her my sketchbook and encouraged her to create her own designs in the book. Although she never said, I felt it gave her a sense of calm and perhaps control.

It was Wednesday morning, and I was settling into the daily life of rural Brittany, but also knew that we would return home in just a few days. I tried not to think about it as I would miss my cousins terribly and didn't know when I'd see them again.

I was sitting with Odile down by the stream that ran along the foot of the farm, braiding her hair and telling her about all the glamorous women in Paris and what the fashions were like, when Rachelle came and sat down beside us.

'Where have you been?' I asked. 'We were looking for you earlier.'

Rachelle gave a raise of her eyebrows and glanced towards Odile, who had her back to us while I fixed her hair. 'Oh, just had to run an errand for Maman,' she said. 'Odile, your hair looks so pretty like that. I'll have to get Nathalie to show me how to do it.'

'I just need to fasten it here at the end,' I said, admiring the braids and the way I had woven them into each other like a bun. 'There you go, all done.'

Odile patted the back of her hair and turned to face me. 'Thank you, Nathalie. You really must show Rachelle how to do it.'

'Of course I will.'

'Why don't you show Maman?' suggested Rachelle. She got to her feet and heaved Odile up by the hand. Then they both pulled me up. We began walking, and as the farmhouse came into sight, Odile broke into a run.

'Maman! Look at my hair!' she called as she neared the house.

Rachelle and I both laughed – it was lovely to see Odile animated for once.

'So where have you really been?' I asked as we crossed the courtyard.

'I had to run an errand, but I also had to check for a message.'

'A message?'

'Yes, if there's a chalk mark on the gate, it means Gaston wants me to go to the woods.'

'And was there a mark today?' I asked, intrigued by the simplicity yet effectiveness of the underground network going on right under the noses of the Germans. I felt honoured just to know these things.

'Yes. It's a sign that Gaston needs you to do the sewing.'

'At last. I was worried he would not ask me before I go home,' I said.

'We have to go tonight,' replied Rachelle.

'That's fine with me.'

As we entered the door of the farmhouse, it surprised

me to see Maman sitting at the table with her suitcase at her feet.

'Ah, there you are,' said Clarice. 'Come in, girls.'

I looked at Maman and she gave a small smile, but I could tell something wasn't right. 'What's wrong?' I asked. 'Why have you got your case?'

Maman took a deep breath. 'I'm going home today,' she said.

'Today? Not today. We're not supposed to be leaving until Saturday.' It was then I realised Maman had only her own case with her.

'Your mother and I have been talking,' said Clarice. 'We think it's safer if you stay here with us for a while.'

'Paris isn't as safe as it used to be,' said Maman. 'Your father and I have already spoken about this, and we feel you need to stay out of the city for a while. Besides, now Gaston isn't here, your aunt and uncle need as much help as they can get on the farm.'

I didn't know what to say. While the idea of staying on the farm was wonderful, I hadn't mentally prepared for it. 'But I haven't told Alphonse. He'll wonder where I am.' It was a weak excuse, and I wasn't sure why it bothered me.

'I can tell him and you can write a letter for me to give to him. It won't be for long. Just a couple of months.'

'A couple of months!'

I felt Rachelle's hand on my arm. 'It will be nice to have you here, Nathalie,' she said.

With that, Odile, rather less gently than her sister, grabbed at my other arm. 'Please say you'll stay.'

I looked down at Odile and her beautiful green eyes, which had been so dull since I'd arrived. There was hope on her face and who was I to crush that hope? Besides, it didn't look like I had any choice. It appeared the adults had already decided my fate. I smiled back at Odile. 'I'll stay.'

Odile squeezed me tight. 'Thank you, Nathalie. Thank you.'

Maman got to her feet and, after I had extracted myself

from my cousins, she hugged me. 'Thank you for making that far easier than I expected,' she said. 'It's for the best and only a couple of months.'

'I'll miss you and Papa,' I said, as an unexpected feeling of sadness washed over me.

'You'll be too busy to miss us,' Maman said with a smile. 'Now, quickly write Alphonse a note, as I must go to get the train soon.'

I was also worried about my brother. How would Edgar know I was here? What would happen if he needed my help? I couldn't voice this to Maman though.

A short time later, as I watched Maman head down the road, accompanied by Uncle Philippe, I had a mix of emotions, both sadness and happiness. I realised the sadness was because I'd miss Maman, but not Alphonse. I couldn't quite put my finger on it, maybe I was a little relieved that I wouldn't be seeing him. In my letter to Alphonse, I had just briefly said I was staying to help my uncle on the farm and I would let him know when I was coming back to Paris. I didn't make any promises to write to him or say that I would miss him. I couldn't bring myself to do it, and I realised it was because I just didn't feel it. And if I didn't feel it, I couldn't say it.

Chapter 10

Darcie

Darcie had trouble sleeping that night and she wasn't sure whether it was the excitement of the meeting with the House of Chanel or having met Matthew Langdon or worrying if the vintage black-and-white polka-dot dress with the red neckerchief she'd brought to wear for the Chanel meeting was professional enough. Whatever it was, she woke on Monday morning feeling like she had a hangover. Thank goodness for the black coffee she was now sipping in the café just along the road from her apartment.

The waiter brought over a croissant and Darcie took a moment to relax, taking in the Parisian street around her that was in full swing. She had opted for a table on the pavement and, from behind her sunglasses, she surreptitiously observed the other patrons. A couple of men in suits sat at one table, and although she couldn't catch what they were saying, it sounded like a serious business meeting. She momentarily mused why a suited Frenchman could look so much more attractive than an Englishman.

She turned her gaze to a middle-aged couple who were sitting at another table, studying the screen of the man's phone, speaking in English. Darcie assumed they were tourists. A car beeped impatiently at a delivery lorry that had blocked the road and this followed a somewhat robust exchange between the two drivers accompanied by several internationally recognisable hand gestures. A scooter zipped its way through the traffic, hopping onto the pavement at one point to avoid the warring factions, and finally the lorry driver conceded and moved his lorry out of the way.

Darcie loved people-watching and as much as she could stay there all day, drinking in the scenery and atmosphere of the city, she didn't want to be late for her appointment.

She took the Métro and walked the five minutes to the hotel. She realised she was just around the corner from where the fashion show was taking place that week. She was surprised that Christophe Padgett had wanted to meet her during such an important week, but decided maybe it was a good sign.

Darcie introduced herself to the receptionist, and they indicated for her to take a seat. The foyer was understated luxury, with a centrepiece fountain and deep-seated velvet chairs and sofas for guests to sit in. Darcie perched on the edge of the seat, but feeling self-conscious, tried to go for a more relaxed look and shuffled back a little. Then, worried she wouldn't be able to get out of the seat with any grace or decorum, resumed her original position. She took out her phone just to look busy, rather than looking like she was waiting outside the head teacher's office at school to be told off again for coming in late.

Several minutes ticked by and Darcie was just beginning to think they had forgotten about her when the clipping of heels across the marble floor had her looking up. A woman in a business suit smiled as she approached.

'Miss Marchant?' she asked, coming to a halt in front of her.

'Yes, that's right. *Oui*.'

'I'm from the House of Chanel. If you'd like to follow me, I'll take you to meet Monsieur Padgett.'

Darcie gathered up her bag and, pulling her suitcase behind, followed the woman across the foyer and into the mirrored elevator. They got out on the ninth floor and Darcie was shown into a room on the left. 'Monsieur Padgett will be with you shortly. Can I get you a coffee or would you prefer tea?'

'A glass of water would be fine,' replied Darcie, not trusting herself to take on board any more caffeine.

'There is some already on the table.' The woman smiled and then left Darcie alone in the room.

A large smoked-glass table occupied the centre of the room, with enough chairs around it to accommodate an entire football team, plus reserves. A silver tray with a glass decanter of water and four glasses were at one end. Darcie poured herself a glass and, leaving her bag and suitcase near one of the chairs, she went over to the floor-to-ceiling windows and looked out over the Parisian skyline.

She could hardly believe she was here. She wished Lena and Chloe were with her, not just so they could give her moral support, but so they could see the views. She took out her phone and snapped a few pictures before turning around and taking a quick selfie. Of course, at that moment, the door opened and in walked a man. He was dressed in what was clearly an expensive suit, with a crisp white shirt and a pale blue tie in the perfect Windsor knot. The scar that ran through his eyebrow and hooked its way around to his cheekbone seemed at odds with the well-tailored man, in his mid-fifties, striding across the room and smiling at her.

He stopped as Darcie quickly stuffed her phone into her pocket. '*Bonjour*,' he said after what seemed like the longest second ever. He walked around the table and held out his hand to Darcie. 'Christophe Padgett. You must be Darcie Marchant.'

Darcie was relieved he spoke excellent English and shook his hand, noting the gold ring on his finger and gold vintage Cartier watch on his wrist. 'Pleased to meet you.'

'Are you happier speaking in English?' He indicated for her to take a seat.

'If that's all right?'

'Certainly.' He gave a smile as he took the seat adjacent to her at the head of the table. He opened the leather-bound

79

file he had with him, which housed an A4 notepad, an expensive-looking fountain pen, and a copy of what looked like her email to Chanel. 'Thank you for agreeing to meet in Paris. I realise it's out of your way, but I'm here for the week and then I'm off to New York and I'm the expert in identifying genuine Chanel garments.'

'It's no problem. I'm glad you've been able to take time out of your busy schedule.'

'I haven't got much time. It's haute couture fashion week, as I'm sure you know, so let's get down to business straight away.' He glanced down at Darcie's bag. 'I take it you've brought the dress with you, together with the sketchbook?'

'Yes. Absolutely.' Darcie took the sketchbook out first and handed it over. Padgett looked closely at the signature initials and several times went back and forth through the pages. 'The dress I emailed about is here on this page . . .' Darcie leaned over and turned a few pages until she got to the blue evening gown. 'This looks identical to the one Coco Chanel is wearing in this photograph.' She placed the photograph alongside the book, leaving Padgett to inspect it while she opened the suitcase properly and took out the dress.

Padgett took the dress from Darcie, laying it out on the glass table. He stood up and with his chin in the forefinger and thumb of one hand, with his other hand supporting his elbow, he stared at the dress, cocking his head one way and then the other. After a few moments, he put his glasses on and began a closer inspection of the dress, looking at the seams and the way it had been constructed, checking the back of the neck, Darcie assumed, for a label.

He paused for a moment and glanced up at Darcie. 'You came by this in a lost-luggage sale?'

'That's right. In England. An old railway station waiting room that had been closed since the 1980s.'

'Well, I have to say, it certainly looks like a Chanel dress.' He turned the dress over. 'It has some of the classic Chanel signatures in terms of design.'

Darcie swallowed hard as the excitement rose a notch. 'That's what I thought, too. This is a classic Chanel shape.'

'The sewing is very good,' said Padgett. 'It looks like the right kind of thread and the stitching is typical of the era and the type of sewing machine used. It looks and feels very authentic.'

Darcie knew she was on the point of holding her breath. The anticipation was almost too much to bear until she saw the expression on his face. One of sympathy. The excitement leached away. 'But what?' she prompted.

Padgett shook his head and frowned. 'There's something about it that's not right. There's no label for a start and this zip, it's too long. For the era you're thinking of, early 1940s, Chanel fashion just wasn't using them. The longer ones were about, of course, but Chanel still favoured the shorter zips.'

'When you say Chanel wasn't using them, do you mean at all or just not in their mainstream clothing lines?'

'As a rule, they were still using the shorter ones.'

'Do you think this could have been put in at a later date? Say, if the original zip broke?'

'No,' answered Padgett. 'There are no signs of repair to the zip.' He turned the dress inside out and inspected the sewing line. 'If this zip was replaced, whoever did so must have been highly skilled. There are no signs of a previous stitching line or anything to indicate the dress has been unpicked.'

'But what about the picture?' Darcie picked up the photograph. 'Chanel is definitely wearing this dress.'

'We can't say if it's this exact dress,' said Padgett, turning the dress back again. 'This could simply be a reproduction made at a later date by a fashion student.'

'But the fabric is vintage. You said yourself it felt authentic,' said Darcie. 'It's not modern. There's no nylon in it.'

'It's not enough to convince me.' He looked over the rim of his glasses. He turned his attention back to the sketchbook, looking intently at the drawing of the dress.

Darcie sat forward in her seat, waiting for his reaction.

The Frenchman was taking a good deal of interest in the book as he went from page to page, inspecting all the sketches. Finally, he looked up. 'I'd like to have another expert look at this,' he said. 'Someone who will be able to confirm the age of the work, the ink used, the paper, and so on.'

Darcie frowned. 'I think it's clear the dress and the sketchbook belong together.'

'Yes, I agree, and having the sketchbook dated would give us an idea of the age of the dress.'

Darcie could see his logic but, for some reason, she was reluctant to leave the sketchbook. Padgett had a proprietorial hand on the now-closed book.

'I can see the benefit of that,' said Darcie. 'Whereabouts is your contact based?'

'He's in New York. I could take it with me and have it looked at while I'm away,' said Padgett, now picking up the book.

Darcie felt a flutter of panic in her chest at the thought of the book not only leaving her hands but the country too. She stood up and reached across the desk, grasping the corner of the book before Padgett could whisk it away. 'I'd sooner keep it myself,' she said, offering what she hoped was a relaxed smile while her fingers held firm. 'I can arrange for someone to date it, authenticate it and then I can get back to you. I have contacts in England I can ask.'

For a moment she thought Padgett was not going to release the book and a fleeting look of displeasure crossed his face.

Whatever his intention, he managed a smile and removed his hand. 'Of course,' he said, smoothing down his tie. 'I trust you have a safe place for it.'

'Yes. I do,' replied Darcie, not wanting to admit she'd been simply carrying it around with her.

'Please do contact me if you change your mind,' said Padgett.

Darcie stood up, slipping the book into her bag and the

dress into the case. 'Thank you. I will. Oh, there is just one thing.'

Padgett gave a questioning look. 'Yes?'

'Are you able to find out if a Nathalie Leroux ever worked here in Paris at the Ritz during the war? Maybe for Coco Chanel herself?'

A frown creased his forehead. 'Nathalie Leroux? What makes you ask that?'

'I believe Nathalie Leroux had a connection with the Ritz hotel, Paris, and Coco Chanel,' she said, trying not to sound desperate. 'There was an envelope in the case, with The Ritz, Paris stamped on one side and her name written on the other.'

'That was all?'

'Yes.'

'Maybe she was a guest. I don't know. Leave it with me and if I find anything out, I'll be in touch,' replied Padgett briskly. 'Now, if you excuse me. I do have to go. My assistant will show you out.' He held his hand out to Darcie. 'It was a pleasure to have made your acquaintance, Miss Marchant.'

'Likewise,' replied Darcie, shaking his hand once again.

With her suitcase trundling along behind her, Darcie followed Padgett's assistant out of the boardroom and down to the ground floor.

'Thank you,' said Darcie as the assistant all but escorted her off the premises.

As she made her way along the pavement back towards the Métro, she heard someone calling her name.

'Hey! Darcie Bytheway!'

She turned and saw Matt jogging towards her. She waited as he caught up with her.

'Hey,' he said, coming to a stop in front of her. 'I thought that was you. I was in the museum, getting set up.'

She forced a smile, not sure if this was a good or a bad encounter. She hadn't yet made up her mind about him. 'Hey,' she replied simply.

He looked down at the suitcase and frowned. 'You leaving?'

'Not exactly,' said Darcie wondering how she was going to explain her presence.

'What are you doing here?' He looked confused for a moment. 'Oh man!' He pressed his hand against his forehead. 'Did you think I was getting you a ticket for today's show? I'm so sorry. I obviously didn't explain properly.'

'No. It's fine. Honest. I know you said tomorrow.'

He looked even more confused now. 'So, why are you here and what's with the case?'

Darcie tapped her nails on the handle of the suitcase and for no other reason than she couldn't think of a reason not to, she said, 'I had a meeting with Christophe Padgett. He's—'

'Padgett! Christophe Padgett?'

'Yes, from the House of Chanel.'

'I know where he's from,' said Matt, clearly impressed or surprised at this revelation. 'He's one of the main men. His speciality is vintage Chanel: sourcing, buying, and selling.'

'I know,' said Darcie. It was her turn to be amused.

'Wait. You had a meeting with Padgett and you're pulling a suitcase along with you.' He flicked his forefinger between Darcie and the case. 'Does that mean you have something in there that he wanted to see?'

'Certainly does. Only . . . I still have it.'

'Can we backtrack for a second? Have I missed some vital part of a conversation we had yesterday? Am I in some sort of time warp where I've missed you telling me that piece of information?'

'I didn't say anything yesterday.' She suddenly felt guilty for keeping it a secret. 'I wanted to see how the meeting went first. Didn't want to jinx it.'

'So, you have a Chanel dress or what you thought was a Chanel dress?'

'Yes. Padgett says it's not an original. That it's a copy.'

'He knows his stuff,' mused Matt. 'But that doesn't mean he knows everything. He's been wrong before.'

'I also think there's a connection to the Ritz hotel during the war,' said Darcie. 'But I don't even know where to start looking for answers about that.'

'Sounds intriguing,' said Matt. He glanced at his watch. 'Look, I gotta go. You're not leaving Paris yet, are you?'

'No.'

'Cool. Can I call you later?' He was walking backwards now, in the hotel's direction. 'I'll have that ticket for you. And I might be able to help you with the dress.'

Darcie found herself replying that it was fine and she'd love to see him. Yes, he should contact her either through social media or the mobile number on her website.

With that, he broke into a jog again and disappeared back inside the building.

As Darcie made her way back to the Métro, she couldn't deny the little flutter of excitement that had pitched up in her stomach. Surely, it wasn't just because Matt was calling her later? And what did he mean, he might be able to help? She muttered under her breath at how easily she'd agreed to it all. She really was a pushover.

Chapter 11

Nathalie

The evening was colder than it had been since I'd been at the farm and the grass was damp underfoot as we scuttled across the field towards the forest, the moon being our only guide. I was glad I'd put on my thicker cardigan when we had sneaked out. We'd left the house earlier this evening than we had before. Apparently, rain was due overnight and Rachelle didn't want to have to explain wet and muddy clothes to her parents.

Rachelle led the way, and I followed silently behind her. It wasn't long before the lookouts in the forest confronted us as before. This time, they were more comfortable letting us through, as I assumed Gaston had already told them we were coming.

The camp seemed busier than it had done the last time I was there.

'Ah, cousin and sister,' greeted Gaston, emerging from a different, larger hut than before. He held his hands out wide and hugged us both at the same time. 'Everything all right?'

'Yes. No problems,' replied Rachelle.

'Come this way,' said Gaston, gesturing back towards the hut.

Two lanterns hung inside the hut above an old sewing machine. To one side was a large table with several items of clothing spread out and a block of fabric. A movement to the side startled me and out from the shadows of the room stepped Marcel. 'I didn't see you there,' I said, trying to compose myself under his watchful gaze.

'You should always be aware of your surroundings,' he said, taking a cigarette packet from his pocket and offering it to me.

I shook my head at the French cigarettes and was surprised when Rachelle took one. He took a box of matches from his pocket and casually threw them her way.

Rachelle lit the cigarette and drew deeply before exhaling. I moved my head away to avoid the unpleasant smell of smoke. I glanced at Marcel and could see a small look of amusement on his face.

'So, where did you learn French?' I asked. 'Your accent is quite good.'

'Quite good?' Marcel raised his eyebrow, and I still got the feeling he was finding me amusing, which annoyed me.

'Yes, I suppose you could fool a German, but not a native speaker.' I sounded more prickly than I'd intended, but this didn't appear to have any effect on his disposition.

'As long as we fool the Jerries,' came Marcel's laconic reply. He headed for the door but paused and turned to me. 'Let's see if your sewing skills can do the same. Wouldn't want a weak link.'

'Weak link!' I couldn't help the indignation in my tone as Marcel exited the building.

Gaston gave a laugh. 'Take no notice, Nathalie. Marcel is teasing you.' He put his hand on my shoulder. 'Now, come over here and I'll show you what needs to be done.'

It turned out to be relatively straightforward and the old treadle sewing machine performed much better than it gave the impression it would. I started with the hems on the trousers of the uniform and stitching the buttons on a shirt.

'We haven't got long,' said Rachelle. 'We mustn't be out any more than a couple of hours.'

'Maybe I can leave the jacket until tomorrow night,' I said, as I examined what needed to be done with it.

'No. We need it finished tonight,' said Marcel, who – much

to my annoyance – had returned to the hut a few minutes earlier. 'Did you do that shirt?'

I looked at Gaston for some sort of backup, but he gave a shrug. 'We need them done tonight,' and then, as an afterthought, he added, 'Sorry.'

I realised there must be something planned for tomorrow night. They either had some sort of operation or the clothing had to be taken somewhere. '*D'accord*. I'll go as quickly as I can,' I said. I picked up the shirt that Marcel had asked about and handed it over to him.

The sound of someone calling Gaston had my cousin on his feet. 'I'll be back in a minute,' he said.

I was glad the light was dim in the hut so Marcel wouldn't see me blush a little. Marcel had taken his jumper and shirt off and was now standing there with just a white singlet on. I looked away and Marcel let out a loud laugh.

'I'm not exactly naked,' he said.

I kept my gaze on the jacket, fiddling with the sleeve but not really looking at what I was doing. In the couple of seconds I had looked at Marcel, I hadn't failed to notice his toned body, the muscles of his arms, and the broadness of his shoulders. If the Germans caught him, they may believe by the clothing he was French, but without his shirt, it was obvious Marcel had not been deprived of food or nutrition in the recent past, unlike some of my fellow countrymen.

'I didn't realise the shirt was for you,' I said, daring to look back up and thankful that Marcel now had the shirt on, if not buttoned up.

'That's why I needed the collar adjusting,' he said as he fiddled with the top button. 'Can't have a German officer in an ill-fitting uniform. Damn it. I can't fasten this button.'

I put the jacket down and went over to him. 'Let me help you.' Despite my earlier fluster at Marcel being half naked in front of me, his comment about the ill-fitting uniform sobered me and knocked all thoughts of childish embarrassment away. He was obviously about to do something dangerous and brave, and here I was blushing like an idiot because he'd taken his shirt off. I was very aware of our proximity as I, too, struggled with the button. 'The buttonhole is too small,' I said finally. Then I inspected the rest of the buttons. 'No, actually it's the button that is wrong. It is bigger than the others. It needs to be changed.'

'Have you got some more buttons?'

'Not that I saw. But I can use this button at the bottom of the shirt. Just make sure you keep your shirt tucked into your trousers.'

'Yes, ma'am,' he said with a mock salute. 'I suppose I should take this off. Just thought I should warn you, so you're not shocked this time.'

'Who said I was shocked?'

There was that small smirk of amusement again, and this time his dark brown eyes danced with a sense of mischief. 'My mistake.'

'Yes.'

He looked at me for what seemed like a long second before he spoke. 'You might want to let go of my shirt so I can take it off.'

I looked down and realised I was still gripping the bottom of the fabric. I pulled my hand away. 'Hurry up. I haven't got much time.' I turned back and went over to the sewing machine, aware my heart was thumping just a little more than it should have.

'Here, catch!'

The shirt came flying in my direction, landing almost in my face. 'I don't think anyone has ever given me their shirt like that before,' I commented.

He lit another cigarette and went to sit down on the chair Gaston had vacated, but then as I wrinkled up my nose at the smell of the smoke, he stubbed it out on the ground. 'Didn't really want it anyway,' he said.

I wasn't sure if that was strictly true, but I appreciated the gesture. Within a couple of minutes, I had removed the bottom button and had sewn it onto the collar. I threw the shirt back at him and couldn't help laughing when it hit the target, landing right in his face.

'I guess I asked for that,' he said.

'Now I need to finish the jacket,' I said, purposely averting my gaze as he changed.

'There, I'm decent,' he announced a few moments later. 'That's much better.'

'Good. I am pleased to hear it. Now let me measure you for the sleeve.'

Without an actual tape measure, I had to hold the sleeve up against Marcel and pin the minor adjustments needed. 'How come this jacket didn't have a sleeve in the first place?'

'Maybe it was damaged,' suggested Marcel.

I paused mid-pin. 'You mean ruined?'

'Possibly. It is an authentic jacket,' said Marcel. 'But having it ripped and bloodstained would give the game away.'

I felt a little sick at the thought of another man, albeit a German, wearing this uniform and having his arm injured so badly the sleeve needed replacing. It reminded me of the reality of war. It was easy to forget young men on both sides were injured and killed daily.

It didn't take me long to fit the sleeve into the jacket and repair the lining. 'Where did these come from?' I asked, handing the jacket over to Marcel.

Before he could answer, Gaston and Rachelle returned to the hut.

'We have to hurry,' said Rachelle. 'Are you finished?'

'Yes. Just this minute. I was waiting for Marcel to try it on.'

We all turned and watched Marcel shrug the jacket on and fasten the buttons. 'How do I look?' he asked, standing straight like he was on parade.

'Perfect,' I said enthusiastically and then realised my cousins had both looked at me. Rachelle raised an eyebrow. I pretended to study the jacket. 'It's a perfect fit. I was just asking Marcel where you got the jacket from.'

'Need-to-know basis,' said Gaston. 'Now, you two had better get back to the farm. It's nearly midnight. Do you need an escort?'

'No. It's fine, we can manage,' said Rachelle.

'Thanks for this,' said Marcel, tugging off the jacket. 'You're pretty good at this sewing lark.'

'You're welcome,' I said. 'Hope whatever you're doing goes well.'

'Me too,' said Marcel. 'Me too.' He gave me a smile. 'See you again soon.'

Gaston walked with us to the edge of the camp. 'You seem to have made an impression on Marcel,' he commented.

'I'm not sure about that,' I replied, although secretly I was pleased if it was the case. 'He was just being polite.'

'Maybe more than polite,' teased Rachelle.

'Friendly,' I retorted. 'He was just being friendly.'

'Which is very unlike him, so I refer you to my first statement,' said Gaston. 'You made an impression on him.'

We had reached the edge of the camp now and I was glad when one of the men appeared, offering to escort us back to the farm.

'Just keep a safe distance,' ordered Gaston. 'If they're spotted, it's best they are on their own.' He turned to us. 'Take care, you two.'

'And you,' replied Rachelle.

I didn't miss the knowing look pass between brother and sister and guessed Gaston had revealed more to Rachelle than I was privy to.

We hurried back through the forest and as we reached the edge of the farm, we both looked back to wave to our escort. Through the trees, I saw him raise his hand before disappearing back into the shadows.

'So, we have a small treat today,' said Clarice the following day when we sat down for lunch. 'The chickens have laid a few extra eggs.'

I looked at the plate of mashed Jerusalem artichokes, which had become a staple diet over the past week. On its own, it wasn't appealing but add an egg and it turned the meal into a feast.

Before we could tuck into the meal, there was a knock at the door. Rachelle jumped up and looked out of the window. 'It's Monsieur Pellon.'

If it were not for the grave tone of her voice, I wouldn't have paid attention, but I could tell something was wrong. I saw Rachelle and her mother exchange a concerned look.

Clarice hurried out to the front door.

'Who's Monsieur Pellon?'

Rachelle didn't answer me. Her face was as white as the enamel kitchen sink.

'Monsieur Pellon runs the post office,' said Odile, putting down her cutlery. Her voice was flat, with no trace of emotion. 'He brings telegrams when there's bad news.'

The kitchen door opened, and Clarice stepped into the room. Her gaze settled on me, and I could see tears in her eyes. Her hand shook a little. 'A telegram,' she whispered. 'I'm so sorry, Nathalie.'

My legs felt heavy as I moved across the kitchen. It was like wading through deep water. I took the piece of paper and tried to focus on the words. It was several lines long. I couldn't believe what I was reading. The words swam on the page in front of me. I tried to concentrate, to understand what I was reading, but it felt alien, as if it was happening to someone else.

'No,' I whispered to no one other than myself. 'Please, no.'

I clutched the telegram to my chest, as my heart broke in two. My legs gave way, and I collapsed on the floor. I have no recollection of what happened after that. The next thing I was conscious of was being carried from the kitchen into the living room by Philippe and being placed on the sofa.

Clarice was at my side with a glass of water and my cousins looked on from the doorway.

I grabbed Clarice's hand, almost spilling the drink. 'Please tell me it's not true,' I begged. 'Please tell me Edgar is alive.' I looked around, searching for the telegram. I needed to see the words again. Surely, I'd read it wrong. I must have made a mistake.

Rachelle stepped forward and handed the crumpled piece of paper to me.

Terrible news. Edgar arrested by Gestapo yesterday. Questioned. Executed today. Our hearts are broken. Please tell Nathalie. Will telephone when possible. Your brother-in-law, Théodule

I allowed myself to be taken upstairs, and the grief of my loss overwhelmed me. All I could think about was my darling brother and what he must have gone through at the hands of the Gestapo, how frightened he must have been when he was executed. I wanted to be home with Maman and Papa. I wanted my mother to hold me and to comfort me. I wanted to be there for her. Instead, I allowed Clarice to hold me in her arms, stroke my hair, kiss my head, and tell me how brave Edgar was and how she understood because she had lost a brother in the Great War.

Eventually, I cried all the tears possible and, after Clarice had pulled the blanket up over my shoulders, I allowed sleep to take me. It was a welcome escape.

When I awoke two hours later, it took me a moment to remember what I was doing in bed during the day and when the memory hit me, it didn't make me cry this time, but made me angry. I don't think I had ever been so angry. So frustrated that I couldn't change what had happened. I felt powerless. And I didn't care for that feeling. If my younger brother was brave enough to take a stand against the invasion, then I should be brave too. I despised myself for being passive and compliant. This was not what being a Frenchwoman was about. I sat up in bed with a sense of purpose that had been missing until that point. I was going to make a difference.

I wasn't stupid enough to go rushing into anything. I had to be careful and cunning. I was going to avenge my brother's death. I would find who had killed him, and I would exact the same fate on them. The thought filled my heart, and I took a deep breath to compose myself. Yes, I was going to take revenge.

First, I'd have to learn how to use a gun. There was one person who could teach me that and they owed me. I stood up and walked over to the window, looking out at the forest beyond the farm.

Chapter 12

Darcie

After her meeting with Padgett and bumping into Matt, Darcie didn't want to use up her precious time by traipsing back across the city to her accommodation to drop off her suitcase. So, she took the decision to leave it with the hotel in their secure locker. The irony of placing left luggage in another left-luggage store didn't escape her – this time, though, it wouldn't be forgotten.

She didn't expect to hear from Matt until later in the day and wanted to make the most of her time, so decided to take a stroll along the River Seine which, according to the map on her phone, was approximately a twenty-minute walk away. It was a very warm day and as she made her way through the Parisian streets, Darcie couldn't help smiling to herself. She was here in the city she'd longed to visit since she had watched the 1950s film *An American in Paris*, starring Gene Kelly. She had imagined herself walking here so many times, it was hard to believe it was now a reality.

Darcie stopped and browsed the book-stall set up along the pavement and took her time to look at the artwork further along the way. They were all aimed at tourists, with watercolour prints of the famous Parisian landmarks such as the Eiffel Tower, Arc de Triomphe, Sacré-Cœur and Le Louvre. She particularly liked the vintage poster art, which would be a nice addition to the decor in her shop, but it was all a little bit steep for her pocket.

She took the steps down from street level to the path that ran alongside the river. There was a group of teenagers sitting with their feet dangling over the edge, their backpacks strewn out, and they chatted and laughed. A cyclist cruised towards her, and she moved out of the way. Other tourists strolled along, one couple stopping to take their picture with the Eiffel Tower in the background. It really was just how she'd imagined it.

Her thoughts turned to the Chanel dress, as she was now referring to it, and she wondered how different Paris would have been under the German occupation. Would it have been much different to how it was today? She knew that the city had all but welcomed the Germans on the surface, but underneath there had been a growing disquiet that eventually led to stronger resistance in the latter days of the occupation. Coco Chanel herself was thought of as a collaborator, having taken up residency at the Ritz for most of the war and even taking a German lover. Where did Nathalie Leroux fit into all this? Darcie wished she could find out more about this elusive fashion designer.

After walking along the riverbank, Darcie found herself opposite Le Louvre and the Jardin des Tuileries. It would be a lovely spot to sit and do some people-watching. She grabbed a coffee and another croissant. At this rate she was going to turn into a pastry.

Her phone pinged an alert to a text message. It was from Matt. He must have got her number from her website.

Matt: Hey. How's your morning?

She smiled at the casual, easy-going message – rather like Matt himself.

Darcie: Doing some sightseeing. River Seine and now at Jardin des Tuileries. You?

Matt: Crazy here. As always.

With the message came a picture from inside the Chanel fashion show. It was a cheeky snap of the runway and in the foreground the backs of the heads of several people, who Darcie assumed were other journalists.

Matt: Not exactly showcasing my photographic skills but not supposed to take any sneaky pictures here.

Darcie took a picture of her view and sent it to him.

Darcie: Not going to lie – my picture is technically superior to yours.

She added a laughing face emoji on the end and smiled at her phone.

Matt: No contest. You win.

Another message came in straight off the back.

Matt: Gotta go. Carla Maldini has just hit the runway. See you on the Pont Notre Dame at 6. There's a nice café nearby where we can get supper.

Darcie sent back a quick message saying she'd look forward to it, and then, tucking her phone back in her bag, began to make her way back to the apartment. On the way, she took a detour onto the Île de la Cité, where Notre Dame was situated. She knew from her research there were little boutiques on the island and it would be nice to look at the cathedral too. It had been ravaged by fire several years ago and restoration work was still very much underway. The building was covered in scaffolding and plastic sheeting. Darcie remembered watching the news and the images of the cathedral burning furiously, and then the spire collapsing. It had been a cultural and architectural disaster.

The little lanes and boutiques on the island were a delight to walk around, and Darcie once again had to mentally pinch herself to believe she was really here. She wanted to take a gift home for Lena, Chloe, Hannah, and her grandmother as a thank you, for without them she certainly wouldn't be here, literally living one of her dreams.

The afternoon passed quickly, and Darcie had thoroughly enjoyed herself, despite having to backtrack to the hotel to collect her suitcase. She'd arrived at her apartment, had a quick freshen up and was now at the bridge, waiting for Matt.

She'd only been there a few minutes when she spotted him crossing the road. He waved and smiled broadly and she found herself returning the smile with equal enthusiasm. There was something about him that was so easy-going that she felt like he was someone she'd known for years rather than just a day.

'Hey, good to see you.' He leaned in and gave her a quick peck on the cheek.

Darcie was sure she was blushing. 'Hi. How was your day?'

'Busy. But I like it that way.' They stood at the pavement's edge, waiting for a gap in the traffic. 'Cross now,' said Matt, taking her hand. They had to break into a jog to avoid an oncoming motorcyclist who blasted his horn at them.

'Do you always live dangerously?' asked Darcie. 'I thought you Americans didn't jaywalk.'

'It's the French influence on me,' replied Matt with a grin.

He let go of her hand, and Darcie had to pretend to herself that she wasn't just a tad disappointed. They took a seat outside and studied the menu for a few minutes before the waiter came and took their order.

'It's so lovely here,' she said, her gaze wandering across the riverbank to the Île de la Cité where she had been earlier that afternoon.

'Yeah, sure is,' he said.

Darcie was certain he was still looking at her. Fortunately, the waiter chose that exact moment to return to their table with their food and a bottle of wine.

'Oh, I didn't order wine,' said Darcie. She had no idea if it was expensive or not.

'I did, but you don't have to have any if you don't want.' Matt smiled as if to reassure her. 'Don't you drink?'

'No. It's not that.' This was far more awkward than Darcie imagined. She didn't want to make a fuss about the cost; she'd just have to suck it up and if it meant skipping a meal tomorrow, then so be it.

'I'm not trying to get you drunk,' said Matt.

'I know. I didn't think for one minute you were,' said Darcie. 'I'm here on a budget. I have to watch my pennies, plus I don't enjoy freeloading and I would never expect that just because I was out with a man, he would automatically pay for everything. Just for the record, I fully intend to pay half the bill this evening.'

'Is that right?'

'Yes. It is, as it happens.'

'OK.'

Darcie looked at him, taken aback by the one-word reply. 'OK?'

'Yeah, OK.'

She flattened her napkin and refolded it for no particular reason other than it gave her hands something to do. 'That's good, then.'

'Listen, I'm sorry if I made you feel awkward,' said Matt. 'I didn't think.'

'It's fine. Honestly, don't worry about it.' She smiled at him to show no hard feelings.

'So, this dress you took to Chanel today, what made you think it was one of theirs?' said Matt. 'And you said something about a connection with the war and the Ritz.'

Darcie was glad of the change in conversation and went

on to explain the background to the dress and how she'd come by it. 'There was an envelope in the case, which had the name *Nathalie Leroux*, and *Ritz Paris* on it, but I can't find out a single thing about her. I asked Christophe Padgett but he didn't really seem interested. I think by then he just wanted to get rid of me.'

'Where does the war come into all this?'

'There was also a train ticket dated 1942. Oddly, that was for a station in England.' Darcie gave a sigh at the seemingly unconnected pieces of information. 'Earlier, you said you might be able to help.'

'I know someone who's an editor with a magazine. They specialise in World War Two and the fashion in that era. They might be able to fill in some gaps. If they don't know, they might know someone who does.'

'What magazine?'

'*The History of Us.*'

Darcie was sure her eyes had nearly bulged out of her head. *The History of Us* was a global publication that focused on the world wars. It was critically acclaimed by historians around the world and a great reference source for amateurs and professionals alike. It was to historians what *Rolling Stone* magazine was to music lovers. 'You know an editor at the magazine?'

'Yeah. Kind of.'

'Kind of?'

'My mother works for the publication.'

Darcie raised her eyebrows. 'Impressive.'

'I do actually know Myles Hoffer,' said Matt. 'I'm not cashing in on my mom's name. It's not my style.'

Darcie appraised Matt for a moment. She sensed it might be something of a raw nerve for him, not dissimilar to her need to pay her own way. She didn't push the matter further with him.

'I appreciate it even more. Thank you,' she replied.

Chapter 13

Nathalie

'What are you doing?'

Rachelle's voice made me jump. I was hiding behind the chicken house, keeping a careful watch on the field beyond where I knew Philippe would come from soon for his lunch. It was a day since I'd received the news about Edgar, and I was eager to put my plan in place.

'Nothing,' I replied, not looking at my cousin.

'It doesn't look like nothing,' said Rachelle.

'What are you doing here, anyway?' I asked, trying to divert the conversation.

'I saw you from the landing window when I was putting the linen away.'

'I'm just getting some fresh air.'

'Behind the smelly chicken house is a funny place for fresh air.'

I let out a big sigh. 'Look, Rachelle, if I don't tell you what I'm doing, then you won't have to lie for me or get into trouble.'

My cousin eyed me for a long time before speaking again. 'You're going to see Gaston, aren't you?'

'Please, Rachelle.'

'He won't help you,' continued Rachelle. 'It's one thing asking you to do some sewing for him, but it's another expecting him to help you get some sort of revenge for Edgar.'

I looked down at my feet and felt the ball of grief lodge

itself in my throat and tears rush to my eyes. 'It's that obvious, is it?'

'I may not have seen you for a long time, cousin, but it doesn't mean I don't know you and understand how you are feeling. I would be the same.'

My tears spilled over as the tenderness in her voice touched me. Rachelle pulled me towards her and I clung to her, fighting back the tears as the anger at what had happened to my brother overwhelmed me once more. I pulled away. 'I have to do something,' I said. 'Every time I think about Edgar, my heart is filled with pain and my belly with anger. I want the person who killed him to pay for what they did.'

'And as I said, Gaston will not help you and you are wrong to ask him.'

'What do you mean?'

Before she could answer, the sound of the gate clanking open alerted us to Philippe coming through from the field. I looked at Rachelle. Without saying a word, so as not to give us away, my eyes pleaded with her to stay quiet. She leaned back against the side of the chicken shed and we both held our breath as Philippe trundled by with the horse and cart.

As soon as he was out of earshot and across the backyard of the farm, Rachelle turned to me. 'If you ask Gaston, he will have to say no and he won't like saying no to you. It will upset him and you have no right to do that.'

It was probably the first time Rachelle and I had disagreed about anything, but I wasn't about to give in. 'That's for Gaston to decide,' I said. 'Now, I'm going to find him.'

'You don't know the way.'

'I have an idea and eventually, one of Gaston's men will find me.'

'Not if the Germans find you first.'

I must admit I hadn't thought of that, so intent was I on seeing my cousin. 'I'll be careful,' I said, knowing I sounded naïve and belligerent all at the same time.

'You have no idea what you're doing,' said Rachelle. 'You're really going to go, aren't you?'

'Yes.'

She let out a sigh and rolled her eyes. 'Then I had better take you myself.' She grabbed the sleeve of my cardigan. 'Come on, quickly. We won't have much time.'

I couldn't deny I was grateful for Rachelle's help. I knew my plan was flawed in that I didn't know how to get to the camp, even though I had tried to memorise the way so if I came again, I'd be able to find my own way. I didn't want to get Rachelle into trouble for helping me, but every time I thought of a reason why I shouldn't be doing this, the pain of Edgar's death came back, hitting me harder than before, knocking away any rational thoughts. I harnessed the anger. It was the only way to get through this.

It didn't take us long to get deep into the forest, all the time listening out for any German patrols. When we came up against the camp guards, I was relieved as it meant we were close.

'Does Gaston know you're coming?' asked one of them after he recognised Rachelle.

'I don't need an appointment to see my own brother,' replied Rachelle, with rather more bravery than I suspected she had. 'It's important we see him.'

'It needs two of you?'

'Just let us through,' said Rachelle.

After a moment's consideration, the Frenchman took us through to the camp. 'Hey, Gaston. Your sister and the other one are here!' he called out.

Gaston was leaning over a wooden table with a group of other men, studying several maps. The men turned, and I noticed the one next to Gaston was Marcel. He made eye contact but didn't acknowledge me. Gaston strode over to us.

'Rachelle? Is everything all right?' he asked immediately, the concern etched on his face.

'Yes. Well, no, but it's personal. Is there somewhere we can talk?'

'Of course.' He led us over to the cabin where I had worked on the German uniform. The room was empty. 'What's wrong?' he asked once we were inside.

'Do you want to tell him?' asked Rachelle.

I nodded. 'We had some bad news yesterday. Very bad,' I said. 'Edgar has been killed.'

'What? How?' Gaston visibly paled at the news.

'He was arrested. I don't know the details. My father sent a telegram.' I took the piece of paper from my pocket and handed it to Gaston, who quickly read it.

He sat down heavily in the chair. 'Edgar,' he whispered to himself before running his hand down his face.

I wasn't sure if I should comfort him or not, but a small shake of the head from Rachelle told me not to. Gaston took a deep, steadying breath and got to his feet. He embraced me in his arms, holding me tight. 'I am so sorry, Nathalie.'

The one small act of sympathy and kindness nearly sent me over the edge again and I fought to keep the emotion back. I didn't want to fall to pieces here at the camp, not when I needed Gaston's help, and showing any kind of weakness would not help my cause.

'I'm all right,' I said eventually, pulling back from my cousin. 'He died a brave and courageous Frenchman who did not bow to the Germans. He was proud of what he was doing. We were very proud of him too.'

'Of course. And rightly so,' said Gaston. 'Edgar was always one to stand up against power and bullies. I remember him getting into a few scrapes with the locals when he came to stay here during the summer. He stuck up for a young lad in the village who was being picked on by some older boys. Edgar didn't care they were bigger than him. He just saw the injustice in what they were doing.'

The recollection warmed my heart. It was comforting to hear such good words spoken about my brother. 'He

104

was always like that,' I said. 'He had a great sense of right and wrong.'

We all stood without speaking for a moment, lost in our own memories of Edgar. It was Gaston who broke the silence first. 'I'm sorry, but I need to get back to my meeting. Thank you for coming to tell me in person, even though I would prefer you didn't take unnecessary risks.' He gave Rachelle a pointed look.

'It wasn't my idea,' said Rachelle. 'Nathalie was coming, regardless. I thought it was best if I at least took her the right way so she wouldn't get lost.'

Gaston nodded as if accepting his sister's explanation. '*Alors*, be careful going back, then.'

'Oh, we're not going back yet,' said Rachelle.

Gaston frowned and looked between Rachelle and me. 'You're not?'

Rachelle raised her eyebrows and nodded in my direction. 'Nathalie is here for another reason.'

Gaston's eyes narrowed. 'Why do I get the feeling I'm not going to like this other reason?'

'Because you won't,' said Rachelle, folding her arms and leaning back against the wall, as if ready to watch the show that was about to take place.

'Nathalie?' Gaston turned to face me fully.

'I need you to help me,' I told Gaston, ignoring Rachelle.

'You know I will always help you if I can,' said Gaston, taking a cigarette packet from his pocket.

'You don't know what she's going to ask you,' said Rachelle.

'True.' Gaston lit his cigarette.

'I want you to teach me how to shoot a gun,' I said.

Gaston choked on the smoke he'd just drawn. He spluttered and looked at me incredulously. 'You want to learn to fire a gun?' he repeated. He exchanged a look with his sister. 'Is she serious?'

'Deadly,' said Rachelle.

'Why on earth do you want to know how to do that?' asked Gaston, composing himself.

'Because I want to join the Resistance and find the person who killed Edgar and then kill them myself,' I announced with a confidence I didn't feel. In my head, it had sounded like a reasonable proposition, but out loud, it sounded naïve.

Gaston's burst of laughter only confirmed my thoughts. When he realised that neither I nor Rachelle had joined in, he controlled himself.

At that point, Marcel entered the room.

'It sounds like fun in here,' he said, looking around the room.

A silence descended, and the air felt heavy, as if someone had sucked all the atmosphere out into the forest.

'It would be funny if my cousin wasn't actually quite serious,' said Gaston, the amusement not quite gone from his voice.

'Care to share the joke?' asked Marcel.

'Nathalie wants to learn how to fire a gun so she can kill a German officer, probably one in the Gestapo,' said Gaston.

'Stop!' I almost shouted. 'Don't make fun of me.'

'I'm not making fun of you,' said Gaston, the humour truly gone from his voice now. 'It's a ridiculous idea and I am certainly not going to help you get yourself killed. One dead cousin is enough for me.'

'What am I missing?' Marcel asked, looking around the room.

'The Gestapo have killed my brother,' I said. 'I want to avenge his murder. I want to know how to fire a gun so I can go back to Paris and—'

Before I could finish, Gaston cut in. 'And get yourself killed, too. How do you think your parents will feel when both their children are dead?'

'They will be proud of what I've done,' I retorted, although not entirely sure that would be their overriding emotion. I pushed the thought of my mother crying as my father tried to comfort her from my mind. This was not a time to be sentimental.

'I don't know why you brought her here,' said Gaston to Rachelle. 'Did you really think I would agree to this?'

Rachelle pushed herself away from the wall. 'No, but if I didn't bring her, she was going to come on her own and I was worried she'd get lost and meet a German patrol.'

'You can't criticise your sister for that,' said Marcel. He looked at me. 'Your brother has been killed, you say?'

'Yesterday,' I replied.

Marcel inclined his head a fraction. 'I am sorry for your loss.' He looked at Gaston and Rachelle. 'And to you both as well.'

'Thank you,' I said, willing away the tears that were once again threatening to gather.

'I understand you want revenge,' said Marcel, 'but I think your cousin is right. It would be foolish to go after the man who killed your brother.'

'It would be suicidal,' said Gaston. He placed a hand on my shoulder. 'Please do not pursue this any further.'

As was becoming the pattern of my emotions, after the wave of grief for Edgar came the anger. I shrugged Gaston's hand away. 'I thought I could rely on you.' I noted the fleeting look of hurt cross his face, and for a second it was satisfying. As I brushed past him and out of the door, I was already regretting it, but my anger and my pride would not allow me to turn back and apologise.

I marched across the clearing, but before I had even reached the campfire, the sound of booted feet on the ground catching me up had me turning around. It was Marcel.

'Nathalie, wait,' he said, coming to a stop in front of me. 'Gaston has your best interests at heart. You're his cousin. Of course he's not going to encourage you to put yourself in danger. You cannot be too harsh on him.'

My shoulders slumped. 'I know. I will say sorry.'

'Yes. Quite right, too.'

I eyed Marcel. He was much taller than me and his eyes looked darker than they had before. There was a small cut on the side of his cheek that I hadn't noticed before in the hut.

'What happened to your face?' I asked.

Marcel's hand went to his cheek. 'Oh, that. Nothing. Got into a scuffle. You should see the other chap.'

'Was it the other night, on your . . . whatever it was you were doing dressed as a German officer?'

'You know I can't tell you that,' said Marcel. 'Everything is on a need-to-know basis, plus if ever you're questioned, you can't let slip what you don't know.'

I nodded. Of course I knew that. Everyone did. 'I'm glad you're not more seriously hurt,' I said.

He gave me a half-smile, as if he didn't quite know what to make of me. 'Yes. Me too,' he said. 'Look, why don't you make peace with your cousin? He thinks a lot of you. He was telling me about how you and your brother would come and stay with them every summer.'

'He was, was he?' I raised my eyebrows. 'What else did he say?'

Now Marcel really did smile. 'Need-to-know.' He tapped the side his nose.

I couldn't help returning the smile, but then I grew serious again. 'Do you have any brothers or sisters?' I asked. The question obviously caught him by surprise, but he answered.

'Yes, I'm one of four brothers. I'm the eldest.'

'If something happened to one of them, you'd feel the same as me, wouldn't you?'

'Without a doubt.'

'You understand my need for revenge?'

'Yes, I understand but . . .'

'Then teach me how to fire a gun. Get me a handgun I can use. Small enough to keep in my bag so that I can have it with me all the time.'

'I really don't think that's a good idea,' said Marcel. 'Just because I understand, doesn't mean I approve. I'm with your cousin on this.'

I had a feeling he wasn't going to budge. 'All right.'

'All right?' He looked questioningly at me.

'Yes. All right.'

'Is that it? After all the shit you gave Gaston, now you're just accepting it from me without any argument?'

'You should count yourself lucky,' I replied. 'Anyway, if no one here will help me, I'll find someone who can.'

With that, I strode off back across the opening to the hut, just as Gaston emerged with Rachelle.

'If you've come for another argument, then save your breath,' he said, folding his arms across his chest.

'I've not come for a fight. I've come to apologise,' I said. The relief on his face was clear. His shoulders relaxed, and he dropped his hands. 'I'm sorry for asking you to help. I realise now it was wrong.'

'Glad to hear it,' said Gaston, although there was a note of suspicion in his voice. 'And that's it?'

'Yes. You don't have to worry about me. I'm sorry and I'm sorry Rachelle had to bring me out here.'

Gaston nodded. 'As long as you make it back to the farm safely, then no harm done.'

'Yes, we should get back,' said Rachelle. 'I'm just going to quickly see one of the boys from the village. I have a message from his mother. Won't be long.'

I hadn't realised that Rachelle was a messenger for the group and their families. She'd never said, but as everyone around me was keen to point out, everything was on a need-to-know basis. I felt a swell of pride for my cousin and, if I was honest, a fraction of me was jealous that she was actively playing a part in the Resistance. She was doing something which, on the face of it, seemed minor, but in reality was a very important role. Passing messages back and forth kept morale and spirits high. It meant families didn't feel estranged from their loved ones and loved ones didn't feel alone. It reminded them of what they were doing and why.

It was something I wanted. I wanted to do something meaningful.

Gaston said his goodbyes and went back over to the group of men, waving Marcel over.

Marcel stopped in front of me. 'You made your peace?'

'Yes. All sorted.'

'But you're still going to go ahead with your crazy idea of getting revenge, aren't you?' It wasn't so much of a question as a statement from Marcel.

I couldn't resist tapping the side of my nose. 'Need-to-know basis.'

He cursed under his breath and let out a long sigh. 'Look, if you're determined to do this, then let *me* help you. Let me teach you.'

'What? You've changed your mind suddenly?'

'I'd sooner you were taught by the best than by some French farmer who has only ever used a twelve bore.'

'Thank you,' I said as relief and anticipation fought for first place.

'You have to let me teach you properly, though, and it won't take five minutes. It takes a long time to get good at it.'

'That's fine. I'm here for the next few weeks, anyway.'

'Damn. I'm going to regret this, I can tell.' He let out a sigh and looked up to the sky, giving a slight shake of his head, before heading off to join Gaston.

Chapter 14

Nathalie

I had agreed to meet Marcel the next day on the edge of the forest at one o'clock.

I had already prepared a cover story in case anyone, especially the Germans, should appear and ask me what I was doing. I had a stick with me and I would say I was scaring off the fox that kept hanging around the chicken coop.

I heard someone whistle from the trees and paused to see if it was repeated. If so, then I would know it was the signal that Marcel was there. The whistle came again, and I gave a quick look around to make sure no one was watching me before I made my way into the forest.

'Psst. Over here,' whispered Marcel.

I spun around but couldn't see him. 'Where are you?'

'Here,' the voice came from a different direction. Then again from somewhere else, this time followed by a chuckle.

'You're not funny,' I whispered.

Then he stepped out from the left of me, not where I had thought he was. 'Sorry, I was just having a bit of fun.'

I frowned. 'This is a serious matter.'

'You're right, but we still have to find some light-hearted moments when we can, no matter how insignificant they seem.'

I couldn't help agreeing with him. 'Very well. But we need to do something serious now.'

'Of course. Follow me,' said Marcel, heading back through the trees.

I had to run a little to catch up. 'Does Gaston know you're helping me?' I asked.

'He hasn't asked, and I have volunteered the information,' said Marcel.

'And if he does ask?'

'Then I shall tell him. It wouldn't do me any good to get on the wrong side of your cousin. He needs to know he can trust me.'

'Well, I'm grateful and I'm sorry if it causes you any problems,' I said, more out of courtesy than sincerity.

Marcel laughed. 'You're not that sorry, really.' He looked over his shoulder at me and grinned.

His smile was infectious, and I couldn't help returning it. 'Not that sorry, no.'

We tramped through the undergrowth of the forest for about another fifteen minutes. The trees were denser and taller, allowing less light to filter through the branches. I didn't know where we were, but I had a sense we were travelling away from the camp. Eventually, Marcel came to a halt, and I stood beside him. We were on the edge of some sort of ravine that overlooked a clearing about twenty metres below.

'We just need to get down there and we should be far enough away and sheltered from any unwanted attention,' said Marcel.

'How long have we got?'

'Thirty to forty minutes.'

It didn't seem long enough for me, but then all I really needed to know was how to aim and fire. We made our way down into the gully, Marcel holding out a hand to steady me as we navigated some rocks and uneven ground.

'Aren't we making ourselves vulnerable down here?' I asked.

'Not really. There's enough coverage to protect us from any prying eyes and there are several ways out of the valley. We're not sitting ducks. I'm not that stupid.' Marcel held my hand a little tighter and longer than necessary now we were over the rough ground.

'Sorry, I didn't mean to imply you were.'

'Good.' He let go of my hand and, from the bag he'd slung over his shoulder, pulled out a small pistol. 'Now this little beauty is ideal for women as it's small enough to fit in your purse, but it means you have to be pretty close to someone to use it effectively. It's got a silencer. If you go for the head shot, you're likely to be sprayed with blood, skull, and brains. You all right with that?'

To be honest, I hadn't considered the blood and guts part of killing someone. Pulling the trigger had been as far as I'd thought. 'Yes. I'm fine,' I replied, not entirely sure if I sounded convincing enough.

Marcel continued. 'So, if you're facing your target, you're going to need to be close enough that they will make eye contact with you. Their eyes will be surprised and then plead with you. It will all happen in a second, before you can register it, but your subconscious will take in all those thoughts. Don't let that deter you. You have no time to think of them. You've got to pull the trigger before you even think. A clean head shot. Blow their brains out.'

I swallowed. It sounded so barbaric. 'And if I shoot from behind?' This seemed a coward's way of doing it and I wanted to see that fear, that surprise, and that pleading in the eyes of whoever had killed my brother.

'From behind. Well, first you will have to get close enough that they don't hear you and spin around. In all honesty, that will lower your chances of a clean hit. They will effectively be a moving target once they turn.'

'I want to see the look on their face,' I said. 'I want to say my brother's name. I want them to recognise the name and realise I have come to get them.'

Marcel let out a low whistle. 'That second you hesitate gives them the chance to react. They might have a gun too. They might overpower you.'

'I'll be ready,' I said. 'What other options are there, other than this little pistol?'

'There's the .38 Special revolver. You can be further away from your target. But the further away you are, the more accurate you have to be, the bigger the margin for something to go wrong.'

'Until I know the target, I won't know which one I'll use,' I said. 'I need to learn how to use both.'

'In thirty minutes, that's a tall order, but we can give it a go.'

'Let's not waste any more time.' I went to take the pistol from his hand, but Marcel moved his hand away.

'Before we go playing the Wild West, I need to show you how to handle this safely, so you don't shoot your own fingers or toes off or plant a bullet in your own side. And yes, it's been done before, so listen up.'

After several minutes of going through the parts of the weapon and how to make it safe, how to get ready to discharge it, Marcel was confident I knew what I was doing. I weighed the gun in my hand after successfully loading, unloading and reloading the bullets quickly enough and accurately enough for Marcel's liking. 'So, you need to show me how to fire this thing now.'

From his bag, Marcel took out an apple and walked over to a large bolder. He placed it on top at roughly his own eye level. I wanted to say what a waste of an apple, but in the circumstances felt it was a justifiable waste.

'It's relatively simple,' said Marcel. 'Hold the gun out in front of you, not close enough that they can grab the barrel and twist it out of your hand or, even worse, overpower you and turn the gun on you.'

I did as I was instructed. I was surprised at the weight in my outstretched hand, but also felt a surge of anticipation. 'Like this?'

'That's good. Now look down your arm and along the barrel. Line your arm up with your sight.' He came over and stood behind me, his body in close contact with mine. He placed one hand on my shoulder and the other down the length of my arm. His head was touching mine and I could feel his breath on the side of my face. I was aware I was breathing heavily. 'Try to keep your breathing steady,' he said softly. 'Take a deep breath and gently squeeze that trigger. Not now. When I tell you to.'

I nodded and whispered a yes, fully aware of how close he was to me and how much I liked it.

'When you pull that trigger, you're going to feel a jolt as it gives a little kickback. It's all perfectly normal. Pull the trigger, hold your aim and absorb that kickback. Let it travel up your arm and let your shoulder be the cushion. Understand?'

'Yes.'

'Now gently squeeze. The gun's loaded, as you know. It's going to fire and you're going to hit that apple.'

'I admire your confidence in me,' I said.

'I'm here helping you. Trust me. You do trust me, don't you?'

The question seemed more loaded than the gun I was holding. 'I'm here in the forest with you. I think that shows I trust you,' I whispered back. He didn't speak for a moment, and I sensed he was looking at me from the corner of his eye, but I remained focused on the gun and the apple, as well as trying to keep my breathing steady.

'Breathe in. One. Two. Squeeze. More. Squeeze more.'

The gun fired, and the noise and the kickback made me jump. I gave a small yelp of surprise and immediately felt embarrassed. The bullet caught the side of the apple, taking a gouge of flesh out. 'We did it.' I was delighted with the result.

'Not bad for a first attempt,' said Marcel. 'Let's do it all over again.'

And we did. Several more times. With each attempt, I became more and more relaxed at handling the gun, expecting the sound and the kickback, while simultaneously becoming more and more aware of the closeness of Marcel's body. On the last go, his lips were grazing my jawline, and I had to do everything I could to stop myself from turning around and kissing him. I had no idea where that thought came from and I shied away just as I pulled the trigger, sending the bullet somewhere way off the target.

'Hey, don't get twitchy,' said Marcel, holding me against him. I tried to wriggle away, but he held me tighter. 'Relax.'

How on earth was I supposed to do that? 'I'm all right,' I said. 'You can let me go now. I was just distracted.'

Marcel dropped his arms away, hooking his thumbs in his belt loops. 'Distracted?'

'Yes. A bird or something. I don't know.'

'Is that right?'

'Yes,' I insisted, looking away in case I was blushing. 'Now, what about the other gun?'

He didn't answer immediately, and I intently studied the pistol in my hand so I didn't have to look at him. Finally, he spoke. 'All right. Let's try the thirty-eight.'

We repeated the procedure as we had for the pistol. I tried to concentrate on aiming and firing rather than the proximity of Marcel. I was sure he was fully aware of it too, but he remained professional.

'You're going to have to get some more practice in if you intend on using this one,' he said. 'Look, we'd better be getting back. We've been here long enough.' He stepped away from me and, taking the weapon, made it safe before putting it back into his bag.

We made our way out of the gully, taking a different route out to the steep bank we had come down, but it was still a strain on the calf muscles. I was relieved when we reached the top. 'Oh, that was—'

'Shh.' Marcel cut me off mid-sentence. He had stopped suddenly, and I could tell he was looking at and listening intently to our surroundings. 'Get down,' he whispered.

My heart began to beat hard against my chest as I heard

the distant sound of voices. I couldn't make out what they were saying, but they were male, calling out to one another every so often. 'Germans?' I whispered to Marcel.

He looked back at me and nodded. 'No more talking. Just do whatever I say, without question. Understand?'

I went to speak but stopped myself and nodded earnestly. Marcel reached back and took my hand. 'It will be all right. I promise.'

It was a bold promise, but I did trust him.

I could hear the voices growing louder as the patrol made its way towards us. Marcel gestured back the way we had come and, still holding my hand, stepped around me and, keeping low, began moving away. I mimicked his stance, but I pulled my hand away. Not because I didn't enjoy it, but I knew it would make moving slower and more awkward. I gave him a quick smile of reassurance. Within a few minutes, we were back in the gully and, keeping to the edge where the trees were denser, we skirted the perimeter before reaching a track.

'You all right?' asked Marcel, pausing momentarily.

'Yes. I'm fine,' I reassured him. I had always been very athletic and could match Edgar for speed and agility when we were teenagers.

'I can't hear them,' he said. 'This is a longer way back, but it's safer. We'll come off the track soon and then we'll head for the east side of the farm. It's about twenty minutes at a run. You think you can manage that?'

'Yes. No problem.'

I may have overestimated my abilities somewhat and after about ten minutes, I noticed Marcel had slowed his pace so I could keep up. He was barely breaking a sweat, but I was breathing heavily now. I stumbled over a tree root at one point but managed to stay on my feet, my dress catching on a branch that ripped the fabric. Again, I reassured Marcel I was all right.

'You're doing great,' he said. 'One last push.'

Finally, we came to the edge of the forest. I could see the farm on the other side of the field.

'We can cut through the maize. It will give us good cover,' said Marcel.

'You don't have to come with me. I'll be all right now. You should get back to the camp as soon as possible.'

'I want to make sure you're safe.'

'And I will be. There are no Germans in the maize field. You're the one who needs to be careful. And I won't even know if you get back safely.'

The corner of his mouth turned up a fraction. 'Anyone would think you're worried about me.'

'Of course I am.' I tried to keep my voice neutral. 'I'd be worried about anyone.'

He was still smiling – a knowing smile – and then more seriously, he said, 'Thanks.'

'What for?'

'For worrying. When you've been out here for a while, it's easy to forget how to care about each other as individuals.'

'That's what makes us better than them.'

He nodded. 'I don't want you to worry about me, but it's nice to know.' He held his hand to my cheek and brushed my face with his thumb. 'It reminds me how to care about others.' With that, he leaned forward and kissed my forehead.

I leaned into him and took a deep breath. I wanted to lift my head to meet his lips with mine, but he pulled away, although his hand remained on my face. I covered it with my own. 'We must always care.'

He nodded, and then – with a sigh – pulled back. 'And on that note, I'm taking you across the field. No arguing.'

We weaved our way through the maize crop and were soon crouched at the boundary of the farmyard. 'Please be careful going back,' I said, suddenly feeling both relief and fear.

I don't know what possessed me. Maybe it was the adrenaline of the moment, the danger we'd shared or just emotions running high, but I leaned forward and kissed him on the mouth. A chaste kiss, but a kiss, nonetheless. And then immediately felt mortified at my boldness. I couldn't read his expression and I jumped to my feet, ready to flee, but Marcel caught my hand and pulled me back down.

We locked eyes and his gaze was intense and I could feel some sort of invisible force binding us together. 'Look for the chalk mark,' he said.

I nodded, my throat too tight with emotion and longing to allow my voice to escape. He kissed me gently on the lips before letting go of my hand.

I took one last moment to look at him before standing and slipping back out through the crops and into the farmyard.

Chapter 15

Nathalie

It was a couple of days before a new chalk mark appeared on the wall. I rubbed it off to show that I had spotted it and the excitement at the prospect of seeing Marcel again sent my stomach into a whirl.

'Someone is looking very happy with themselves,' said Rachelle as I came back into the kitchen. 'What are you up to?'

I assumed what I hoped was a look of innocence. 'Nothing.'

'Liar,' said Rachelle good-humouredly. 'You're up to something.'

'I am not.'

'It wouldn't involve a certain Englishman going by the name of Marcel, would it?'

'Shh,' I hissed, looking around to make sure Clarice wasn't about.

'Oh, don't worry. Papa has taken both Maman and Odile into the village,' said Rachelle. 'So, am I right?'

'You're not supposed to ask me anything like that,' I said. 'Remember, we must only know the bare minimum so we can't accidentally pass on any information.'

Rachelle rolled her eyes. 'I suppose I could come with you and then I'd see for myself.'

'Rachelle! Stop.' I hugged my cousin. 'Don't ask and don't follow. I promise you I'm being careful.'

Rachelle eyed me sceptically. 'I will have to trust you, but if anything happens to you, my mother will murder me. And if she doesn't, your mother will.'

We shared a smile. 'I will do everything in my powers not to get you murdered,' I said, looking at the kitchen clock. 'I should go.'

Knowing my uncle had taken Clarice and Odile into town on the horse and cart, I felt far more at ease crossing the farmyard and weaving through the maize field. Still, I was cautious when I got to the edge, just in case there was anyone who might spot me. It was a sad fact of the war that neighbours had taken to reporting on each other to curry favour with the Germans in the hope they would be rewarded with extra rations or a travel pass or something to make their lives easier. Times were becoming increasingly difficult under German occupation and every week there was another rule restricting the freedom of the French people.

I was now at the edge of the field, with just two rows of crops in front of me. A movement to my left caught my attention, and I saw Marcel appear.

My heart gave an extra bump, and a surge of excitement swept through me. He looked particularly handsome today, but I wasn't sure why or whether it was just because I was more aware of him, or more aware of my reaction to him being near.

'*Bonjour*,' I said, realising I sounded formal. '*Salut*.' There, that sounded more casual and friendly. He was standing in front of me now, looking down at me, with his brown eyes a rich shade of coffee.

He kissed me on each cheek. 'That's how I'm supposed to do it, isn't it?'

I shrugged. 'If you're French, I suppose it is.'

'As Marcel, I am.'

'And when you're not Marcel?'

There was a pause between us, and then, slowly, Marcel leaned into me. 'It's only ever Marcel here.' His lips brushed mine and then he moved away. He took my hand. 'Come on, you want to learn how to shoot. We'd better get going.'

I took his outstretched hand and ran alongside him across the fields. All I could think of was the touch of his lips on mine and how that small but intimate gesture had sent ripples of desire through my body.

We didn't go to the gorge where we'd been before. Marcel explained he had been monitoring the area since we'd had a near run-in with the German patrol and they were making daily tours of the gorge now.

'Instead, I thought I'd teach you some hand-to-hand combat,' he said. 'You never know when you might need it. I'll show you how to disarm someone with a gun.'

'I hope I never have to get that close to a German.'

'But if you do, I want you to be able to protect yourself,' said Marcel. 'Besides, we can't risk firing any shots today. Not only did they attract the interest of the Germans, but Gaston asked me if I knew anything about them.'

'What did you say?'

'That I'd heard them too, but they were on the other side of the river.' He looked at me. 'So, I didn't lie, but I didn't tell all the truth.'

'Do you think he guessed?'

'Possibly. Probably. But I'm not about to make the same mistake. I can get myself out of danger pretty easily, but I don't want to be responsible for anything happening to you.'

We walked on and soon came to a small clearing. I had to confess to only having a very general idea where we were in relation to the camp. The farm was behind us in a westerly direction.

'You seem to know your way around the forest,' I said, as I watched Marcel take off his jacket and roll up his shirt sleeves.

'I've made it my job to know this place like the back of my hand. If I need an escape route, I don't want to be running into dead ends, cliff tops or places where I can't cross the river. I don't like surprises.'

It made sense. I took off my cardigan and hung it over a nearby tree trunk that had fallen over.

'So, we're going to start with what to do if someone comes at you head on,' began Marcel. 'Always expect the unexpected. Never relax. That's the first rule. Always suspect the other chap wants to kill you.'

I had to keep reminding myself that Marcel was teaching me lifesaving skills, and I wasn't to get distracted by the closeness of his body to mine.

'Concentrate,' Marcel reminded me several times.

I forced myself to focus and as Marcel came towards me from behind, wrapping his arm around my neck, I threw all my weight and strength into the move he'd been teaching me, launching him over my shoulder.

Marcel let out a groan as he hit the ground. I slammed my body weight onto him, pinning him with my knee in his throat.

'All right. All right,' he wheezed.

I removed the pressure. 'Have I passed the test?'

Before I knew what was happening, Marcel had flipped me over onto my back and was straddling me, just lifting his weight from my stomach. My hands were pinned above my head.

'Never let down your guard,' he said. Then he lowered his head and kissed me on the forehead, before getting to his feet and, still holding my hands, pulling me up.

I wasn't about to let him get the better of me and I hooked my foot around his leg, catching the back of his knee so his leg crumpled. He grabbed me and we both fell to the ground. Once again, I found myself pinned underneath him.

'Second rule. You need to know when to quit,' said Marcel.

This time, when he helped me to my feet, I didn't try any sneaky moves on him.

'You win,' I said.

He smiled. 'I always win.'

It was amazing how his smile could inject heat into my face as I felt a small blush creep up my neck. I looked away, brushing forest debris from my clothes. 'If my mother could see me now, she'd die,' I said. 'She would despair of me even more than usual.'

'Even more than usual?' Marcel unscrewed the lid of his water bottle and offered it to me.

I took a long sip before handing it back. 'She wants me to marry and have children and have a normal life.'

'And you don't want that?'

'Maybe one day, but I don't want just that. I want more,' I explained. 'I want to be a fashion designer. I want to have my own fashion house.' I paused, looking for amusement on his face or some sort of patronising expression, but there was none.

'I've only seen your sewing skills on a uniform,' he said, as I handed him the water bottle. 'I'm no expert, but it all looked pretty good to me. I've no doubt you can be whatever you want to be.'

'You don't disapprove?'

'It's not my place to disapprove, but if my wife had skills like you, then I'd happily support her to make something of her life.' He took a swig of water from the bottle before screwing the lid back on.

'You're the first man who hasn't laughed at me or dismissed me.'

'Who else has laughed at you?'

'Alphonse. He's my . . . boyfriend, I suppose.'

Marcel raised his eyebrows in question. 'You suppose?'

'I don't think he is anymore,' I confessed, looking down and scuffing the ground with my foot. 'He wants to marry me.'

'And you don't want to marry him?'

I shook my head. 'No. He's not as understanding as you are. He's very traditional. We don't really have anything in common and the war, the occupation, has just highlighted that even more.'

'How do you mean?'

I looked up and met Marcel's gaze. 'He's a policeman and he's very loyal to the Vichy government.' Marcel didn't reply, just gave a small nod of understanding. I continued. 'He was asking me a lot of questions about Edgar before I came here. There was also an incident and he scared me.' I gave an involuntary shiver as I remembered Alphonse holding the gun to the back of my head.

'Do you trust him?'

I looked away, feeling embarrassed at my connection with Alphonse. 'No. I don't.' It was only because Papa had spoken up that Kranz had ordered Alphonse to take the gun away. I couldn't be sure he wouldn't have pulled the trigger if Kranz had ordered him to shoot me.

'Does he know how you feel?'

I shook my head. 'I haven't told him yet. Being away from him has given me a clarity of thought I haven't had before. Despite the distractions here.'

'Distractions?'

I didn't need to reply. Marcel knew I meant him. He closed the gap between us and wrapped his arms around me, holding me to his chest. I didn't resist. I wanted to feel his body against mine.

He breathed in and let out a slow breath. 'I know what you mean by distractions.' He tipped my chin up with his finger and kissed the tip of my nose. 'We should start heading back before anyone notices you're missing.'

'Thank you for doing this for me,' I said as we began walking back through the forest.

'Are you still determined to go through with this revenge thing?'

'It's not a thing and yes I am,' I replied.

'I was hoping you'd change your mind.'

'I can't. I owe it to Edgar.'

'But would he want you to do this for him? Who are you doing this for?'

I didn't answer him. It was hard to even admit it to myself, but I was doing this for me, to extinguish my anger and inflict the same penalty on the person who'd killed my brother. It wasn't a trait I particularly liked, but it was there – the need for retribution.

'Plus, I don't want anything to happen to you.' Marcel stopped and looked at me. 'I'd feel it was my fault.'

I looked him straight in the eyes. 'Whatever happens, please know this is not your fault.' I began walking again.

Marcel caught up with me, taking my hand in his. 'It's not just that. I shouldn't really say this. I mean, I don't believe in getting involved romantically with someone in these sorts of circumstances, not to mention the fact that I barely know you, but I care about you, Nathalie. Probably more than I should.'

I squeezed his hand. 'And I about you, but whatever is happening between us, life around us is still going on and we have to be involved. I need to do something. I can no longer be a bystander.'

His hand came up to my cheek, and my breathing quickened. I covered his hand with my own. I wasn't scared. I wasn't afraid. I felt brave and desired.

He closed his eyes as if steeling himself and let out a long breath with frustrated undertones. He went to move his hand away.

'Nathalie. I'm sorry. I can't,' he began.

I gripped his hand tightly so he couldn't move it from my face. 'Don't,' I whispered. 'We mustn't think about the future. Everything can change in a moment. We must only think about now.'

'But you deserve better than me.'

'Don't say such a thing. I don't care for noble comments like that. Now is the time to be honest.'

He leaned in, his forehead resting against mine. 'All this is new to me. How I feel about you . . . it's unnerving.'

'The unflappable British serviceman is unnerved,' I said

with amusement and then more softly: 'I don't believe in regrets. Not anymore. Not when life is so precious and can be taken away without warning.'

'You're making it very difficult for me to think with a level head.'

'Don't think too hard.'

'I can't say no to you,' replied Marcel, his voice gruffer than I'd heard before. 'Whatever you ask, I'll agree to. I knew that from the first moment I saw you. I knew you were special, but I didn't think you were mine to take.'

'I belong to no one,' I said. 'I give myself. No one takes me.'

His breathing was becoming faster. 'I want you,' he whispered.

'I want you too.' My voice was ragged, and I could feel my body reacting to his. It felt natural and spontaneous.

I didn't wait for him. I took the initiative and kissed him. He responded immediately as we matched each other's hunger and desire.

Chapter 16

Darcie

Despite feeling pretty tired from all the excitement, not to mention all the walking the previous day and the evening out with Matt, Darcie didn't sleep that well. She wasn't quite sure what was disturbing her the most. Christophe Padgett had come across as uninterested and indifferent to the dress, and yet the way he had wanted to keep hold of the sketchbook, to the point of her having to force it from his hands, made her think he wasn't being honest with her in some way. Then there was the excitement that Matt had another contact. On top of that, there was the thrill of attending the Chanel haute couture fashion show later.

She showered and dressed, choosing to wear a pair of 1940s white wide-legged trousers that had been in her shop for a couple of months, together with a white short-sleeved blouse. Darcie folded a colourful headscarf into a hairband and tied her hair back. Before leaving, she texted home to make sure everyone was OK. Chloe replied almost immediately.

Chloe: All good here. Stop worrying and enjoy your holiday! We love you. Xx

The show wasn't until later in the afternoon, so Darcie planned to spend the morning at the La Galerie Dior, which had long been on her wish list of places to visit.

The Dior museum exceeded every one of Darcie's

expectations, from the beautiful glass staircase showcasing fashion accessories in a spiral of rainbow-colour blocks to the amazing evening dresses in various shades of cream, gold, and white.

She left the building in something of a daze and was glad of having a couple of hours to sit and have some lunch before meeting up with Matt for her next round of fashion extravaganza.

Lunch was a much more grounded affair of a pastry and a hot chocolate, giving Darcie time to reset herself. After checking the route and making sure she had allowed enough time, she set off to the fashion show. It took her nearly an hour to get there but she actually arrived early. She didn't mind and only had to wait ten minutes before Matt showed up.

'Great, you're here,' he said, once again giving her a peck on the cheek.

She liked it and it made her feel warm inside. 'Told you I wasn't going to stand you up.'

'Come on, let's go inside.'

Darcie followed Matt, along with the other photographers, into the building. She thought she was going to have to pinch herself, to believe she was there. Her stomach was somersaulting with excitement. Looking around at the faces of the photographers, she could tell this wasn't their first time attending one of Chanel's shows.

Going through a set of double doors, Darcie almost stopped in her tracks. The fashion show was being held in a large exhibition room, with white walls, floor, and seating. Around the edge of the room were three layers of boxed and terraced benches for viewing. In the centre of the room, set out in a triangular formation, were soft, rounded bench-like cushions. Instead of a traditional catwalk running down the centre of the room, there were a series of large white steps cascading gently down the wall on the far side, leading out onto the ground floor. The catwalk would essentially flow around the centre seating, thus giving everyone a full

360-degree view of the outfits. Dotted around the ceiling hung clusters of highly polished silver domes and discs.

Matt guided Darcie towards a cluster of seating reserved for the press, directly opposite a huge plasma screen mounted on the far wall. Within a few moments of settling themselves, the screen came to life, showing a musician sitting in front of a pared-down drum kit.

'That's Pharrell Williams,' said Matt. 'American rapper, record producer, singer songwriter.'

'That's so cool,' said Darcie, watching as Pharrell opened the show with his music. He was wearing a silver bomber jacket, which was in keeping with the futuristic feel of the show.

Darcie had watched live-streaming of Chanel haute couture shows on YouTube before but it was nothing compared to actually being there in person. The atmosphere, the setting, the outfits and the sheer luxury were hard to comprehend. She wanted to savour every moment of it. She knew she wouldn't get an opportunity like this again. This was definitely a once-in-a-lifetime experience. She closed her eyes and inhaled deeply, feeling the atmospheric charge of the room.

She opened her eyes a moment later just as the first model descended the staircase, followed by a procession of other models.

They were dressed in the classic Chanel style of a two-piece women's suit: some in skirts, some in trousers, some with long coats and others with shorter versions. Despite the different colours, the distinctive silver buttons running down the centre of the garments, together with the breast pockets, all clearly oozed the Chanel brand of sophistication, luxury, and understatement.

Matt had already told Darcie she could take photos on her phone but she didn't want to see the garments through the lens of a camera, she wanted to experience them with her naked eye.

'I can always look at your photos to remind myself

afterwards,' she'd told him. 'I want to see them for real.' And that's exactly what she was doing.

Much as she loved the classic Chanel pieces, it was the long evening dresses that she was most taken with. The effortless flow and lightness of the fabric betrayed the amount of work that had gone into creating such pieces of art. Darcie thought back to the sketchbook and the long evening dress, which she was sure would not have been out of place among all these spectacular ones today.

All too soon, the show was over. Darcie hadn't been able to take her eyes from the catwalk and the disappointment there were no more clothes to view was palpable. But she was also on a high at having been to such an event. She wished she could do it all over again, right there and then.

'Did you enjoy it?' asked Matt as they left the building.

'Oh my God, are you serious?' replied Darcie. 'It was out of this world. Thank you so much.'

Matt grinned, obviously sharing in Darcie's delight. 'It was all my pleasure.'

'Now, I want to treat you to supper,' said Darcie. 'As a thank you.'

'You don't have to do that.'

Darcie held up her hand. 'I know I don't, but I want to.' She was pleased when he didn't argue.

The restaurant was a bit more upmarket than the café they'd been to previously, but not so much that Darcie felt awkward and out of place or had to worry about whether she could afford it or not.

After a quick look at the menu, they ordered their food and chatted comfortably about the show. 'That outfit at the end.' Darcie sighed. 'It was like a sculpture. It was hard to believe it was made out of fabric.'

'I liked the one that was folded like a piece of origami. I would say it was the cream-coloured one but all of the clothes were cream.'

'They were amazing. You probably know of the Japanese

fashion designer Issey Miyake and the fashion label Comme des Garçons – they're both very famous for their geometric and origami-inspired styles. I studied them at school for my Textiles project.'

Their food arrived and they ate in companionable silence for the most part, making small talk about some of the photographic assignments Matt had undertaken. 'I'm still looking for the big one,' he said.

'Aren't we all?' replied Darcie. 'I thought I might have it with the dress.'

Matt's phoned pinged a text message. 'Do you mind?' he asked, taking his phone from his pocket.

'No. Carry on.'

'Just in case it's important.' He studied his phone, read a text message, tapped out a reply and placed his phone on the table, before putting his cutlery together and pushing his empty plate to one side.

Darcie looked up at him to see he was grinning at her. 'What?' she asked.

'That was Myles Hoffer. He has some information about Nathalie Leroux.'

Darcie was sure her eyes were about to bulge from their sockets. 'He does?'

'Yep.'

Darcie pushed her plate away. 'Tell me. Don't keep me in suspense.'

Chapter 17

Nathalie

The next few weeks passed far too quickly. I met with Marcel whenever I could. Clandestine meetings in and around the forest. Rachelle had stopped asking me where I was sneaking off to and if Clarice suspected anything, she never said so. I knew my time in Morbihan wouldn't last forever, but with each passing day, I became acutely aware of how my feelings for Marcel were growing. It was only when I thought of Edgar that my desire to return to Paris made any sense. I didn't want to leave Marcel, but I comforted myself with the thought that once I'd done what I set out to do, if I was lucky enough to escape, then I would be right back here with him.

It was therefore surprising when one morning Philippe said that now the harvest was over, I would be going back to Paris. I couldn't help wondering if my mother was struggling to deal with Edgar's loss and was lonely now neither of us were there. I knew the day to return home would come, but the rush of panic at leaving Marcel hit me harder than I imagined it would.

'Don't be upset,' said Clarice, misreading the tears that gathered in my eyes. 'Your mother has missed you. She wants you home.'

I could only nod.

'What's wrong?' Marcel looked down at me. We had met in the forest later that morning. Despite my best intentions not to be overwrought with emotion, as soon as I saw him, I felt my heart crumple.

'I'm being sent back to Paris,' I said, trying not to let the sob escape my throat.

Marcel frowned. 'When? Why?'

'Next week. The harvest is over and I'm an extra mouth to feed. My mother wants me back home.'

Marcel pulled me in to his chest and wrapped his arms around me, kissing the top of my head. He didn't say anything. I wanted him to say he was going to miss me and that he didn't want this to happen. That he had some way to fix it so that I could stay. But he said nothing.

'I don't want to go,' I said, almost prompting him to agree with me. 'I want to stay here with you.' I pulled away from the embrace. 'Aren't you going to say anything?'

'I'm thinking,' he said, a frown creasing his forehead. Then his expression changed and his eyes lit up. 'This could be a good thing.'

'A good thing?'

'I've been looking for an opportunity to get closer to the Germans in Paris. We need more intelligence about what they have planned,' said Marcel. 'I need to speak to my contacts, but with your help, I think I know how we could do this.'

I looked at him, momentarily lost for words, but then they came. 'Is that all you can think of?' I asked. 'Does it not worry you I am leaving?'

He closed his eyes for a moment and drew his hand down his face. When he looked at me again, there was sorrow in his expression. 'I'm sorry, Nathalie. I'm such an idiot. Come here.' He cupped my face and kissed me gently on the mouth. 'I got ahead of myself.'

'Is that all you see me as? A source of information?'

'Of course not. I promise you.' He took in a deep breath and exhaled slowly. 'You mean so much more to me than that. The thought of you leaving here hurts terribly. It terrifies me but I can't forget the bigger picture. The reason I'm here. It wasn't to fall in love.'

I knew what he was saying was right and I couldn't deny that it hurt, but the last sentence took the sting out of it somewhat. 'Fall in love?'

His thumbs stroked the sides of my face. 'Yes. I've fallen in love with you and that was never meant to happen.'

Any anger or sadness I felt disappeared. Marcel loved me. I covered his hands with my own. 'I love you too,' I whispered. Tears filled my eyes, partly because of the relief of saying the words to each other and partly because I knew we only had a week left together. 'How are we going to do this?'

He kissed me on the mouth again. 'I've no idea,' he replied. 'But I'll think of something. Hard as it might be, we're going to use this to our advantage. I promise I'll be here for you. I'll do everything I can to be near you, somehow. Just leave it with me. I need to speak to the right people, but I have to know if you're willing to help?'

I knew in that moment that I would do anything for Marcel, but I wasn't doing it purely for him. I was also doing it for my country and for Edgar. 'I'll do whatever I can. Whatever you ask of me, I'll do it.'

The next week passed by in a blur. I saw Marcel every morning and sometimes again in the evening. We knew it was risky, but we also knew we had limited time with each other. We made love whenever we could and each time was more intense, more urgent and more loving than the one before. I had no doubt in my mind how much I cared for this man, even though I didn't know his real name or anything about him.

On the last night before I was due to go back to Paris, I crept out of the farmhouse to meet with Marcel.

'I never want to let you go,' I said as I snuggled under the blanket in his hut at the camp. 'I wish I could stay here in the forest. I could help the other women.'

'I wouldn't let you do that,' replied Marcel. 'Much as I love you, this is no place for a woman. If it were down to me, then there wouldn't be any women here.'

He squeezed me against his chest. 'I had news today,' he said, as he lit a cigarette with his free hand. 'There's a job for you at the Ritz when you get back to Paris.'

I sat bolt upright, the blanket dropping from my shoulders. 'The Ritz?'

Marcel smiled. He sat up, too, and reached for my blouse, draping it over my shoulders. I slipped my arms in and he slowly fastened the buttons. 'Yes, the Ritz.'

'What will I do there?'

'Housemaid.'

'Cleaning?'

'Yes. I'm sure you know how to do that but, of course, we both know the real reason you'll be there,' he said, pressing the end of my nose with his forefinger. 'You will be our eyes and ears. Don't tell anyone you speak fluent German. You just need to stay in the background, not draw attention to yourself, be like a ghost. All you have to do is report back what you see and hear.'

I thought about what Marcel said as I got dressed, pulling on my underwear and stockings, before fastening my skirt. He made it sound very simple. The only reservation I had was not being able to help Papa in the shop. I countered this concern with the knowledge he had managed all the time I was here in Brittany, so perhaps it wouldn't matter so much if I worked elsewhere.

'Is it really worth going to all the trouble of getting me a job at the Ritz? I'm sure I could be more effective doing something else.'

Marcel stubbed out the cigarette and pulled me back onto the bed, my head in his lap as I looked up at him. He kissed me. 'I'm sure you could be effective elsewhere but this is more important than you realise and doesn't come without its dangers.'

'Everything is dangerous, it's just that some things are more dangerous than others.'

'I won't see you again, will I?' I suddenly felt vulnerable and frightened as the reality of what lay ahead appeared crystal clear.

'Don't think like that,' said Marcel, moving closer to me. 'I can't say anything, but we will see each other again.' His breath was warm on the nape of my neck. 'Just trust me.'

I did trust him. I really did, but I just couldn't see how it was going to be possible. The walk back through the forest was sombre. We held hands tightly all the way, savouring the last moments with each other. When we reached the edge of the farm, I kissed him hard and long, and clung on to him until he was forced to remove my arms from around his neck.

'Please be careful,' I said, somehow managing to hold back the tears.

'I'm always careful,' he replied. 'You must be the same for me.'

I nodded. 'Always.'

Chapter 18

Darcie

'It seems there is some confusion and some sort of secrecy about Nathalie Leroux,' said Matt. 'Her father, Théodore Leroux, was a tailor. He owned a shop in Paris. I've got the address here.' He showed his phone to Darcie. 'Myles texted it over.'

'That must be where Nathalie got her talent for design from,' said Darcie. 'I wonder if she was ever a fashion designer then or whether she just did this as a hobby.'

'I don't know, but we can go to the shop and see if the family still own it,' said Matt.

'Oh, could we? That would be amazing. They might know more about Nathalie's connection to the Ritz.'

'That's if she ever told anyone, or if the family still own the shop,' said Matt.

Darcie knew he was erring on the side of caution and she should, too. She shouldn't be getting carried away. She was talking about something that happened nearly eighty years ago. 'Do you think Nathalie had anything to do with the Resistance?' she asked. 'I mean it was during the war when the city would have been crawling with Germans.'

'Let's take one step at a time,' said Matt. 'We'll go tomorrow and see what we can find out. Oh, there is one other thing.'

'What's that?'

'Might be nothing, but apparently Padgett has political aspirations. Myles didn't seem that impressed by Padgett. I guess they've come across each other in the past.'

Darcie gave a shrug. 'I can't say I particularly warmed to him myself.'

The evening was mild when they left the restaurant and they strolled back towards Darcie's accommodation.

'I've had a really nice evening,' said Matt.

'Me too,' replied Darcie. She was aware they were walking very close to each other, their shoulders almost touching. In a way, she wished it was a cold evening and she could have snuggled up to him for warmth.

'Do you want to meet tomorrow afternoon and visit the address?' asked Matt.

'Do you really need to ask me that?' Darcie grinned at him.

'Just checking.' Matt gave her shoulder a gentle nudge with his own. 'What time and where shall we meet?'

'I could wait for you after you've finished at tomorrow's show.'

'Sounds good to me.'

There was a pause in the conversation and, probably for the first time that evening, a slightly awkward one. Darcie looked down at her feet and then back up at Matt. 'Thank you for getting me the ticket today. It was a wonderful experience. I really appreciate it.'

'You're more than welcome.' He leaned forwards and kissed her cheek. 'Sleep well, Darcie Bytheway.'

Darcie went into the building smiling at not just the kiss but the little nickname he'd adopted for her.

It wasn't until she got up to her room, she remembered about the dress. She hadn't shown it to Matt. She had been meaning to, even though he hadn't asked. She was sure he would be interested but was probably worrying about being too forward. She quickly sent him a text message.

Darcie: I was going to show you the dress. Sorry. I forgot.

Matt: No worries. Probably a bit late for me to come back now.

Darcie: I'll send you a couple of pictures. Maybe you can send it to that person you know. I'll show you the actual dress tomorrow.

She had already taken some pictures on her phone, when she had originally emailed the House of Chanel, so she quickly sent them to him, together with a screenshot of Coco Chanel wearing it.

She got a text message back just a few minutes later.

Matt: Wow! They really are the same dress. I'll let Myles see them. Get some sleep now.

Get some sleep – that was easier said than done as she went over the day and the evening. So many exciting things had happened to her in the few days she'd been in Paris, it was almost unbelievable.

Darcie didn't have to wait for long outside the fashion show the following day. Matt was probably one of the first photographers out of the building. Today had been the last day of the three-day haute couture show.

As was becoming his custom, he greeted her with a warm smile and a kiss on the cheek. It was feeling more natural and she actually looked forward to the momentary close contact. It felt personal and genuine.

'How was your day?' Darcie asked. She hadn't heard from Matt all day and assumed he must have been busy.

'Glad it's over. I find the fashion shows a bit tiring after a few days, if I'm honest. There were a few celebs there today, which makes it busier.'

'I thought you liked doing these sorts of things?'

'Not especially, but they pay well and I can't be too fussy and turn my nose up at these gigs.'

Darcie couldn't imagine ever being fed up watching fashion shows but then it was her thing and Matt's was photography not fashion. 'So, the tailor's, is it far?' she asked.

'Not too far. We can get the Métro or we can walk, if you prefer. It's only about fifteen minutes on foot.'

'I think a walk would be nice,' said Darcie.

They made good time and soon they were in the right street. 'It should be just along here,' said Matt, checking the door numbers and coming to a halt outside a shop. 'Here we go.'

There was a door in the centre and two windows each side. One displayed a formal arrangement of shirts and ties while the other window was more relaxed with the mannequin dressed in an expensive-looking navy-blue suit, white shirt and pale blue tie.

Darcie looked up at the sign: *Clavette of Paris*. 'There's no mention of Leroux at all,' she said, feeling a little disappointed.

'Let's go inside and ask,' said Matt. 'How's your French?'

'Not great. What about yours?'

'Passable. I'll do the talking.'

They were greeted by an older gentleman, probably in his late sixties. He was impeccably dressed in his suit and tie, his grey hair was coiffed back, and a pair of steel-rimmed glasses perched on the bridge of his nose. A tape measure hung around his neck.

'*Bonjour, monsieur, madame,*' he said as they walked into the shop.

If he felt they were clearly not his usual customers, then he did a good job of hiding his feelings.

Darcie listened while Matt spoke in what, to her, sounded like very good French. She could get the general idea of what he was saying as he explained the situation and that they were looking for the Leroux family who used to own this shop.

The man nodded throughout the explanation, seemingly unsurprised by the request. He replied in fairly rapid French to Matt, which Darcie found hard to follow. However, he appeared to be saying something positive as Matt conversed with him and they both smiled their way through the conversation. After a few minutes, the man went out to the back of the shop.

'Where's he going?' whispered Darcie.

'Says he has something for us,' replied Matt. 'I'm not sure what.'

'What's he said so far?' Darcie tried to peer through the door the gentleman had left ajar, which led into a workroom. She could just see the edge of a sewing machine and a table.

'He was telling me how it's been a tailor's for over a hundred years, but that his father bought the shop in the late Forties.'

'How old is he? He's obviously not old enough to have been born then.'

'No, he did say it was before he was born.'

Before Darcie could ask any more questions, the man came back into the room, holding a notebook. He spoke to Matt in French and then proceeded to open up a brown leather-covered book. Darcie couldn't make out the writing as it was all handwritten and in an older cursive style. Matt took out his phone and took a picture of the page before the tailor copied out one of the entries onto a piece of paper. His handwriting looked much easier to decipher. He folded the paper in half and handed it to Matt.

'*Merci beaucoup, monsieur,*' said Matt.

Darcie thanked him in French also, but had no idea what she was thanking him for and managed to contain her excitement until they were out of the shop.

'What did he say?' she blurted out no sooner than Matt had closed the door behind them.

'Come on, let's grab a coffee and I'll tell you.'

There was a café just across the road and as soon as they'd ordered and their drinks arrived, Darcie couldn't contain herself any longer. 'Come on, you have to tell me now.'

'Sure. So, the shopkeeper said his father bought the shop in 1947 from a Monsieur Théodule Leroux who had taken over the shop from his own father. It has been a tailor's since the beginning of the 1900s apparently.'

'Leroux? So related to Nathalie Leroux. He has to be her father. It would make sense and that would be why she was into fashion and design.' Darcie checked herself from sounding disproportionately excited at this little nugget of information.

'It does make sense. The current owner doesn't remember the daughter's name, but he said he thought there were two children. His mother mentioned them from time to time when they spoke about buying the shop but the current owner wasn't even born when this happened.'

'Maybe we can find Nathalie through her father. Like on one of the genealogy sites,' said Darcie. 'It's likely that she married.'

'More than likely.'

'What did the man write on the piece of paper?' Darcie had almost forgotten about that. She looked up at Matt and could see a spark of excitement in his eyes.

Matt took the piece of paper from his pocket and, after unfolding it, he placed it on the table, turning it around so Darcie could read it.

GRANDIS, Philippe & Clarice
La ferme verte
Ploërmel

'Grandis? Who are they?' asked Darcie.

'The address book was left in a box with other things concerning the business and a forwarding address. The Grandis family is related to the Leroux family.'

'OK,' said Darcie, not sure she understood the significance. 'And where is Ploërmel?'

Matt was now tapping into his phone. 'According to Google it's a small town in Southern Brittany, department 56.'

'Brittany? And the Grandis family?'

'They are related to the Leroux family and they might know what happened to Nathalie.'

'Wow. What are we going to do? Call them? Would you be able to do that? I couldn't manage a conversation in French on the telephone. I hate speaking on the phone in English, never mind a foreign language.'

'Sure. I'd be happy to if we had a phone number.'

'There wasn't one in the book?'

'No. It wasn't unusual. Not everyone had a phone in those days,' explained Matt, which seemed logical to Darcie. Matt was busy on his phone again and she finished her coffee in silence, not wishing to disturb him. After a few minutes he put his phone down. 'No luck with a phone number.'

'Really? Oh, what a shame.'

'We could go there.'

'To Brittany?'

'Yeah. I could drive us.'

'You have a car?'

'I do, although I never really use it in the city. It's too much of a pain in the ass for parking.'

'How far away is Brittany from here?'

'About a four-and-a-half-hour drive.' He looked at Darcie. 'You up for that?'

'What? Drive to Brittany? Oh, I couldn't ask you to do that,' she said. Not that she wouldn't love to take him up on the offer, but it seemed too much.

'You don't have to ask. I'm offering.'

'Honestly, it's really kind of you, generous, but I couldn't.'

Matt frowned. 'I want to. I'm invested in the story of Nathalie Leroux and the dress now. I want to help.'

'Why do you want to help so much?' she asked.

Matt shrugged. 'I guess I always like rooting for the underdog. No offence.'

She laughed. 'None taken.'

'I don't like to see the big fat cats eat up the little guys,' he said. He paused and fiddled with the teaspoon for a moment, before looking up at here. 'There's something I haven't told you.'

Darcie's heart dropped a little. She knew Matt was too good to be true. 'What's that?' she asked. She might as well find out now.

'Well, you know I told you my mom works on a magazine, well, my dad – he's a CEO,' said Matt.

'Right,' said Darcie. 'So are you trying to tell me you're not really a struggling photographer but the son of a businessman and, oh, I don't know, heir to a wealthy corporate empire?' She went to laugh but realised Matt was deadly serious. 'Shit. You are, aren't you?'

'It's not quite like that,' said Matt. 'I walked away from the family business because working out of an office isn't my jam. I want to make my own way in life. I don't want to live off my father's name or handouts.'

'That's very noble of you.'

'I'm not trying to be noble,' said Matt, looking a little offended. 'I like to be independent. Just like you.'

Darcie wasn't sure what she made of Matt's financial disclosure. 'I didn't choose to be poor,' she said. 'You have. You can do that in the knowledge that if things get tough, you can walk away from money problems back to a trust fund or a job with your father. I don't have that luxury, so it's not just like me.'

'Ouch,' said Matt. 'That's told me.'

Darcie realised she was probably being disingenuous. 'I'm sorry. I didn't mean to be touchy,' she said. 'I'm being oversensitive.'

'Maybe, but you have a point,' said Matt. He blew out a long breath. 'Look, if you don't want anything to do with me anymore, I understand that. I'll go, but I do genuinely want to help you find out more about this dress. It sounds an amazing story and, as I say, I'm not into the big guns dictating to the little guns.'

Darcie believed him. She didn't know why – she barely

knew him – but she always prided herself on being a good judge of character. She thought of the dress and the mysterious Nathalie Leroux. She wanted to find out more. No, make that she needed to find out more, and Matt was offering to help.

'OK,' she said at last. 'But I'm not a charity case. I want to pay my way.'

'Sure,' said Matt. 'That's cool with me.'

He held her gaze and she knew she was going to agree. 'In that case, I'd love to go.'

Matt squeezed her hand. 'Excellent. This could be the breakthrough you need.'

When he moved his hand away, Darcie couldn't help feeling a little sad, but the thought of going to Brittany more than made up for it.

Chapter 19

Nathalie

When I returned to Paris I had never felt so conflicted. I hated leaving Marcel when I felt I had only just found him, found someone I truly loved. But seeing my parents was more emotional than I had imagined. Despite everything, I had missed them greatly, but on seeing them, the idea that we were now a family of three felt an unwelcome reality.

Coming home brought Edgar's death into sharp focus, and I could see the loss had taken its toll on Maman. Her clothes hung from her and were clearly at least one size too big for her now. I made a mental note to alter her dresses, so they fitted her better.

'I am glad you're home,' said Maman as we sat down for our evening meal of bread and cheese. My aunt had insisted I take some food home with me as rations in the city were worse than ever. 'The apartment is too quiet without you or your brother.'

I looked across at Papa and couldn't help noticing the drawn look in his face. His cheekbones were more pronounced and his eyes looked like they were sinking into his face. There was a bleakness that hadn't been there before, and his presence that once filled a room had diminished. I couldn't explain it, but it was as if part of his soul had died and left behind a man shrouded in an aura of grief.

'Is everything all right? You look tired, Papa.'

There was an uncomfortable silence as my parents

exchanged looks. 'Not tonight,' said Maman. 'We will talk tomorrow.'

'Talk about what?' I asked, now alarmed at their behaviour.

Papa shook his head. 'We might as well say now.'

'Please, tell me,' I urged.

Papa couldn't look me in the eye; instead his gaze was fixed on the food in front of him. 'I've had to close the shop,' he said.

I frowned, not quite understanding the implications. 'Today? Why?'

'Not just for today,' he replied.

I looked at Maman. 'I don't understand.'

Maman let out a sigh. 'We have been targeted,' explained Maman. 'The Germans believe we are somehow involved with whatever Edgar was up to. They have stopped coming to the shop and last week, we received orders we were to cease trading.'

'That is terrible,' I said, putting my fork down. 'They can't do that.'

Papa tutted. 'Of course, they can. And they have.' He reached out and placed his hand over mine. 'I am so happy you are home. I know your mother has missed you but all of a sudden everything is so uncertain. Maybe you should have stayed in Brittany after all. We only have a small amount of money. After that . . .'

He didn't finish the sentence.

Maman spoke. 'After that, we all may have to go to Brittany.' Tears filled her eyes and she grappled for a handkerchief to wipe her face. I knew how much Paris meant to Maman. She would hate to have to leave her home and her beloved city.

'Please don't cry, Maman,' I said. 'It will be all right. There is something I haven't told you.'

Both my parents looked up at me and I tried to keep the smile from my face.

'What is it?' asked Papa.

'I have been offered a job at the Ritz hotel,' I said, sitting up straighter. 'I begin the day after tomorrow. So you won't have to worry about money. I will be earning.'

'A job at the Ritz?' said Maman. 'But how?'

'A friend of mine knows the manager and he has guaranteed me work as a maid.'

'But the place is full of Germans,' said Papa.

I shrugged, trying to negate their worry. 'It will be safe. I promise. I am only there to clean their rooms. Lots of girls work there.'

'But working for the enemy,' protested Papa.

I had to hold down the bubble of anger. 'It is no different from you opening the shop to the Germans,' I said, keeping an even tone. 'We have to do what we must. And this is too good an opportunity to turn down.'

'Nathalie is right,' said Maman. 'We cannot force her not to work there and we do need the money. I don't like it any more than you do, but it is a fact.'

Papa nodded. 'Very well.'

My heart went out to my parents. I had never seen my father look so defeated. The death of Edgar and the loss of the shop were hard for him to deal with. It was a reversal in roles. It was now my mother who was strong and pragmatic, despite the grief of losing Edgar. She understood what needed be done.

Work at the Ritz was harder than I had imagined. Twelve hours a day, six days a week.

The hotel was a magnet for high-ranking German officers and some of the wealthy Parisians who had decided to make the Ritz their home during the war. Of course, the most prestigious guest resided in room 304 – Coco Chanel. Her relationships with German officers were well known within the hotel but none of us dared speak about them openly. I remember Marcel telling me to trust no one and I reminded myself of that on a daily basis.

It was the end of September and I still had not had any contact from Marcel. With each passing day, I began to imagine the worst. I swayed from him being captured or returned to England, to him not wanting anything to do with me and that I had been hoodwinked.

The only thing that kept a small flicker of hope alive was the fact that I had been given this position. It had been all arranged and the hotel manager, Monsieur Tache, had given me a minimal interview and I had signed my contract there and then on the spot. He hadn't of course said anything outright, but I got the feeling from his comments that he was letting me know he was sympathetic to the Resistance.

'This is your contract. Sign here. That's if you're willing to take the position?'

He looked at me and I didn't miss the weight of his words on the last sentence. 'I'm more than willing to take the position,' I replied with absolute certainty. I didn't know if Monsieur Tache had any idea why he was hiring me or how involved with the Resistance he was, but on the chance he might provide feedback to them, I wanted to be sure my position on the Vichy government and the German occupation and my dedication to my country were crystal clear.

'The work here is not for the faint of heart,' pressed Monsieur Tache. 'The tasks you will be required to undertake are difficult and demanding. At all times you must, however, keep your composure. Our guests must not have an inkling of any hardship. You need to move around the hotel with a ghost-like presence, so you are barely noticeable. You need to fade into the background, unseen. You must carry out your duties in the manner in which I expect.' He paused again. His gaze drilling into the back of my eyes. 'You do realise what you're undertaking, don't you?'

'*Oui, monsieur.*' My voice was firm.

'You won't let me down, will you?'

'*Non, monsieur.*' Even firmer this time.

He held the pen out to me.

I took the pen from his hand and, as I signed my name at the bottom of the paper, I thought of Edgar. I hoped he would be proud of me, and I hoped I would be able to avenge his death in some way.

Three weeks on from that day, after a long shift at the hotel, I lay in bed and stared at the bedroom wall that separated my room from Edgar's. Just knowing it was empty, and that Edgar would never come back, brought more tears to my eyes. Coming home had only highlighted what we had lost.

I turned my back on the dividing wall, not wanting to acknowledge the depth of my grief. In my heart, my dear younger brother was still with me. His loyalty to France and his determination to fight for his country filled the chasm his presence had left behind.

Instead, I turned my thoughts to someone else I loved: Marcel. I may have only known him a short time, but my heart had no brakes and I had fallen head over heels for this mysterious Englishman who I knew so well and yet knew nothing about at all. If I had learned anything from this war, then it was to love with a fierceness and an intensity that couldn't wait because we had so little time and life was a fragile gift. My feelings for Marcel had also clarified my feelings for Alphonse insomuch that he wasn't the man I wanted to spend the rest of my life with. Marcel was the only man for me.

The head housekeeper, Madame Bochette, was turning out to be my least favourite person at the hotel. She was in her mid-fifties, with her dark hair scraped back from her face, accentuating her long sharp nose and pointed chin. The skin around her mouth, where it was pinched, looked like a ploughed field, and the lines splaying from her eyes looked like they had been scoured out with a knife. Her appearance matched her persona. Sharp. Brusque. Harsh.

'Don't get on the wrong side of her,' whispered Collette – one of the maids who I had become friendly with. 'She's a witch and a Nazi sympathiser.'

Neither of these statements surprised me. For the first week, I'd shadowed Bochette, while she taught me how to fold the linen, how to make the rooms up, and all the things I might be asked to do at some point. All of which I had to do with ease, without hesitation, with no indication that I was new. I suspected straight away that Bochette was using the first week as an excuse to weigh me up, to gauge what kind of person I was and where my own sympathies lay.

I was careful to answer her questions with just the right amount of deference to the occupying army, balanced with a sadness and patriotism to France so that she didn't suspect me of being too loyal to my country. Even that felt like a betrayal, but I reminded myself it was all part of the game.

Now I was at the hotel, I would have more chance to find the man who killed my brother so I could plot my revenge.

As it happened, I didn't have to wait long before a series of events unfolded and fate brought the opportunity several steps closer.

One day I arrived at work and was about to start cleaning my usual set of rooms, when Madame Bochette stopped me.

'Go to room 211. Collette is off sick today. I need you to take over her rooms.'

'Yes, madame,' I replied.

'Just so you're aware, the rooms are occupied by a very important guest. I can trust you, can't I?'

'Of course, madame.' I gave a subservient nod of my head. I knew several high-ranking German officers were based on that floor.

'Well, hurry along. Don't keep anyone waiting.'

I took the back staircase up to the room and knocked, hoping the officer wasn't in his room and had gone off to do whatever it was they did all day.

'Enter,' came the reply from behind the closed door.

I went into the room, which was a reception area. The

double doors through to the bedroom were open. 'In here!' the voice came again.

I gulped. Going into an officer's bedroom was not what I wanted to be doing. I hesitated. 'Do you want me to clean the living room?'

'No! If I wanted you to do that, I wouldn't have called you. Now, come here.'

I obeyed the command. 'Sorry, sir,' I said, keeping my head down and my gaze fixed on the carpeted floor.

The officer tutted and let out a long sigh. 'Don't start with all that shy business. Where's my usual girl, Collette?'

'She's off sick today,' I replied.

'Are you any good with a needle and thread?'

This question had my attention. 'Yes.'

He picked up a pair of trousers that were draped over the end of the bed. 'Fix those. The pocket has a hole, and the seam has come undone.' He threw the trousers at me and I just managed to catch them. 'They're my best pair of trousers. Can you fix them so the repair won't be seen?'

I looked up at the officer; I took in a sharp breath. It was Kranz. The one who had been to the shop asking for Edgar.

A second passed between us as recognition dawned on Kranz's face. 'Ah, well, if it isn't Mademoiselle Leroux. I didn't expect to see you here.'

'Monsieur,' I kept my voice steady as I acknowledged him.

'How long have you been working here?'

'Three weeks.'

'And they've sent you to me already. Well, Madame Bochette must think highly of you.' He gestured to the trousers now in my arms. 'I expect the repair to be invisible, bearing in mind your background. You can do that, can't you?'

I inspected the tear in the fabric. 'Yes. I can do that.'

'Good. Have them done by midday.' He straightened his tie. 'Now, get on with your duties. You'll find a needle and thread in the drawer over there. Collette sewed up a hole in the pocket, but she didn't make a very good job of it. I hope your skills are superior.'

He strode past me but paused at the doorway. 'Oh, I am sorry about your brother.'

I looked up. 'Edgar?'

'Unless you have another brother you haven't told us about.'

I shook my head. 'No.'

'You shouldn't have tried to protect him that day I came to your home,' carried on Kranz. 'It was all for no purpose.' A smiled played at the corners of his mouth. 'Foolish boy. He may have been big and bold when trying to impress you, but you know what? He was cowardly and spineless. It took very little to get him to talk.'

The rage soared through me and I had to do everything in my power to stop myself from flying at the German bastard in front of me. I swallowed hard, gripping the trousers tightly in my balled-up fist. 'You interrogated him?' I had to know. Was it Kranz who had killed my brother?

'Interviewed him. There's a difference,' said Kranz. 'As I say, too cowardly to put up much of a resistance. Rather ironic use of the word.'

'My brother was not a coward.' I ground the words out, even though I knew I should keep my mouth shut. This was not keeping a low profile like Marcel had instructed. This was not being a ghost, as Monsieur Tache had warned me to be. But I couldn't let Kranz disrespect my brother.

There was amusement in Kranz's eyes, which only served to infuriate me more, but I managed to bite my tongue.

Kranz wagged his forefinger at me. 'You should really learn to watch what you say. If you want to keep your job and especially if you want to keep your tongue.'

With that, he strode out of the apartment, letting the door bang closed behind him. 'Ignorant pig,' I muttered by way of defiance, even though I wasn't quite brave enough to say it out loud just in case he carried out his threat. Besides, I needed to keep my job if I was to avenge Edgar's murder.

I went over to the dresser where he'd indicated the needle and thread were and it was then I noticed a briefcase tucked alongside the piece of furniture.

I paused, considering my actions. My finger tapped against the side of my thigh. I glanced over my shoulder. The door to the suite was closed. I looked back at the case. My heart was picking up speed. Before I had time to talk myself out of it, I nipped across the room and flicked the lock on the door.

I hurried back to the case and laid it flat, looking at the catches. I flicked the locks, and the mechanism pinged open on both sides. My hands shook as I lifted the lid. I did not know what I was going to find, if anything, but this was part of the reason I was here. If and when someone contacted me, I'd be able to share anything of importance that I found. I had to keep providing the Resistance with information to keep my position here valid, which would enable me to do what I needed to do.

The case was full of handwritten letters on all sorts of paper. Some formal-looking and some on scraps. I picked up the first one and scanned the contents. The second was much the same, as was the third.

My breath caught in my throat as I realised what I had found. Letters from Parisians reporting on other Parisians for various violations of the laws. Some were minor infringements, such as using a ration book that belonged to a dead relative, having an endless supply of cigarettes, getting meat on the black market. Others were more serious offences: out after curfew, speaking out against the regime, hiding Jews, being part of the Resistance.

Tears stung my eyes. How could one Frenchman do this to another? It was beyond me. Were people so desperate that they resorted to reporting their neighbours, hoping to get something in return? A lot of these letters were anonymous, though – an opportunity to cause trouble for someone who had once crossed you. It was horrendous. And there weren't just four or five; there were tens and tens of the hate mail. Maybe fifty letters or more.

I didn't think these would be of any use to the Resistance and I dug down beyond the letters to see what lay beneath. But there was nothing other than a single sheet of paper folded in half.

I opened it out.

The White Lily
Basilica Sacré-Cœur Crypt

It said nothing else. I turned the paper over to check, but it was blank. The White Lily. What did that mean? It felt important, but I didn't know why, or how I was going to tell anyone. I wished Marcel or someone else would make contact; then I could pass the information on.

I replaced the piece of paper, together with the raft of poison pen letters. Shame for my fellow countrymen washed over me, quickly replaced by anger that one person could do that to another. I wouldn't have believed it if I hadn't seen it with my own eyes.

I clicked the lid of the briefcase closed and slid it back against the side of the cupboard. Locating the needle and thread, I set out to repair the trousers.

Once the repair was done, I left the trousers on the end of Kranz's bed. The unexpected sewing had taken up a lot of time and I would probably have to work late to get everything done. I knew Madame Bochette would not be pleased at all.

The hands of the clock crawled their way through the morning. My feet ached and my back was killing me. As I was unloading my cart of dirty linen, all I could think about was soaking my feet in a bowl of warm water when I got home later that evening.

'Nathalie!' It was Madame Bochette. 'You're wanted.'

'By who?' I dropped the bedsheet into the basket.

'Hauptmann Kranz.'

I muttered an expletive under my breath, which obviously wasn't as muted as I'd thought – Madame Bochette raised her eyebrows and I offered her an apology.

'I hope you have done nothing wrong,' snapped my superior. 'The last thing I want is to upset our guests. Did you break anything? Touch anything you shouldn't have?'

I felt a warmth to my neck as I thought of the briefcase. 'No,' I replied. 'I repaired his trousers, though.'

Madame Bochette looked surprised. 'You did what?'

'He asked me to repair a tear in his trousers.'

'And what qualifies you to undertake such a request? You should have brought it down here for one of the experienced seamstresses to do.'

'Kranz asked me to do it,' I explained. 'My father is a tailor and I've worked in his shop for many years. I'm skilled at that sort of work.' I could hear the pride in my voice and I sensed that this nugget of information had taken Madame by surprise.

'Why didn't I know about this?' she demanded.

'No one asked.'

'Well, you'd better hope you're as good as you think you are. Come along, I'll go with you in case there's a complaint. You will end up looking for another job if there's any problem.'

Chapter 20

Nathalie

Of course, there was no complaint about my work. In fact, Kranz was most complimentary and I could see Madame Bochette's demeanour change from apprehension, to surprise and then to satisfaction and, dare I suggest, pride. One of her staff had made a perfect repair.

Just as I thought the meeting was over, there was a knock at Kranz's door and, without waiting for him to answer, the visitor entered. I did a double take and somehow managed to withhold my gasp of surprise.

Coco Chanel waltzed in, and that is the only way I could describe it, straight into Kranz's apartment. She paused to offer her hand, which Kranz took to his lips, bowing as he did so.

Madame Bochette made a small squeaking sort of sound in the back of her throat before regaining her composure and going into full deference mode. I thought for one moment she was actually going to curtsey.

Chanel looked over at us. 'Ah, so this is the little seamstress you've been keeping all to yourself.' She looked me up and down as if eyeing a garment she had been offered to inspect. Her dark hair was fashioned off her face, exposing her fine and chiselled features. I wasn't sure if she was beautiful or handsome, but she exuded an elegance and determination that sat comfortably alongside each other. 'Your name?'

I realised she was addressing me. I cleared my throat. 'Nathalie Leroux.'

Chanel took a cigarette from the silver case on the table and Kranz hurried forward with a lighter, holding it close to the tip. Chanel's red lips drew on the cigarette before she spoke to me again. 'And where did you learn to sew like that?'

'Her father is a tailor,' supplied Madame Bochette.

Chanel didn't take her gaze from me as she replied to the head housekeeper. 'I was asking the child.'

I wasn't sure I cared for being referred to as a child but was aware I looked younger than my years. I could feel Madame Bochette's embarrassment as she muttered an apology.

I filled the awkward space with a reply. 'My father had a tailor's shop in the city. He taught me everything I know.'

'Who is your father?'

'Théodule Leroux.'

Chanel glanced over at Kranz, who replied to the unspoken communication. 'Leroux is well known among the officers of the Luftwaffe. We frequented the shop often when it was open. It has recently closed.'

I didn't reply, unsure where this conversation was going. Chanel sat down on the brocade sofa and took another draw on her cigarette, before exhaling the smoke into the air. 'So, Madame Bochette, how long has the child been working here?'

'She's new, madame,' replied Bochette. 'Been here just a few weeks.'

'And is she a good worker?'

I felt uncomfortable at this dissection while I was standing there.

'She does what she's supposed to do. Doesn't give me any trouble, and the guests like her,' replied Bochette.

Chanel appeared to be weighing up this information. 'Very well. I want her to attend my room from now on.'

'But I have other staff,' replied Bochette. 'More experienced. If you're not happy with Sophie, your current room maid, I can arrange for someone else.'

'No. I want . . .' she waved her hand in my direction

'. . . Nathalie,' she said, as if finally remembering my name. 'I want her to attend my room.'

'Very well, madame,' said Bochette with a nod of her head. She shot me a sideways look, which clearly said she wasn't happy about this and I'd better not let her down. I also knew that without a shadow of a doubt, I'd be out of a job if anything went wrong.

'It's an honour, and I'd be delighted to. Thank you, madame,' I replied and dipped my head in the way I'd seen Bochette do.

'Come to my room at 7 a.m. sharp. I hate lateness,' said Chanel.

'Yes, madame,' both Bochette and I said in unison.

With that, Chanel got up from the sofa and stubbed the cigarette out in the glass ashtray. 'Will I see you for supper?' she asked Kranz.

'Certainly.'

Chanel wafted out of the room, leaving a trail of her perfume scent in the air.

The following morning, I was standing outside room 304 at two minutes to seven. I smoothed down my apron and patted my hair to make sure it was all in place, before knocking on the door.

'Enter!' came the voice from inside. I stepped into the apartment and through to the living area where Chanel was sitting at her writing desk, with several letters, a writing pad, and a pen in front of her. 'Ah, Nathalie.' She gave me another of her appraising looks. 'Glad that Bochette freed you up. She can be quite tiresome with her rules and regulations, but I suppose that's what keeps everything afloat and why she's trusted.'

I just nodded, not sure if Chanel wanted to get into a conversation or not. My training had told me not to comment unless directly asked a question. A lot of our guests simply spoke at us rather than to us.

Chanel got up from her writing table and plucked a cigarette from her beautifully engraved silver cigarette case. She cast her gaze around. I realised she was looking for a lighter and produced one from my pocket, flicked it and held the flame towards her.

She leaned towards the flame, drawing on her cigarette before pulling away. 'Do you smoke?'

'No, madame. I just keep it with me.'

She nodded. 'Not just a pretty face.' Chanel wandered over to the window. 'You'd better get on with your cleaning duties.'

'*Oui, madame*. Where would you like me to start?'

'The bedroom, then the bathroom. I have clothes I need laundered. I'm going out for dinner this evening, so I need to choose something to wear. Once you've tidied my room, lay all my evening dresses out on the bed.'

I made sure I didn't rush with tidying and cleaning, but I could hardly contain my excitement when I opened the wardrobe and my eyes were greeted with dress after dress of pure luxury, elegance, and class. I took a moment to enjoy the sight before me and, taking a deep breath, I slowly ran my hand across the fabrics.

'You like what you see?'

I spun around to see Chanel standing in the doorway. 'Sorry, I was just taking a moment to admire them. They are beautiful,' I said.

'Hurry up and get them out and we can have a proper look at them. You can help me choose which one to wear tonight.'

I was sure my eyes must have bulged so much they nearly fell out of my head. Chanel gave a small smile of amusement and gestured towards the wardrobe.

'What sort of party are you going to?' I gazed at the dresses hanging in the wardrobe.

'It's a dinner with Kranz. Just the two of us, and then we are going to the theatre afterwards,' replied Chanel.

'So, perhaps a long evening gown.' I ran my hand across the top of the hangers, inspecting the dresses, taking out first a long black gown, then a silver gown, another black one followed by a peacock blue. I laid them out on the bed, side by side, inspecting each one.

'You have good taste,' said Chanel, nodding towards the clothes on her bed. 'So, with your expert eye, you tell me which one you think is the most expensive.'

I looked up at Chanel and I could see that amusement in her eyes again. I took a closer look at the dresses, examining the stitching, which was all perfect.

'Well, the ones with the jewels would appear more expensive, but they are not necessarily real.' I looked at Chanel to gauge her response, hoping I hadn't insulted her, but she gave a nod of approval.

'I'm impressed.'

I carried on with my analysis. 'However, looking at the fabrics used, I can see that the one with the pearls, or maybe not real pearls, has not been made with the same quality fabric as the plain black dress with the scooped back and the thin velvet belt around the middle.' I picked up the black dress.

'This fabric is not the typical satin and silk that you buy in the everyday department store,' I continued. 'In fact, I'd go as far as to say this fabric came from abroad, possibly the Middle East. The understated look and the subtlety of the expense, to me, indicates that this is the most expensive dress.'

Chanel clapped her hands. 'Bravo!' The compliment didn't come with quite as much enthusiasm as one might receive at an award ceremony, but as it was coming from Coco Chanel herself I was going to take it as a huge compliment, far better than any compliment or gratitude I had received to date for my work with a needle. 'Now we know which is the most expensive one. My next question is, which one should I wear?'

'It depends what you want to achieve by the end of the evening.' Her compliment had made me a little bolder than I might otherwise have been. Again there was the amusement in her eyes and the corners of her mouth twitched.

Chanel took a draw on her cigarette and slowly exhaled the smoke.

'I have high hopes for this evening and for Kranz himself,' she said.

'In that case,' I said, laying down the expensive evening dress and picking up the peacock blue one, 'this one is your satisfaction dress.'

'Satisfaction dress!' Chanel burst out laughing. 'I'm not sure I've ever heard a dress described like that before. But you have an eye for things, child, and this dress is my best bet for satisfaction. Have you ever made anything like this?' she asked.

'Nothing as beautiful as this,' I replied with a sigh. 'I've dreamt of making things like this before, and my sketchbook is full of such designs. I'm working on a dress at the moment,' I confessed.

Chanel took a long draw on her cigarette. 'Bring them here tomorrow. I'd like to see your work.' I spent the rest of the day swaying between excitement and nerves that Chanel wanted to see my work.

As I walked to work the next day, I hoped I would impress Chanel with my drawings, which I now clutched in a folder in my hand, together with the evening dress I'd almost finished. She had asked to see them and although I knew they were to a high standard, having someone such as Chanel look at them was quite intimidating. She would have seen sketches by the top fashion designers in not just the country, but all of Europe. I wasn't sure how mine would compare, but it was a great opportunity to find out whether the designs were actually any good.

I filled my walk with fantasies of seeing my work in a collection, admired by the famous and glamorous women of Hollywood who would fawn over the garments and commission me to make one-off pieces for them.

Arriving at the hotel, I went straight up to Chanel's suite and knocked on the door. With no response, I quietly let myself in. The rule was to knock, wait for a reply and, if none was forthcoming, to enter but ensure I was silent as the guest might still be in bed.

As I walked into the apartment, I could see the doors to the bedroom were closed. I looked around the living room, surprised to see how much cleaning and tidying was needed. It was clear from the empty bottles of wine and two redundant wine glasses that Chanel had brought Kranz back here the previous evening.

I glanced towards the bedroom and wondered whether he was still in there. It wasn't unusual to find an extra body in a guest's bed in the mornings, especially when servicing the room of a German officer. It was quite the pastime for them, according to the other girls I worked with. We were to turn a blind eye and carry on as if it was quite normal.

The ashtray on the coffee table was full of cigarette ends and, ensuring none were still smouldering, I tipped the contents into the rubbish bin on the small cleaning trolley I had with me, along with the empty wine bottles.

I spent the next hour cleaning the main sitting room and was just beginning to wonder whether I should knock on the door and ask if Chanel wanted coffee, when the door opened. It was Chanel, looking rather bleary-eyed.

'Where are my sunglasses?' she croaked, a frown creasing her forehead. She pushed a straggly strand of hair from her eyes and pulled the belt tight around her silk dressing gown. 'Coffee. I need coffee. Then run me a bath.'

She went to walk back into her room but stopped and turned to look at me. 'Did you bring your sketchbook and the dress?'

'Yes, madame,' I replied.

'Good. Leave them on my desk – I shall look at them later.' With that, she disappeared back into her room.

I was a little disappointed I couldn't show my work to her myself, but I did as she requested and left the sketchbook and dress on her bureau.

While the coffee brewed, I tapped on the bedroom door and let myself through to run the bath for Chanel. I had to make a conscious effort not to stare at the other person lying fast asleep in bed, snoring his head off. It was, indeed, Kranz.

'God. I can't bear the noise,' said Chanel, shoving the sleeping German to get him to roll onto his side. Kranz groaned and shifted position.

'I was just going to run the bath for you,' I said, moving through to the bathroom.

'Make it nice and hot. I need a soak.'

A few minutes later, Chanel appeared in the bathroom. 'I can't put up with him snoring like a warthog. Make sure he's gone by the time I come out.'

She waved me out of the bathroom, leaving me alone in the bedroom with the semi-conscious officer.

'Monsieur,' I ventured, not really knowing how I was going to extricate him from the bed. I moved to the bedside. 'Monsieur Kranz,' I said, leaning closer to him. 'Wake up. It's time to leave.'

Still he didn't move. I stood up, surveying the sweaty snoring pig in front of me. It disgusted me to look at him and disgusted me further when I thought of how he was responsible for killing my brother.

I glanced at the pillow on Chanel's side of the bed. How easy would it be to place the pillow over Kranz's face? Did I have the strength to pin him down and smother him? Probably not.

It was then I saw his pistol in the holster, lying on the dressing table.

I knew how to fire one, thanks to Marcel. I could easily take the gun and place the muzzle against his head. But what about the noise? I'd have to silence it with a pillow. I remembered Marcel telling me that much. He'd also told me it would save me from seeing all the blood and brains sprayed out on the pillow and from looking him in the eye.

My breathing became faster as I considered the opportunity I was presented with. I could do this. I could kill Kranz here and now. I looked over at the bathroom door. It was firmly shut. I looked back at the pistol.

I could do this. I would do this. I'd do this for Edgar. For France. I reached out my hand.

'I wouldn't touch that if I were you.'

I spun around at the voice behind me and let out a small yelp of alarm as I was confronted with Kranz propped up on one elbow, pointing a small pistol at me. It was a tiny silver gun, small enough for a handbag, and I assumed it must be Chanel's.

The corners of Kranz's mouth curled but not into a smile. They formed something rather more sinister, and there was a hint of depraved pleasure.

Kranz threw back the covers and swung his feet down onto the floor, before standing up. He was naked, and I looked down at the floor, not wanting to see him. He revolted me in every possible way.

Kranz made a scoffing noise. 'Don't insult me, otherwise I might be inclined to show you a thing or two.' He strode over, purposely coming close to me, his arm brushing against mine as he reached around me for the gun. I could smell his breath. His body odour. Stale alcohol, sweat, and sex. 'I'm going to enjoy making you pay,' he whispered in my ear.

I could hear the pleasure in his voice, and I wanted to vomit.

'Just stay there and don't move,' he ordered as he stepped away. 'Pick up my clothes and lay them out on the bed.'

I did as I was told, unsure of what was happening now. 'Turn around and kneel on the floor,' he snapped.

Again, I complied. In any other situation, I would have expected him to execute me there and then, but I was certain he wouldn't do that in Chanel's suite, let alone her bedroom. No, Kranz had other plans for me. I could hear him dressing and a minute later, he was dragging me to my feet.

'Consider yourself under arrest. Now move.' He shoved me out of the bedroom and out of the suite. With his hand gripped tightly around my upper arm, he marched me down the corridor and into the elevator. The tears were welling up in my eyes. I should have just shot him. I shouldn't have hesitated. I hated myself for being such a coward.

Monsieur Tache, the hotel manager, must have been alerted to what was happening, but even as he tried to protest as Kranz marched me across the hotel lobby, his pleas fell on deaf ears.

Kranz barked an order at a soldier on duty outside the hotel and a car instantly appeared.

'You are I are going to spend some time together,' said Kranz. 'Now get in.'

Chapter 21

Darcie

Before Matt had even pulled up, Darcie knew that the black Audi TT cruising to a halt in front of her apartment was his. He buzzed down the window and leaned across the passenger seat.

'Wanna ride?' He grinned and winked at her, before jumping out and opening the boot.

'You should be careful, I'm sure kerb crawling is an offence here.'

'Let's get outta here, then,' said Matt, emphasising his American accent to comedic effect.

'I've only brought the sketchbook with me,' she said, handing Matt her bag to put in the car. 'I didn't want to cart the dress around with us.'

'Good thinking,' said Matt, closing the boot and then going around to open the passenger door for her.

The traffic was slow going out of the city, but eventually they were cruising along the main route out of Paris with the air con blowing gently and a Glenn Miller CD playing, which Matt said he thought she would like.

Darcie smiled at the music. It reminded her of the shop and the reason why she was in France in the first place. She hoped Lena and Chloe were all right. She hadn't phoned them since she'd arrived, more at their insistence than her choice, but she couldn't deny she was enjoying not having the responsibility of being chief carer. Almost immediately, a wave of guilt rushed over her for even thinking such a thing.

'You all right?' asked Matt, throwing a glance in her direction.

Darcie forced a smile. 'Yeah. Just enjoying the scenery.'

Matt looked over again, this time with a questioning expression before reverting his attention back to the road. 'You sure? We're on a motorway and all I can see is tarmac and trees.'

'Just nice to be out of the city,' she said. Even to herself it sounded unconvincing. 'So, what time do you think we'll arrive in Ploërmel?'

'About another three hours,' said Matt. 'We can stop on the way and have some lunch. In typical French style, I've brought a picnic. Just some bread, ham, salad, that type of thing.'

'Sounds great. I hope you've also brought a picnic table and tablecloth.'

'I even have wine,' said Matt, 'but we can drink that later when I'm not behind the wheel.'

Another hour of driving and Matt pulled into a picnic area.

'This looks popular,' said Darcie, noting the numerous cars, vans, and caravans parked up. In the centre were the restroom facilities and a large grass area with picnic benches spread out. She got out of the car, stretching her arms and breathing in the warm Breton air.

Matt went to the boot and took out a cool box. 'Can you manage this?' he asked.

'Sure.' Darcie took the box and watched on in surprise as Matt proceeded to take out a fold-up table and two chairs. He set them up on the grass under the shade of a large birch tree. Darcie followed with the cool box. 'I didn't actually think you'd do this.'

'Like I say, we can be properly French.' Matt delved into the cool box and pulled out a tablecloth.

Darcie laughed. 'Oh, Matt, this is brilliant. This would be so OTT in England, but here . . .' she spread her hand out, taking in the other French families set up for lunch in the same way '. . . here, it's no big deal. I love it.'

'Would madame care for a seat?' Matt pulled the chair out for Darcie.

'*Merci, monsieur,*' she said sitting down, watching as Matt laid out the lunch he'd brought. 'Did you make these?' she asked, looking at the French stick stuffed with salad and ham.

'Of course. I'm more resourceful than you think.'

Matt was indeed resourceful and had not just brought a baguette and ham, but a mini buffet of French delights, albeit pre-packed from the supermarket.

'There's enough here to last a week, never mind one meal,' said Darcie, plucking a grape from the bunch and popping it into her mouth.

'We can keep what we don't eat for later,' said Matt.

Darcie wondered whether he was being this practical-minded for her benefit.

'You're doing that thing again,' said Matt.

Darcie looked up at him. 'What thing?'

'That thing where you're thinking about something else. Something that doesn't sit easy with you.'

Darcie raised an eyebrow in his direction. 'I don't know what you mean.'

Matt's usual easy-going expression had been replaced by one that Darcie couldn't quite pinpoint, but it was far removed from his engaging relaxed smile she liked so much.

Matt lifted his glass. 'I think you do.' He sipped his water and looked over to the other side of the picnic area. 'Do you want to see what's over there?'

Darcie was glad of the quick change in conversation and grasped it. 'There's a noticeboard. I keep seeing people look at it and then walk off down that path.'

'Looks like it takes you over the bridge,' said Matt. 'Let's get this put away and we can go and explore. We can spare half an hour.'

Within a few minutes the picnic was all packed away in the car and they headed over to the noticeboard. There was a white bollard painted with a red star in front of the board.

'It's where the American troops came after the D-Day landings,' said Darcie. 'Come on.'

They followed the path, which took them over the bridge and out to a small clearing that overlooked the countryside below and beyond. It was breath-takingly beautiful.

'Wow,' said Matt. 'This is amazing.'

'Does it make you feel connected to the past?' asked Darcie. 'Especially because it was Americans who came this way?'

'I guess it does,' said Matt, his gaze travelling the vista in front of them, before he crouched down and picked up a small handful of dust, letting it trickle out through his fingers. 'In theory, they could have walked across this very dirt.'

He stood up and brushed his hands together.

'That's how I feel about the dress,' said Darcie. 'When I touch it, I feel I'm being transported back in time. I imagine Nathalie Leroux handling the fabric and I even imagine Coco Chanel herself touching it, undoing the zip and stepping into it.' She stopped, feeling a little embarrassed at her fantasy. 'Sorry, I'm getting carried away, I know.'

Matt turned her towards him, his hands on her shoulders. 'Hey, don't be sorry. What you said is exactly that. It's connecting with our past, not just through our knowledge, but through our hearts and minds. Don't ever apologise for that.'

Darcie smiled and as they walked back to the car, she felt Matt's arm rest on her shoulder. She moved into him, enjoying the feeling of closeness.

Matt, ever the gentleman, opened the car door for her and Darcie climbed in.

He walked around the front of the car and Darcie tracked him. He glanced through the windscreen at her, winking before sliding into the driver's seat.

'All good?' he asked softly.

She nodded. 'All good.'

They pulled out onto the motorway and drove on in a comfortable silence.

The further away they were from Paris, and the closer they got to their destination, the more green and lush the passing fields and wooded areas became. Brittany had always been a popular tourist spot for Parisians, with many owning second homes in the area. With the roads so much clearer than those in the UK, the journey felt effortless and rapid.

'Thanks so much for driving,' said Darcie. 'I really appreciate it.'

'I enjoy driving. I don't often get the chance in Paris. Not much call for it,' said Matt. 'I did think about the train, but then we're restricted to timetables and reliant on the train running on time.'

'Oh, look. A sign for Ploërmel,' said Darcie sitting more upright in her seat. She remembered Matt saying that the Grandis farm was near there.

'Just a few kilometres away,' said Matt.

'Are we going straight to the Grandis address?'

'I was planning on doing that, but if you'd rather not or you've changed your mind, that's OK.'

'I feel nervous all of a sudden,' confessed Darcie as her stomach fluttered.

'Nervous as in fear or nervous as in excited?'

'Both.'

Matt smiled at her. 'And that is perfectly normal. I feel excited too.'

'You'll have to do most of the speaking,' said Darcie hurriedly, her nerves definitely getting the better of her.

'Sure.' He reached across and squeezed her hand. 'Don't worry. I've got this.'

Darcie appreciated the reassurance and wasn't ungrateful for the handhold either. In fact, it wasn't until he needed to change gear that he moved his hand away and she definitely felt disappointed by that.

Darcie wasn't quite sure what was going on between them but did know that she liked Matt's company. Correction. She liked Matt. A lot.

'Hey, don't look so worried,' said Matt.

'Sorry, I'm not really. Only a little.' No way was she going to tell him what she'd just been thinking. Not yet, anyway.

The satnav guided them through the centre of Ploërmel, where an array of shops lined each side of the road as it twisted around the buildings, past the cobbled square of the church and over several mini roundabouts, before dropping down and passing a retail park on the outskirts of the town. The directions guided them out on the road that wrapped itself around the lake, Lac au Duc.

'That looks a nice place to stop. Maybe we can call in there on the way back?' said Matt.

Darcie craned her neck to see over the wall and down to the lake. 'It's massive,' she said. 'There are boats and all sorts down there. And a beach. Oh, we should definitely stop if we have time.'

Matt took the directions from the satnav, leaving the lake in their rear-view mirror. 'Just down this road and we should be there,' said Matt, taking a right turn.

They travelled down the narrow road, with fields of maize on either side. As they turned a bend, a farmhouse came into view about fifty metres on the left.

'Is that it?' whispered Darcie.

'Yep.'

Matt pulled up outside and got out of the car, going around to open the door for Darcie, who hadn't summoned up the courage to get out. She wasn't sure why she felt nervous, but she did. Matt took her hand and led her up to the door. He didn't let go as he rang the doorbell.

After a few moments, the door opened and a woman who looked to be in her late fifties appeared. '*Oui?*'

'*Bonjour, madame,*' began Matt, giving the woman a deferent nod. Darcie listened as he went on to introduce himself and her, and then explain the reason for their visit. It was easier to follow what he was saying, when she already knew the story, but as the conversation expanded and the woman began replying with what sounded like questions, Darcie was lost. Matt had long since let go of her hand and she studied their expressions and looked for clues in the tone of their voices and their body language to gauge how the conversation was going. It would appear Matt was gradually winning her over, and why Darcie thought he would do anything less was beyond her – Matt was amiable and charming. Now the woman was smiling. Not just at Matt, but at Darcie too.

Darcie smiled back, hoping it was the right thing to do. She watched on as Matt finished his conversation and said goodbye to the woman, handing her his business card.

'So, what's the news?' asked Darcie. 'You're grinning like the proverbial Cheshire cat.'

'Let's get down the road and I'll tell you,' said Matt. He waved at the lady, and turning the car around, drove out of the farm and back down the lane.

'You're such a tease,' said Darcie. 'Tell me. Please.'

'Patience, patience.' Matt refused to say any more until they had reached the lake at Ploërmel and had parked the car. As they walked towards the water, he took Darcie's hand again before coming to a stop at the edge of the sandy man-made beach.

'You have to tell me now,' said Darcie.

Matt turned to face her. 'So, that was Elaine Vachon. She's lived at the farm all her life. She lives there with her husband and family, also her mother and until recently, her great-aunt.'

'Matt! You're really dragging this out on purpose.' She couldn't help laughing at her own frustrations and his teasing.

'I love it when you get animated,' he said with a grin.

'Oh my God, if you don't tell me right now, I swear I'll . . .' she looked around '. . . I'll take you out in that boat and tie you to the buoy out there until you break.'

'OK. OK.' He held up his hands in surrender. 'Elaine's

174

great-aunt is called Odile Grandis. Her father Philippe Grandis owned the farm during the war.'

'Does Odile still live at the farm?'

'No. She's in a nursing home.'

'OK,' said Darcie slowly.

'Odile is ninety-five, almost ninety-six, and her memory isn't great. She's hasn't got dementia or anything but, as far as Elaine knows, Odile hasn't spoken about the war for a long time.'

'So, is visiting her a possibility or not really?' asked Darcie.

'Elaine is going to speak to her mother and, if she's agreeable, she's going to arrange for us to visit Odile.'

'Wow! That's so generous. I don't know what you said, but you obviously charmed her.'

Matt looked very pleased with himself. 'I'm hoping Elaine isn't the only one my charm is working on.' His expression changed to one less sure of itself.

'Don't look so worried,' said Darcie. 'I think your charm offensive is going just fine.'

He placed a hand on her cheek and then dropped a kiss on her forehead. 'Good. That's what I like to hear. Now, how about we get a coffee and something to eat? I don't know about you, but I'm pretty hungry.'

'You mean you don't have another picnic stashed away? I'm disappointed,' said Darcie, this time taking the initiative and slipping her hand into the crook of his arm.

'Sorry to disappoint.'

'I'm not sure disappoint is the right word.'

'Looks like there's a café further around the lake. We can get some food there.'

They walked along the shoreline to the café and Darcie felt totally comfortable with Matt. Her phone broke the silence that had settled between them.

'I'd better get it, in case it's Chloe,' said Darcie, opening her handbag and quickly locating her phone. She stopped and looked at the screen. 'Unknown caller,' she said.

'You going to answer it?'

Darcie swiped at the screen, taking the seat Matt had pulled out for her. 'Hello.'

'Ah, is that Miss Marchant?'

'Yes, that's right.'

'Hello, my dear, it's Christophe Padgett here. We met earlier in the week to discuss the dress you found.'

'Oh, hello. How are you?' Darcie looked at Matt and mouthed Padgett's name at him, which earned a raise of the eyebrows from Matt as he sat down next to her.

'*Ça va bien,*' came the reply. 'Now, I have a little proposition for you regarding the dress you came to me about.'

'Oh, I didn't realise you were interested in it,' said Darcie. She put her phone on speaker and laid it on the table between her and Matt.

'I couldn't help thinking about it yesterday. It played on my mind,' explained Padgett. 'And even though I can't authenticate it, I wouldn't like to think of the dress just being thrown out or put in a second-hand sale. It doesn't seem fitting for such a beautiful garment.'

'I agree,' said Darcie. 'Although I had no intention of throwing it away.'

'So, I would like to make an offer for the dress. How does ten thousand euros sound to you?'

'Ten thousand euros.' Darcie had to repeat the sum to make sure she was hearing right. She glanced at Matt who didn't look quite as impressed as her with the figure.

'That's correct. And that's to include the sketchbook too,' said Padgett.

'To include the sketchbook,' repeated Darcie looking to Matt for his reaction. He frowned and shook his head.

'It means you don't have to worry about getting the book authenticated,' continued Padgett. 'Obviously, that's an expensive exercise. As is having the dress forensically scrutinised.'

Darcie glanced again at Matt who was shaking his head

firmly this time. Darcie hesitated for a moment before replying. 'I need time to think about it.'

Padgett tried to hide the impatience from his voice but didn't quite mange it. 'More time? But it's a generous offer for a home-made dress and a sketchbook.'

'I appreciate that,' said Darcie. 'But I don't want to rush into any decision. Can I just ask, did you find out anything about Nathalie Leroux?'

'Oh . . . err . . . No. Nothing. There are no records. I don't think she could have worked at the hotel.'

'Strange that her name is on the envelope with the Ritz stamp.'

'Yes. Anyway, back to my offer for the sketchbook.'

'And dress,' said Darcie.

'Yes. Of course.'

'What would happen to the dress and the book? Would it go into the Chanel museum or some sort of exhibition? Because, like you, I wouldn't want it to be forgotten about. You know, shoved in the back of a cupboard and never see the light of day again.'

'It's something I would certainly consider,' said Padgett.

Darcie got the feeling he was avoiding giving her a straight answer. 'I think there are certain terms I'd like agreed beforehand. Would you be able to put the offer in writing?' Matt tapped her on the arm and pushed his phone towards her where he'd typed a message in the Notes application. Darcie quickly scanned it and nodded at him. 'Also, I'd need a solicitor to liaise with the legal team at the House of Chanel to agree terms.' Matt gave her the thumbs-up sign.

'A solicitor?' said Padgett. 'Do you really think that's necessary? It's simply a sale transaction.'

'I would prefer it that way.'

'Hmm, well, I can do that,' said Padgett. 'Just so there is no misunderstanding, this offer is from me personally so it won't be the House of Chanel's legal team.'

'You personally?' Now that was a surprise. 'I thought you were acting on behalf of Chanel.'

'Sorry if I didn't make that clear.' Padgett coughed. 'I am passionate about my work and I do have my own small collection of vintage designer garments. As I explained earlier, I would hate to think of the items being discarded – hence my offer. It's a good outcome for both of us and the sketchbook.'

'Well, thank you for the offer,' said Darcie. Padgett's admission under pressure was unsettling. 'Like I said, I need time to think about it.'

'Very well,' replied Padgett tersely. 'My offer only stands for twenty-four hours.'

'OK, thank you,' said Darcie, although not entirely sure why she was thanking him. 'I have your number. I'll be in touch this time tomorrow.'

She ended the call and blew out a long breath. A waiter appeared and took their order for drinks, before leaving them alone again.

'Wow,' said Matt, in that understated way of his. 'So, Padgett wants the dress for his private collection.'

'I don't think he wanted to tell me that bit,' said Darcie. 'He was happy for me to believe he was acting on behalf of Chanel.'

'All a bit weird,' said Matt.

'Definitely. I'm not sure what to make of it.'

'He was very dismissive of Nathalie Leroux,' said Matt. 'Like he didn't want to talk about her.'

'I noticed that too,' said Darcie. She fiddled with the teaspoon on her saucer. 'I can't help feeling there's more to Nathalie Leroux than just this book and dress, but I don't know what. I'm sure Padgett knows more.'

'I get that feeling too,' said Matt. 'He almost seemed more interested in the sketchbook than the dress.' Before they could continue the conversation, Matt's phone rang. He looked at the screen. 'It's Madame Vachon.'

'Ahh! I hope it's good news.' Darcie waited patiently while Matt spoke with Elaine Vachon, but couldn't tell from his poker face how the conversation was going.

Finally, he ended the call. He looked up at her. 'It's good and bad news.'

Chapter 22

Nathalie

The room was cold and the air felt damp. They had stripped me of my uniform and left me in just my underwear before tying me to a wooden kitchen chair. I was blindfolded and had no idea what sort of room I was in, but I could sense the vastness.

Once Kranz had bundled me into the car and blindfolded me, he spoke in German to the driver, obviously not realising I could understand him, and instructed the driver to take us the long way around the city to the centre. I did not know what the centre was, but guessed it was some sort of interrogation facility as opposed to the centre of Paris. We certainly weren't sightseeing.

Once we had stopped, I had been dragged along by Kranz and I felt sure we were passing other people, but no one said a word. I wondered if that was a tactic they used to prevent anyone arrested having any perception of where they were. It added to the fear of the unknown.

I sensed I was alone in the room, but time had no meaning. It could have been minutes or it could have been hours.

Finally, I heard the door open and the sound of boots on the stone floor.

The blindfold was snatched from my head and I blinked at the brightness of the single overhead lightbulb above me. I squinted at the person in the room. It was Kranz.

'Water?' he asked, gesturing to the table in front of me.

He lifted the jug and poured some into a glass.

I shook my head. Not because I wasn't thirsty – I was – but because I didn't trust him not to have put something in the water.

He chuckled as if reading my mind before lifting the glass and swigging down the entire contents. 'You should trust me. Shall we try that again?'

Out of stubbornness, I shook my head. Kranz tutted and let out a sigh. 'Nathalie, I'm not in the business of hurting women, and I don't want to start now.'

I looked warily at him, not understanding the implications of the statement. If he didn't want to hurt me, what on earth was I doing there?

Kranz continued, 'I need to know that I can trust you. I can't have you working at the hotel, for Coco Chanel, near me or any of my comrades if I think you are untrustworthy. Going on your brother's past record, I have to be especially careful around you.'

'What do you want from me?' I asked, finding my voice.

'You need to prove to me you can be trusted. That you do not have any connections with the Resistance or, if you do, what those connections are. If you want to go back to work, to go home to your parents, then you need to give me something.'

'I have nothing to tell you. I know nothing.'

'Oh, in that case you'd better go home,' he said. For a moment I believed him, but then I realised he was being sarcastic. He laughed out loud. He walked around the chair and stopped behind me. I resisted the urge to turn around. 'Tell me, what did you know about what your brother was up to?'

'Nothing,' I replied without faltering.

'I don't believe you. Please be careful how you answer.'

'I didn't know what he was doing,' I insisted.

'You were very close to your brother. I could tell that from when I first encountered you.'

'Yes, that's true,' I replied, feeling a sense of pride and loss at the same time.

'So, he must have confided in you.'

I shook my head. 'He didn't because he didn't want to get me involved. He loved me and wanted to keep me safe. I asked him, but he always refused to say anything.'

'How very noble. And I'm expected to believe you?'

'I don't know what else to say to make you believe me.'

'Why did you want to shoot me?' Kranz walked slowly around, coming to a halt in front of me. He leaned back against the table, his hands cupped the edge.

'I didn't. Honestly. I wouldn't do that. I was just cleaning.' As I spoke, I looked at him straight in the eye. He needed to believe me. There was no way I could die in this room. I thought of my parents and how heartbroken they'd be that another child of theirs had been killed by the Germans. I couldn't let that happen to them. 'I don't even know how to hold a gun, let alone fire it. Besides, why would I choose to kill you in Coco Chanel's room?' I asked. 'I wouldn't make it out of the hotel. It would be suicide.'

'Maybe you don't care if you're killed? Maybe you have a false sense of loyalty to your brother and you think dying for his honour will make a martyr of you.'

'Not at all,' I replied. 'I have no desire to die for anyone or anything.' The dryness of my throat was making talking painful.

Kranz poured water into the glass and handed it to me. This time I accepted, and the relief was significant. 'Thank you.'

Kranz gave a nod of acknowledgement and placed the now empty glass back on the table. 'Tell me, Nathalie,' he began, 'how did you come to get a job at the Ritz when before you were working in your father's shop?'

'I needed to earn some money for the family, especially now my father's shop has closed,' I said.

Kranz appeared to consider my reply. Then he spoke again. 'And just how did you get the job?'

I silently thanked Marcel for having had the foresight to prepare me for any such questions. 'A neighbour works at the hotel and she told me about the position. She put in a good word for me with Monsieur Tache.'

'And who is this kindly neighbour?' There was a glint in his eye, as if he had caught me out.

I didn't hesitate to respond. 'Madame Segal – she works in the laundry room.'

'You know I shall check up on all these details?' Kranz made notes on a piece of paper on the table.

'You'll find everything to be in order,' I said with confidence. Kranz was on the prowl again. 'Does the name Marcel Reynard mean anything to you?'

I tried not to hesitate, to keep my composure, to not gulp, to not spin around and look at Kranz as my mind raced with all the reasons he might be asking about Marcel. 'I don't know the name,' I replied, hoping the momentary hesitation went unnoticed.

'Are you sure about that?' He came to rest on the table once again.

'I'm positive.'

'What about the Blacksmith circuit? Do you know what that is?'

'I don't know what you're talking about.' Sweat gathered under my arms and I could feel a droplet of moisture track its way down my spine.

'Come now, you must have heard of the Blacksmith network. After all, you have recently returned from Brittany where I understand your cousin, Gaston Grandis, is part of the Resistance movement there.'

'I was there to help my aunt and uncle with the harvest for a few weeks. I never saw my cousin.'

'So, you never saw your cousin. You don't know who Marcel Reynard is. You've never heard of the Blacksmith circuit. Is that right?'

'Yes. That's right.'

'You have two more cousins, Odile and Rachelle. Sisters of Gaston. That's right, isn't it?'

'Yes.'

'At this very moment, my comrade is speaking to them.'

I wanted to vomit. I wanted to scream out 'NO!' To demand they leave my cousins alone. I knew Rachelle would be strong, but dearest Odile – she wouldn't be able to withstand any form of interrogation. Even though she knew nothing, the Gestapo wouldn't necessarily believe her. I blinked back the tears that threatened to betray my impassiveness, but it was impossible. 'They know nothing either,' I forced myself to say.

'Come now, Nathalie, don't cry. If what you say is true, then no harm will come to them. They will be safely tucked up in their own beds this evening.'

He walked around to the other side of the table and sat down in the chair. Leaning back, he crossed one ankle over his other knee and took out a packet of cigarettes and lit one. Then he tossed the packet across the table towards me.

I didn't move.

'You don't smoke or you don't want to take a cigarette from a German officer?'

'I don't smoke,' I replied.

'Wise girl.' He drew in a lungful of smoke and exhaled slowly. 'You see, I do know you're wise so you'd be very wise not to keep any information from me. If you care about your cousins, especially the young one, then you will share any knowledge you have. That would be the wise thing to do.'

'I don't have any information to share. I don't know anything,' I insisted. 'I don't know where Gaston is and I don't know anything about the Blacksmith circuit.' I wanted to sound confident and non-confrontational. I didn't want to come across as weak, as if I was scared and was trying to hide something. I tried for a different tack. 'I know you arrested my brother Edgar, but I had no part in whatever he was involved in and I do not condone what he did. He was a fool, and he broke my mother's heart.'

Kranz cocked his head. 'Doesn't do to break a mother's heart.'

'If I could have stopped him, then I would have done,' I continued, warming to this distorted version of events. 'I would not have let him leave.'

'Is that because of what might happen to him or because of your political beliefs?'

I didn't hesitate when I told my biggest lie to Kranz. 'Because I believe France will have a better future under German rule. Because I believe in the ethos of the Third Reich. Because I am sympathetic to the cause.' I wanted to bite off my own tongue for such lies. I quelled the nauseous sensation in my stomach and I begged a silent forgiveness to all those who had already died at the hands of *les Boches*.

Kranz raised an eyebrow. 'Is that so?'

'Yes,' I replied firmly. 'That is why my father continued to run his shop for as long as possible. That's why you and the other officers frequented the family business. It's not just because my father is, of course, the finest tailor in the city. Another reason my brother's treacherous actions broke my mother's heart.'

Oh, how I wanted to cry at the words leaving my mouth.

Kranz gave me a speculative look. He put his feet down and leaned towards me on the desk. 'How do I know you're not lying?'

I hesitated before I replied. 'You don't know.'

Kranz threw his head back and laughed out loud, before looking back at me again. 'You are a funny one,' he said, amusement still in his voice. 'I don't know if you're stupid or brave.' He stubbed his cigarette out in the ashtray. 'Just how devoted to the cause are you, I wonder?'

I maintained my steady gaze at him. Several silent and heavy seconds passed between us. I certainly wasn't going to offer to prove myself in any way. This was Kranz's game, not mine.

'I know,' he declared, looking very pleased with himself. 'You give me some information on the Blacksmith circuit and if this matches up with the information your cousins give me, then I'll allow you all to go free.'

'But they don't know anything,' I said, with a nonchalance I didn't feel. 'It would be impossible for me to prove anything. My cousins know nothing.'

'And that implies that you do.'

'It implies that I could find something out,' I corrected, still feigning an indifference despite my heart racing with fear at the prospect of Odile and Rachelle being held to ransom.

'I'll tell you what I want. I want the British operative who is running the Blacksmith circuit. I want you to arrange a meeting with him. Of course, I shall be part of the reception committee.'

'The British operative?' I repeated, my voice fainter than before.

'Yes. Do you have a problem with that?'

'There are layers and layers of secrecy. I'd never be able to find out.' I was grasping at straws and Kranz must have known it.

He gave a shrug. 'I don't think it's as hard as you're making out. I'm sure you'll be able to use your charms to make the meeting happen.'

'Whoever it is won't want to meet with me. I'm nothing.'

'Then you need to become something.' Kranz tapped the edge of the desk with an agitated finger. 'I'll give you some information to pass on to the circuit. It won't be significant in the grand scheme of things, but enough to authenticate you. After that, you can meet with the British agent.'

'I don't know if it will be that easy,' I said.

'I don't care about how hard or easy it is. You just bring me the British agent and I'll ensure your cousins are released.'

'But it will take several weeks. I can't just win their trust in a matter of days. If you want me to do this, then you must release my cousins immediately.'

Kranz chuckled. 'I knew there was more to you than the demure housemaid. Very well, I don't see any reason why your cousins shouldn't be freed. As a gesture of goodwill and a show of my honour, I'll instruct that your cousins are free to go home. Of course, if you renege on our agreement, I will have them arrested, tortured, and then shot. Am I making myself clear?'

'Yes. Perfectly.'

'We have an agreement, then, Mademoiselle Leroux?'

'We do.'

Chapter 23

Darcie

'Good and bad news?' repeated Darcie as she looked across the table at Matt after he ended the call with Elaine.

He put his mobile phone down on the table. 'Well, good news and a little bad news, which could actually turn out to be good, depending how you look at it.' There was that mischievous twinkle in his eye again.

Darcie rolled her eyes good-humouredly. 'You need to tell me and tell me now.'

Matt grinned. 'OK, so here's the deal. Elaine has spoken to her mother, Paulette, and while she's a little reluctant for us to see Odile alone, she's agreed to a meeting as long as she can be there.'

'That sounds perfectly reasonable to me,' said Darcie. 'I'd be exactly the same if someone wanted to question my mum. So, was that the bad news?'

'Not exactly. The bad news is that we can't go and see Odile until tomorrow.'

'But we're supposed to be going back to Paris today.'

'Exactly. Hence the bad news, but we could stay the night and before you say anything, yes, I know that will involve booking a room and, yes, I know you won't be happy about that and, yes, you will want to pay your way even if you can't really afford it. So, before you throw all those objections at me, let me say this.' He took a deep breath. 'I will pay for all these things and you can pay me back when you get the

188

money from Chanel and if you don't sell the dress to Chanel, you can pay me back by sending me one of your best vintage dresses or fancy handbags or pieces of jewellery that I can give to my sister who will be blown away if it's come from England. Especially, if it was worn by a duchess or a princess or someone titled . . . you get what I mean.' It was Matt's time to roll his eyes and Darcie couldn't help laughing.

Knowing his offer had come from a good place and was genuine, she agreed. 'OK. It's a deal.'

'It is?'

'Yes. Sure.'

After they had finished their meal and were taking their time over their coffees, Matt got on with booking somewhere for them to stay the night.

'Finally,' he said, putting down his phone after the fifth time of trying. 'Everywhere is really booked up, but I've managed to get us somewhere here in Ploërmel for the night. There's a small château just on the outskirts of the town.'

'A château?'

'Just a small one. We can check in at about four o'clock, once they've got everything ready.'

'Great.' Darcie felt a little awkward about asking whether he had booked one or two rooms. She studied her coffee cup as she worked out how to word the question. When she looked up, she saw Matt was smiling at her. 'What?'

'I'm sorry. I'll put you out of your misery,' he said. 'I've booked two rooms so you don't have to worry about asking me.'

'I wasn't even thinking about it,' she protested. 'It didn't even cross my mind about the whole one or two room thing.'

'Methinks the lady doth protest too much,' said Matt.

'Methinks the gentleman is far too cocky for his own good,' retorted Darcie, but she couldn't help laughing even though there was no way she was going to admit he was right.

They finished their coffees and walked back along the

beach, where once again, Matt casually put his arm around her shoulder. 'All good?' he asked looking down at her.

'All good,' she replied. And right at that moment she felt inexplicably comfortable in Matt's company.

Matt gave her another long-considered look, before cupping her face in his hands and kissing her. One small kiss, before he moved back slightly, so he could look her in the eyes.

She couldn't deny she was enjoying being kissed by Matt, and if her body's reaction was anything to go by, she wanted more. He kissed her again and this time it was longer and deeper.

Darcie felt she was melting into him. Or at least, she wished she could.

They walked on further around the lake, past the pedaloes, the windsurfing school, and the man-made beach, which was now busy with afternoon bathers and beachgoers.

They sat down on the grass at the edge of the sand for a while, just relaxing in each other's company.

'This is nice,' said Darcie, closing her eyes against the glare of the mid-afternoon sun. 'I feel so relaxed.'

'Do you get much downtime when you're at home?' asked Matt.

Darcie felt herself tense up. With the mention of home, the guilt rocked up that she was here enjoying herself and had not really given Lena and Chloe much thought for most of the day.

'Hey, Darcie, you OK?' asked Matt, as he ran a finger down the length of her arm.

'Yeah. I'm fine.' She forced a smile but knew her heart wasn't in it. She let out a sigh. 'I was thinking about my mum and sister. More specifically, I was thinking how I hadn't thought about them since first thing this morning until just now when you asked about getting any downtime.'

'Ah,' said Matt knowingly. 'And you feel guilty, right?'

'Yes, I do. I'm here, swanning around France, enjoying fancy food, great company, about to spend the night in a château and they're in a little market town in England, probably having beans on toast.'

'I'm sure they would be delighted if they knew what you were doing.'

'They probably would, but it doesn't make it any easier for me.'

There was a short silence before Matt spoke again. 'Why are you so hard on yourself all the time?'

'Honest answer?'

'Always.'

'Because I'm the only one I can rely on. Mum and Chloe rely on me. I can't let either of them down.'

'Why do they rely on you so much?'

Darcie realised she hadn't actually explained Lena's condition to Matt. 'My mum is . . . she has mobility issues. She was in a car accident when we were kids, and as a result she lives with chronic pain.'

'I'm really sorry to hear that,' said Matt. He reached over and squeezed Darcie's hand.

'I ended up taking on most of the caring,' explained Darcie. 'We're a small family. There's only my maternal grandmother and she lives down in Cornwall. It just kind of fell to me.' Unexpected tears filled her eyes and she swallowed hard and blinked them back. She had no right to feel sorry for herself. 'I was glad to do it. I am glad to do it. I get pleasure from caring for my mum.'

'I get that,' said Matt. 'But would I be right in thinking that because of this weight of responsibility you've carried around with you since you were a kid, you're scared to go out and live your life? You feel too guilty if you're having fun? Is it like that?'

The tears made a comeback and this time Darcie couldn't stop them from falling. No one had ever said it out loud like that to her. No one had ever been so precise in hitting the nail on the head. She could barely admit it to herself, because even having those thoughts made her feel guilty.

'She's my mum – I shouldn't resent it,' she said through her tears. 'It's not my mum's fault, and if she could change what happened, she would, but I owe it to her. She would never walk away from me, so I can't walk away from her.' She buried her head in her arms as she hugged her knees to her chest.

Matt shuffled closer to her, wrapping his arm around her shoulders and holding her head against him with his other hand. He made comforting, soothing noises, kissed the top of her head and stroked her hair.

He didn't try to argue with her, to stop her from crying; he just held her and soaked up all the anguish, all the emotion and all the tears both metaphorical and physical.

'Oh God, your shirt is soaked from where I've been crying,' said Darcie when she eventually pulled away. She fished in her handbag for a tissue and wiped her face. 'I'm sorry. I don't know what came over me.'

'I didn't mean to upset you,' said Matt. 'And I'm sorry if it was all a bit too close to home, but I meant what I said: you shouldn't feel guilty for living your life and enjoying it at the same time.'

'I know. I do know that, but it's hard. I can't help it.'

'Can I ask you one question and then I promise we don't have to talk about it anymore?'

'OK.'

'You spend all your time putting your mum first, putting your sister before you. You are the one who does all the caring, right?'

Darcie nodded, unsure where he was going with this. 'Yes, but like I said, I don't mind.'

'I wasn't going to say that,' said Matt gently. 'You care for your mum and sister, but who cares for you? I don't mean your mum and your sister, but who outside of the three of you, looks after you? Who is your support system? Who hugs the hugger?'

This only brought more tears to Darcie's eyes. She shrugged. 'No one.'

'Exactly. You don't have anyone looking after you.'

'I can manage.'

'Can you? Can you really? We all need someone to hug us,' said Matt. 'Christ, even I do.'

'Who looks after you, then?' she ventured, not even bothering to wipe the tears from her face now.

'My sister's pretty good at it. She's down to earth and while she can't give me a real hug, she does good virtual hugs.'

'You can't beat real human contact, though,' said Darcie. 'Having said that, I don't want you starting to get all fussy over me.'

He pulled her closer into his body. 'Right now, it's my job to look after you.'

As Darcie allowed herself to sink into him, she had never felt more vulnerable and yet more protected and cared for than she did right at that moment.

The château was every bit as gorgeous as Darcie imagined. OK, it didn't have a moat and it certainly wasn't on the scale of some of the fairy-tale images in glossy magazines and those renovation shows on the TV, but it was beautiful in its compactness. Three storeys high with modest turrets on each corner and a half-flight of stone steps up to the main door, it still had a unique French magic.

They were greeted by the owner, who insisted they call her Yvette. She spoke good English, with Matt only having to fill in with his French every now and again.

'Your rooms are on the first floor,' Yvette said. 'Do you have any luggage with you?'

'Erm, no,' said Darcie. 'It's an unexpected overnight stay.'

'If you need anything, there is a supermarket not far, but I can provide you with toiletries.'

'Thank you, we just called in there,' said Matt.

'Ah, *c'est bon*,' said Yvette, seemingly happy. '*Alors*, here is the first room. It's the blue room and next to it is

193

the yellow room. I'll let you decide who has which room. Both rooms have a double bed.'

Darcie wasn't sure if Yvette raised her eyebrows at Matt or not.

'Thank you, Yvette,' said Matt, taking both sets of keys.

With one last look at them both, as if she couldn't quite figure out what the situation was between them, Yvette went off back downstairs.

'I think we've confused her,' said Darcie.

'I think so too.'

Darcie pressed her lips together and wrapped her arms around herself. 'I guess we are confusing.' After kissing the hell out of Matt today, she wanted to take things further, but she wasn't sure she was ready to, not that night.

'Don't overthink things,' said Matt with an easy smile. 'Try to relax and just go with the flow.'

She nodded. 'It's just, well, I don't know.' God, she felt like a teenager, not being able to express herself properly.

'Why don't you take a look at the room next door and then choose which one you prefer?' suggested Matt, holding the keys out to her.

He was so sweet, so understanding, Darcie once again felt a swell of appreciation for him. 'I'm sure it's equally lovely,' said Darcie. 'I'll go next door.'

'Try to get some sleep. Stop worrying about everything and everyone,' said Matt. 'Night, Darcie. See you in the morning.'

As she went into her own room and closed the door, Darcie wasn't quite sure how she was going to be able to sleep, knowing Matt was just on the other side of the wall. She checked her watch. It wasn't too late to call Lena, but as she took her phone from her bag, she paused. She didn't need to check. Maybe she'd just send a quick text. No. That was checking. Who was she trying to kid? Instead, she showered in the en suite and indulged in a fantasy that this was her reality and she was some aristocrat living the high life.

Even though it wasn't particularly late, she decided to try to get some sleep. She put her phone on charge for the night, grateful that she had thought to pack her adapter, and was just about to put the phone down, when she noticed she had an email alert. Opening it, she saw it was from Christophe Padgett but this time from what looked to be his personal email address and not the House of Chanel.

Dear Miss Marchant

I just wanted to follow up on our telephone conversation and my latest offer. As I stated before, there is a cut-off time for this offer so please give it your full consideration. I am sure the generous sum involved would go a long way to helping your own business and making life more comfortable for you and your family. I look forward to hearing from you.

Yours

Christophe Padgett

'What a bloody cheek,' said Darcie out loud. How rude and presumptuous. Pompous even. And openly referring to her business was one thing but bringing her family into it was another. Not only that, but she didn't trust him. He was hiding something and she wanted to know what it was. She was sure it was to do with Chanel and Nathalie Leroux.

Chapter 24

Nathalie

I wasn't released until later that afternoon, but Kranz made sure I was taken back to work. As soon as I entered the laundry room, Bochette pounced on me.

'Where have you been? What have you been up to? I thought I told you to keep a low profile?' She stood blocking my path.

'I was taken for questioning,' I replied. I was exhausted and the heavy feeling in my heart at the act of treachery I faced weighed heavier than anything I had ever known. I had tried to talk myself out of a situation, only to talk myself straight into another where I was expected to betray the man I loved. If I didn't, then I couldn't bear to think what would happen to Odile and Rachelle.

'Why were you questioned?' persisted Bochette.

'Thank you, Madame Bochette.' It was Monsieur Tache, the hotel manager. 'I'll take this from here. You can return to your duties.' He looked at me. 'Come with me.'

The head of housekeeping gave me a final look up and down but didn't protest and stepped aside, allowing me to pass.

Once we were inside Tache's office, he motioned for me to sit down and then, from the drawer of his desk, he produced a bottle of brandy. He poured two glasses and pushed one across the oak desk to me.

'Drink that,' he said. 'You look like you need to steady your nerves.'

With a shaking hand, I accepted the drink. The warm liquid burned my throat a little, and it made me cough. But the second sip went down much easier.

'Thank you,' I mumbled.

'Are you all right?' enquired Tache. 'Have they harmed you in any way?'

There was a gentleness in his voice that reminded me of my father. An enquiry that came from a genuine place of concern and the sympathy it carried was enough to open the floodgate of tears.

Tache waited until I had finished crying. 'I'm sorry,' I said. 'I didn't mean to cry. And in answer to your question, I am all right. I wasn't hurt in any physical way.'

'Sometimes the physical hurt is preferable to the mental torture,' he said.

I nodded. I wanted to confide in Tache the deal I'd struck with Kranz, but I daren't. Not yet. I needed time to think it all through. To understand the implications and to work out if I needed to tell Tache or whether I needed to keep quiet. I wished, not for the first time, that Marcel was there. He would know what I should do.

'Thank you for your concern,' I said to Tache, placing the now-empty glass on the table. 'I'm sorry if I've caused any problems today. I'll work late to finish my duties.'

'No need,' said Tache. 'I had one of the other girls attend to Madame Chanel. She was very concerned about you. She's asked that you go to see her as soon as you return. Once you've been to see her, you're to go home and report back here in the morning for duty as normal.'

'*Oui, monsieur.*' I rose to leave.

'Nathalie, if you need to speak to anyone about what happened this afternoon, you can speak to me.' His gaze fixed on mine. 'I am your confidant here. You know that, don't you?'

I studied his face for a moment. 'Yes. I do. Thank you, Monsieur Tache.'

Suzanne Fortin

After stopping at the restroom to make sure I was presentable, I went up to room 304. Coco Chanel opened the door and surveyed me from head to toe before speaking.

'Are you all right?'

'*Oui, madame.*'

'Good. You'd better come in and tell me what happened.'

There was nothing I wanted to do less right at that moment, but I had no choice, and standing in front of her in the living room, while she sat on the sofa, I relayed the day's events.

'And so, I was released and am back here,' I concluded. I omitted to tell her about the deal I had struck with Kranz, only that I had been questioned because he believed I was working for the Resistance.

'When I see Kranz I shall make it clear to him that I wasn't very happy to finish my bath and to find my room empty and that he had whisked you away without so much as telling me,' she complained. 'I am sorry that happened to you but . . . is there another reason why you have ended up here at the Ritz?'

'I needed a job,' I replied.

'I like you, Nathalie,' said Chanel. 'And while you were gone, I looked at both the drawings and the dress you brought with you.' She nodded towards her writing desk where my sketchbook was open. 'You have a good eye for detail and a flair for bringing your creations to life on the page. And your sewing skills really are very good. Even though the dress isn't finished, I can see the high level of skill you possess. In fact, had I not known these were yours, I might have thought they were from a professional designer and far more experienced seamstress. I like them very much indeed.'

For a moment, I was speechless at the praise Chanel heaped on my work. Never in my wildest dreams would I have imagined she would have been so enthused by them. 'Thank you, madame,' I said, not knowing what else to say.

'Don't look so surprised,' she replied, getting up from the sofa and walking over to her desk. She flicked through several pages, coming to a stop at an evening dress I was in the process of making. 'This is particularly appealing. Your choice of fabric is perfect. It's the exact choice I would have made and in this glorious colour, a deep inky blue, it really will be magnificent.' She turned to me. 'So, you have my congratulations.'

'Thank you,' I repeated.

'Now, I've been thinking,' said Chanel, her tone warmer. She picked up my sketchbook. 'I would like you to make a replica for me.'

I blinked hard. Had I heard her right? 'You want me to make you that dress?'

Chanel gave a chuckle. 'Yes. That is exactly what I want. Now, I've already spoken to Tache and he has agreed to my request that you set up a workshop in the room next door.'

'A workshop here?'

'It's easier than you having to take the dress home with you every day and bring it back for fittings and adjustments. Besides, I'd like to be able to see you at work. That way I can guide you, if I think something needs to be done differently.'

'I don't know what to say, madame.'

'There's nothing to say.' Chanel smiled. 'I assume you're happy to do this.'

'Of course,' I stammered. 'Absolutely.'

'Very good. Tomorrow you shall start. I'm prepared to allow you to use the last hour of your working day, working on the dress instead.'

I could barely believe that Chanel wanted me to recreate my design for her. Not only that, but she was organising a workshop for me and she would mentor me. I couldn't help feeling a little guilty too. Here I was, living a dream of mine and yet, around me, a war was raging; people were dying of starvation, being tortured and executed. It was a sobering thought.

'Now, I've had someone else in here today, so I've no need

for you anymore this evening.' She looked over at the gold carriage clock on the mantelpiece. 'It's nearly six o'clock. I'm dining out tonight. With Kranz.' She gave me a pointed look. 'Can you get my black evening gown with the gold belt out? Some suitable shoes and a jacket. You decide. I trust your judgement.'

I scurried off into the bedroom, amazed at yet another compliment I had received from Chanel. Taking the dress from the wardrobe, I paired it with a pair of black kitten-heeled shoes and a short fox-fur coat. Although Chanel hadn't asked about any other accessories, I took it upon myself to select a pair of earrings with a matching necklace and a black leather handbag.

Chanel surveyed my choices. 'As I said, I know I can trust your judgement. You'd make a very good apprentice. Just need this damned war to be over.' She turned and faced me with a smile, one I don't think I had received from her before. 'That will be all. Get some sleep and I'll see you in the morning. Seven o'clock sharp.'

'*Oui, madame.*'

'Oh, and if Kranz is here, don't even so much as look at his gun this time.'

'*Non, madame.*' I dipped my head and left the suite.

I practically skipped down the back staircase as I replayed Chanel's comments in my head and the last one about what a good apprentice I'd make. Could it be true? Was there a chance I could work for her?

I was so lost in my daydream that I didn't notice Bochette at the foot of the stairs until it was too late and I crashed into her.

'Sorry, madame!' I gasped.

'Look where you're going, girl,' she snapped. 'Haven't you got yourself into enough trouble for one day?'

'Sorry.' I went to sidestep her, but she moved into my path, blocking my way.

'I don't much care for what happened today,' she hissed.

'You may have fooled Tache and won some sympathy from him, but I don't trust you.'

Her breath was stale and smelled of coffee. I looked down, but she grabbed my hair and yanked my head up.

I gave a cry of pain, grasping her hand to stop her from pulling me any further. 'You're hurting me.'

'Shut up,' she snapped. 'I'm going to be watching you very closely from now on. You had better not put a foot wrong. Do you understand?'

'*Oui. Oui.*' I stammered as she gave my hair another yank.

The sound of footsteps on the tiled floor behind Bochette had her letting go of my hair. It was Tache.

'Is everything all right?' he asked, giving Bochette a questioning look.

'*Oui, monsieur,*' replied Bochette. 'I was just making sure everything was all right with Leroux.'

'And is it?' Tache looked at me.

'*Oui, monsieur. C'est bon,*' I replied.

'Good. Has Chanel finished with you?' he continued.

'She has.'

'You can go home now. You've had a tiring day. We shall see you in the morning.'

I couldn't get out of there quick enough. To be out in the fresh air of the Paris evening, under the open skies.

I strode quickly along the back alleyway of the building and out into the crowds, taking deep gulps of air. Suddenly, I felt a hand on my arm.

'Nathalie.'

'Alphonse! You frightened me,' I said with a gasp.

'Tache told me what happened today. I've been out of my mind with worry. I was so relieved when he said you had been released. I've been waiting for you.'

While I was touched by Alphonse's apparent concern, it wasn't him I wanted to comfort me. I wished Marcel was there instead. However, I forced a smile. 'I'm all right. It was just a misunderstanding, that's all.'

'Could have been a costly misunderstanding,' Alphonse replied with a frown.

'You're not in uniform,' I said, noting his civilian clothes.

'My night off. Do you want to have a drink?'

'I'm sorry, Alphonse. I'm so tired from today. I just want to go home.'

Alphonse looked disappointed. 'But I've barely seen you since you've been back. I am beginning to think you are avoiding me.'

The truth was, I had been avoiding Alphonse, but I was putting off the inevitable.

I stopped walking and turned to the young man in front of me. 'Alphonse,' I began. 'We should talk.'

'I'm not sure I like the sound of that,' he replied.

'Another day, after work,' I said, ignoring his comment. 'When I'm not so exhausted. I need to go home to sleep tonight.'

'At least let me walk you home,' he replied.

'Thank you. I'd appreciate that.'

He held out his arm, and I slipped my hand in the crook of his arm, before we continued our walk in silence. I wasn't sure whether I was being paranoid, but I kept getting the sensation we were being watched or even followed. Every now and then I found myself turning around or scanning the street.

'What's wrong?' asked Alphonse.

'Nothing. I'm just on edge,' I replied.

'Were you really going to kill Kranz this morning?' asked Alphonse as we turned the corner onto the road where I lived.

'No. Not at all,' I replied quickly. 'I was cleaning, that's all. He jumped to conclusions.'

We came to a halt outside the door of my apartment.

'I know when you're lying,' said Alphonse, a note of irritation creeping into his voice. 'If this is anything to do with Edgar, then you need to stop. I can only protect you so far.'

I looked at Alphonse. 'I'm not asking you to protect me.'

'I think maybe you should.'

'What does that mean?'

'I love you, Nathalie. Make no mistake about that, but don't underestimate how much I love our country.'

'I need some sleep,' I said, too tired to continue the discussion. 'Thank you for walking me home.'

He went to kiss me, but I turned a fraction and his lips met the side of my face. He moved back, and I could see the hurt and annoyance in his eyes.

He coughed and straightened up. 'Goodnight, Nathalie.' With that, he turned and walked back down the street.

As I watched, a movement from the other side of the road caught my attention and I snapped my gaze in that direction, but no one was there. Again, that uneasy feeling of being watched swept over me.

With one last look at Alphonse and then the street, I quickly hurried through the main entrance and up the steps to our apartment.

My parents didn't appear to know what had happened to me during the day and greeted me as normal. I rushed to the window that overlooked the street below. A dark figure slipped out of a doorway from across the road, and with their head down and coat collar turned up, hurried down the street.

I was right. I was being followed. And I would recognise that figure anywhere.

Chapter 25

Nathalie

I didn't sleep well at all that night, despite how tired I felt. My mind was filled with the events of the previous day, the conversation I'd had and the one I needed to have with Alphonse and, most of all, the man I'd spotted in the street.

It was Marcel. I was certain of that. More certain than I had been of anything. He had been following me from the Ritz. It made me both hopeful and fearful.

I had longed for him every day and every night since I had been back in Paris. I had almost given up on seeing him again, but his promise on the last night we spent together, that he would find me, kept that hope alive. But now that he was here, it was the most dreadful timing. Not just because he would have seen me with Alphonse, but because of what Kranz wanted me to do.

I wanted to cry and jump for joy all at once. I didn't know how to find Marcel and would have to wait for him to come to me.

Of course, I needed to speak to Alphonse at some point and tell him our relationship was over but needed some breathing space before that happened.

I felt like I was being hemmed in on all sides and I didn't know how to escape.

There was no sign of Marcel when I arrived at the hotel. I had kept a lookout for him, in case he was hiding in a doorway, and I half expected him to appear at my side, but he didn't and I was more than disappointed.

As I hung my coat up, Monsieur Tache came into the staff quarters. 'Ah, Nathalie. I've been waiting for you. Come this way please.'

I followed Tache along the corridor and up the servants' staircase. 'The sewing room Chanel requested is ready. I'd like you to see it. If there's anything you need that's not already there, you can let me know.'

The sewing room was amazing. How Chanel had managed to fill it with all the resources I needed in such a short space of time was beyond me. The room was only small – it had been a storeroom – but it contained all that I needed.

'I've had everything moved to another floor,' explained Tache, standing in the doorway. 'Sorry there is no window, but it's the best I can do. It is a very unusual request.'

'Thank you, Monsieur Tache,' I said, running my hand along the workbench and inspecting the sewing machine that was next to it. 'This is wonderful. I appreciate you allowing this.'

Tache cleared his throat and stepped further into the room, closing the door behind him. 'I couldn't really say no,' he said, and then lowering his voice. 'As it happens, it's something we can use to our advantage.'

'Our advantage?' I gave my superior a questioning look.

From his pocket Tache withdrew a pen and a small vial of clear liquid. 'This is for you to use,' he said. 'It's invisible ink.' He eyed me as I took in the implication of what he was saying. I went to speak but he held up his hand. 'No need to say anything out loud. Of course, you and I are working for the same cause.'

I nodded. All my suspicions about Tache being part of the Resistance were now confirmed. I felt relieved I no longer had to second-guess him. 'What do I need to do?'

'Write anything you hear in your sketchbook. Use the invisible ink. Each week, I shall come up to the room and tear out the sheet of paper and pass it on. You will need to write in code and that code is here.' He passed over a piece of paper to me, which looked like someone had jotted various numbers and equations on it.

'How do I use this?' I asked. It reminded me of the notebook Papa had in the shop where he wrote measurements and fabric lengths, and worked out costs.

'It's simple. Let me explain.'

Tache spent five minutes showing me how to work out the code using the six times table and the back of a sewing pattern he also provided me with. 'Cross-reference against this. Keep your message short. Stick to the facts. We can interpret it from there. If clarification is needed, someone will be in touch.'

I had to marvel at the ingenuity and simplicity of the code. In a sewing room where there were pattern pieces, mathematical equations, random numbers and sums dotted about, it would be difficult to work it out.

'If there's no new information, leave the book face up,' he continued. 'If there's information, leave it face down.'

'It sounds very straightforward.'

'It is. The best plans are simple.' He took a deep breath. 'I must go and you must get on with your work.' He paused in the doorway. 'Be careful.'

I looked at the closed door and then back to the pen and ink Tache had given me. It was a stark reminder of what was important. It wasn't about the dress or the designs or how much Chanel admired my work, this was about life and death. This was about fighting for what was right and fighting against the Germans.

I hid the pen and ink at the back of a drawer, and using the key Tache had left in the door, I locked the room behind me.

It wasn't long before I was called to action to use the invisible ink and secret code for the first time.

The following evening after I'd finished work, I was in the sewing room working on the dress, when a knock at the door startled me and I was surprised when Monsieur Tache walked in. I rose from my chair.

'Don't stand up,' said Monsieur Tache, waving his hand for me to remain seated.

'Is everything all right, monsieur?' I asked, noting the bundle of three towels in his arms.

'I need you to do something,' said Tache.

'Of course.'

'Kranz is down in the dining room, having dinner with another officer,' explained Tache. 'I need you to go to his room with some clean towels.'

I frowned. I knew Kranz's room was serviced by Collette but it wasn't for me to ask questions. 'Do you need me to do that now?'

'Yes, but while you're there, I need you to look inside Kranz's briefcase for a document. It's an agenda for an important meeting that he is attending on Friday with some very high-ranking German officers. We need to know where they are meeting, what time and what they will be discussing.'

I nodded. 'How long do I have?'

'About thirty minutes. No more. I've only just received this instruction myself.' He placed the key to Kranz's room on the sewing table.

I got to my feet, pocketed the key and then took a sheet of paper from my sketchbook. 'Write on here,' I said. 'As if it's a note telling me what I need to do. I'll take it with me so if I'm caught in his room, I have proof but I'll use the paper to write down everything I can find out about the meeting. I'll use the invisible ink.'

Tache nodded his approval and wrote on the paper: *Clean towels to Kranz's room* and followed that with his signature before handing it back to me. 'If anyone asks I'll tell them I had carried out a spot check on the room,' he said.

I folded the note and pushed it into my pocket, along with the pen filled with invisible ink.

I waited only a few moments after Tache had left before picking up the towels and heading down to Kranz's room.

As soon as I was safely inside, I scanned the room and located the briefcase at the side of the desk. Before I did anything else, I went into the bathroom, and taking one of the towels I opened the window and ran the towel along the outside window ledge, leaving a dirty streak across it. Then I folded it back up and placed it on the side of the bath, before going back into the main room.

Kneeling, I opened the case and started carefully flicking through the contents. I didn't know exactly what I was looking for and also didn't want to miss any other information that might be useful to Marcel.

There were three folders, the first of which contained several pages of timetables and schedules for troop movements between Brittany, Paris, and the south of France. If I had time, I'd copy the information down. I moved on to the second folder. This looked to be internal reports on several interviews with Parisians. I didn't recognise any of the names and from what I could tell, as it was all written in German, no significant information had been gained from the interviews. Mostly, the interviews appeared to be based on suspicions rather than any hard proof.

I opened the final folder and there was the agenda for the meeting. Perfect. Without wasting any time, I copied down the names of the six other officers who were attending. As the ink was invisible I had to keep my left finger on the piece of paper to track where I had written the information so I didn't write over it. This made the process a lot slower but finally I had copied the names and the agenda down.

I checked the clock on the desk. I'd been in the room for twenty-five minutes already. I didn't dare try to copy any of the other information down and, with shaking hands, placed the folders back in the case, leaving it at the side of the desk as I'd found it.

I'd just got to my feet when I heard voices outside the door. German voices. It was Kranz and another man. I scooped up the towels as the door opened.

Kranz stopped in his tracks as he saw me. 'What are you doing here?'

'Towels,' I said, trying not to stutter as my breath laboured. 'Monsieur Tache asked me to bring new towels.'

Kranz's eyes narrowed. 'Is that so?'

'Yes. I have instructions from him.' Holding the bundle of towels with one hand, I took the note from my pocket and handed it over.

Kranz inspected it.

The other officer looked over his shoulder and then spoke in German, suggesting Kranz inspect the towels in the bathroom to see if they really did need changing. Kranz smiled and said he thought it was a good idea.

Of course, I had to pretend I didn't understand them. Kranz shoved the note back in my hands and strode into the bathroom, emerging a few moments later with the dirty towel in his hand. He spoke in German again to the officer, saying that indeed the towel was dirty. Then he threw it at me.

'Get on with it,' he said.

I hurried past him into the bathroom and set about changing over the towels. I could hear them speaking again.

'Yes, as I was saying,' said Kranz, 'I have my own currency I use to buy the locals here. The head housekeeper is rather fond of jewellery. Look at this.'

I heard Kranz open a drawer in the desk. 'A nice gold ring. Belonged to a Jewish bookkeeper. Let's just say, he won't be doing any more accounting these days. And he certainly doesn't need this. I've swapped several items with Bochette for information. She's very good at supplying names of interest. She had an angel statue the other day as payment. The time before, a gold bracelet. I like to keep her sweet.'

'Erm, Kranz, the maid,' said the other officer in an uncertain voice.

'What? Oh, don't worry about her. She can't speak German. She doesn't have a clue what we're saying,' said Kranz with a laugh.

'Are you sure?'

'Of course. Watch this.' He then called out to me in French. 'Nathalie, come here.'

I did as I was told. 'Yes?'

'You don't understand what I'm saying do you?' he said in German.

I looked at him blankly. 'Sorry, I don't understand.'

Kranz laughed. He nudged the other officer. 'See I told you.' Then he looked at me again. 'You're nothing but a French whore. A filthy slut.'

I had to force myself not to react. I couldn't give anything away. 'Please, I don't understand,' I repeated.

Both men laughed. Then the other officer spoke. 'Let me try.' He looked at me. 'If you're a French whore then you won't mind spreading your legs for me.'

I looked from one man to the other as if I had no clue what they were saying. This caused them both to laugh out loud.

My heart was racing. There was an atmosphere in the room that was rapidly turning from amusement to something more sinister. The officer threw some more insults at me, together with vile and vulgar suggestions. It took every effort not to react. To not show them that I understood.

'That's enough now,' said Kranz. 'We can't upset Nathalie, here. She's Chanel's little pet and I don't want Chanel to decide I'm no longer welcome in her suite.'

'Oh, I see,' said the officer, eyeing me up and down. 'Maybe another time, then.'

Kranz held the door open. 'You should leave now,' he said to me.

I didn't need telling twice and hurried from the room.

As soon as I was safely back in my sewing room, I wrote down what I'd heard Kranz say about Bochette in my sketchbook using the invisible ink. I didn't know if this information would ever be worth anything, whether there would come a time that it could be held against her, but I knew it was important and certainly information Bochette would not want anyone to know about, least of all the Resistance or the Allied forces. One day, she would get her reckoning and I wanted to make sure every scrap of evidence could be used against her.

Chapter 26

Nathalie

I loved spending time in the sewing room Chanel had arranged for me. It reminded me of being back at the shop and working for Papa in the days when life was easier, simpler, happier, and when Edgar was still alive. The only good thing about now was that I had Marcel and although one didn't counter the other, my feelings for Marcel reminded me that life was still worth living and fighting for.

That morning I had arrived at the Ritz early so I could spend an hour working on the dress before my day's work began. The sewing room had come to be something of a sanctuary – a place where I could immerse myself in creating the dress for Chanel, and for just an hour or so, I could forget about the war and all the wretchedness that came with it.

However, when I entered Chanel's suite later that morning, I was reminded of the real reason I was here: Kranz. He sauntered out of the bedroom, fastening the top button of his shirt.

'Ah, here comes the little assassin,' said Kranz with a laugh.

'Erich, don't tease the staff,' scolded Chanel, walking around him and sitting on the sofa. I placed the tray I was carrying with the fresh coffee onto the table.

'It's just a bit of fun,' said Kranz, clearly amused by himself. 'Fortunately, her skills lie with the needle and thread, rather than a pistol; otherwise I might not be here today. Now, wouldn't that be a shame?'

'A shame, indeed,' said Chanel. She turned to me. 'And how are you enjoying the sewing room?'

'Oh, it's wonderful,' I replied, pouring the rich coffee into the cups.

'Glad to hear it. You can show me how you're getting on later,' said Chanel. She took a sip of her coffee. 'If you can start in the bedroom today, please.'

'And don't worry,' said Kranz. 'I haven't left my gun lying around this time.' He laughed at his attempted humour.

'Erich,' scolded Chanel. 'That's enough. Leave the girl alone.'

I was relieved to get away from Kranz, vowing that if I had the chance again, then I wouldn't hesitate to use the gun. Oh, how I would love to see the look on his face as I fired it.

I had only been in the bedroom cleaning for a short while when the telephone in the sitting room began to ring. There was an extension on Chanel's beside table, which was also ringing. I was debating whether I should answer it when I heard Chanel take the call.

After a quick exchange with the caller I heard her speak to Kranz. 'Erich, it's for you. It's Göring.'

'What?' said Kranz. I imagined him jumping to his feet and saluting the receiver. 'Herr Reichsmarshall,' he said, taking the call.

I looked at the telephone by the side of the bed. My heart raced as, with a shaking hand, I carefully picked up the receiver and held it to my ear.

The two men were speaking in German and it only took a few seconds to tune my ear in. I placed one hand over the mouthpiece, scared they would hear my breathing. All the time I kept my eye on the door in case Chanel should come into the room, while at the same time, I listened intently to what was being said.

I could understand nearly everything, and anything I wasn't familiar with, I could take an educated guess. Göring was very unhappy about a large batch of leaflets that had been distributed throughout the city in the night. Allied propaganda. Kranz was taking something of a telling-off as Göring demanded Kranz arrest those involved.

'I have a new name,' Kranz was saying, trying to appease his superior. 'There is a pharmacist who we have persuaded to work for us. He's been supplying the Resistance with chemicals for the printing presses. He's proved quite a talkative man. We know all about the White Lily circuit at Sacré-Cœur now.'

'I want results,' demanded Göring.

'And I will have results for you very soon,' assured Kranz. 'There is a meeting next week and we will be waiting for them.'

'Good. Don't let me down.' Göring ended the call abruptly and from the other room I heard Kranz drop the handset into the cradle.

I held my breath as I lowered my receiver onto the telephone, hoping Kranz would be too distracted to hear the small ding the main phone would make as the call was disconnected. He was busy talking loudly to Chanel and I guessed he was making his way out of the apartment.

I spent some time cleaning the bedroom and bathroom, emerging later to find Chanel sitting on the sofa where she'd been earlier. 'You should ignore Kranz,' said Chanel, not looking up from the newspaper she was reading. 'He's easily amused, like most men.'

'*Oui, madame.*'

Chanel put the paper down. 'You seem distracted today. Are you all right? Are you ill?'

'I'm not ill, madame.'

Chanel let out an impatient sigh. 'Do I have to drag everything out of you? What is bothering you?'

I shook my head. 'It's nothing important.'

'I think it is. Let me guess. It's a man.'

I looked up, startled at how accurate she was. Chanel continued. 'I tell you, men are at the root of all our troubles. Now, what is wrong? Has something happened to your boyfriend?'

Something made me want to confide in this woman, but I knew I couldn't tell her everything. I had to protect Marcel at all costs, but Alphonse, well, I could speak about him.

'I do have a boyfriend, but I don't love him anymore,' I ventured.

'Ah. And you haven't told him about this change of heart?'

'No. I haven't had the chance yet, but I will when I next see him.'

'At least you're going to be honest. I assume he must work for the Germans.'

'He's a gendarme.'

'I see. You know sometimes, we have to put matters of the heart to one side and do things that we wouldn't normally do. Things that keep us safe and ensure that we survive this war.'

'Is it possible to go against the heart, though?' I asked, thinking of Alphonse and Marcel at the same time.

'We have to be strong,' insisted Chanel. 'Paris won't always be like this and despite what the German war machine spouts, we must never give up hope that one day we will live in peace. The war will be over and then we can let our hearts rule our heads. But at the moment, we just need to survive and do whatever it takes to stay alive.'

Chanel motioned for me to pour some more coffee, and I obliged. 'What I'm saying,' she continued, 'and this is strictly between us . . .'

'Of course, madame.'

'Take Kranz, for example. He's a nice enough man to look at, good in bed . . . oh, don't blush . . . but I know he's married and when this war is over or his posting is over, he'll be going home to his wife and children. But all the time he's here with me, he's keeping me safe. I am surviving. Neither of us is naïve enough to think our relationship is anything other than human desire, a basic need and, I have to admit, on the whole, good company. Except when he's teasing you.'

Chanel's candour surprised me, and it encouraged me

to be open with her. 'But that is good because you both understand that. Sometimes, it can be one-sided.'

'True. But again, Kranz is not my first lover and nor will he be my last. Not everyone has been or will be as understanding, but all the time, I am keeping myself safe so I come out the other side of this war alive.' She pointed her cigarette at me. 'And you need to do the same. I'm not suggesting you sleep with every German soldier, but this young man of yours could be useful to your survival. Remember that.'

Chanel picked up her paper, and I took this as a signal the conversation was over.

When I had finished work for the day, I went up to the sewing room and, using the invisible ink, I wrote down the details of the earlier conversation between Kranz and Göring.

It was a long and time-consuming process as the codes were unfamiliar to me and I had to check and double-check every letter. Eventually, though, I was finished and I left the sketchbook face down on my desk for Tache to tear the page out later that evening.

It gave me a deep sense of satisfaction and accomplishment. So much so, when it came to working on the dress for Chanel, my usual enthusiasm was overshadowed.

By the time I left the hotel two hours later, I was exhausted. All I wanted to do was to go home to bed, and when I spotted Alphonse waiting outside the back of the hotel, my heart sank.

'I wasn't expecting to see you,' I said, as he approached.

'I've been thinking about you. I wanted to make sure you were all right,' said Alphonse. 'I hope you don't mind.' There was a trepidation in his voice.

Chanel's words of advice about using men in power to my advantage came back to me. It was different for her. I wasn't thinking about keeping myself alive. Out of all the lives that depended on me, mine wasn't the priority. Odile and Rachelle's lives were. And maybe not even Rachelle. She would understand the position I had been put in, but

Odile, I couldn't betray her. Dear, sweet Odile who had already been damaged beyond repair by this war. How could I betray her?

'No. Not at all,' I replied, taking the arm he offered.

'I thought we could stop at the café around the corner from your father's shop,' he said. 'That way, you won't have far to go.'

We walked down the road and we exchanged details of our day – superficial conversations about nothing in particular and no one in particular. We were both skating around the real issue of our relationship.

All the time we walked, I couldn't help glancing from one side of the road to the other, wondering if Marcel was lurking in the shadows or following us. I hated that he might think I still had feelings for Alphonse or that I might be double-crossing him. Not for the first time, I wished I was with him.

'Are you all right this evening?' asked Alphonse as we neared the café. 'Only you seem a little on edge. You keep looking around all the time.'

'I'm sorry. It's just after being questioned, it's unnerved me,' I explained, hoping Alphonse would accept my word.

'I know it was awful but I was able to speak to Kranz. I assured him you were not a threat,' said Alphonse.

I looked incredulously at Alphonse. I wasn't sure if I believed him or he was making such a claim to impress me. 'I had no idea,' I said finally.

Alphonse looked very pleased with himself. 'Kranz and I are on good terms. He values my opinion and the contacts I have.'

He said the last sentence with a pride that made my stomach churn. What Alphonse meant was he would readily betray his fellow countrymen, and he was proud of it.

I had to use every ounce of self-restraint to stop myself from slapping Alphonse across the face. He was so proud of what he did. I despised him and everything he stood for.

'I need to use the bathroom,' I said as soon as we entered

217

the café, and hurried through the tables to the back of the building. Simply being in Alphonse's company was making my skin crawl. I would willingly walk away from him, but Chanel's words of advice came back to me. Instead of making an enemy of Alphonse, maybe I should remain close to him. I didn't care about myself but as long as I was alive, I would have some vague chance of keeping my cousins and Marcel safe. If I was dead or arrested, I would be completely powerless.

The toilets were in the restaurant's backyard, and I was glad of the fresh air. I leaned against the wall of the small courtyard.

'That was quick. Wasn't expecting you out here so soon.'

The voice startled me, but I knew at once who it was without even looking.

'Marcel?' I whispered.

From the side of the outhouse, the dark figure of Marcel emerged into the half-light of the moon.

I rushed forward and threw myself at him. He pulled me to him and stepped back into the shadows again.

'Nathalie,' he murmured before kissing me. His mouth was firm on mine and his hands clasped me tight.

Eventually, we pulled apart. 'I knew you were here in Paris,' I whispered. 'I saw you follow me the other night.'

'Really? I'm not such a good spy after all.'

'It's only because I could sense you.' I held his face in my hands, barely able to make out his features in the darkness. 'I can't stop long. Alphonse is in the café.'

'Ah, the boyfriend.'

'Yes. But it's not through choice,' I said. 'I was arrested.'

'I know. I heard.' Marcel held me against him and kissed the top of my head. 'I have never been so terrified in my life. I'm just glad you're safe now.'

'I need to tell you something,' I said, pulling back from him. 'I've got to keep Alphonse on side. It is better I know what he is thinking and doing, and the only way I can do that is to pretend I still have feelings for him. I'm sorry.'

Marcel's body tensed and I knew he did not like the idea. 'I wish it didn't have to be this way,' he said at last.

'There's something else,' I said. 'They know about you. They know the name of the circuit. They know Marcel Reynard is heading it up. They want me to give you up. If I don't, then they will kill Odile and Rachelle.'

'Bastards.' Marcel hissed the word. He pulled back and turned away. I couldn't see his face but his anger cut through the darkness like a torch beam. I could feel the rage in the space between us. He inhaled heavily and held his breath for several seconds. The release of air was slow and controlled.

I put my hand on his arm and steered him back to face me. 'I can't give you up, but I can't let something happen to Odile and Rachelle. I need you to get them out of Brittany. To safety somehow.'

'And you?' His face was etched with fear. A raw and visceral emotion, so intense and so pained.

I put my hand to his cheek. 'It doesn't matter what happens to me,' I whispered. 'Just as long as they are safe. And you are too. If it means I have to sacrifice myself, then so be it.'

'No. I won't let you do that.'

I held his gaze and shook my head gently. 'Let's not end with cross words.'

'We need to talk about this some more,' said Marcel at last. 'Not here. Not tonight.' He took my hand and kissed my knuckles. 'Look, you'd better get back before you're missed.'

'When will I see you again?' I gripped his arm, not wanting him to leave so soon.

'In the next day or two. I'll leave a chalk line on the wall across the road. You'll be able to see it when you leave your house. If it's there, I'll meet you by the bridge Pont Neuf at the water's edge at either eight p.m. or six-thirty in the morning on your way to work. Whichever comes first. If you need to contact me, you do the same.'

219

A wave of fear and desperation washed over me as I realised Marcel was about to leave. 'Please be careful.'

He took my hand. 'And you. Don't annoy the boyfriend. I need you to stay out of trouble and to stay alive.' Then he pressed a small white pill into my palm. 'You know what this is, don't you?'

I shivered involuntarily and nodded. 'A suicide pill.'

'Or as we call it, the L-pill. Lethal,' he replied. 'I don't want to give this to you, but it's the only way I can protect you if things go wrong.'

I felt a wave of nausea wash over me and I took a deep breath, before closing my fingers over the pill. 'Thank you.'

'You have to crack it between your teeth. Crunch down on it.'

'Will it take long? Will it be painful?'

'A minute or two. That's all.' He reached over and cupped my face. 'It's better than the alternative.'

I put the pill into my skirt pocket.

With that, he kissed me again before hopping over the wall.

Chapter 27

Darcie

Breakfast at the château was nothing short of a feast. Darcie wasn't sure she'd ever seen so much food on a single table in all her life. There was fresh fruit, yoghurts, Breton butter cake, pastries of so many varieties it looked as if the local patisserie had opened up a shop at the château.

'I'm stuffed,' said Darcie, after politely declining another slice of the Breton cake. 'Cake for breakfast is rather decadent.'

Matt smiled at her. 'It's very French,' he said. He dropped his napkin onto his empty plate. 'So, have you had any more thoughts about Padgett's email?'

Darcie had sent him a copy of it last night before she went to sleep.

'I just don't trust him,' she said. 'There's something off about him that I can't put my finger on.'

'I agree,' said Matt. 'I did a bit of digging on him last night. Seems Padgett is heavily involved with the right-wing political party and, as I mentioned before, has aspirations of going into politics himself.'

'Leaving the House of Chanel?'

'I guess so. Maybe that's why he wanted to purchase the sketchbook for himself – because he's leaving his employment,' suggested Matt.

'Wonder what's so important about the sketchbook rather than the dress, which he seems less bothered about,' mused Darcie.

'Maybe Odile will be able to shed some light on it.'

'I hope so.' She sighed and looked out of the window across the gardens, where hydrangea bushes lined the gravel path. Something like that would look nice in the courtyard of the shop back home.

The thought of home was something of a reality check. It would mean she'd have to say goodbye to Matt and probably wouldn't see him again. The realisation they only had limited time together made her feel sadder than she expected.

'What are you thinking?' Matt gave her hand a gentle shake.

'I was just thinking how little time we had together before I have to go home.' She looked down at their hands. 'I'll miss you.'

'Hey, that's not for another, what, ten days? We should make the most of our time, rather than let it get us down.'

'Yes, you're right. I know. Ignore me.' She smiled broadly, in an attempt to lighten the mood. 'So, today's the day,' she said, taking her hand away and pouring a cup of tea, one she didn't really want but it kept her busy.

'Yep. Today is the day. I checked out the address and directions last night when I went to bed,' said Matt.

'You didn't sleep well?'

'Not really. You?'

She shook her head. 'Not great.'

Matt held her gaze for a long moment. 'It was a big bed for one person.'

Darcie took a steadying breath. 'That's what I thought too.'

'Shame we have to go back tonight.'

'Yes, it is really.'

'I guess we could stay until tomorrow,' said Matt, leaning his elbows on the table and stretching his hand out.

'Two rooms would be expensive.'

'We could cut costs in half.'

Darcie looked at his hand and back up at Matt. Was she

really going to do this? Of course, she was. She didn't want to regret this trip and she felt she'd regret not making the most of her time with Matt. She didn't want to think too far into the future. She had enjoyed being in France, where she felt free and away from all responsibility. There would be plenty of time for commitments and grown-up real life when she was back home.

'I think that would be a great idea,' she said reaching across the table and once more holding his hand. She was sure she could feel sparks of energy zinging back and forth between them.

'No pressure,' said Matt, rising in his seat to lean across the table towards her. 'We go at your speed. At your say-so.'

'Thank you,' she whispered, tilting her head upwards to meet his lips.

It was at that moment Yvette chose to come back into the breakfast room. '*Ooh là là,*' she said with such exaggeration, Darcie was sure it was something she perfected just for English tourists. 'It is hot in here, no?' She went over to the windows and opened them wide. 'I think we all need to cool down. So early in the morning as well.'

Darcie had to suppress a giggle.

'Jesus,' muttered Matt. He shook his head as he sat back heavily in the chair, but there was a grin on his face.

'Jesus?' repeated Yvette, making the sign of the cross. 'What are you calling him for?' She didn't wait for an answer. 'Now, I will let you get your things together so I can strip the beds as soon as you have left.'

Darcie exchanged a grin with Matt. Yvette was charming in her outspoken French way.

Matt straightened the expression on his face. 'Actually, Yvette, we were wondering if we could stay another night.'

Yvette stopped fussing with the net curtains at the French doors. '*Bien sûr.*' She looked at their hands, which Darcie realised were still entwined across the table. 'Is it the one room or both rooms?'

Darcie dipped her head, not able to look at Yvette.

Matt cleared his throat. 'Just the one tonight. My room?' He looked at Darcie who shrugged to indicate she didn't mind. He looked back at Yvette. 'Just my room.'

Yvette pursed her lips, her forefinger pointing at their hands, she wagged it from side to side. 'But for two people, no?'

'Yes, for two people,' said Matt.

Yvette smiled. '*C'est bon.*' She said something else in French to Matt, which Darcie didn't understand but caused Matt to tamp down a laugh. Then she left the room, humming Edith Piaf's '*Non, Je Ne Regrette Rien*'.

'What was that she said?' asked Darcie.

Matt shook his head again. 'You don't want to know.'

'I do! Tell me,' insisted Darcie.

'Words to the effect of what took us so long and could have saved her sheets if we'd stayed in one room last night.'

Darcie burst out laughing. 'Oh my God, she's hilarious.' She paused and looked at Matt. 'She does have a point though.'

Matt sighed. 'She certainly does. But we shall just have to make up for lost time.'

Darcie grinned. And carried on grinning as they left the room to get her bag and toiletries from what would soon be the redundant bedroom.

'I'm so nervous,' said Darcie as she hopped from one foot to another in the car park of the care home. They had arranged to meet Elaine Vachon and her mother at eleven o'clock.

'Nothing to be nervous about,' reassured Matt, rubbing her upper arm. 'Just be your usual charming self and all will be fine.'

'I think you're the charming one,' said Darcie. She looked up as a car pulled into the car park.

'Eyes looking,' said Matt. 'They're here.'

Elaine was driving and her mother occupied the passenger seat. Elaine lifted her hand in acknowledgement and smiled, which Darcie took as a good sign. When they got out of the car, it was clear they were mother and daughter, the family resemblance of blonde wavy hair, blue eyes and a straight nose were evident. They even held themselves in the same way.

'Thank you so much for coming,' said Darcie in French. 'I'm Darcie Marchant.' She shook hands with each of the women, who then greeted Matt.

Paulette seemed pleasant if a little more guarded than her daughter but it was to be expected, thought Darcie.

Paulette spoke in French and Darcie guessed she was giving them instructions about the care home. She looked at Matt for confirmation who translated an abridged version.

'Odile is expecting us,' said Matt, 'but Paulette said to remember she's ninety-five and has been through a lot.'

The staff member in the nursing home reception greeted them, asking them to sign the visitors' book and sanitise their hands. Once they'd all done that, she took them through to a small lounge that overlooked the lake. Darcie could make out the beach and the café on the other side where she and Matt had been the day before.

'Please sit down,' said Paulette, indicating to the sofa. 'My English is not very good.'

'Oh, no need to apologise. My French isn't very good,' said Darcie. 'Good job I have Matt with me.'

Paulette nodded in understanding.

It was something of an awkward silence that followed while they waited for the care assistant to bring Odile down to them. Matt gave Darcie's hand a reassuring squeeze and started up a conversation with Paulette about the weather, from what Darcie could tell. Bless him, he was really trying to make this go smoothly and soothe anyone's nerves. Whatever he was saying, it seemed to have the desired effect as Paulette gradually relaxed into the conversation and even laughed at something Matt said. Darcie caught Elaine's eye and the younger woman gave her a reassuring smile.

Fortunately, it wasn't long before the doors opened and a nurse wheeled in an elderly lady with white hair, combed neatly back in a bun.

'Aunt,' said Paulette getting up and greeting Odile. Thanking the nurse, Paulette wheeled Odile over to them. They spoke in French and appeared to be recapping on why they were there before Paulette introduced Darcie and Matt.

'We cannot stay long,' said Elaine. 'Odile's attention isn't what it used to be and my mother doesn't want to tire her out.'

'I am not that tired,' said Odile, her voice surprisingly clear for someone her age.

Darcie nearly fell off her chair. Odile spoke excellent English, even though her French accent was heavy.

'Odile has always been able to speak English. She spent a lot of time in England,' explained Elaine. 'She switches between the languages.'

'That's amazing,' said Darcie. She leaned forward towards Odile. 'Thank you for seeing us, madame.'

Odile raised her head and her green eyes, although a little watery, were bright. 'I do not get many visitors,' she said. 'It is nice to see someone new.'

Paulette said something to Matt.

Darcie looked to him for translation. 'She wants us to get on with it,' he explained.

Darcie took a breath and began to explain how she'd bought the contents of a luggage locker in England and the book and dress in the case. She took the sketchbook from her bag and passed it to Odile. 'This was the book I found,' she said. 'The designs are signed and we think they're by Nathalie Leroux – your cousin.'

Odile's fingers trembled a little as she took the book with

her age-spotted hands. She ran her fingers, twisted a little from age and arthritis, across the cover before opening it. Her mouth appeared to be working but no sound was coming out.

'Aunt?' queried Paulette leaning closer. 'What is it? Do you recognise this book?'

Odile shook her head. 'Nathalie. Nathalie.' Her voice broke and a tear streaked its way down her face.

Paulette grabbed a tissue and wiped her aunt's face. 'This has to stop,' she said. '*Arrêtez*. I do not want my aunt upset.'

Darcie knelt in front of Odile. 'I'm sorry for upsetting you,' she said. 'Do you know Nathalie?' She knew she was pushing her luck when Paulette had already asked them to stop but she was desperate to know about Nathalie.

'I said *enough*,' said Paulette.

'Maman, let Odile answer them,' said Elaine.

Odile gave a heavy sigh. 'She should never have gone there,' she said, her voice crackling as she spoke. 'I didn't want her to go. It was too dangerous.'

'Where didn't you want her to go?' asked Darcie, holding Odile's hand.

'To Paris. The Ritz,' Odile replied, her gaze fixed on the book in her lap.

Darcie's breath caught in her throat and she glanced up at Matt, who nodded his understanding of the significance. So far Darcie hadn't mentioned the hotel. 'What happened at the Ritz?'

Odile shook her head. 'I loved Nathalie. She always took care of me.' She smiled at a memory. 'She taught me to sew. We made a quilt together.'

'That's lovely,' said Darcie. 'Do you still have the quilt?'

'I think we have it,' said Elaine. She looked towards her mother, who frowned without passing comment.

'What happened to Nathalie at the Ritz?' Darcie ventured, hoping to bring Odile back around to Nathalie.

Odile looked up at Darcie. She blinked several times and she placed her other hand over the top of Darcie's. 'It was dangerous. Spies. You can't trust people. They betray you.'

'Did something happen to Nathalie there?' asked Darcie, excitement and anxiety vying for pole position.

Odile's hands began to shake again and tears welled in her eyes, before running down her face.

Paulette took the book away, dropping it onto the carpet. 'Enough. No more questions.' She continued in French, clearly agitated and although Darcie couldn't understand, the message was clear.

Darcie felt Matt's hand on her shoulder. She wanted to ask Odile more, but she could see how distressing it was for the older woman. 'I'm sorry for upsetting you,' she said. 'It's just very important to me that I know more about Nathalie Leroux and the dress and her designs.'

Odile was dabbing her eyes with a handkerchief and Paulette scowled at Darcie. She turned to Matt and spoke in rapid French, too fast for Darcie to follow.

Elaine came over to Darcie. 'My mother is very protective of her aunt.'

'I know and I would be the same. I'm my mother's carer and I would want to protect her too.'

Elaine relayed the message to Paulette and it seemed to have a calming effect. She blew out a breath and spoke to Matt again.

Matt translated. 'She understands but doesn't want to upset Odile. She's going to speak to her after we leave and will phone me. We might be able to come back tomorrow morning before we leave.'

'Oh, thank you. *Merci, madame*,' said Darcie, grateful the door hadn't been fully closed on them. 'It is very kind.'

Elaine smiled. 'Thank you for understanding.'

'Can I say goodbye to Odile, please?'

Elaine nodded.

Darcie knelt down in front of Odile and once again held the woman's hand. 'Thank you for talking to us,' she said softly. 'I hope we can talk again tomorrow.'

Odile looked at her but said nothing, only nodded. Darcie got to her feet and watched as Paulette wheeled Odile away.

As they left the nursing home, Darcie glanced back to where Elaine was standing in the doorway, watching them. They exchanged a small smile. Darcie hoped she'd be able to see Odile again. Their meeting had been so brief and Darcie still had a raft of unanswered questions.

'What did you make of that?' she asked Matt as they walked towards the car.

'Odile definitely knows who Nathalie is, but whether we will get a chance to ask her anything significant, I don't know. Paulette is very protective.'

'Something happened at the Ritz though. Something bad. I've no idea what or how the dress and sketchbook are connected but we are definitely onto something.'

'Hopefully, tomorrow we can get some more info from Odile,' said Matt. 'And before Paulette says it's too much.'

'Yes, I do feel bad pressing Odile with loads of questions. I totally get where Paulette is coming from, but Odile actually remembered Nathalie.'

Instead of going back to Ploërmel town, Matt drove them out to the small village of Malestroit, where they sat in the square next to the church and took a leisurely lunch.

Matt was busy tapping on his phone while Darcie messaged home to check Lena and Chloe were OK. Darcie had been very good at not constantly phoning and messaging, but having seen Odile, her resolve waned.

She got a reply almost straight away from Lena, telling her she was fine and that Chloe was doing an excellent job of looking after her.

Despite the reassurance, Darcie was aware of a certain pang of something she couldn't quite pinpoint. While she was glad Lena and Chloe were managing fine, it also made her feel dispensable, something she wasn't at all familiar with.

She messaged Hannah to ask about the shop and again, although relieved that Hannah seemed to be managing the shop just fine without her, it left Darcie with a sense of having no purpose.

She'd spent years being the prime carer, the indispensable one, the one everyone needed and now she had been away for a few days and everyone was managing without her. And it bothered her, more than she realised and more than she cared to admit.

She put her phone back in her bag and realised Matt was watching her from over the top of his sunglasses. 'Everything OK?' he asked.

'Yes. All fine,' said Darcie. She knew she was brooding and she hated that sense of realisation. 'Apparently, Mum, Chloe, and Hannah are all just fine and managing perfectly well without me.' She crossed her legs and her foot jiggled in agitation.

'That's good, right?' said Matt slowly.

Darcie folded her arms. 'Yes. It is good.' She looked beyond the church at the Tudor-framed building, which was shrouded in scaffolding while repairs were being carried out. 'It's perfect. So perfect, I don't know why I ever worried they'd miss me.'

Matt gave a chuckle, which had Darcie snapping her head around to look at him. 'What's so funny?'

'You are.'

'I don't see why.' It was in fact a lie. She knew exactly what Matt was finding amusing and she hated herself for showing too much. She let out a sigh. 'Ignore me. I'm just being a princess.'

Matt shuffled his chair closer to her and leaned forward, his forearms resting on his knees and his hands together while his fingertip brushed her knee.

'You're not being a princess,' he said softly. 'You're just having a moment of realisation.'

Darcie let out a sigh. 'What makes you such an expert?'

'We all have moments like that.' He sat back and absent-mindedly toyed with the teaspoon. 'I had one when I realised I didn't want to become CEO of my father's company. I spent weeks agonising over it, how I was going to tell him, what he'd say, all the usual.'

'And what did he say?'

'Well, I went to see him with a speech I had rehearsed so many times, to make sure I was getting my point across without being disrespectful, so that I'd make it as easy as possible. I had lined up all the arguments he'd make and how I would respond to them. I had it all straight in my head. Every scenario covered, except for one.'

'Was he really angry?'

'Nope. The opposite. I went through everything and I ended along the lines of "I'm really sorry but it's just not for me but I can stay on until you find a replacement,"' replied Matt. He gave a self-deprecating laugh. 'I didn't want to leave him in the lurch so I told him all this and he simply said, "I appreciate you telling me. I wondered how long it would be before we had this conversation. So I'm prepared for it and you can leave at the end of the week. I have your replacement already lined up."'

Darcie's eyes widened. 'Wow. He didn't even try to talk you out of it?'

'No. I mean, we have spoken about it since, briefly, and my mom has spoken with me at greater length, and basically Dad didn't want anyone there who didn't want to be there. If my heart wasn't in it, he didn't want me taking over as CEO one day. He wanted someone as passionate as he was.'

'And you didn't realise that until then?'

'No. I thought he'd put up a fight, but it turned out I wasn't indispensable. It didn't mean he didn't love me, or thought any less of me, but it did show me that the show goes on, no matter what. No one is indispensable.'

'And that goes for me too,' said Darcie, looking down. 'Part of me is relieved but part of me is sad. Maybe a little confused.'

'It's natural. You have given yourself that narrative for so many years, even if it wasn't true, or at least not totally true, you've kinda believed your own hype.'

Darcie didn't answer straight away as she tried to get her head around what Matt was saying. 'I don't mean to sound conceited, but I always thought I played an important role, a vital one that no one else could fulfil, but I think I've got that wrong.'

'Oh, your role is important and it is vital but none of those things are exclusive to you.'

Darcie sat back in her chair and looked up at the clear blue sky. 'I feel like I've just been to therapy.'

Matt rubbed her calf. 'Don't be too hard on yourself. You can't just adjust your mindset over one coffee. It takes time.'

Darcie leaned forward, her hands cupping Matt's face. She kissed him on the mouth. 'Thank you for being so wise and so kind.'

'You're welcome.'

'I'm looking forward to discovering more of your skills,' she said, kissing him again.

Matt laughed. 'I'm more than happy to share them with you.'

'What are your thoughts on afternoon naps?'

'Naps? Or nap-naps?' He emphasised the last two words.

It was Darcie's turn to laugh. 'Both. I really could do with a snooze right now.'

'What are we waiting for?' asked Matt getting to his feet, throwing a couple of twenty-euro notes on the table, which was more than enough to cover their coffees and food, before taking Darcie by the hand and off in the direction of their car.

'How quickly can you get back to the château?' asked Darcie, fastening her seat belt.

'Legally, twenty minutes.'

'Illegally?'

'Fifteen. Hold on!' He put the car into gear and broke every speed limit possible getting back to Ploërmel.

Chapter 28

Darcie

Waking up the next morning, not only in a strange bed, but also not on her own was something of a novelty for Darcie. She hadn't spent the night with someone since her last relationship ended and that was three years ago. Since then she'd had a very brief fling with some guy she knew from the pub in Petworth but that was over a year ago. She hadn't pegged herself as someone who could do relationships. Usually, once boyfriends realised she was committed to looking after Lena and putting her first and foremost, above everything else, their interest had waned.

Now, here she was, lying next to Matt, and for some reason, she didn't want it to end. A bizarre train of thought seeing as they had only just begun and in just over a week, she'd being going back to England and it would all be over. She was used to living for the moment where her personal life was concerned; she hoped Matt realised this.

He stirred in his sleep and pulled Darcie closer to him, his arm wrapped around her shoulders.

Darcie snuggled up, the hairs on his chest tickling the side of her face, but she didn't mind. He smelt warm and the faint tones of his aftershave lingered on his skin.

He stirred again and rolled over to face her, his eyes opening. He smiled and kissed her.

'Morning,' he said. 'Just making sure I wasn't dreaming.'

'Definitely didn't dream yesterday afternoon or last night,' said Darcie, returning the smile.

'I think we need to cement it in our memories again,' said Matt.

Darcie wasn't going to argue with that idea.

Afterwards, they'd tested out the shower and, yes, it was big enough for two people, if a little snug.

Yvette greeted them when they finally went down for breakfast. 'I wasn't sure if you two were going to make it.' She gave a raise of her eyebrows and Darcie felt her cheeks burn red with embarrassment, which seemed to amuse Yvette no end. 'You will need a big breakfast now to regain your strength. Eat up!'

'She's terrible,' Darcie said with a laugh after Yvette had left the room.

'She does have a point though,' said Matt. 'I'm famished.' His phone began to ring before he had time to even pour a coffee. Matt answered the call. He looked up at Darcie and gave her the thumbs-up sign. It must be Elaine ringing about seeing Odile again. Darcie listened eagerly to Matt's side of the conversation and although he was speaking French, she was able to get the gist of it. Matt ended his call.

'Was that Elaine? What did she say?' asked Darcie, not giving Matt the chance to take a breath. 'Can we see Odile again?'

'Yes. We're to be there at eleven this morning,' said Matt, checking his watch. 'That doesn't give us much time. We have about ninety minutes.'

'Did Elaine say if her mother was going to be there?'

'That's the best bit. Apparently, Paulette can't make it this morning so Elaine is going to meet us on her own.'

'I hope Odile is all right,' said Darcie. 'I don't want to upset her by stirring up old memories but I'm desperate to know more about Nathalie Leroux.'

After finishing their breakfast, they checked out of the château, promising Yvette they would stay with her again if they were ever in the area.

'And I want an invite to the wedding!' she called, as they climbed into Matt's car.

Darcie shook her head but was laughing at the same time. 'She's way ahead of herself,' she said as Matt started the engine and pulled away, tooting his horn as he went.

'Has there ever been anyone serious?' asked Matt, not taking his eyes off the road.

Darcie was a little startled by the question, but she supposed it was going to come sooner or later now they'd taken their relationship to another level. She was actually quite curious about Matt's past. 'There was one. Kyle. We went out for about eighteen months. Didn't live together or anything like that,' said Darcie, keeping a light tone to her voice.

'Eighteen months is quite a long time. You didn't ever think about moving in together?'

'Not really. I couldn't leave my mum. I'd feel too guilty.' As she spoke, yesterday's conversation with Matt in the square popped into her mind. Maybe she should re-evaluate the notion that she was indispensable. Not right now, but when she had a bit more time. She looked across at Matt. 'So, do I get to ask you about your love life now?'

'Sure. Fire away.'

Darcie wasn't sure if Matt was as enthusiastic as he was trying to make out, but she appreciated the effort. 'OK. Have you ever been in a serious relationship? Who with? How long? Why did it end?'

'That's a lot of questions, but here goes. I've had two serious relationships. The most recent, was Emma. Back home. I wanted to go travelling and do this supporting myself thing; she didn't. She wanted to stay in her comfort zone. She gave me an ultimatum. Her or Paris.'

'Do you regret your choice?'

'Not at all. We were convenient for each other but we were very different in a lot of ways as it turned out.' Matt manoeuvred the car onto the main road. 'Anyway, she's engaged now. Getting married to some Harvard graduate and getting a house in Maine or the Hamptons or somewhere like that.'

'I don't know much about the US, but I do know that's where a lot of money is,' said Darcie. 'Do you think you'll go back to America, to live, eventually?'

Matt was thoughtful for a while and Darcie wasn't sure if he was going to speak, but she sat the silence out and eventually it paid off when Matt answered her. 'I'm not sure. I miss my family, but I can always go back and visit or they can come out here. I don't miss the lifestyle though. I like Europe; it feels right for me.'

'And you'll always stay in Paris?'

'For now, but I'd like to go to some other countries.'

'You're lucky you can do that.' Darcie looked back out of the window, hoping she didn't sound too spiky.

'I know, but there is a trade-off,' said Matt.

'What's that?'

'It can get kinda lonely. Sure, I have made friends here, but they've always felt transient.'

'Like me, you mean.' She said the words she had meant to keep to herself.

'I'll be honest, I wish we could have more time together,' said Matt. 'You'll note I used the past tense when I said they've always felt transient. That's because up until I met you, that was true.'

Darcie looked down at her hands. This was no time to be shy and lack confidence. 'I feel the same but in a week's time, or just over, I'll be back in West Sussex, looking after my mum and sister while running a business. That's my reality. Being here with you in France, that's my dream, my make-believe.'

Matt reached for her hand and they drove in silence for the rest of the journey. What was there to say? It was true. Darcie couldn't pretend it was anything other than that. Much as she'd like to think Matt was going to sweep her off her feet and they were going to travel Europe together, the fact remained she had responsibilities and he didn't. They were worlds apart. He hadn't argued the point either or tried to make some childish promise that they could have it all. He knew the score. It was something of a sad acceptance they both understood.

Twenty minutes later and they were pulling up outside Odile's care home, parking next to Elaine's car.

'She must have gone in ahead of us,' said Darcie.

They were let in by the nurse who'd seen them yesterday and were just signing in the visitors' book when Elaine appeared in the hallway.

'Oh, I am glad I have seen you. I'm very sorry but you can't see Odile.'

Darcie exchanged a confused look with Matt. She turned back to Elaine. 'Is everything all right with Odile?' God, she hoped the older woman was OK and hadn't taken ill or been disturbed by their visit the day before.

'Odile is fine but she can't speak to you anymore.'

'I'm so sorry if we've upset her in any way,' began Darcie.

'It's not you,' said Elaine.

'What's happened?' asked Matt.

'Look, I can't tell you, but circumstances have changed since yesterday, since I spoke to you earlier in fact, and Odile doesn't want to talk with you.'

'Doesn't want to or has been told not to?' It was Matt again.

'I can't say any more,' insisted Elaine. 'I shouldn't even be saying anything. My mother would be very cross if she knew.'

'I don't understand,' said Darcie.

'We should leave,' said Matt. He thanked Elaine and put his arm around Darcie's shoulder.

Darcie paused and turned back to Elaine. 'Odile is the only living person who can tell us what happened to Nathalie Leroux. If you feel you can share anything with us, can you call me please?' She pulled her purse from her bag and took out a card, which she handed to Elaine. 'That's my business card. It has my phone number and email.'

'Has something happened this morning to change Odile's mind?' asked Matt.

Elaine shook her head. 'I can't comment.' Her gaze shot towards the visitors' book before looking pointedly at Matt. 'Now, please, I can't say any more.'

With more reluctance than Darcie thought possible, she left the nursing home, leaving Matt to sign them straight back out of the visitors' book.

'I don't understand what happened,' said Darcie, when Matt joined her in the car park. She genuinely felt like crying. The words felt prickly in her throat and she swallowed hard to stop the tears from gathering in her eyes.

'Odile had a visit from two men from a law firm based in Paris this morning,' said Matt. 'I saw it in the visitors' book when I signed us out. Did you see the way Elaine glanced at it when she said she couldn't comment? She was trying to tell us. My bet is Padgett sent them.'

Darcie stopped in her tracks. She turned to face Matt, looking from him to the care home and back to him again. 'What?' She closed her eyes momentarily and shook her head. 'Padgett has sent his lawyers to see Odile? Why?'

'Think about it, Darcie,' said Matt, holding her shoulders and looking intently at her. 'This week you've been to Padgett about a dress, which he says they're not interested in. Then you get an email from Padgett, not Chanel, but Padgett on his private email, offering you a lot of money for the dress, which, by the way, you're on a deadline to reply to. Then we speak to Odile who obviously knows something but found it too upsetting to say and anyhow was stopped by Paulette. Then Odile agrees to see us today. We get here and all bets are off. Suddenly, in a matter of less than two hours, she's changed her mind and doesn't want to speak to us.'

Darcie took a moment to process everything Matt was saying. 'And you think it's to do with the dress?'

'What else can it be?'

'That means the dress must be important. More important

than Padgett wants to admit but not something he wants to go through the official Chanel channels.' Darcie's heart began to pick up speed. 'He wants that dress and doesn't want us finding out the truth.'

'Exactly!'

'Oh God. That must mean it really was the dress Coco Chanel was wearing.'

'There's definitely more to this than he's letting on.'

'I feel awful,' she said. 'I've no idea what those men said to Odile, but it was enough to make her not want to talk to us. What if they frightened her in some way? Threatened her? I hate the thought it was my fault.'

'You can't think like that,' said Matt. 'You've done nothing wrong. You've showed complete and utter respect for Odile.'

'But I pursued this whole idea about the dress, I've dragged you into it and ruffled the oh-so-sleek designer feathers of Christophe Padgett.'

'Don't do that to yourself. You are not the bad guy here.'

'I can't help feeling guilty. I know my logical brain says it's not me, but my conscience has a pretty loud voice.'

'I'm going to try to find out what was said to Odile. I'm not one for using contacts but, in this case, I have no qualms. I'll just have to swallow a bit of pride, that's all.'

'Well, you know what they say about swallowing your pride?'

'What's that?'

'It won't choke you.'

He kissed the top of her head. 'There's probably some saying about taking your own advice. I just can't think of it right now.'

Chapter 29

Nathalie

I looked at the small capsule in the palm of my hand. The cyanide pill Marcel had given me. I knew today I was going to put it to use.

I slipped it back into the pocket of my apron, pushing it into the corner where it would be safe.

'What are you doing standing around?' It was Bochette. How that woman seemed to appear from nowhere amazed me. I was at one of the laundry cupboards that was tucked away around the corner from the laundry presses.

'I was just getting a tablecloth,' I said, taking one from the cupboard. 'Madame Chanel is dining in her suite this evening and needs a fresh one.'

Bochette's eyes narrowed and she nudged me out of the way with her hefty shoulder before peering into the cupboard. She lifted several of the tablecloths and when she wasn't able to find anything, she dropped the linen back into place and closed the door. She turned towards me. I took a step away, my back now up against the wall. She moved closer, so she was only inches away from my face. 'Remember, I'm watching you. Hauptmann Kranz has asked me to pay special attention to you.'

Her face was so close to mine I wanted to vomit at the nearness. She grabbed my face, squeezing it between her thumb and fingers. 'You may think you're clever, and have Tache to protect you, but one word from me and he can be removed.' Her grip tightened, causing the flesh of my cheeks to dig into my teeth. 'You'll do well to remember that. Now, get back to your duties.' She released her grip but didn't move.

I could feel the burn of tears in my eyes, but I was damned if I was going to cry in front of her. I felt dirty at her touch and nearness. I rushed from the laundry room, ignoring the concerned look from Marie, who was pressing sheets.

Bochette was a despicable woman and if I ever had a chance to pay her back, I would.

The incident in the laundry room just made me more determined to carry out my plan.

It was late afternoon, and I was setting up the dining table for Chanel and Kranz. Neither of them was in the apartment and I was glad as I didn't want my nerves to get the better of me.

I had just put the finishing touches to the table when Chanel and Kranz returned. Chanel had asked me to wait for dinner to be brought to the room, which was unusual, but I couldn't help thinking that it only served to help me execute my plan more easily.

'Good afternoon, Nathalie,' said Kranz with such ease, it was as if nothing had happened and I hadn't been arrested. 'I'm glad I've seen you. I wanted to check on your well-being. Madame Bochette told me that she spoke to you today.'

'Yes,' I replied, not meeting his or Chanel's gaze.

'Was everything all right?' he asked.

'It was a brief conversation,' I replied. 'She said something about being able to talk to her.' I made a point of hesitating and looking uncertain.

'What is it?' asked Kranz.

I glanced at Chanel as if asking for approval, and she nodded her consent. 'Speak up, Nathalie,' she encouraged.

I wrung my hands together. 'I don't like speaking out of turn but . . .' Again, I made a point of hesitating.

'But what?' I had Kranz's full attention.

'She said I could trust her, that she had connections.'

'What sort of connections?' came Kranz's clipped question.

'She didn't say exactly, but said she knew people who could help fight against what was happening.'

Kranz looked startled. 'The Resistance?'

I shrugged. 'I'm not sure what she meant.'

'Oh, I don't think Bochette is involved in the Resistance,' said Chanel, seemingly uninterested as she lit a cigarette. 'You know how much she adores you, Erich. It's really quite charming.' She gave a laugh.

'It's not a laughing matter,' said Kranz. His brow furrowed as he considered my revelation.

'Thank you. I shall make a point of speaking to Bochette.' He turned to Chanel. 'Now, if you will excuse me, I will return shortly for supper.'

After Kranz had left, Chanel looked at me. 'I understand you don't like the woman, but it's best not to make an enemy out of her. I don't expect she'll take too kindly to being questioned by Kranz.'

'*Oui, madame,*' I said, rather sheepishly, feeling embarrassed at being caught out.

'Now, I'm going to bathe. Is my bath run?'

'*Oui*. It's ready now.'

'*Bon*. And my clothes?'

'I'll do that now, madame.'

As I picked out the clothes Chanel had already instructed me to have ready, I couldn't help wishing I was a fly on the wall when Kranz spoke to Bochette. Casting some doubt over her was the only act of revenge I could exact.

Of course, it could all be academic within a few hours.

Kranz was back at suite 304 by 5.45 p.m. and Chanel was just putting the finishing touches to her appearance. I fastened her necklace for her. She looked beautiful in the long, figure-hugging silk gown. It reminded me of the dress I had cut up in my father's workroom just a couple of months ago and how I had repurposed it for the women and children in the neighbourhood.

Chanel gave herself the once-over in her full-length mirror and sprayed some perfume on her neck. Then she wafted out of the room, leaving a trail of the scent in her wake. I hurried after her, knowing the evening meal would soon be on its way up to the suite. I needed to intercept it.

'Where are you going?' asked Chanel as I headed towards the main door.

'To wait for your food.'

'Can you pour some drinks first?' She gave me a pointed look and I could feel her eyes track me across the room as I went to the drinks cabinet.

'I spoke to Bochette,' said Kranz, as I handed him the drink. 'I think there has been some confusion somewhere. However, I have warned her that I am keeping a close eye on her.'

I didn't know what to say, so just gave a small nod of acknowledgement.

'I've never liked the woman much myself,' said Chanel. 'I don't trust her, but then we don't know who we can trust these days, do we?'

Again, I avoided any eye contact. The atmosphere in the room was charged with unspoken words and subtle meanings.

'No, you can't even trust those who are blood-related, can you, Nathalie?' said Kranz.

'What do you mean?' asked Chanel.

'Nathalie's brother. He was a traitor to the French government. Silly boy. Joined the Resistance but just wasn't clever enough to outsmart me,' said Kranz, with obvious pleasure in his voice. 'Nathalie and I were talking about that. How he was a traitor. He was a coward, too. As soon as any pressure was put on him, he betrayed all those around him. And he cried like a baby. Pissed his pants.'

'Erich!' scolded Chanel.

I couldn't stop myself physically jolting at Kranz's remark, causing me to slosh the drink I was pouring over the tray.

'Nathalie!' It was Chanel again. 'Be careful what you are doing!'

'Sorry, madame. Very sorry.'

'Kranz, stop talking about her brother. Can't you see it's upsetting her?'

'Maybe blood really is thicker than water,' mused Kranz, obviously pleased with the effect his words had on me.

A knock at the door brought the conversation to a halt. It was the waiter with their evening meal. He pushed the trolley into the lobby.

I breathed in the smell of roast lamb and wondered where on earth they had managed to get such a treat from when the rest of the city was surviving on a diet of vegetables.

'Thank you, Charles,' I said to the waiter. 'I'll take it from here.'

'But . . .' began Charles. It was customary for the waiters to take the food into the dining room, and my instructions were out of the ordinary.

'She's in there with her lover,' I whispered to him and widened my eyes.

Charles replied in kind, his eyes even wider than mine. '*D'accord.*'

'I'm to take it in when she calls me,' I said, to shore up my story. 'You can go now. Thank you.'

As soon as Charles had left the room, I quickly lifted the lid off the plate on the right-hand side. I could hear Chanel laughing with Kranz, while the soft tones of music filled the air. This was going to be my only chance.

I dug my hand into my apron and pulled out the oval-shaped cyanide capsule. It was made of glass surrounded with rubber to protect it from accidental breakage. I didn't want to risk crunching it between my teeth, so I picked up the two dessert spoons and placed the ampoule between them. After a little pressure, the capsule broke and I quickly sprinkled the white powder over the food, mixing it into the gravy that covered the meal. My hand was shaking furiously and even my knees felt jelly-like. There was no going back now.

Just as I was removing the remains of the capsule from between the spoons to slip into my pocket, to my shock, Chanel appeared in the hallway.

I looked up at her. Our eyes locked. I felt the heat of guilt surge up my neck, inflaming it a bright red.

'What are you doing?' asked Chanel, her eyes flicking to the trolley, my hands and then back to my face.

'I . . . I was just getting your food ready to bring in,' I stammered. I held on to the handle of the trolley to steady myself as the space around me seemed to move.

Chanel rushed forwards. 'You stupid girl,' she hissed.

She grabbed the plate and threw it to the floor. The crockery shattered on the tiles, sending food splattering up my legs, across the floor and up the wall.

I let out a scream. At least I think it was me.

'Nathalie!' cried Chanel. 'You clumsy girl! Look at the mess.'

The next thing I knew, Kranz appeared in the lobby. 'Whatever is happening?' He surveyed the carnage before him. 'Is that my dinner?'

'I'm sorry,' I said through a sob that had somehow escaped my throat.

'Get this cleaned up immediately,' ordered Chanel.

'And get some more food ordered,' added Kranz.

'No. We will dine out instead,' said Chanel. 'I don't want to wait.' She turned to me. 'Get my coat.'

'Of course, madame,' I said, scurrying through to the bedroom and returning immediately with her fur coat.

Kranz snatched it from me and held it out for Chanel to slip her arms into. 'Make sure you clean this up properly,' he snapped. Then he stopped and stared at the floor. 'What's that there?'

To my horror, he was looking at the broken pill capsule. I must have dropped it when Chanel caught me. Before I could think of a reply, Chanel spoke.

'Oh, that was mine. My doctor gave it to me earlier. I had a headache. Thought I was getting a migraine. I'd just come to fetch it from my bag.' She gestured to her handbag on the hall table.

'You never said anything,' Kranz said. I couldn't tell if he believed Chanel or not, but at that moment I wanted to hug her and thank her for her quick thinking. I don't know why she covered for me, but she did.

'I didn't want to worry you,' said Chanel. 'Now, come on, let's go. Clean this up and then go home, Nathalie. I will speak to you in the morning.'

'*Oui, madame.*'

As they left the apartment, I leaned back against the closed door and slid to the floor. The tears came. Tears of relief. Tears of guilt. Tears of regret.

'I'm sorry, Edgar,' I whispered, burying my head in my hands. 'I'm so sorry.'

Chapter 30

Nathalie

'Have you heard from Aunt Clarice?' I asked Maman, trying to sound casual as we sat at the breakfast table the following morning.

'Not this week,' replied Maman. 'The post isn't very reliable. Why do you ask?'

I couldn't tell her I was worried about Rachelle and Odile. I didn't want to alarm her or my aunt; neither did I want to confess to being dragged off and questioned recently. It was a worry my parents could do without.

'I was just wondering,' I said, breaking a piece of stale bread from yesterday's baguette. 'I miss them, that's all.'

'Maybe you would like to go back and stay with them again,' suggested Maman. 'It is safer in Brittany.'

I nodded. 'I'll think about it.'

'It's not possible,' interjected Papa. 'It would be a burden to Philippe and Clarice. An extra mouth to feed. At least here, Nathalie is with us and earning some money.'

'What good is money when there is nothing to buy?' replied Maman dejectedly. 'It is becoming a daily challenge to find food in the city. And even with ration books, after queuing for hours, there is often nothing left. I never thought the day would come when the people of Paris were starving. And those German pigs . . .' she made a faux spit to the ground '. . . they dine out every evening. They never go short of food.'

'Therese, don't upset yourself now,' said Papa, patting my mother's hand. 'It won't always be like this.'

'How can you say that?' cried Maman.

'Because it can't always be like this. That's why,' I said, holding Maman's other hand. 'Something will happen. Something will change.'

'But it will never be the same, not without Edgar.' Maman gave a sob and hurried from the room.

I exchanged a look with Papa and I could see my pain, despair, and hope mirrored in his eyes.

I left for work a little earlier than usual. The previous evening on my way home I had left a chalk mark on the wall to let Marcel know I needed to speak to him.

As I walked by the end of the wall, I noticed another chalk mark below mine and my heart leapt with excitement. It was an indication that Marcel knew of my sign and wanted to meet me.

I went via the river path, walking as fast as I dared without drawing attention to myself. It was dark under the bridge, but as I passed beneath the archway, I could see Marcel standing there.

He looked tired, and he had dark circles under his eyes and stubble on his chin.

I threw myself into his arms and ignored the scratchy whiskers as he kissed me.

I heard him draw in a deep breath. 'Ah, Nathalie. I've missed you,' he said. 'It feels so good to hold you.'

It startled me to hear him speak like that. It wasn't Marcel's usual confident way. 'What's wrong?' I asked, taking a step back so I could study him properly.

'I've been up all night. I'm just tired.'

'Up all night?'

'Working.'

I realised what he meant. 'Are you safe?' I asked.

'Yes. Don't worry about me. Now what is it you needed

to see me about? Or could you just not bear to be apart from me for another day?'

We both knew that the joke he was trying to make fell a little flat. I held his hands. 'I did something last night, and it went wrong,' I began.

'Nathalie, what did you do?'

'Please don't be cross.'

'I can never be cross with you, but I need to know what happened.'

I gave Marcel an abridged version of events, including the run-in with Bochette and how I'd set her up to be spoken to by Kranz.

Marcel let out an exasperated sigh. 'Oh, Nathalie. What am I going to do with you?' He pulled me to his chest, wrapping his arms around me.

'I'm frightened,' I confessed.

'I won't let anything happen to you,' said Marcel. 'If it's the last thing I do on this earth, it will be to keep you safe, but you have to help yourself along the way and that doesn't mean doing your own thing. You were put in the hotel to spy on the Germans, not draw attention to yourself and certainly not to kill one of their officers.'

His criticism stung me, but I knew deep down that what I had done was reckless and I hadn't kept the low profile that he and Tache had told me to keep.

'I'm sorry,' I said, 'but I saw an opportunity.'

'You can't go around doing things like that. Acting on impulse, it will get you killed and could jeopardise the safety of others. This war isn't about settling individual personal scores,' he said. 'It's about the greater good.'

'I know. From now on, I will be careful. I promise.' I hugged him tightly. 'I have to go. If I'm late, I'll be in even more trouble. I don't want to give Bochette the opportunity to tell me off about it.'

'We need to change our meeting place,' he said. 'Meet me at Vallée Suisse in the Jardins des Champs-Élysées.

Same time tomorrow morning.'

I kissed Marcel goodbye and hurried on through the tunnel and out the other side to work. I knew it was a risk meeting with Marcel but it was one we were both willing to take to see each other. We just had to be careful; that was all.

Arriving at the hotel, I went straight up to Chanel's room. I was half expecting Kranz to be in there but Chanel was alone. She was sitting on the sofa in her satin dressing gown, smoking a cigarette.

'I got rid of Kranz early,' she said. 'I need to talk to you.' She rose from the sofa and we faced each other across the living-room rug. 'Actually, it's more to warn you.'

I gulped. 'Warn me?'

'Kranz is suspicious of you. He doesn't trust you. He told me that last night. Now, I don't want you to tell me what you were doing with the food last night because then I will have to tell Kranz. I like you, Nathalie, but you're not cut out for whatever it is you're attempting to do. If it's some foolish notion of revenge for your brother's death, then you must stop, as it will not end well for you. Of that I am certain.'

I felt light-headed, and I was sure the colour drained from my face. I reached out for the side of the armchair as I felt the floor move beneath me.

'Sorry,' I said, trying to stand up straight again.

'Take this as a warning,' continued Chanel.

'I will. Thank you, madame.'

I carried out my duties for the rest of the morning and managed to avoid crossing paths with Bochette. I was glad when lunchtime came and I could feel myself relax a little as I chatted across the table with the other maids who were also taking their break.

I had only been sitting there for about five minutes when, to my surprise, in walked Alphonse. The look on his face sent a shiver down my spine.

I got to my feet. 'Alphonse, what are you doing here?'

He removed his hat and nodded at the other girls before addressing me. 'I need to talk to you.'

This wasn't a lovers' tête-à-tête. I could tell that from the serious look on his face and the austere tone in his voice.

'Of course,' I said, sliding out of my seat and following Alphonse out of the building into the rear courtyard. 'What's the matter?' I asked, standing in front of him. A sudden thought that Alphonse was here to give me some sort of bad news about Maman and Papa hurtled to the fore. I gripped his arm. 'Has something happened to my parents?'

Alphonse shook his arm free. 'No. Nothing. They are fine.'

I took a step back as I studied the man in front of me. His face was hard, his jaw tight, but his eyes were a mix of anger and sadness. 'Alphonse, what is it? Tell me.'

'I saw you,' he stated.

'You saw me?' A whole host of possibilities ran through my mind, but it could only settle on one that would evoke this sort of reaction in Alphonse.

'This morning. Under the bridge.' His eyes bored into mine. 'With a man.'

I looked down at the ground, not only with shame but also to bide my time for a few moments as I gathered my thoughts. He said a man. He didn't say Marcel Reynard.

'The man. He was a friend of Edgar's. That's all,' I said, wondering just how much Alphonse had seen.

'A friend of Edgar's? He looked much older than your brother.'

'Look, Alphonse, it's hard at home sometimes, especially when Maman is so upset about Edgar. I miss my brother terribly and needed some time to myself. It was pure coincidence that I just happened to bump into Edgar's friend. Anyway, why didn't you make yourself known, instead of spying on me?'

'I wasn't spying,' protested Edgar. 'I was on the other side of the river. I saw you walk under the bridge.'

'You have good eyesight.'

'Not good enough. I didn't recognise the man.'

'You couldn't possibly have seen him.'

'No, but I saw you walk out a few minutes later and then shortly after, the man emerged. I could tell he knew you. You looked back, and the man hesitated.'

'So you were just guessing?' I was annoyed with myself for being caught out so easily. I could have denied it. However, I was past that point. 'Like I said, we spoke briefly and then I carried on to work.'

'What did he say?'

'He asked me how Edgar was. He didn't know what had happened to him. I wish I hadn't met him, as it just made me feel worse.'

Alphonse looked at me, indecision etched over his face. 'I don't know.'

'Don't know what?' I demanded, sounding as indignant as possible.

'I don't know whether you are telling me the truth.'

'Why would I lie to you? I'm actually quite offended by the accusation.' I looked at my watch. 'I have to go back to work.'

'Wait.' Alphonse caught me by the arm.

I looked down, and he had the decency to look embarrassed and remove his hand. 'I want to believe you,' he said.

'Why can't you?'

He gave an awkward shrug. 'Kranz doesn't believe your story about supporting the new government.'

I raised my eyebrows. 'So, you let yourself be guided by Kranz now, do you? When you're the one who knows me, not him?'

'You're not denying it.'

'Oh, can we please stop this?' I implored. 'We are going around in circles. You either believe me or you don't. And if you don't, then we definitely don't have a relationship.'

That took the look off his face. 'You mean that?'

'Of course I do.' I was far too aware of the double standards. I was asking Alphonse to believe me when I was, in fact, the liar. I was in love with another man and giving Alphonse false hope.

'There's something you're not telling me,' pressed Alphonse. There was a slight note of menace to his voice. 'I don't know what it is, but please, Nathalie, don't keep things from me.'

'I have to go.'

'What was his name? The man you met. Edgar's friend.'

'I really need to go back to work.'

'I don't believe you.' Alphonse's voice stopped me in my tracks. 'I don't believe you,' he repeated, this time quieter, which was somehow more unnerving than him shouting at me in anger.

I turned around to face him. There were tears in his eyes. I took a step closer. I went to speak but stopped. What could I say? I could only protest my false innocence and lie even more. 'I'm sorry,' I said, swallowing down a ball of guilt as my own tears gathered in my eyes.

'It was him, wasn't it? It was Reynard – the one Kranz is looking for.'

'How do you know?'

'It's obvious. It can't be anyone else. I wish you hadn't gone to Brittany.' He drew in a long slow breath, held it for a second, before releasing it. 'Are you in love with him?'

'Please don't ask me,' I said so quietly I wasn't even sure if I'd said it out loud.

'*Merde*. Why can't you deny it? Why can't you argue and persuade me I am wrong?'

'I'm so sorry, Alphonse.'

He nodded, and we both knew we had come to an impasse. 'Me too.'

'How long have I got?' I asked, the tears freely falling now.

'Twenty-four hours at the most.'

It was my turn to nod. 'Thank you, Alphonse. Goodbye.'

'Goodbye, Nathalie.'

I didn't look back as I went inside and I was sure Alphonse didn't either. The sound of his unfaltering footsteps striding across the rear courtyard echoed around the buildings.

The vultures were circling, closing in on me, coming from all sides. I didn't know who would strike first. Alphonse had given me twenty-four hours' head start, and I needed to make every hour, every minute, every second count.

Chapter 31

Darcie

Before they had even set off for Paris, Matt had already made some phone calls to his mother and to Myles Hoffer, assuring Darcie that he was certain at least one of them would come good.

'I don't like leaving, thinking Odile has been pressured in some way,' confessed Darcie as Matt drove through the Breton countryside, heading for Paris on the N24.

'It's despicable,' said Matt. 'It wouldn't make for a good story if it ever got out.' He gave her a sideways look. 'You could use it as leverage when you go back to Padgett.'

'I was thinking the same,' admitted Darcie. 'I'm not going to let him off the hook so easily, and I'm certainly not going to negotiate with him on the sketchbook and dress. It's a matter of principle now.'

She took out her phone and fired off an email to Padgett asking if she could meet with him as soon as possible.

'He'll think you're ready to cave,' said Matt. 'I'd love to be a fly on the wall when you tell him no.'

'Why don't you come with me?' suggested Darcie. 'Safety in numbers and all that. Not that I'm frightened of him.'

Matt gave a grin. 'I'd love to be there.'

By the time they had arrived back in Paris, nearly five hours later, Darcie had received a reply from Padgett.

'He wants to meet tomorrow at eleven-thirty,' said Darcie, scanning the email.

'He's keen.'

'Can you make it?'

'Sure. I've a few days free between jobs, so not a problem.'

'Thanks.'

'Hey, listen, do you want to stay over at mine tonight? No pressure, though.'

'I'd love to stay over,' said Darcie without hesitation.

'Phew. I was hoping you'd say that.'

Darcie sat back in the seat, a feeling of contentment settling over her where Matt was concerned. It was something she didn't think she'd felt before. It was good and although she knew she shouldn't get used to it, she gave herself permission to enjoy the moment.

The morning came all too quickly and Darcie had no desire to get out of bed. Neither did Matt as it happened, but eventually his mobile rapid-firing text message alerts forced him up from the comfort of the duvet.

'It's from Mom,' he said, looking at the screen.

Darcie propped herself up on one elbow. 'She's got news already?' She looked over at the bedside clock. 'It's only eight-twenty.'

'Did I not mention that my mom is a workaholic?' said Matt, sitting on the edge of the bed.

Darcie pulled on her clothes from the day before and sat down next to him. 'What's she say?'

'As we thought, it was Padgett's lawyers who went to see Odile yesterday.'

'How does your mum know all this?'

'She knows someone who knows someone who knows Padgett's secretary. Or something like that.' Matt kissed Darcie on the cheek. 'It's a small world. My mom's been in and around the fashion industry for a long time. She's like a walking Rolodex of who's who and who works for who. She makes it her business to know everyone's business.'

'Wow. She sounds more like a secret agent.'

Matt laughed. 'She wants to know when she can meet you.'

Darcie was sure she had turned white at the thought. 'What?'

'Mom figures I must be serious about you if I'm asking for help.'

Darcie wasn't sure how to respond to that. A flutter of excitement pitched up in her stomach. She liked the idea that he might be serious about her. She realised that Matt was looking at her. 'Oh, right, well whatever she figures, thank her for me.'

Matt smiled at her. 'I'll make coffee.'

'I should go, really,' said Darcie, suddenly feeling flustered. It wouldn't do to get too attached to Matt. She'd be back in England in a week and the last thing she needed to be taking back home with her was a broken heart. 'I need to get some fresh clothes.'

'Just give me a half-hour and I'll come with you. Then we can go to the meeting together,' said Matt. 'That's if you still want me to?'

'Yeah. OK.'

'You sure? You're not sounding that OK.'

'Sorry. No. I'm fine. And yes, I'm sure.' She forced a smile. She needed to keep on top of her emotions. Head over heart. That's all she had to remember.

When they arrived at Padgett's office, they were shown through to a boardroom by a secretary.

The room was situated on the corner of the building and overlooked the Paris streets below. A pitcher of water was on the table, together with two glasses. The secretary added a third glass from a cabinet in the room, placing it on the silver tray alongside the others.

'Monsieur Padgett will be along shortly,' she said in excellent English before leaving the room, the sound of her heels cushioned by the deep-pile carpet.

'Hey, why don't you sit down?' said Matt, coming over to Darcie. He rubbed the top of her arm.

'I'm suddenly really nervous,' she confessed.

'You have nothing to be nervous about.'

'I just don't know how we're ever going to get to the bottom of this if basically Padgett is denying the story and Odile isn't talking.'

Before Matt had a chance to offer any answer, the door opened and Padgett appeared in the room, together with two other men in suits, all of them carrying matching leather-bound document wallets.

'*Bonjour,* Darcie.' Christophe Padgett beamed, clearly thinking Darcie had decided to take the payment and this meeting was a mere formality.

'*Bonjour,* Christophe,' replied Darcie. She looked pointedly at the two other men as she lowered herself into a seat on the opposite side of the table to where Padgett was standing.

'These are my lawyers,' explained Padgett. It was his turn to direct an enquiring look to Matt.

'Matthew Langdon. He's a friend of mine,' said Darcie.

With an exchange of nods, all four men sat down on their respective sides of the table.

'So, Darcie, I assume you've come to a decision about the dress and sketchbook,' began Padgett. 'I was pleased to hear from you yesterday.'

One of the lawyers coughed. 'Before we go any further with the conversation, can I just confirm that you're here to accept the offer made by Monsieur Padgett in an email sent out to you as per this copy?' The lawyer whipped out a printed copy of the email from Padgett offering ten thousand euros.

Darcie looked at the email, the sum of money standing out amid the text. She was about to turn down ten thousand euros. She looked at Matt from the corner of her eye. His expression the epitome of poker face. A small surge of excited anticipation swelled inside her and she looked up at the three Frenchmen opposite her.

She smiled. Padgett returned a patronising smile, while the lawyers both appeared to physically relax.

'Gentlemen,' she began. 'This email has given me much to think about. I was amazed at the generous amount offered.' She waited as Padgett nodded and settled back into his chair. She felt Matt nudge her foot with his, but she ignored his unspoken gesture to get on with it – she was enjoying herself far too much. 'But I expect ten thousand euros is really small change for someone like Monsieur Padgett.'

The lawyer who had spoken let out a sigh. 'I wondered when we'd get to this.' He flicked another page over. 'We can get straight to the point.'

Padgett gave a nod to the lawyer, who continued. 'So, we can extend our offer, without prejudice, as a gesture of goodwill to a maximum amount of twenty thousand euros.'

'Wow. That is generous,' replied Darcie. 'But what I was getting to was that . . . I don't want your money.'

Padgett sat forward. 'What do you mean?'

Matt repeated what Darcie said in French. 'Just for clarity,' he added.

'I know what she said!' retorted Padgett, clearly ruffled by the exchange.

The second lawyer spoke. 'What is it you do want?'

'I want the truth,' said Darcie.

'You have the truth,' said Padgett.

'I don't think I do.' Darcie shifted in her seat. 'I believe you're withholding the truth. You're frightened I'm going to make some discovery, of what I don't yet know. What I do know is you silenced an elderly lady in her nineties.'

'What foundation do you base that allegation on?' asked the second lawyer. 'There is a law against slander.'

Darcie felt Matt's hand on her arm. 'Darce,' he said softly. 'Careful now.'

She wanted to shrug off his hand. She wanted to jump to her feet and tell Padgett just what she thought of him and how intimidating an old woman was morally out of order. Unethical. But she did none of that. 'If you have nothing to hide, then you won't care if I take my story to the papers,' she said.

'No one will be interested. You need proof. There's no truth without proof,' sighed Padgett as if bored of the conversation now. 'Why don't you just take the money, give us the book and dress and we can all get on with our lives and you'll be twenty thousand euros better off. I'm sure that will go a long way to making your mother's life more comfortable.'

Darcie gasped. How did they know about Lena? 'You leave my mother out of this!'

Padgett looked at Matt. 'You seem a reasonable young man. Why don't you speak to Mademoiselle Marchant? The offer is still open until close of business tonight.'

Darcie got to her feet. 'Over my dead body.' She stormed from the room and out through reception. It wasn't until she was racing down the staircase that Matt caught up with her.

'Jesus, Darcie, when did you turn into Flo-Jo?!'

She couldn't help but smile at his joke. 'I'm sorry, but he just got under my skin. I should have kept my head.'

'I'm sorry he brought your mother into it,' said Matt, taking her hand so they were now descending the stairs at a safe walking pace.

'It's scary that he did,' admitted Darcie. 'I mean, he must have looked into my background, my personal life. I don't like it one bit.'

'We can just walk away from this now,' said Matt. 'Or take the deal.'

'I'm not doing either.' They were now out in the main reception area. Silently, they walked across the marbled floor and out onto the street. 'What all that means is that they have something to hide.'

'They're powerful men,' warned Matt.

Darcie shrugged. 'The truth is more powerful.'

'Sure, but we need to find a way to get to the truth,' said Matt. 'Come on, let's grab a drink and something to eat. We can work out what we do next.'

'Don't try to talk me out of this,' said Darcie.

'I wouldn't dream of it.'

They stopped at a café a little further down the road, and Matt convinced Darcie to have some crêpes at the very least, even though her appetite had left her.

'I'm sorry,' she said as they finished their coffee. 'I'm not very good company.'

'Hey, no worries. You look tired. Why don't you get some rest this afternoon?'

Darcie gave a sigh. 'I think I might have to. Do you want to come back to mine? Just to chill.'

Matt gave a smile. 'Sure. I'd like that. I can sort through some photos on my laptop and then maybe we can go out for dinner tonight or, failing that, I can cook.'

'You can cook?'

Matt frowned, but then the corners of his mouth curled up. 'I'd sooner that was a statement, not a question.'

Darcie laughed. 'It's both. But I'm very happy for you to dispel any questions I might have.'

'It's a deal.'

They made their way back via the Métro to the Montmartre area and took the short walk from the station to rue Ordener and Darcie's apartment.

'You don't like the elevator?' asked Matt, as he moved over to one side of the staircase to allow two men, who were on their way down, to pass.

'I'm trying to walk off those crêpes I had for lunch,' said Darcie. 'At this rate, I'll be charged for excess baggage at the airport.'

Going home was a sobering thought and she wished she hadn't mentioned it as the mood immediately shifted between them.

She stopped outside her room. 'Sorry. I seem to be surpassing my own expectations of not being good company.'

Matt pulled her into his chest, wrapping his arms around her. He looked down and gave a small kiss on her mouth. 'You don't have to apologise. You just need some sleep. I'm glad you feel you don't have to put on an act for me,' he said. 'Now, how about you let me look after you?' He put his finger to her lip to quell any protest.

She relaxed into him. Maybe she could switch off and let someone else take up the slack for a change. And who better to look after her than Matt?

'Come on, then. I need tucking up with a hot chocolate,' she said.

She opened the door and as she walked into the apartment, she let out a gasp.

The whole room had been turned upside down. It had been ransacked. Cushions pulled off the sofa and chair, the foot stool turned over, books pulled from the bookshelf, cupboard doors open and a couple of smashed mugs on the floor.

The high-sleeper bed above the sofa had fared no better and she was distraught to see her personal effects scattered across the duvet.

'Shit,' muttered Matt.

She turned to look at him. 'I hope you're good at hugging,' she said, before bursting into tears.

Once again, she was in Matt's arms and he stroked her head and her back, murmuring soothing words into her hair. 'It's OK, Darce,' he said. 'Shhh. It's OK.'

She pulled away and looked around at the mess. It was true what people said when they had been burgled – that they felt violated. Every item of hers was now contaminated by an unknown person's touch. 'I'll have to wash everything before I can wear it,' she said. Even her underwear had been unceremoniously strewn across the floor. Good job she and Matt were past the point of wondering what sort of pants each other wore.

'You'd better check nothing has been taken,' said Matt. 'I'll phone the police.' He went to take out his phone and then stopped in mid action. 'Darcie?'

She looked up at him. 'Yeah?'

'Where are the dress and sketchbook?'

Chapter 32

Nathalie

After Alphonse's ultimatum, I went back inside the hotel, wiping my eyes, ignoring the questioning look from one of the other maids. Bochette was sitting at the table and I had no desire to spend any time with her, so left, going straight back to work.

Chanel had already informed me she wouldn't be at the hotel for dinner and was leaving mid-afternoon, so when I went to her suite at 5 p.m., I knew it would be empty.

I tidied and cleaned the rooms as I normally would, ending with turning the bedcovers back, ensuring her nightwear was laid out for her, and that all the lotions and potions she liked to use were arranged in readiness for her return.

Once that was done, I crossed the room to the bedside cabinet. Surprised that my hand wasn't shaking and I wasn't feeling any nerves whatsoever, I opened the top drawer and felt to the back. My fingertips made contact with the hard metal and, after pulling it into the palm of my hand, I withdrew the small pistol that Kranz had pointed at me.

Remembering how Marcel had taught me, I checked the barrel to make sure it was loaded and, satisfied it was, I slipped it into my pocket.

On my way down to the laundry room, I went via the floor where Kranz's room was, hoping to bump into Collette who usually cleaned his room.

'Nathalie,' she said warmly, but also with a degree of surprise, 'what are you doing here?'

'I'm on my way down to the laundry room. I'm staying out of Bochette's way,' I said. 'I've just finished Chanel's suite. She asked me to make sure there was wine in her room. I suppose that means Kranz will be back there tonight.'

Of course, we weren't supposed to gossip about our guests, but we did, all the same.

'He's there so much. I hardly have to do anything to his room these days,' said Collette.

'It's a wonder he hasn't moved in with Chanel,' I said, giving an eye-roll.

'Well, he won't be there all night tonight,' said Collette, unwittingly giving me the confirmation I needed. 'He's got an early start and has requested his uniform be set out ready for him. He's ordered breakfast in his room at six forty-five sharp, which means I'll have to come in early.'

'Oh, that's annoying.'

'Yes, especially as I'll have to leave my little sister on her own an extra half an hour before my neighbour will have her. I hate asking her. She's quite elderly and Cissy doesn't enjoy going at the best of times.'

'Look, why don't I come in early for you?' I suggested, trying to keep the excitement from my voice. This was a golden opportunity that I hadn't expected. 'I don't mind. I could bring his breakfast up.'

'Oh, I couldn't ask you to do that.'

'You're not asking. I'm offering. All you have to do is say yes.'

'Are you sure?'

'Perfectly.'

'Thank you so much.' Collette gave me an impromptu hug. 'That's so kind.'

I left Collette to finish her chores and congratulated myself on how much easier I was making this. Step two of my plan was in place.

Lost in my own thoughts and what I needed to do next, I let my guard down, and it wasn't until I'd been into the laundry room to dump the towels and sheets and then walked into the staffroom to get my jacket, that I realised that the room was empty.

Empty except for Bochette, that was.

It was the sound of the lock turning that made me spin around. She was standing there with the key to the corridor held between her chubby fingers. She shoved her hands and the key into the pocket of her apron.

'Here's the little Resistance whore.' She spat on the floor in my direction. 'Been telling tales about anyone else? Been getting anyone else questioned?' I hadn't noticed earlier, but standing in front of her, I could see a bruise around her eye and a slight swelling of the eyebrow.

'No more than you have,' I retorted, determined not to let her intimidate me. The knowledge of what I planned to do in the next twelve hours gave me a courage I hadn't felt before. 'You're the one who's as good as sleeping with the enemies of France. Or at least wish you were.'

Rage filled her face and I realised I may have overstepped the mark. 'You'll regret saying that.'

'I doubt it.' I reached for my coat but made sure I kept my gaze trained on her.

'You need to be taught a lesson. You need to be taught how to comply. I'm your superior and you need to be punished for speaking to me like that. Opening your legs for the Resistance. Maybe you should open them for your superiors.'

'I'm not sure Monsieur Tache will be pleased to hear about this,' I said. 'You could end up losing your job.'

Bochette let out a laugh. 'Oh, I don't think Tache will be bothering me anymore. At this very moment, he is being arrested and taken for questioning by the Gestapo.'

'What?' My thoughts raced to keep up with this new information. Had Tache really been arrested? Or was Bochette just saying it? Would Tache give up my name to the Gestapo? It was only a matter of time before a person cracked under interrogation.

'So, you little bitch, there's no one here to save you now, is there? No Monsieur Tache.' She pulled a mock sad face. 'So we can have a bit of fun. Well, at least I will.'

'You leave me alone,' I said with as much force as I could muster.

'Don't be like that,' said Bochette. Her face cracked into a greedy smile, showing her yellowing teeth and the gap at the side where two were missing. She took a step nearer, taking her hands from her pockets. It was then I saw a glint of metal reflecting the amber glow of the overhead light bulb. She had a knife in her hand.

I thought about screaming or shouting, but down here in the staff quarters, no one would hear me. The kitchen was too far away and even if anyone was in the laundry room, they wouldn't be able to hear me above the noise of the spinners and wringers that were constantly in use to cater to the needs of the guests. I ran towards the door that led out into the courtyard, grabbing the handle. But it was locked.

Bochette let out a cackle of laughter.

I spun around, my back pressed up against the door as I frantically scanned the room, looking for something to defend myself with.

I had a fleeting thought of regret that I hadn't brought the little silver pistol down with me. I had been wary about being stopped at a checkpoint and having it found in my purse. I had hidden it at the back of one of the laundry cupboards on Kranz's floor.

Bochette was taking slow, deliberate steps towards me, enjoying every moment of trapping her prey.

On my second scan of the room, I saw the poker used to stoke the open fire. I looked at Bochette. Her eyes flicked towards the fireplace and back to me. The poker was nearer to me and I lunged for it a split second before Bochette pounced.

I grabbed the poker from the hearth and somehow swerved my body away from the blade, leaving Bochette stabbing the air.

With no conscious thought, I spun around, a little unsteady on my feet, and with all my might, I slammed the iron poker down onto Bochette's arm.

She let out an almighty roar of pain but amazingly didn't drop the knife.

I staggered back. The adrenaline pumped hard through my veins as Bochette snatched up the coal shovel and advanced towards me, swinging it back and forth in front of her. I tried to smash the shovel from her hand, but she held fast. It was like some ludicrous sword fight but without the appropriate weapons.

Bochette was faster on her feet than I expected and her robust frame was an easy match for my light and petite one.

I would not get many chances at this. I backed into the table but skirted around the end to keep a safe distance between us.

'I promise you, I can keep this up all evening,' said Bochette. 'No one will come down here for hours. I've told them the door is jammed and can't be fixed until tomorrow. Everyone will leave through the kitchen.'

I had to give her credit for her foresight. It was clearly superior to mine.

'What do you think you're going to do, kill me and just leave me here?' I demanded, wondering, even if I managed to disarm her, how on earth was I going to physically fight her and get the key from her.

She rolled her eyes. 'I'm not going to kill you. That I'll leave for Kranz. He can have some fun with you, after I have, of course. By the time we're both finished with you, you'll wish you were dead anyway. Just like your snivelling brother, Edgar.'

'Shut up!' The rage ignited deep inside me, setting my insides on fire. 'Don't you dare even speak my brother's name.'

Of course she didn't stop. 'Oh, how he cried, just like a baby. In fact, he called for his mother just before the end. It was one of the last words he said. Maman. Maman,' she mocked.

I'm not sure what happened next. All I knew was I was screaming at her, running towards her, the poker raised above my shoulder. I swatted the shovel like swishing away an annoying fly.

Bochette cried out and lunged towards me with the knife. I threw my body to the side, bringing the poker up and smashing it down again on her shoulder. And again, for a third time.

It was this blow that caught the side of her head and Bochette crumpled soundlessly to the floor. The only noise was the knife clattering to the floor.

I kicked it away from her, sending it sliding under a cupboard. As it did so, I noticed a stain of red on the blade. Suddenly, a white-hot heat seared through my left side. I looked down and saw a bloom of red seeping through my blouse. I'd been stabbed. I clasped my hand over the wound.

I dropped to my knees, dizziness taking over. I swayed. How bad was it? I took a deep breath and gingerly lifted the fabric. The wound was about an inch wide and blood was pumping out.

I pulled my apron from me and bundled it up against my side, pressing it with my hand. Trying to clean my hand of the blood, I rummaged in Bochette's apron and found the key.

I knew adrenaline was keeping me going at this point. I just needed to get out of the hotel and home, where Maman would clean me up. I focused on what I had to do. Taking a deep breath, I got to my feet, wincing at the pain. I needed something better to dress the wound with. I was certain it wasn't fatal, but bad enough that I needed it attended to.

My scarf was in my coat pocket and, using the apron as a pad, I wrapped the scarf around me before putting on my coat and holding my arm to my side to keep everything in place.

I took one last look at Bochette and felt no remorse. She didn't deserve my pity.

Unlocking the door, I was out in the fresh air. Again, I took a deep breath to steady myself and walked calmly away from the hotel. Someone would find Bochette but they wouldn't know it was me who delivered the fatal blow. There were no witnesses. I just had to hold my nerve. I still had things to do before I was finished here.

Chapter 33

Nathalie

My side throbbed, and it took every ounce of effort to stop myself from doubling over from the pain that shot through me every now and then. The walk home had never felt so far. Fortunately, I didn't encounter any random checks, and it was not without much relief that I barrelled in through the door to our apartment.

It was only then I allowed myself to crumple and cry with pain.

Maman and Papa rushed out from the living room.

'I've been injured,' I managed to say, before wincing in pain once more.

They helped me to my feet and into the bathroom and, as I sat on the side of the bath, we all inspected my wound.

'What happened?' gasped Maman. 'What did you do?'

Papa was kneeling in front of me, looking at my injury. 'You've lost a lot of blood and it doesn't look like it's stopping.'

'Can you sew it up?'

'What sort of question is that? We need a doctor,' said Maman.

I looked at Papa and gave a small shake of my head. 'No doctor,' I whispered.

'This is ridiculous . . .' began Maman and then stopped mid-sentence. 'Oh, Nathalie, what have you been doing?'

'I was attacked,' I began. 'At the hotel, by the housekeeper.'

'Then it must be reported,' said Maman, still not quite understanding the situation.

'No. Don't ask me what happened, but no, it can't be reported,' I said.

Papa squeezed my hand. 'You need stitches,' he said.

'I don't know anyone better with a needle and thread,' I replied.

'Oh, you cannot . . . no . . . no,' gasped Maman.

Papa got to his feet. 'Stay calm, Therese. It needs to be done. I need you to clean the wound while I prepare everything.'

Maman hesitated, but then sprang into action. 'I have some iodine in the cupboard here.' She opened the bathroom cabinet and sifted through several bottles before producing the one she was looking for. 'Now, warm water and a sterile cloth. And you, Théodule, need to wash your hands properly. I'll boil some water. Nathalie, you need to lie down. I'll put a towel on the sofa.'

Maman went into full mother mode – the role she loved best – and soon had us organised.

Papa came and sat beside me, passing me a small glass of brandy. 'For emergencies,' he said. 'And for medicinal purposes. Drink it in one.'

I gulped the liquor down and then lay back. Maman held my hands, and I braced myself for the pain. The cleaning was bad enough, but the actual stitching was horrendous. It was all I could do to stop myself from screaming out.

Several excruciating minutes later and Papa was dressing the now sewn-up wound. 'You did well.'

I don't remember anything else as I felt myself pass out.

I awoke to the sound of hammering on the door to our apartment and Maman frantically waking me up.

'Sit up, sit up,' she said urgently, helping me to get upright. She whipped the towel out from underneath me and folded it up with lightning speed before placing it on the side with some clothing she had been ironing.

The hammering grew more insistent and I could hear someone shouting from the other side.

'Open the door! Now!'

'*J'arrive! J'arrive!*' called Papa. He glanced back down the hallway and Maman nodded at him, before she dropped a book in my lap and then sat down beside me with her knitting needles.

No sooner had Papa opened the door, than in marched two German soldiers. They came straight into the living room, their guns waving around the room, before coming to rest on us.

'Monsieur Leroux, I'm sorry for the lateness of my call.'

The voice was unmistakable. It was Kranz.

I froze. What on earth was Kranz doing here? He was supposed to be out with Chanel tonight.

'Is your daughter in?' Kranz asked.

I swallowed hard as the officer's footsteps clipped down the hallway. He came through the doorway, stopping in front of the sofa where we were sitting. His whole being occupied the room, and I felt the walls close in and the air leach away.

'Madame Leroux,' said Kranz, nodding towards my mother. And then to me. 'Mademoiselle Leroux.'

'Good evening,' I replied, my voice somehow sounding much calmer than I felt.

He rocked back on his heels for a moment, as if deciding on his words. He smiled. The smile worried me more. 'So, this evening, as you know, I was dining out with a friend. When we arrived back at the hotel, I was told of an incident concerning a member of staff. Madame Bochette.'

'Madame Bochette,' I repeated. 'What sort of incident? Is she all right?'

'She has sustained a very serious head injury. At this moment she is in the hospital being operated on. She may not survive.'

A morass of emotions swirled inside me. Relief that I hadn't killed her, but also fear that I hadn't killed her. If she was still alive, she'd tell Kranz what had happened and then I'd be arrested and I had no doubt I would be tried and found guilty of attempted murder, despite the circumstances. No one would believe it had been self-defence. 'I'm sorry to hear that,' I said at last, realising Kranz was waiting for my response.

'Are you?' he questioned.

'Of course.' I met his gaze.

'She had been attacked in the staff quarters with a poker,' said Kranz. 'It appears you might have been the last one to see her.'

I shook my head. 'I didn't see Madame Bochette this evening. I saw her when we had our break, but other than that, I haven't seen her.'

'You and Bochette have an interesting relationship,' said Kranz. 'You have both indicated to me that the other is a traitor to Germany. That the other is feeding information to the Resistance – that they are spying. It is well known that you two do not get on.'

'Madame Bochette has a vivid imagination,' I said. 'But I am not the traitor. I stand by what I said.'

Kranz's gaze toured the room. I gripped my book a little tighter to stop my hands from shaking. The tension was building in the room. He looked at the towel folded on the chair and then wandered over, picking it up by the corner.

The pale pink blood stain from where Papa had sewn me up stood out against the whiteness of the towel.

'What is this? It's fresh blood.'

'That is mine,' said Maman quickly.

'The blood?' asked Kranz.

Maman dipped her head before looking back up at the German. 'Monthly bleeding,' she said.

If the situation hadn't been so strained, I might have laughed at the look on Kranz's face as he dropped the towel back where he had found it. He returned his attention to me.

'You will need to make a statement in the morning. One of my officers will be at the hotel. Report to him.'

'Of course,' I replied.

'Goodnight, *madame, monsieur*,' he said to my parents. And then to me: 'Make sure you tell the truth. If Madame Bochette regains consciousness, she will no doubt tell me everything.'

'Of course,' I said, repeating my earlier response.

After Kranz and the soldiers had left, Maman turned to me. 'Nathalie, what are you going to do? You can't go back there tomorrow. They will arrest you.'

'I have to go back,' I said.

'You have to tell the truth,' said Papa. 'I can't see any other way around this. You should have told Kranz tonight.'

'Even if you tell the truth tomorrow, you'll be in trouble for not doing so now,' said Maman. I could hear the anxiety racking up in her voice.

'You can't go back,' said Papa. 'It will be too dangerous.'

'What is she supposed to do?' Maman got to her feet, wringing her hands together.

'I have to go in tomorrow,' I insisted. 'There's something I need to do.'

'What? What could you possibly need to do?' demanded Maman, quite frantic now.

'I can't tell you. Just trust me. I have to go back one more time.'

Maman went to say something but a small shake of the head from Papa stopped her. He gave a long sigh. 'You'd better hope that Madame Bochette doesn't recover from her injury.'

'It's not something I would wish in normal circumstances,' I said. 'I'm sorry.'

Papa came and sat down beside me, placing an arm around my shoulders and kissing the top of my head. 'I'm sorry you are in this position. I'm sorry we could not protect you from what happened. We can only hope and pray that one day soon, this war will be over. What we do now is not what we would normally do. The war brings out the best and the worst in a person and I am truly sorry you must live through this.'

Chapter 34

Nathalie

The following morning, I left for work early so I could wait for Marcel at the newly agreed meeting spot. The sun was out, but there was a chill to the air that day and I wrapped my coat around me. My side was still very sore from my injury and I had winced as I had fastened my apron that morning. Somehow, Maman had managed to get the bloodstains out and although it was still a little damp, it was wearable.

There weren't many people in the park that morning – it was no longer a place for leisurely strolls and afternoon picnics. The few people I passed were either on foot or on bicycles, hurrying their way to work or to the food queues.

I walked towards the Palais de la Découverte. The red flags with the German swastika now adorned the front of the building, waving in the early morning breeze. I wanted to rip each and every one from its mast.

Tucked away in the park's corner was the sculpture of the nineteenth-century poet Alfred de Musset. It was rather appropriate to be meeting my lover here. The expanse of white marble depicted the poet daydreaming about his former lovers. I followed the path to the right of the sculpture and took the stone steps that led down to the Vallée Suisse, as yet untouched by the Germans. There at the bottom was a pond, complete with waterfall.

No one was there, and my heart dipped. I was desperate to see Marcel. I turned at the sound of approaching footsteps, and relief flooded through me as he appeared.

'Nathalie,' he whispered, embracing me. 'I was worried. I heard there had been an attack at the Ritz.' I winced as his hand slipped to my waist. Marcel's face was full of concern. 'Are you all right?'

'Don't worry.' I cupped the side of his face with my hand. 'I am fine.'

'You don't sound fine to me. What the hell happened last night?'

'Bochette attacked me. She wanted to teach me a lesson for getting her arrested.'

'Attacked you!'

'With a knife. I fought her off with a poker.' I looked down at the ground. Much as I hated Bochette, I wasn't proud of what I had done. 'I hit her. She's in hospital with a serious head injury. I don't know if she'll regain consciousness but if she does . . .' I left the rest of the sentence unspoken.

'Bloody hell,' muttered Marcel, understanding the implications immediately. 'We've got to get you out of here.'

'I can't. Not yet.'

'What do you mean, you can't?'

'I have to go to work today. There's something I need to do.'

'No, Nathalie. I don't know what you have planned but I'm saying no.' Marcel's voice was firm. It reminded me of the first day in the forest in Brittany when I'd met him.

'Please, Marcel, let's not argue.' I held his hands in mine.

'You're going after Kranz, aren't you?' he said.

I let out a sigh. 'If I don't, then he won't stop. If I don't, he will force me to give either you or my cousins up and I can't do either of those things.'

'I should never have got you into that hotel,' said Marcel. 'God, why did I do that? I put you in danger.'

'It's irrelevant. There's no point wishing we could change things.'

'I just ask one thing,' said Marcel. 'Please, think about your brother. Would he want you to put your own life at risk?'

A little of my resilience faltered. Edgar certainly wouldn't want me to do this, but I couldn't let his death be for nothing. 'Even if I wanted to back down now, I couldn't,' I said eventually. 'It's gone too far.'

'It hasn't, though,' insisted Marcel. 'You can walk away now. I'll make sure you're safe. And your cousins.'

I shook my head. 'I have to go to work. I've agreed to work a shift for Collette. If I don't turn up, she'll be in trouble.'

'You're just making excuses,' said Marcel.

'There's something else,' I said. 'Kranz has papers in his briefcase. I've seen them before. The papers detail the movement of personnel and arms from Brittany to the rest of France and he gets an up-to-date list every week. I can get that list for you.'

Marcel gave a low whistle. 'That information would be gold.'

'I know. It will be the only chance I'll get.'

'I still don't like it. Is there nothing I can say or do to make you change your mind?'

I shook my head. 'I'm sorry. Please don't be angry with me.'

Marcel kissed the top of my head. 'I'm not angry with you. I'm just scared for you.'

'I need you to help me later, though.'

'Anything.'

'After today, I need to get out of France. I also need my cousins out of France,' I said. 'We can travel the pipeline to northern Brittany and get a boat from there. Or if it comes to it, travel south into Spain and then safe passage to England after that.'

'You've given this thought, haven't you?'

I nodded. 'Please, Marcel. Help me, because I'm going to do this anyway.'

'That sounds awfully like emotional blackmail.'

'I don't mean to make it sound like that. I'm just being honest.' I rested my head against his chest and could feel his heart beating. I closed my eyes and thought of our nights together. How I longed for those again.

'Meet me under the bridge at seven-thirty this evening,' said Marcel.

'No. Not the bridge.'

Marcel looked at me. 'Why?'

'It's been compromised,' I admitted, thinking of Alphonse. My twenty-four hours would be up by then, and once he didn't find me at work or home, he'd go to the bridge.

'You sure know how to make life complicated,' muttered Marcel, running a hand through his hair. 'Meet me here instead.'

'I need Odile and Rachelle safe as well,' I reminded him.

'Leave it with me. I'll do everything I can.'

'Thank you, my darling,' I said, rising to my tiptoes to kiss him.

'Please be careful, Nathalie. I want to see you again. To hold you. To make love to you. To grow old with you.'

I wanted to cry at his words. They filled my heart with so much joy and hope. 'So do I.'

I was at work with five minutes to spare to take Kranz's breakfast up to him. There was no sign of Tache and I hoped he was all right. The deputy manager was on duty.

'Have you heard anything about Madame Bochette?' I asked.

'No change, as far as I am aware,' he replied. 'The police are coming today to take statements, so make sure you don't go home before they speak to you.'

I didn't let on that I was well aware of that, but I planned to be long gone by then. Before going to Kranz's room, I ran up to Chanel's floor and into the sewing room. The sketchbook was now face up and when I checked the back, I could see Tache had removed the last page.

Quickly, I gathered the original dress I had made, leaving the one I had been working on for Chanel hanging on the rail. It would be my parting gift to her – a way to thank her for having faith in me as a person and as a designer even though, ultimately, I was letting her down. I stuffed both the dress and the sketchbook into a laundry bag, together with the pen and vial of invisible ink.

I hurried down the stairs to where Kranz's room was located and left the bag on the cleaning trolley. Checking no one was about, I opened the laundry cupboard and felt to the back for the pistol, before slipping it into my pocket. Steadying my breathing, I walked along to Kranz's room.

There was no answer when I knocked, so I let myself in with the master key. The room wasn't a suite like Chanel's, but it had a sitting area on one side and a double bed on the other, with a bathroom beyond that.

The bed was empty, and I could hear whistling coming from the other side of the door. His briefcase was on the desk in the corner with the catches open. I'd grab that to give to Marcel once I had done what I came to do. I scoured the room for Kranz's gun. It was there on the back of the chair, in its holster.

I moved across the room to the chair and took the gun from the holster. My fingers fumbled with the barrel and it took two attempts to open it and empty out the bullets, which I shoved into my apron pocket. I returned the gun to the holster.

The water running in the bathroom stopped and after a few moments, Kranz emerged from the bathroom, patting his face – the smell of spicy aftershave wafted around him.

He stopped in his tracks when he saw me. His eyes immediately went to the holster and although he tried to hide it, I didn't miss the slight relaxation in his shoulders when he saw his gun still in place.

'Good morning, Nathalie,' he said. 'This is a surprise. Where's Collette?'

'She couldn't get in early today, so I'm here instead.' My voice wobbled a fraction.

Kranz eyed me with caution for a moment, before tracking across the room and taking his tie from the end of his bed, looping it around his neck under his shirt collar.

'I'm glad I've seen you,' he said, adjusting the tie until he was happy with the length of each end. 'How are you getting on with finding out the information I asked for? It's been a few days now and I only have a limited amount of patience.'

I swallowed hard before I replied. 'I need to know my cousins are safe first.'

He stopped in the middle of fastening the tie. 'I'm not sure that's how it works,' he said, going back to pulling the end of the fabric through the knot at the collar. 'You give me the information. If said information turns out to be unreliable, then I'll instruct my colleagues to re-arrest your cousins.'

'Re-arrest?'

'Yes. They were released and if you provide me with the true identity of Marcel Reynard, they will not be bothered again. You have my word.' I wasn't sure Kranz's word meant very much, but I kept my thoughts to myself. 'So,' he continued, 'what have you found out? I trust that is why you're here, really.'

'I have found nothing out,' I said. 'And I have no intention of doing so.'

His eyes narrowed. 'What do you mean?'

I had come too far to turn back, even though every nerve ending in my body was screaming with fear. I took the gun from my pocket and pointed it at Kranz. The end of the barrel wavered as my hand shook, unable to keep it steady.

Kranz looked at the pistol and gave a laugh. 'I take it that's the pistol from room 304. I thought as much. Do you really think I'd leave that there with live ammunition in it for you to pick up?'

I was confused. The gun was loaded. I had checked. 'Do you think I'd aim a gun at you with no bullets?' I returned.

'Oh, it may have bullets, but they're not real. They're fake.'

I could feel the confidence slip from me. Was he telling the truth? Had he outsmarted me? 'You're lying.'

Kranz shrugged. 'Pull the trigger and we will both find out.' He turned to pick up his own holster. 'Then I'll use mine.' He gave a smug smile.

'Do you think I'd leave your gun there loaded?' I said, experiencing a small sensation of victory at my foresight.

Kranz eyed me and then the holster. Slowly, he took the gun out and inspected the barrel. 'It would seem not.' He put the gun down and clapped his hands together. 'Bravo. Bravo. You win that round.'

We stood facing each other. All I had to do now was pull the trigger. 'Turn around,' I said.

'You want me to turn so you can shoot me in the back without looking into my eyes?' said Kranz, this time sneering. 'Is that the sort of coward you are? I shouldn't have expected anything less of you. You're a coward, just like your brother.'

'Turn around!' I said, this time louder.

'You seem to forget your gun has blanks in it. Now, put it down before you make this any worse than it has to be.' He took a step closer.

'Stay back!'

'Nathalie, put the gun down.' He took another step.

Sweat was trickling down my face. I still held the gun out, one hand steadying the other as it wavered up and down, back and forth. He came closer, his words losing any meaning. All I could hear was the blood rushing through my ears. I squeezed the trigger. Nothing happened. I squeezed again, closing my eyes.

There was a loud bang.

I opened my eyes and saw Kranz standing there. The gun had indeed fired blanks. Kranz smiled and reached down to his ankle, producing another pistol, not dissimilar to the one I was holding. I had no doubt his was loaded with live ammunition.

The next thing I knew, there was a crashing noise from behind me. I spun around.

A German officer bowled through the door, a gun in his hand, aiming straight ahead. I looked back at Kranz with his pistol aimed at me.

'Put the gun down,' shouted the officer. It was then I recognised the voice. I did a double take. It was Marcel in a German officer's uniform.

'Well, who have we here?' mused Kranz, not in the least perturbed by the stand-off. 'Marcel Reynard, I presume. You know the penalty for impersonating a German officer is instant execution.'

Marcel didn't take his eyes off Kranz. 'Shut up and put the gun down.'

Kranz gave a chuckle. 'Or you'll do what? Shoot me?'

'That's exactly what I'll do.' Marcel's voice was steel-like and as I looked at Kranz, a flicker of hesitation crossed the German's face.

'Not before I've killed the girl,' said Kranz.

I watched as if time had slowed to just a fraction of its speed and Kranz's finger began to squeeze the trigger.

I heard Marcel shout my name. It sounded muffled and far away. I turned towards his voice, but my head felt heavy and my body moved slowly as my heart bumped a muted beat.

Marcel was throwing himself at me, catching me at the waist. We fell to the ground as simultaneously a shot rang out almost immediately followed by another one.

I landed on the floor with Marcel on top of me, knocking the wind from my lungs. I fought to catch my breath and then suddenly all my senses were alive and time rushed back to its normal speed.

My side burst into pain. I gasped for air and, opening

my eyes, I screamed as I saw Kranz lying on the carpet next to me. His eyes were wide open. A single bullet hole in the middle of his forehead.

Marcel turned my head away and rolled me to my other side. 'Are you all right?' he asked, his words jarring.

'I think so,' I said, mentally checking over my body.

Marcel groaned and moved to a sitting position. It was then I noticed he was cradling his left arm. 'Damn it,' he muttered.

'You've been shot!' I scrambled over to him.

'I'll live.' Marcel got to his feet. 'We need to get out of here.'

'What made you come?' I asked. 'And what's all this?' I gestured towards the uniform.

'Had to get in here somehow.'

'But you also need to get out,' a voice said from the doorway.

We both looked up and there was Alphonse. As Marcel before him, Alphonse was holding a gun in his hand. He stepped into the room, closing the door behind him as he surveyed the scene.

'Alphonse,' I began.

'Don't speak,' he snapped.

I could see Marcel look to the floor where, after shooting Kranz, he had dropped his weapon as he bundled me to safety.

I knew he was thinking about making a grab for it. 'Don't,' I said, resting my hand on his arm.

Alphonse waved the gun at Marcel. 'Keep your hands where I can see them.' He then moved around us and picked up Marcel's gun.

'He was going to shoot Nathalie,' said Marcel.

Alphonse pursed his lips. 'And I'm guessing, Nathalie, you were going to shoot Kranz?'

I nodded. There wasn't any point denying it, not to Alphonse. 'It was a stand-off,' I said.

'And that's when you arrived.' He looked at Marcel. 'You knew she was going to do this?'

'I tried to talk her out of it.'

'She didn't listen to you either,' concluded Alphonse.

'What are you going to do?' I asked Alphonse. 'Are you going to shoot us?'

Alphonse looked shocked. 'Shoot you? Do you think that little of me? I know you don't love me and you hate what I represent, but surely you know I'm incapable of killing you.'

'I'm sorry,' I said, and I meant it. I was sorry I had rejected Alphonse and hurt him. I was sorry I had been pig-headed and determined to avenge Edgar's death. I was sorry Marcel had got involved. The only thing I wasn't sorry about was Kranz being dead.

'Dearest Nathalie. You know I would have taken care of you,' said Alphonse. 'I would have looked after you. I could have made you happy.' He let out a deep sigh. 'I'm not the heartless man you may think I am.'

'I know you're not, but we . . . we want different things,' I said, feeling genuine sorrow but at the same time relief.

I could sense Marcel getting agitated. He grunted as he moved from one foot to the other, his injury obviously hurting him.

'What's wrong with you?' asked Alphonse.

'Shot in the shoulder,' said Marcel.

'He pushed me out of the line of fire,' I explained.

'And caught a bullet for you. How romantic,' replied Alphonse.

'He needs a doctor.'

Alphonse studied us for what seemed a long moment before speaking. 'What I am about to suggest is not because I don't still believe in the German ethos, but because I still care about you, despite everything.'

'What do you mean?' I asked.

'I promised you yesterday that I would give you twenty-four hours.' He looked at his watch. 'That still leaves you one hour and ten minutes.'

I couldn't believe what I was hearing. 'Do you mean you're going to let us leave?'

'Yes. But before you go,' he said, looking at Marcel, 'you need to punch me and then shoot me. In the leg.'

'What?' I cried. 'We can't shoot you.'

'Yes we can,' said Marcel. 'If we don't make it look realistic, then he won't be believed.'

Alphonse held out Marcel's gun to him. As Marcel went to take it, Alphonse hesitated and kept his grip on the weapon. I watched as a silent agreement passed between the two men and then Alphonse released his hold.

'You'd better punch me first,' said Alphonse. He braced himself in front of Marcel who, without hesitation, landed a right hook on Alphonse's jaw, sending the younger man backwards onto the floor. He got to his feet, rubbing the side of his face. 'Now you need to shoot me.'

'I'll try to avoid any bones,' said Marcel. 'So it's just a flesh wound.'

'I hope you're not left-handed,' said Alphonse, nodding towards the wounded shoulder.

'I came top of my class in small firearms,' said Marcel. He raised the gun and without warning fired off a shot, the silencer doing its job once again to avoid detection.

Alphonse cried out in pain, and for a second time, fell to the floor. He gripped the top of his thigh with both hands. 'It went straight through,' he said. 'Now you had better go.'

I crouched down next to Alphonse and put my hand on his arm. 'Thank you, Alphonse.'

'Just don't get yourself caught or killed,' he said, clearly in discomfort from the wound.

'Nor you.'

I got to my feet.

Marcel and Alphonse exchanged another look. 'You get her out of here now. Make this worth it.'

'I will.'

Marcel paused. 'The briefcase. Where's the briefcase?'

I grabbed Kranz's case, which had all the documentation the Resistance could need. With that, Marcel took my hand and we were out into the hallway, closing the door behind us.

Everything had happened in a matter of minutes. I scooped up the laundry bag I'd left on the trolley earlier as Marcel hurried me along the corridor. The hotel was still silent. 'Take the staff staircase,' instructed Marcel. 'I'll go out through the main entrance. It will look suspicious if we go together. Meet me at the back.'

I kept my composure as I hurried down the stairs and was grateful the staffroom was empty as I exited the rear of the hotel for the last time. There would be no going back now.

As I walked out onto the main road, a car pulled up and the door opened. Marcel was sitting in the back. I climbed in and the driver sped us away through the streets of Paris.

'Where are we going?' I asked.

'First, I need to get this shoulder cleaned up,' said Marcel, kissing the top of my head. 'Then we'll quickly call to your home to grab some clothes before heading to Brittany.'

'Brittany? My cousins?'

'Yes. We're going to get you and them out of the country to England where you'll be safe.'

'And what about you?' I asked, suddenly panicked that we might be separated again.

'Well, I'm going to be out of action for a while. If all goes well, we can stay with my mother.'

'All of us?'

'She has a big house.'

'She has more than a big house,' chipped in the driver. 'His mother has a bloody great mansion. She's titled and everything.'

'Titled? A mansion?' I knew little about the English class system but I was sure that all sounded very upper class.

'We'll get to that later,' said Marcel. 'Once we're in England, I'll be allowed to tell you, but not while we're still out here in the field.'

'I suppose I will have to get used to calling you by something other than Marcel.'

'Don't worry about that now. We've got to get out of here first, and that could take a few days, or even weeks.' He squeezed me into his chest. 'Try to rest. We've got a long drive ahead.'

I snuggled into his body, suddenly feeling exhausted as the events of the past hour caught up with me. As we sped through the streets of Paris, I thought of Alphonse and what he'd done for me, for Marcel. I could never repay him, but I would be eternally grateful for his last act of love for me.

Chapter 35

Darcie

'Oh God, the dress. Do you think that's what they were looking for?' Darcie flopped down on the sofa, among her belongings.

Matt knelt down in front of her. 'Where is the dress, Darcie?'

'Oh, don't worry, that's safe,' she said. 'I left it in the secure luggage store of the hotel next door. I don't know why, but I felt uneasy about leaving it in the apartment.'

'You left it in a locker?'

'It's fine. I did it the other day before we left for Brittany. Don't worry, I have the key.' She smiled at Matt. 'I thought it was a good idea.' The words died on her lips along with the smile. 'It was a good idea, wasn't it?' She grabbed his arm.

'I think it was a damn good idea in light of this. A genius move, in fact,' said Matt. 'Maybe we should go check it's still there as soon as we've reported this.'

'Do you think someone was after the dress?' asked Darcie, looking around the apartment. 'I didn't leave anything valuable here so as far as I can see, nothing's been taken.'

'If the property is well known as an Airbnb, it could be targeted,' said Matt. 'Similarly, if someone is after the dress then it would have to be someone who knew you had it here in Paris.'

'And who would know that? Padgett,' said Darcie answering her own question. 'Oh God, you don't think he's tried to steal it because I refused to the agreement this morning.'

'We need to make sure the dress is still there.'

'But what if I'm being followed? I might be taking them straight to it.' Darcie was pacing the room.

'I'll come with you. Whoever it is will have to get past me first.'

'I don't want you getting hurt,' said Darcie.

'Likewise,' said Matt.

'We should do it now, before whoever it is has time to think of their next move,' said Darcie, grabbing her bag.

'We need to report it too,' said Matt.

Darcie waited while Matt made the call. It was several minutes before he got off the phone. 'We've been given a case number. As nothing's been stolen and there's no sign of forced entry, they're not too bothered about coming out. It's not top of their priority list. They said we could go down to the station and provide a statement.'

'Seems a waste of time,' said Darcie. 'We've got better things to do.'

They left Darcie's apartment and went next door to the hotel and retrieved the bag with the dress in it.

'We should put it somewhere safer,' said Matt.

'Like where?'

'A safe deposit box at my bank.'

In any other circumstances Darcie might have argued that this was overkill but in this instance, it felt the right move. 'OK. Let's do that. Then I need to think what I'm going to do long term.'

'It would make a good news story. You should think about it. Once the story is out there, whether you're able to prove it or not, you'll be safer because everyone will know you own the dress. Padgett can't steal it and would gain nothing by doing so. He wants to stop the story getting out. Once it's out, it's game over for him, regardless of the truth behind the dress's origin.'

'I know what you're saying, but I'm not sure anyone will be interested unless I have proof about the history of the dress and how it came to be left in a locker in England.'

'Maybe we should contact someone else at the House of Chanel,' suggested Matt. 'I'm sure they would be more than interested in what their esteemed Christophe Padgett is up to.'

'I don't know,' said Darcie. 'What if they claim some sort of ownership of the dress and sketchbook. I'm not against that, but I'm frightened no one will be interested in finding out the real story behind it: what happened to Nathalie Leroux and why Padgett is being so deceitful.'

'Fair enough,' said Matt. 'Let's get this dress put somewhere safe in the meantime. I'll feel a lot happier then. Also, I don't like the idea of you going back to that place tonight. Would you consider staying with me, at mine?'

Darcie looked up and smiled. 'I don't need asking twice.'

Letting Matt take the lead on directions, they made their way across the city via the Métro to Matt's bank. Darcie wasn't surprised to see it was an international bank and judging by the security on the door, the bag checking, the marble flooring and air of luxury, this wasn't your average high street financial institution.

'Sorry about all this,' said Matt. 'It's easier than trying to open a French bank account when I'm only here on a visa.'

Darcie could tell he was embarrassed by the obvious wealth surrounding them. She guessed the average customer had to be pretty rich to even get through the door.

It was a relatively straightforward process depositing the dress and Darcie couldn't help feeling a wave of relief once they were out on the pavement, knowing the gown was safe.

Matt's phone rang and they moved to one side, while he

answered the call. He spoke in French and Darcie idly took in her surroundings, enjoying the feeling of calm around her.

At first, she didn't think anything of the car across the road – black saloon cars, Mercedes, BMW, Citroën were very much a part of this banking district landscape. It was only when she inadvertently made eye contact with a man, phone pressed to his ear, standing across the road from her that something on the edge of her memory stirred. She couldn't work out what. It was too far out of her reach, but something about the man looked familiar.

She looked away as she tried to grapple with her thoughts but couldn't summon up anything tangible. When she looked back, the man was getting into the black Mercedes. Another man was behind the wheel of the car and the vehicle pulled away, accelerating down the street.

'You'll never guess what,' said Matt, coming over to her. He stopped when he saw her expression. 'What's up?'

'I don't know.' She frowned, still unsure of what she'd just seen. 'There was a man across the road, on his phone. We made eye contact. I've seen him somewhere before but I can't place him.'

'Where is he?'

'He's gone now. Got into a car.'

Matt looked up the road but gave a shrug. 'Maybe he was someone famous. You get a lot of celebs around here.'

'Yeah. Maybe.'

'Anyway, have I got some good news or what?' He was grinning broadly.

'What? Tell me!'

'I've just got off the phone from Elaine Vachon. Things have changed again. She wants to see us. In person.'

'She does?'

'Yep. Odile wants to speak to us.'

'Oh, Matt, do you think . . . wait, what about Elaine's mother, Paulette?'

Matt winced. 'Elaine has assured me that Paulette won't be a problem and Odile definitely wants to speak to us.'

'Does that mean we have to go back to Brittany?'

'Yeah. We can go tonight, if you want.'

'Oh Matt, I can't expect you to take me there again. I'll get the train.'

Matt pulled her in for a hug and kissed her temple. 'As I said before, I'm as invested in this dress story as you are. There's no way I'm going to let you take the train.'

Darcie slipped her arms around him. 'I don't know what I've done to deserve someone like you or why we met, but I'm so grateful we did.'

'Me too.' Matt looked down and kissed her.

Darcie just wanted to melt in his arms there and then. There was something different about his kiss. She couldn't quite articulate it, but she could sense a deeper level of whatever it was going on between them.

'So, are we going tonight or tomorrow?' she asked when they finally pulled away.

'It might be a bit late to get somewhere to stay tonight when we get there. Let's stay at my place and leave early in the morning. How does that sound?'

'That's fine with me.'

'OK, let's go back to yours, have a tidy-up and get a bag together.'

'And hope we don't have any surprises when we get there this time,' said Darcie.

'Yeah, could do without any more of those,' agreed Matt, taking her hand and beginning to head down the street.

Darcie stopped in her tracks as the scrap of memory she hadn't quite been able to reach earlier burst to the fore.

Matt stopped walking and turned to look at her. 'What's wrong?'

'The man I saw across the street from the bank,' she said, trying to keep her composure. 'The one on the phone who got into the car with another man driving.'

'Yeah. The one you thought you knew,' said Matt slowly.

'They were the two men we passed on the staircase at my apartment. They must have been the ones who ransacked the place.'

Chapter 36

Darcie

'It's going to be all right,' assured Matt for what must have been at least the twentieth time. They were in the car, heading into Brittany.

Darcie had to admire him for not only his patience with her but also his ability to install a sense of calm. She could almost believe him. Almost.

'And there's no way they can get to the safe deposit box,' she said for probably the one hundredth time.

'None at all. There's absolutely no way they can access the box without full identification and the key. I promise you, it couldn't be in a safer place.'

'Maybe I should have left the sketchbook there as well,' said Darcie, looking down at her bag where the book now was. At the time, she'd told Matt she was happier keeping the book with her, but now she was questioning her wisdom.

'Quit worrying. You have it with you. Neither of us are going to let it go anywhere,' reassured Matt. He reached over and squeezed her hand. 'Look, let's focus on the plan. We've got this opportunity to speak to Odile and, after that, we can work out what to do next. Whether that's going to the police with evidence or taking legal advice about the dress or about Padgett and warning his hitmen off.'

'Hitmen!'

'Sorry, I didn't mean it like that. Just an expression.'

'I know you're right.' Darcie had to stop going over

the same ground. She switched the conversation to more immediate things. 'So, how long until we're there?'

'Another thirty to forty minutes,' said Matt. 'Traffic is light. No hold-ups. I've had a message from Elaine confirming it all, so all is good.'

Thirty-five minutes later, they were pulling up in the car park of the care home where Odile resided. Elaine was waiting in her car.

'Thank you for coming,' she said. 'I know it's a long way.'

'No, thank you for contacting us,' corrected Matt.

'Is Odile all right?' asked Darcie. 'I hope none of this has distressed her too much.'

'My great-aunt is much more resilient than her petite frame would suggest,' reassured Elaine. 'I have learned things in the past twenty-four hours that I never would have believed in a hundred years.'

'Sounds intriguing,' said Matt.

'*Oui* and I will let Odile tell you herself.'

'Sorry, can I just ask another question?' said Darcie. 'What does your mother think to all this? Or doesn't she know we're here?'

'She knows. She wasn't very happy, but it's not up to her to decide whether to keep the secrets or to tell them. We have to abide by Odile's wishes.'

'And she's decided not to come today?' asked Darcie, feeling partly relieved but also a little disappointed. She didn't like the idea of upsetting Paulette, brusque as she was.

'My mother feels embarrassed. She will come around though,' said Elaine with a smile.

'So, what caused this change of heart?' asked Matt.

'We had a telephone call from the care home to say Odile had been visited by two men after your first visit. The staff didn't know what was discussed but Odile was upset afterwards and kept talking about her cousin Nathalie.'

'Oh, no. Poor Odile. I'm so sorry,' said Darcie, guilt rolling up in waves.

Elaine made a dismissive tusking noise. 'You have nothing to feel guilty about. You did nothing wrong. *Alors*, the men left their business card. They were lawyers acting for an individual – a collector – who wanted to buy the dress and the sketchbook from Odile. They assumed she had it or could get it from you.'

'Did they say who they were acting for?' asked Matt.

'No. They wouldn't disclose the name. My mother spoke to them. They also offered her a large sum of money in return if the story behind the dress and sketchbook was not . . .' Elaine waved her hand around as if trying to find the right word.

'Disclosed?' offered Matt.

'*Oui*. That's right.'

'Buying everyone's silence.' said Darcie, finding it hard to believe all this. It was like an alternative universe she had landed in. 'Did Paulette agree?'

'She did. She has signed the document,' said Elaine.

'But that contract is between your mother and the lawyers, not Odile,' said Matt. 'Odile hasn't signed anything, I assume.'

'That's correct,' said Elaine. 'And neither have I.'

'Why didn't you want to sign it?' asked Darcie.

'I spoke to Odile and she was very lucid. I was concerned about how upset she had become. I told her more about you. I had looked you up on the internet. Your shop and what you do. I showed it to Odile and I think it . . . erm . . .' Elaine tapped her chest. 'It touched her heart. She said you reminded her of Nathalie. She is adamant she wants to speak to you. I am going to do some shopping and I'll be back in an hour. What you do in that hour, is up to you.'

'Thank you, so much,' said Darcie, spontaneously hugging the Frenchwoman.

'Hurry,' replied Elaine. 'The clock is ticking.'

'Come through. Odile is expecting you,' said the nurse. 'She's looking forward a great deal to see you.'

The nurse led them up to the first floor and halfway along the hall. She stopped at room 34 and knocked on the door before entering. She greeted Odile in French and then left Darcie and Matt to go in.

Odile's room was large with a bed to the right of the door, a bathroom off to the left-hand side and, at the back of the room, a sitting area with doors opening onto a small balcony overlooking the rear gardens.

'*Bonjour, madame*,' said Matt, going in first. '*C'est Matthew Langdon et Darcie Marchant.*'

'*Bonjour.* Come, come.' Odile beckoned them with her hand and pointed to the two armchairs adjacent to her. She looked over the top of her glasses at Darcie. 'It is like looking back eighty years. You remind me of my dear cousin, Nathalie.' She pointed to the sideboard where several framed photos sat. 'That one on the end, that's me, my sister Rachelle, and Nathalie. It was taken at my parents' home during the war.'

Darcie jumped up, eager to see a picture of Nathalie. 'May I?' she asked, touching the frame. Odile smiled and nodded. Darcie immediately sought out Nathalie in the black-and-white photograph. She was smiling at the camera, her hair tied up at the sides but the rest loose over her shoulders.

Darcie felt her connection with Nathalie Leroux stronger than ever before now she had a face to the name. Darcie looked at Nathalie's hands, the same hands that had touched the sketchbook and worked the fabric of the dress all those years ago. The emotion was almost overwhelming and Darcie felt tears prick her eyes. She blinked them away.

Matt joined her. 'I can see the similarities,' he commented. 'Same dark hair and the smile.' He put his arm around Darcie's shoulders and gave a quick squeeze as if he instinctively knew how she was feeling.

'They were happy days,' mused Odile. 'I loved Nathalie coming to visit. She was such a good seamstress. Once she made a dress for my doll out of an old shirt of Papa's. She taught me how to sew, but I wasn't as good as her. Nobody was. She had a gift.'

'I've seen her drawings in her sketchbook,' said Darcie, reluctantly replacing the photo frame on the sideboard. 'And the dress she made. It's beautiful.' She returned to her seat and unzipped her rucksack. 'I have the sketchbook with me. I thought you might like to see it properly, as I didn't get time to show you before.'

Odile made an impatient gesture towards the bag. 'I would very much like to see it.'

Darcie took the sketchbook from her bag and held it out towards Odile. 'Her sketches are amazing. I wish I had her vision.'

Odile took the book and opened it out, turning the pages and taking in the sketches before her. 'I never thought I'd see this again,' she said. Odile stopped at one particular page. She tapped it with her finger. 'Do you notice anything different about this page?' She looked up at Darcie and there was a twinkle in the older woman's eyes.

Darcie knelt at the side of Odile's chair and looked at the page. 'I'm not sure,' she said. 'It looks a bit different to the other pages.'

'You have a good eye,' said Odile. 'I did that drawing.'

'Oh, wow! That's amazing,' said Darcie. It explained why she'd always thought that particular page wasn't drawn by Nathalie Leroux.

'Nathalie was trying to teach me how to create a design. I wasn't very good at it.'

'I think it's a good starting point,' said Darcie, marvelling at how the sketchbook had almost come full circle. It wasn't for the first time she felt like the book wasn't hers, even though she had bought it. She felt guilty having it in her possession. 'Odile, I think you should have this book.'

She could hear Matt almost choke on his coffee, but to his credit he didn't say anything, just shot her a questioning look.

'It's not my book to have,' said Odile.

'But it was Nathalie's and you're her family. That's your drawing on the page. It feels like it belongs to you,' insisted Darcie.

Odile shook her head and with a long look at the page, closed the book and handed it back to Darcie. 'It's never been mine. It's always been Nathalie's.'

Darcie tried a different approach. 'Has Nathalie got any family alive that you know of? Did she marry? Did she have children? Perhaps they would like this.'

Odile reached out and patted Darcie's hand. 'I think it's time I told you everything I know.'

Darcie sat back in the chair next to Matt. 'Only if you want to,' she said, even though every fibre in her body was longing to know. Despite that, Darcie didn't want to pressurise Odile.

'It's about time the truth was told,' said Odile. 'I've never spoken about what happened. It didn't seem relevant anymore, but when those lawyers came yesterday, it reignited all the feelings I've suppressed over the years.'

'We heard they had been,' said Matt.

'They didn't get any satisfaction from me, but they came to an agreement with Paulette,' said Odile. 'I know she meant well, but now the drawings have been discovered, I owe it to Nathalie to tell her story. It's time for me to speak out against the men who are trying to silence her just like during the war when we were suppressed and not allowed to speak the truth. This isn't about the money, it's about making peace with my life and with Nathalie's memory. I wouldn't be doing her justice if I didn't speak out. She was a wonderful and courageous woman and people need to know that.'

Darcie had to blink back tears that unexpectedly gathered in her eyes. 'Odile, I'd love to hear Nathalie's story.'

'It is not a story. It is the truth,' said Odile.

Chapter 37

Nathalie

It was dark when the car pulled up at the edge of the forest where Gaston and the Resistance were hiding out. We had stopped for an hour just outside Paris where a doctor had, without question or protest, let us into his house and removed the bullet from Marcel's shoulder and dressed the wound. The doctor had also inspected my side and had been very impressed with my father's handiwork. He applied a clean dressing and assured me it would heal without any problems but that I needed to make sure the stitches were removed soon. Marcel had changed back into civilian clothes that the driver had produced from the boot of the car.

We climbed out of the vehicle and, with a nod, the driver sped away into the darkness.

'Stay close to me,' instructed Marcel. We clambered across a ditch and scurried into the safety of the forest.

I had just the clothes I was wearing, a satchel slung across my body with a few essential items in it and a small brown suitcase where I had also put the dress and my sketchbook. The dress took up precious space, but I was prepared to forego some of my everyday clothes.

There had been hardly any time to say goodbye to my parents, and that lay heavy on my heart. I had rushed into the apartment, grabbing my belongings while Maman and Papa followed me around, listening as I tried to tell them with as little information as possible what was happening.

I prayed with all my heart that they wouldn't come to any harm because of my recklessness, because that is now how I was viewing it. The satisfaction of revenge had been fleeting. I had hoped to feel some sort of elation at the death of Kranz, but I just felt fear for my parents and my family in Brittany.

We had only been walking for about fifteen minutes when the lookouts for the Resistance appeared from nowhere in front of us.

'It's me, Marcel Reynard. I have Gaston Grandis' cousin with me,' said Marcel.

'Ah, Marcel. We were not expecting you,' said one of the men, emerging from the shadow of the tree.

'Change of plan,' said Marcel.

We walked on until we reached the camp.

Gaston was sitting around the campfire with several other men. He jumped to his feet when he saw us, shaking hands with Marcel and then embracing me.

'*Alors*, it is our little Parisian warrior,' he said, standing back and inspecting me. 'Are you all right?'

'Yes. I'm fine,' I replied, not wanting to tell him about my stab wound.

Before I had a chance to say anything else, there was a squeal of delight from behind Gaston. I looked around him and there was Rachelle, rushing towards me.

'Nathalie! Is it really you?' She hugged me tightly. 'They never said you were coming.'

'We didn't know,' said Gaston. 'What's happened?'

'I'll explain,' said Marcel, before turning to me. 'Why don't you and Rachelle go inside?' He leaned over and kissed my temple. 'Please, rest now.'

'You need to rest too,' I said, eyeing his wounded shoulder.

'I'll be fine. I'll come and see you later.'

Before I could protest any further, Rachelle was dragging me over to the shelter she'd emerged from moments earlier. After a cup of coffee, made from roasted acorns, a hunk of bread and some dried apple rings, I explained to my cousin what had happened.

'I've been so worried about you and Odile,' I finished. 'Kranz said he had arrested you both.'

'Oh, Nathalie, we've been fine,' said Rachelle. 'Nothing happened to us. We were arrested and then just left in the police station for twenty-four hours. They released us without even asking us anything.'

'Is Odile all right?'

'A little shaken, but she is fine,' said Rachelle. I suspected that there was more to it than that, and a wave of guilt swamped me again.

'What is going to happen to you now?' asked Rachelle.

'Marcel is going to get me to England. And you and Odile too.' I gripped her hand. 'You will both be safe.'

Rachelle looked at me for a long moment before finally speaking. 'I can't go,' she said softly.

'But you have to. You can't stay here.'

'I don't want to go,' said Rachelle firmly. 'I've already discussed this with Gaston that I'm going to become more involved with the Resistance. I can't leave now.'

'Rachelle, please,' I begged.

'My mind is made up, Nathalie. You won't be able to change it,' said Rachelle.

'But you'll be in danger.'

'That is why I'm going to be staying here with Gaston.'

'Do your parents know?'

'Not yet. But they will be glad because it is not safe to stay at the farm,' said Rachelle. 'The German soldiers are becoming restless and there have been several incidents involving local girls.'

'Oh no, not that.' I immediately thought of Odile and what she had been through already. 'I can't leave Odile here.'

'No, you can't. In fact, you must take her with you,' said Rachelle. 'I will speak to Gaston and we'll get her here in time.'

'I wish you would come,' I said. 'I feel guilty about leaving.'

'You mustn't feel guilty. If you stay, you are putting yourself in danger and everyone else. They will be looking for you to make an example of you. And no matter how we would like to think your presence would be kept a secret, no offence, but you're not local and the loyalty towards you will not be so strong. People are desperate. Someone will give you up.'

I knew this was true, much as it hurt. Marcel had said as much on the journey when I had tentatively suggested I stay in the forest camp.

The door to the shelter opened and Marcel stepped into the room, followed by Gaston.

'It seems you've been causing quite a stir in Paris,' said Gaston with a wry smile.

'It didn't quite go to plan,' I confessed. 'Not sure what I would have done without Marcel.'

'So, we need to get you out of here and this man home for some medical treatment.' Gaston gave Marcel a slap on the back, causing Marcel to wince.

'What is the plan?' asked Rachelle. 'I've explained to Nathalie that I'm not going.'

'And you're certain about that?' asked Gaston.

'You know I am.'

'I just wanted to check. *Alors*, we need to wait for the next moon, which is three nights' time. There's a plane coming in with supplies. We will swap you two and Odile. Tomorrow evening, we'll bring Odile here.'

'Will she be agreeable, do you think?' asked Marcel.

'She might not like it at first, but she will be happier knowing Nathalie is with her,' said Rachelle. 'I'm sure she would have liked you as a sister instead of me,' she added with a laugh.

'Ah, but we all love our crazy Parisian cousin,' said Gaston good-humouredly.

'We certainly do,' said Marcel, exchanging a grin with me.

Gaston gave a small raise of his eyebrows but then smiled broadly. My heart skipped a beat at this unspoken seal of approval on our relationship.

As predicted, Odile had been hesitant about the plan, but after reassurances from her siblings and blessings from her parents, she had agreed.

I had noticed a decline in Marcel over the last three days and although he didn't say anything and assured me he was all right, I could tell his shoulder was causing him a great deal of pain. He was having to hold it all the time. In the end, I had fashioned a sling from a sheet and insisted he wear it to support his arm.

'Damn thing,' he muttered, but accepted my help.

I could see the collarbone under the skin was at several different angles and realised it must have been shattered by the bullet. 'You're going to need surgery on that.'

'Might be too late, but I expect the military docs will give it a good try,' he replied.

Odile had been brought to the camp the night before and now, twenty-four hours later, we were huddled around the campfire, going over the plan to meet the aircraft.

'The drop and pick have been brought forward an hour,' said Gaston. 'There is cloud coming in tonight and the British don't want to attempt a landing with poor visibility.'

'What time do we have to leave?' I asked.

'In one hour,' replied Gaston. 'Now, we have things to arrange before then. Make sure you're ready.'

As Gaston, Marcel, and Rachelle went off, Odile and I went to our shelter to make sure what few possessions we had were ready to go.

'I'm scared,' admitted Odile once we were inside the shelter. 'I don't know if I can do this.'

'I'm scared too,' I said, going over to her and holding her hands. 'It is the fear of the unknown, but we have to trust Gaston and Marcel. They wouldn't put us in any danger.'

'I don't want to leave Maman or Papa,' said Odile, looking down at the ground. 'What if I never see them again?' Tears tracked their way down my cousin's face.

I put my arms around Odile. She was so tiny and fragile; I daren't squeeze too hard in case she broke in two. 'I will look after you,' I said. 'You will always have me. As long as there is a breath in my body, I will never let you down.'

'Do you promise?'

'Of course. I promise you, Odile, I'll be here for you. Always.' After everything she had been through, I knew Odile's confidence was shattered and as much as I was fearful of what lay ahead, I knew her fear would be greater than mine. 'Your parents want you to come with me,' I continued. 'They want you to be safe and, in England with me, you will be. Once the war is over and it's safe to come home, then we will.'

'But you might be married to Marcel by then and want to stay in England.'

I gave a laugh. 'I don't know if we are at that stage yet. And if we ever do get there, then I will insist we come to live back here in France.'

I turned the idea of marriage to Marcel over in my mind, and it was not an unappealing thought at all.

It seemed no time before Rachelle was at the door to the shelter, telling us it was time to go.

As we followed Gaston, Marcel, and other members of the Resistance through the forest towards the temporary airfield, Rachelle held Odile's hand all the way. They didn't speak, but the unspoken communication of love passed silently between them. My heart went out to Odile, and I hoped with all my heart that I would be able to fulfil my promises to her.

Marcel fell into step alongside me. 'She'll be all right,' he said, as if reading my thoughts. 'I'll look after her as well. We're both responsible for her once we're on that plane.'

I reached for his hand and brought it to my lips, kissing his knuckles. 'You're a good man, Marcel Reynard. Although I suppose once we're in England, I will get to meet the real you.'

He smiled. 'It will be the first thing I tell you.'

We trampled on through the forest for another thirty minutes before coming to the edge of a field, where we crouched down while the group checked around for any signs of a German patrol or, worse, an ambush.

The minutes ticked by and the tension racked up with every second. In the distance, I could hear the small rumble of a plane engine getting louder as it neared us. With a whisper from Gaston, the group moved out into the field and, with well-practised precision and speed, lit the torches that outlined the runway strip.

The plane came into sight and after circling once, didn't waste any time lining up and coming into land on the bumpy farmer's field that had been identified as a makeshift runway.

All at once, Marcel was herding us across the field at a pace. We had only a matter of minutes to unload whatever it was on the plane and for us to get on board.

Rachelle gave me a brief hug and a slightly longer hug to her sister. Gaston did the same and shook hands with Marcel.

We were about to climb on board when suddenly the field was illuminated by a bright light. At first I thought the group had lit more torches, but almost instantly there was shouting. German voices. A rapid fire of gunshot.

And then confusion broke out. There was yelling coming from everywhere. French and German voices bellowing above the noise of the plane engine. Odile had one foot on the steps. The co-pilot was holding her hand. He yanked her onto the plane.

'Get in!' shouted Marcel at me. He pushed me towards the steps. I scrambled on board, ignoring the pain that shot through my side as I overstretched to haul myself up. I looked over my shoulder as Gaston and the group scattered away from the plane, charging for cover of darkness.

'MARCEL!' I yelled at him. The co-pilot pushed me out of the way. The plane was moving.

'SIR! Get in now!' shouted the co-pilot, as he began to move the door into place. 'NOW!'

The plane was gathering speed. I shouted Marcel's name again and for a moment I lost sight of him. Then he was there, jumping into the gap between the plane and the door.

The co-pilot yanked him inside the aircraft, slamming the door shut. I could still hear gunfire above the noise of the engine, but as the speed of the plane increased, the rumble of the engines drowned out the shots.

It seemed an age before we were in the air. The plane banked to the right before setting its course high above the Breton countryside.

Odile was crying softly, and I sat next to her, my arms around her, trying to offer some sort of comfort. Marcel was speaking to the crew and then came to sit beside me a short time later, his arm around me. We stayed huddled like that for the rest of the flight.

I had no idea what had happened to the group. I knew Odile was experiencing some kind of shock. I had no doubt, like me, she could only think of Gaston and Rachelle. Hoping that, somehow, they and the rest of the group had made it out of the ambush.

I lost all track of time as we bunched together in the back of the aircraft. The co-pilot came out and told us we would land at Tangmere airfield in five minutes.

Sure enough, five minutes later, we bumped down onto the airstrip and taxied to a standstill before being helped out of the aircraft.

A British army soldier was waiting to meet us on the tarmac and the crew helped us down from the plane.

'*Bonjour, mademoiselles,*' greeted the soldier. He nodded at Marcel. 'Sergeant.'

'Just give us a moment, Corporal,' he said.

The corporal walked back to the waiting car.

Marcel turned to me. 'Thomas Colvin.'

I looked at him, confused by this statement. 'What?'

'Thomas Colvin,' he repeated. 'I said that would be the first thing I told you once we're on British soil.'

'Thomas Colvin.' I repeated the unfamiliar name, resetting my mind to think of Marcel as Thomas. I smiled at him and rose onto tiptoes, kissing him on the cheek. 'Hello, Thomas.'

Chapter 38

Nathalie

Now safely on British soil, we were taken over to Tangmere Cottage, which was the operations room for the airfield, and given something to eat and a cup of coffee. It had been so long since I'd tasted real coffee that I was almost sick, such was the richness of the taste.

'We have tea, if you'd prefer,' suggested one of the airmen as we sat in the messroom.

'I'm not sure I'm that desperate,' I said.

The airman looked at me as if most offended, and I couldn't help laughing.

'I thought you were serious for a minute,' said the airman.

'It's nice to see you smile,' said Marcel, coming to sit beside me. I corrected my internal thought, reminding myself he was Thomas now.

'What happens next?' I asked.

'We'll be debriefed individually,' said Thomas. 'But before that, I'll be paying a visit to the hospital to get my shoulder looked at.'

'How is it?' I asked. I hadn't missed him wincing from time to time, when he thought I wasn't watching.

'Bloody sore, if I'm honest. But I'll live.' He reached over with his good hand and squeezed mine. 'Everything will be all right. Don't worry.'

'I'm not worried about myself, just you and Odile,' I said. 'She's just a child. She can't be on her own.'

Thomas looked over at my cousin, who had so far refused food and had only accepted a glass of water. 'I'll see what I can do,' he said.

That first night, or what was left of it, Odile and I were given a room upstairs at Tangmere Cottage.

'Where will you be?' I asked, suddenly feeling anxious Thomas might be whisked away from me.

'Once I'm back from the hospital, I'll be in barracks,' he said. 'As civilians, you get the guest rooms.' He laughed at this and I realised it was the British sense of humour coming out. I had seen little of it in France, but now safe on home soil, he obviously felt more relaxed. 'Don't worry, I'll be here waiting to take you to breakfast. There will be questions to answer, but they're going to take us up to Bignor Manor for that.'

'Bignor Manor?' It sounded like we were visiting a country home rather than the local headquarters for the Special Operations Executive and the Secret Intelligence Service.

'It's a safe house where personnel, French in particular, pass through,' explained Thomas. 'Going in and coming out of France. The owner, Tony Bertram, is a major. Speaks fluent French. MI6 persuaded him to open the doors to help the war effort.'

'So many people, both here and in France, are involved in fighting the war,' I said. 'It's not just the soldiers on the ground.'

'Not at all. There's far more going on that we know nothing about.'

I sighed and fell silent for a moment as I contemplated the vastness of the support networks in Britain and Europe. 'What will happen after we've been to the safe house?'

'I hope we get some downtime. I get my shoulder fixed properly, and you and Odile get to stay with my mother. That's if you want to.'

I pressed my lips together. 'I suppose so.' I wasn't quite sure how Thomas's mother would react to Odile and me turning up. 'Will she not mind?'

'Not at all,' declared Thomas. 'She'll love it. Especially if she thinks she is harbouring two spies. She loves that sort of thing.'

I had to remind myself of Thomas's sense of humour – I was still getting used to it. The British didn't seem to take the war as seriously as the French. But, then again, England wasn't occupied, so maybe they didn't have the same sense of desperation as my fellow countrymen and women.

We did indeed go to Bignor Manor that day and were there for a total of five days while we were debriefed, or questioned, as I thought of it. They were all very polite, but they asked the same questions many times.

Odile answered a few questions, but it soon became apparent to them she had suffered at the hands of the Germans and I was relieved when, on the second day, they sent a female member of staff to talk to her. Gradually, over the five days, Odile opened up and was able to answer the questions more freely. It was encouraging to see some of my cousin's confidence return, albeit a much-diluted version.

I was surprised to find two other Frenchmen were also staying at Bignor Manor, courtesy of the Bertram family – Anthony and Barbara, together with their two young children.

The guests had been instructed not to talk about their reasons for being there in front of the children, but to stick to the cover story that they were French airmen recovering from injuries.

'We tell the children and the other people in the village that we are looking after injured French servicemen,' explained Barbara. She nodded across the table to the Frenchman who had his arm in a sling.

The injured man waved and said, *bonjour*, and winked at me, before placing his arm back in the sling. He tapped the side of his nose.

Odile laughed, which pleased me. I had felt a little of the Odile I knew and loved coming back with each passing day.

'We are going to the pub tonight,' said the Frenchman. 'Would you like to join us?'

'That would be perfect,' replied Thomas with enthusiasm. He too was sporting a sling, but his was genuine. Thomas had been assured his arm would heal as long as he rested it and used the sling, which he agreed to, albeit somewhat begrudgingly. He held out his hand to the Frenchman. 'Thomas Colvin.'

The Frenchman reached out and shook hands. 'Jacques Daniel and this is Martin Tremblay.'

Thomas introduced me and then Odile. Although everyone was curious about each other, no one asked any probing questions.

'We're here just until the next moon,' said Jacques.

Everyone knew that was code for being flown over the Channel to France and I could only assume they were going on some kind of sabotage mission.

The White Horse was in Sutton – the next village along from Bignor – and the locals were all clearly used to military personnel from both England and France in the pub. They greeted Jacques and Martin like old friends.

It was quite a surreal evening, and I found it hard to think that just a week ago I had been in Paris and planning how I was going to kill Kranz. Now I was in an English village pub in West Sussex, sipping a glass of wine as if there wasn't even a war going on just across the Channel.

The following morning, Odile and I were helping Barbara in the garden when Thomas came out to find us. He was waving an envelope in his hand.

'I've got our train tickets,' he said. 'Fourteen hundred hours . . . I mean two o'clock this afternoon.'

'Oh, so soon,' said Odile.

I knew Odile had begun to feel comfortable at Bignor Manor. Barbara had really taken to her and spent extra time talking to Odile and showing her how to press flowers and, in return, Odile had darned some socks and mended a patch on the elbow of a jumper. It made my heart expand, and I hoped Odile could find some sort of contentment or happiness in her life one day.

'Do I have to go?' asked Odile, her gaze skipping from me to Thomas and back to Barbara. 'I don't mean to be rude, Nathalie, but I like it here.'

There was a long pause as we all contemplated the possible scenario.

'Well, I don't see why not,' said Barbara at last. 'I'm happy for you to be here. Lord knows I could do with an extra pair of hands, especially when I have a lot of guests. But it's not up to me.'

Thomas spoke before I did. 'I don't have an issue with it. I'm sure there won't be a problem with it back at Tangmere Cottage. But like you, Barbara, it's not up to me.'

I realised all eyes were on me. I spoke in French to Odile, just so I could be sure there was no misunderstanding. 'Is this what you really want to do, Odile? Stay here in Bignor?'

'Yes. It is.' Her reply was the most confident I had heard since we'd been there.

'You can change your mind at any point,' I said. 'I just want you to be happy. I will worry about you, but we can still meet up.'

'I know, and I can telephone you,' said Odile. 'I would just feel happier here with Barbara.'

'Very well. That's agreed, then,' I said. And then in English for clarity: 'I'm happy for Odile to stay here. It's what she wants.'

'Excellent,' said Barbara. 'And now, you'd better get packed. Odile, why don't you help your cousin?'

While I packed, I questioned Odile again, just to be certain it was definitely what she wanted. She assured me it was, so when it came to say goodbye, I had no real worries; at least I knew the Bertram family would look after her well. We planned to telephone each week and for me to come back to see her in a month's time.

Tony Bertram drove us the five miles to Pulborough station and Odile came along for the ride. I hugged her fiercely as we said our goodbyes and we promised to phone every Sunday.

It was easy to forget about the war as the train trundled out of the station towards London; I rested my head on Thomas's shoulder and watched the passing countryside through the window. It was the first time I had felt no fear in a long time.

'And you're sure your mother doesn't mind?' I questioned.

'No. I telephoned her this morning, and she's looking forward to meeting you.'

'Did you tell her about us?'

'Not yet. I'll give her time to get over me being home. Oh, and I've got to go to London on Tuesday for a meeting. I'll be gone for a few days.'

Thomas's mother, Geraldine, was an absolute delight, and she welcomed me into her home without hesitation. I had a room on the first floor, along the hallway from Thomas's room, but on the opposite wing to Geraldine, who I learned spoke fluent French from her days of being brought up by a French governess. Thomas's father had been French and so it had been natural for them all to speak French at home, hence Thomas being fluent in the language.

Every day I was learning something new about Thomas, and every day I was falling in love with him just a little more. When we were walking back from the pub one evening, I told him as much. I have to say I didn't realise how important a role the pub played in everyday British life, but so far it had been a positive experience. I wondered what Gaston and Rachelle would say when I told them, and immediately I felt guilty. It had been an agonising few days while we waited for a coded radio message to confirm my cousins had made it to safety. It was such a relief to know this, but now all I could think was they were stuck in the middle of a forest, living on very little, just trying to stay alive and here I was in England going to the pub and socialising.

I had been staying with Thomas and his mother for two weeks and had just started to relax and feel a little at home. The wound in my side had healed nicely, although I would be left with a scar as a reminder. Thomas's shoulder looked like it was healing well and the army surgeon was confident surgery wouldn't be needed after all.

That day, Thomas had to go to London for a meeting, something that he couldn't tell me about, but he assured me he would only be gone two days and then he'd be back.

'Mother will look after you,' he said, giving me a hug as we stood on the station waiting for the 10.14 to London. 'I wish I could take you with me, but it's just impossible, I'm afraid.'

'So, are you officially back at work now?' I asked, my hand resting gently on his shoulder.

'I'm not fighting fit, but I'm fit to be in the office, so to speak.'

'I'll miss you,' I said. It would be the first time we had been apart since he had rescued me from the Ritz that night. It was beginning to feel normal being around him. We had even made love several times when Geraldine was out, and the previous night, Thomas had even sneaked down the hallway to slip into my bed. I had no objection to that. I wanted to spend every possible moment with him. If this war had taught me anything, it was to appreciate those dear to us and not to be scared to love – because life was fragile and short. I wanted no regrets. Not anymore.

'I'll miss you more than you'll know,' he said. 'When I get back, I've something important I need to talk to you about.'

I looked up at him. 'What?'

'Oh, don't look so worried,' he said with a smile, kissing the top of my head. 'It's something nice. Or at least I hope it will be.' He gave a mischievous wink.

'Oh tell me.' I laughed. 'I hate surprises.'

'Not this one,' he said. 'Besides, I can't tell you yet because while I'm in London, I've got to see someone. Once I've seen them, I'll be home.'

'See someone?'

'Oh, not like that, you silly bean,' he said with a laugh. 'It's a man who has a shop. I've got to pick something up. Ah, here's my train.'

He enveloped me in his arms and kissed me for longer than necessary, much to the amusement of some schoolchildren, but I didn't care. I was madly in love with Thomas Colvin, even more so than I had been with Marcel Reynard. I knew I wanted to spend the rest of my life with him. And I had a feeling I knew just what sort of shop he'd be visiting.

'Take care,' I said. 'Hurry back.'

I stood on the station until the train carrying Thomas had disappeared out of sight. I knew I was smiling to myself, but I didn't care. That was what love did to you.

I don't know what made me look up, but I had a strange feeling that I was being watched. A train was pulling in at the opposite platform as I looked across the two railway tracks. I glimpsed someone, but the train obscured my view. My heart gave a brief flutter and my stomach performed an unwelcome turn.

No. It couldn't be. Surely not. I tried to look through the train windows to see them again, but there were too many people standing up ready to disembark from the train.

I could feel my heart picking up its pace.

I needed to get out of there.

I couldn't stand around.

I needed distance.

I spun on my heel and although I told myself to walk, my feet were paying no attention to the instruction and I ran out through the ticket office and on to the street.

I looked behind me, but all I could see was a small crowd of people exiting the building.

I wanted to calm myself, to think rationally, but I couldn't.

I spotted a bus on the other side of the road and, without thinking, raced across, just managing to dodge the traffic, which earned several beeps of the horn from a bread van.

I jumped on the bus and almost threw myself into the window seat where I had a full view of the train station.

The bus pulled away, and I stared at the ticket office door, craning my neck but I could see no one I recognised and certainly not who I thought I'd seen.

Chapter 39

Nathalie

My brain scrambled with so many thoughts. Had I seen them? Was my mind just playing tricks on me? The more I thought about it, the more I was sure I was imagining things. Still, the uneasy feeling settled on me and, much as I tried to ignore it, to convince myself it was all in my mind, I couldn't.

I arrived back at Geraldine's house, where she was entertaining a friend in the library. She invited me to sit with her and I spent the next hour exchanging polite chit-chat, as Geraldine had described it. Of course, I had a cover story, insomuch as I was a friend of a friend and had escaped France and was staying with Geraldine for a few weeks.

Her friend had given me a knowing look and then said no more. The conversation turned to how Geraldine was going to plough up the rear of the garden and dig for victory, as she called it.

I hadn't realised England was struggling for food as well as the rest of Europe, although I gathered it wasn't on the same scale or in the same desperation as back home. In fact, Geraldine and her friend seemed rather excited at the idea of growing vegetables and went into great detail about how the other gardens in the village now resembled agricultural land.

Later that morning, after Geraldine's friend had left, we were taking lunch in the lounge when the telephone rang. The housekeeper, Lottie, answered it and then came into the room.

'Who is it?' asked Geraldine, looking up from her cup of tea.

'It's someone from the Home Office asking for Miss Leroux,' said Lottie.

Both Geraldine and I exchanged curious glances.

'The Home Office,' I repeated to make sure I'd understood.

'Well, I suppose you had better take the call,' said Geraldine.

I went out to the hall, wondering who on earth from the Home Office would want to speak to me. 'Hello,' I said, glancing back towards the open door to the lounge.

'Nathalie Leroux?' The voice was female and French.

'Yes. That's right. Who is this, please?' I asked in French.

'Nathalie Leroux, the thief. Nathalie Leroux, the murderer. Nathalie Leroux, the spy.'

I thought I was going to vomit right there in the hallway. I glimpsed my reflection in the mirror on the coat stand, and it was as if a ghost was looking back at me. I was so pale. I recognised the voice instantly. It was Madame Bochette. I hadn't killed her that day. Somehow, she had survived.

'What do you want? How did you find me?'

Bochette laughed, but there was no warmth, just menace and evil, laced with enjoyment. 'You're not the only one with connections,' she said.

'But you . . . I hit you . . . you were . . .' I couldn't finish. The words lodged in my throat.

She laughed again. 'You thought I was dead. I suppose I should be, but God has better plans for me and I wanted to let you know that I'm coming for you.'

'You stay away from me,' I hissed. 'I'll have you arrested. You're a spy for Germany.'

'Don't get ahead of yourself, little one. How are they going to arrest me when they don't know where I am?'

'They'll find you.' I hoped I sounded more confident that I felt.

'I wouldn't count on that,' said Bochette. 'I've got into

England without being found. Do you think they'll find me now?'

'What do you want?'

'I want revenge and also you have something that needs to be returned.'

'What do you mean?'

'Come now, don't play the innocent. The sketchbook. We know about the codes.'

'You're bluffing,' I said, as I tried to work out who had told her about the codes.

'Tache turned out to be very talkative in the end,' said Bochette. 'He tried to protect you for as long as possible but there's only so much a man of his age can deal with. Still, he's out of his misery now. Forever.'

My heart wanted to break at the thought of Monsieur Tache being tortured. 'I don't have the book anymore,' I said.

'Maybe I should pay a visit to Bignor Manor. Your cousin might be able to enlighten me on the whereabouts of the book and dress. I'm sure where one is, the other is too.'

I gripped the phone tighter. My legs felt weak. 'You stay away from there,' I hissed, trying to keep my voice down. I glanced back through to the living room and Geraldine gave me a concerned look. I turned away and whispered down the telephone. 'You stay away from there. If you go anywhere near Bignor, I will make it my personal mission in life to hunt you down, and this time I will succeed. Just so we are clear, I will kill you if you go anywhere near Odile.'

'And I'm supposed to fear you and your little bitch cousin? I think I will enjoy visiting her. I think it's me who needs to make myself clear.'

The line went dead. I replaced the receiver with a trembling hand. I felt physically sick. My breathing was coming in short, rapid gasps and finally my knees buckled and I slumped into the chair at the foot of the stairs.

Geraldine rushed out, calling for Lottie to bring some water. Between them, they helped me back into the lounge and once I had assured them both I was all right, Lottie left us alone.

'What's wrong?' asked Geraldine. 'Who was on the telephone?'

'It was the Home Office,' I said, hurriedly thinking up an excuse. 'They want to ask me some more questions about when I was in Paris.'

'Oh dear, you poor child.' Geraldine squeezed my hand. 'I don't know what you've been through, but I know it was bad. Thomas hasn't said as much, but I'm his mother and I can read between the lines.'

I nodded. 'I'm sorry I can't say anything either.'

'No, of course you can't, my dear.' She gave a sigh. 'Maybe Thomas will go with you, so you don't have to go alone.'

'Yes, that's a good idea,' I replied.

'Now, I have to go out shortly. Are you going to be all right today?' asked Geraldine, getting to her feet.

'I'll be fine,' I replied. 'In fact, I think I'll go to my room and have a rest.'

Offering Geraldine a reassuring smile, I went upstairs. Closing the door behind me, I leaned against it. I shut my eyes for a moment and took a deep breath. I needed to work out what I was going to do.

I walked over to the window and formulated a plan. The Sussex countryside stretched out beyond the edge of the garden, the rolling hills, patches of farmland and many an acre of dense woodland. It was beautiful here, and it reminded me of the Breton countryside.

I had to be strong. I couldn't let Gaston and Rachelle down. I couldn't let my aunt and uncle down, either. They had all trusted me to take care of Odile and it was down to me to keep her safe.

I took my suitcase from the top of the wardrobe and began packing away the few clothes I had.

I hated doing this. I hated the thought of running away from Thomas, but once Odile was safe, I'd get a message

324

to him. I looked at the pen and paper on the dressing table and quickly scribbled a note to Thomas.

My darling Thomas,
Forgive me for . . .

I got no further when there was a knock at the door and in came Geraldine.

'Oh, Nathalie, I've brought you . . .' She stopped mid-sentence, the small glass of sherry in her hand. She took in my suitcase, the letter on the dressing table and the pen in my hand.

Her eyes filled with hurt. I went to speak, but she cut me off. 'You know, Thomas will be heartbroken,' she stated.

I looked down, not wanting her to see my shame. 'I don't want to hurt him,' I said.

'But you're running away,' she continued. 'You know he loves you dearly. He's not said as much, but as a mother, I can tell. It's written all over his face. Whatever you're doing, Nathalie, and for whatever reasons, he doesn't deserve to come home to that.' She pointed at the letter.

I looked up at her. 'I can't tell you what's happening, but I promise you, I'll be back.'

'And it can't even wait until this evening when he telephones?'

I shook my head. 'I'm sorry.'

'I am, too,' she said with such disappointment and sadness in her voice, I wanted to cry.

I put the pen down and closed the lid of my suitcase. Taking my coat from the wardrobe, I picked up my luggage and moved around Geraldine, leaving the room.

As I reached the front door, I looked back up at Geraldine on the half landing. I wanted to say I was sorry. I wanted to explain, but I couldn't. I needed to protect her. Instead, I simply said, 'Please tell Thomas I love him very much.'

Chapter 40

Darcie

Odile took a deep breath as if settling herself. She had been gripping on to the book all the time she recounted what had happened.

'Can I get you a glass of water?' asked Darcie, exchanging a concerned look with Matt. Much as she wanted to find out the truth, she wasn't prepared to risk Odile's well-being – that would make her no better than Padgett.

'A coffee,' replied Odile. 'I'd like another coffee.'

Matt obliged and soon a fresh cup was in Odile's hands, Darcie having moved the sketchbook to one side.

'Is there anything else I can get for you?' she asked.

Odile shook her head. 'No. I want to tell you what happened, while I still have it in my mind. At my age, the mind can be a tricky thing. It pretends it can remember things and then, poof! They're gone.'

'If you're sure,' said Darcie.

'*Alors*, I had been at Bignor Manor for several weeks,' began Odile, refreshed after her coffee. 'I very much enjoyed being there. The Bertrams were so welcoming, and I adored their children. All my life I had been the youngest in the family, the one everyone looked after and cared for, which was lovely, but the Bertrams gave me something I'd never experienced before. They gave me responsibility. They trusted me with their children and I became something of an older sister to them. It helped me recover.'

'That's good to hear,' said Darcie softly. 'Caring for someone may be hard work, but it's very rewarding.' She felt Matt's gaze on her and knew he realised she was referring to her own situation.

'I had been there for a few weeks, as I said. Nathalie telephoned me every Sunday and I was looking forward to seeing her the following weekend,' continued Odile. 'So it was something of a surprise when she turned up unexpectedly one afternoon. I was helping Mrs Bertram prepare the tea when there was a knock at the door and there was Nathalie. I could tell straight away something was wrong. I had seen that expression on her face before, even though she was trying to hide it.'

Odile placed her cup on the side table next to her and took a handkerchief from her pocket. She dabbed at her eyes and wiped her nose, her hands a little shaky. 'I sometimes look back and can't really believe what happened next.'

Darcie shifted to the edge of her seat. The tension in the room filled every corner, squeezing them as if the walls were being drawn in all around them. She could barely breathe.

'Nathalie! Oh, Nathalie, how lovely to see you.' Odile threw herself at her cousin, hugging her tightly, before kissing her on each side of the cheek twice. 'This is such a surprise.'

It was then she realised Nathalie's embrace had not been so enthusiastic. Odile took a step back, holding her at arm's length. Panic swept through her as she took in Nathalie's grim expression. 'What's wrong?'

'Odile, I can't tell you now. You have to trust me. You do trust me, don't you?' whispered Nathalie, holding on to Odile's hands.

'Of course I do. I'd trust you with my life.'

Nathalie nodded. 'Good, because I wouldn't ask if it

wasn't important. I need you to get your things and come with me.'

'What?' Odile almost laughed at the suggestion but then realised Nathalie was deadly serious. 'Get my things? Where are we going?'

'I haven't got time to explain.'

'Nathalie, you're scaring me.'

'Odile, you have to trust me.'

'But we're just preparing tea. The children will be home from school soon,' began Odile, but seeing the desperation increase in her cousin's expression, she began to understand just how serious it must be. Worse still, she could see the fear in Nathalie's eyes. 'Can I say goodbye to the children?'

Nathalie shook her head. 'There's no time.'

'Odile! Who is it?' came Barbara Bertram's voice from the kitchen.

'You can't tell her,' hissed Nathalie.

'But if it's so bad, then she needs to know. It's not just me who is hiding here,' said Odile.

'Oh, Nathalie, what a surprise,' said Barbara, walking down the hall towards the front door. 'Do come in. I didn't realise you were coming today.'

'No, I didn't have time to tell you,' said Nathalie.

Barbara stood at Odile's side, her gaze switching back and forth between the cousins. 'Is this something I should be concerned about?'

Odile looked at Nathalie, who gave a small nod. 'Someone is coming for me and Odile.'

Only the small raise of her eyebrows belied Barbara's concern at this. 'Do you have an exit plan?'

'Not an official one, but once we're safe, I can let the right people know,' said Nathalie.

'Are you sure?'

'Certain.'

'Odile has to come with me now,' said Nathalie.

Odile swallowed. She didn't think she'd ever felt so torn.

In the few short weeks she'd been at Bignor Manor, she'd grown so close to the Bertrams, the thought of leaving the safety of the family troubled her.

'Does Odile want to go?' asked Barbara, looking at her guest.

Odile dropped her gaze to the ground before looking back up at Barbara. 'I have to. I can't put you and the children at risk, or the other guests.'

'That bad, is it?' said Barbara.

'Yes.'

'I can get you help,' said Barbara.

'No. We can't wait. We need to leave,' insisted Nathalie. 'As soon as it's safe, I'll bring Odile back.'

Odile wanted to cry, but she knew she didn't even have time for that. Whatever was happening was happening now, not tomorrow, next week or some vague time in the future, it was imminent. She rushed upstairs to grab her case, stuffing what she could into it. She had no idea how long she'd be away from Bignor Manor but as she stopped in the doorway to hug Barbara Bertram goodbye, she wished with all her heart it would be very soon.

Odile followed Nathalie out into the lane. 'Where are we going?'

'We have to get the train to London,' said Nathalie, taking the case from her cousin.

'Where are your bags?'

'I didn't want to have to lug them all the way here and back again,' explained Nathalie. 'They're safe for now. We can collect them on the way.'

'Can you tell me what's going on?' asked Odile as they hurried down the road. She was aware of Nathalie constantly looking over her shoulder as if they were being followed. It added to the tension caused by the urgency of their flight. To where, she had no idea.

'Bochette is here in England,' said Nathalie, without breaking stride or looking at Odile.

'What? I thought you . . .'

'So did I, but apparently not. And she's here for me and the sketchbook.'

'Oh, Nathalie! We should tell the police. Tell Mr Bertram. He'll know what to do. He has contacts with all sorts of people.'

'Yes. And we will in time, but for now I need to get us away from the house.'

'What aren't you telling me?' Odile stopped dead in the road. 'I'm not moving until you tell me everything.' She knew whatever it was, it was bad, but surely it couldn't be worse than what she'd already gone through. Just being at Bignor Manor for a few weeks had given Odile the chance to rediscover an inner strength she didn't know she still possessed. After being attacked back in France, she had wanted to hide away from the world, but here in England, she felt safe and she could feel herself coming back from the dead.

Nathalie stopped walking, and after a moment's hesitation, turned around to face Odile. 'Bochette wants to prove to me that she will stop at nothing to get me and to retrieve the sketchbook.'

'Can't you just give her the book?'

'I can't. There is information hidden in there. Keys to codes and names of spies working for both us and the Germans. If they get their hands on the codes and names . . .'

'Why don't you just destroy the book?'

'Destroy my work? My designs? I know it sounds vain but I couldn't bring myself to do it. I truly didn't believe Bochette would come to England for it.'

'But, Nathalie, you must,' said Odile.

'No, I'm going to give the book to Thomas,' said Nathalie. 'He'll be able to take it to the Home Office and they can decide if they need to extract the information.'

'Can't it wait?' asked Odile.

'No. It has to be done today and I can't risk leaving you

here until this is sorted out. They need to stop Bochette,' said Nathalie. 'Please don't be scared.'

Odile began walking. Now she understood. It made sense. 'I'm not scared anymore,' she said, falling into step alongside her cousin. 'Well, not as much as I used to be.'

'I know,' said Nathalie with a sad smile. 'I just wish the circumstances were different.' She checked her wristwatch. 'We have to hurry, otherwise we'll miss our train. I've bought the tickets already.' She tapped the bag over her shoulder.

The road to the station seemed to go on forever, but eventually they arrived.

'Come on, quickly,' said Nathalie, hurrying Odile along.

Odile followed Nathalie in through the ticket office and out onto the platform. She watched as Nathalie scanned both sides. The platform was surprisingly busy and Odile shuffled back against the wall, her suitcase in her hands, watching her cousin briskly walk up to the end of the platform and back.

The whistle of a train had Odile looking up. She looked over at Nathalie who shook her head. 'Next train. This one doesn't stop!' she called above the noise of the steam engine.

Odile's anxiety levelled out a little and her shoulders relaxed, allowing some of the tension to ease from her neck. She watched Nathalie walk to the far end of the platform and then back as the speeding train approached.

'Stand back!' called the guard, as he walked in the opposite direction along the platform. The noise of the train grew louder as it rumbled its way towards them. It tooted several times.

Odile turned her gaze back to Nathalie and smiled as her cousin turned to meet her gaze.

And then Odile saw Nathalie lurch forwards. She was too close to the edge of the platform. She pivoted on the edge, trying to throw her balance away from the track and the oncoming train. There was a look of horror on Nathalie's face as she realised she was falling backwards.

Another woman stood near the edge, but she didn't try to reach out to grab Nathalie. She just stood there watching.

'NATHALIE!' screamed Odile. 'NATHALIE!' Her cries were smothered by the noise of the train as it bore down and hurtled through the station. Odile watched in horror as Nathalie disappeared from sight. Odile dropped her case and began running towards the edge. She was aware of some women on the platform screaming.

Then someone caught her. Stepped into her path, grabbing her and swinging her around. Strong arms clasped her.

'Where is it?' asked the woman whose grip was vicelike. 'Where's the book?'

All at once Odile realised this was the woman who had watched Nathalie fall, who had no doubt pushed her. This was Bochette.

Odile let out a scream but no one heard her. There was too much commotion going on around her. The train was trying to stop but the engine needed at least half a mile, such was its speed and weight. The squeal and screech of the locked iron wheels against the metal track pierced the air. People were shouting; others were crying. It was chaos.

Odile tried to wriggle free, but Bochette held her tighter. 'Where are the book and the dress?' she hissed.

'Get away from me,' shouted Odile, panic setting in. She fumbled in her coat pocket. Her hand found the hard-cold steel Barbara had slipped into her pocket just before she left.

Odile's fingers closed around the barrel of the handgun and managed to yank the weapon from her pocket.

Something made Bochette look down. She gasped and tried to grab the gun. Odile wrestled with her. She didn't know how long she could hold on to the gun. Bochette was strong and almost flinging her around.

Odile was aware of the trigger being squeezed. A muffled

bang rang out. Bochette locked her gaze onto Odile's. Her body jerked several times before she collapsed into a heap on the platform. Blood spewed from her chest. Her eyes stared up, unseeing, at the autumnal Sussex sky.

Chapter 41

Darcie

'Oh, Odile,' cried Darcie rushing to the side of the Frenchwoman who was now in tears, hunched over, her whole body shaking as she relived that moment. Darcie put her arms around the older woman and cradled her as if she were a child. 'I'm so sorry, Odile. I'm so sorry you had to go through that and I'm so sorry I made you relive it.'

Odile shook her head. 'I just hope Nathalie can forgive me for not telling the truth sooner.'

Darcie held Odile for a long time. What a heavy secret she'd kept for all these years, telling no one. It was some time before Odile stopped crying. Matt made some fresh sweet coffee for her.

'Thank you so much for sharing what happened with us,' said Darcie when Odile had a degree of composure.

The retelling had taken its toll on her and she looked exhausted.

'I'm glad I've told someone,' said Odile.

'There is one thing I can't quite clear up,' said Darcie. 'The picture of Coco Chanel wearing what is clearly this dress, how did that come about?'

'Yes, Nathalie told me what happened,' said Odile. 'She showed Chanel the sketchbook. Chanel was very taken with some of the designs and in particular the evening dress. She took a great interest in Nathalie's ideas.'

'Did Nathalie make the dress for her?'

'Yes. She made a version for Chanel.' said Odile. 'I assume Chanel had the dress finished at some point and that was how she came to be photographed in it. The original, Nathalie took when she fled.'

'Who sent Bochette to get the book?' asked Matt.

'The codes were very important so maybe the Gestapo. But I also believe she was trying to cover her own tracks and get information on any others named in the book to blackmail them, so she could ensure her own safety. The names, the codes were her bargaining chip. That's what Thomas told me later. The codes were to protect herself from the Gestapo and the names to protect herself from the Allies.'

'And the book and the dress were never retrieved from the locker?' asked Darcie.

'We didn't know where Nathalie had hidden them. She never told me. She didn't want me to have any information that might put me in danger,' explained Odile. 'If only we'd known that's where she had stored them.'

'So no one knew the dress Chanel was wearing was one that Nathalie had made for her,' said Matt.

'I'm afraid that is so,' said Odile. 'Of course, I knew Nathalie had made Chanel a dress, but I didn't know what it looked like. It all seemed so unimportant after the war and what happened to Nathalie was just one of many personal stories. It got lost among the bigger narrative of the war.'

'What happened after that day on the station?' asked Matt.

'I don't really know all the details. There was such a commotion. At first, no one realised what had happened to Bochette. Naturally, they were all concerned about Nathalie,' said Odile. 'I remember being taken to the police station. I was left in a cell for what seemed like hours. Tony Bertram, together with someone from MI6, came and got me. I think it surprised the local police, but they were told it was a matter of national security and they weren't to question or discuss.'

'Wow. They must have thought you were a spy or something,' said Matt.

'Maybe. I don't know what story was spun but, of course, I had several days of being questioned by MI6 and then I was allowed back to Bignor Manor. I stayed with the Bertrams.'

'And Thomas? What about him?' asked Darcie.

'He was absolutely heartbroken when he heard the news. He blamed himself. He had been away in London, something to do with the war effort, and he was planning to propose to Nathalie when he came back. He had been to Covent Garden and purchased the most beautiful diamond engagement ring.'

'Oh, that's so sad,' said Darcie.

'Isn't it? I knew Nathalie would have accepted. She loved him very much. I had never seen her so happy.'

'What happened to him, do you know?' asked Matt.

'I believe he did find happiness again and went on to marry. She was a widow. She didn't have any children and she and Thomas didn't have any either. But I like to think he found some comfort in his life.'

'I hope he did, too,' said Darcie. 'Everyone deserves to be happy, even if life doesn't turn out as planned.' She wanted to ask about Odile but couldn't quite bring herself to be so forward.

'And as for myself,' said Odile, as if able to read Darcie's unspoken question. 'When I was young, it was expected that I would marry and have children but I always knew it was something I never wanted.'

'I think being happy is more important than conforming,' said Matt.

'Indeed. I stayed with the Bertrams until 1945 when I was able to go back to France, and Tony Bertram took a posting in Paris. I moved back with my parents and I cared for them until they both passed away.'

'I'm sorry,' said Darcie.

'Don't be sorry,' said Odile. 'I was happy. Maybe not as happy as I was in Bignor, but happy enough. I did consider going back to England at that point, but the Bertrams had moved on and I knew I had to make a life for myself. So I threw myself into being an aunt to Gaston's and Rachelle's children, Paulette being one of them. I've always been at my happiest looking after and caring for youngsters. I really should never have been the youngest in my family.' She smiled at Darcie. 'So, I hope that answers all your questions.'

'I think it does,' said Darcie, warmly. She bent down and gave Odile a hug. 'I'll do my very best to honour Nathalie's memory.'

Odile patted her arm. 'I have no doubt you will. I'm happy the dress and the book are in the hands of someone like you. Nathalie would approve.'

'Sorry, just one more thing, if I may?' asked Matt. 'Did anyone else know about the book and the codes?'

'There was talk of it some years ago,' said Odile. 'I had a visit from a gentleman claiming to be the grandson of someone who worked with Nathalie at the Ritz.'

'Really?' said Darcie. 'Who was that?'

'I can't remember his name, I'm afraid.'

'What did he want?' asked Matt.

'We didn't get that far. All he said was, it was about Nathalie and something she had belonging to his grandmother,' said Odile. 'He made me very uncomfortable. I told him he would have to come back another time when my niece, Paulette, and her husband were there. I didn't see him again. Paulette's husband phoned him and made it clear he was to leave me alone. Shortly after that, my house was broken into. It was very upsetting so I went to live with Paulette before I came here.'

'Do you think it was related?' asked Darcie, thinking of her own experience.

'There was no proof, but it was quite a coincidence,' said Odile. 'It's a wonder I didn't have nightmares about him.

Horrid man with a scar running through his eyebrow, around his eye and onto his cheek.'

Darcie looked incredulously at Odile. 'A scar, here?' She traced her finger around her own eye.

'Yes. Through his left eye and around,' replied Odile. 'He had the most piercing blue eyes I think I've ever seen.'

'It's got to be Padgett,' said Matt. 'It literally can't be anyone else.'

'It must be him,' said Darcie. 'But why does Padgett want the book and dress so badly? And who is his grandmother?'

Chapter 42

Darcie

The journey back to Paris was filled with a morass of emotions. Sadness at the story of what had happened to Nathalie. Joy at finding out the truth about the dress and drawings. Disbelief that Padgett had previously tried to get hold of the sketchbook.

'There has to be something in the book,' said Matt. 'We need to have a closer look at it when we get back.'

'What about just confronting Padgett?' asked Darcie. 'Calling his bluff.'

Matt considered this for a moment. 'I don't think he will fold that easily. He'll want us to prove it. We need to find out more about him and exactly who his grandmother was.'

Darcie spent most of the journey googling Christophe Padgett and the history of the Ritz, following every thread that might lead her to find a connection between them, but drew a complete blank.

'It might be his grandmother went by a different name, if it's on his mother's side of the family,' said Darcie. 'I don't really know how to progress this.'

'The answer is in the sketchbook, I'm positive,' said Matt. 'We need some sort of expert to look at it. Nathalie told Odile there were names and codes in the book. We're not exactly Turing; we won't be able to break the codes or even recognise them. That will need some sort of military wartime expert, but if we can find the names, we might be able to make a connection.'

'Whatever Padgett is up to,' said Darcie. 'I'm pretty sure the House of Chanel know nothing about it.'

'I agree. I don't think they'd be too happy to find out either.'

When they arrived back in Matt's apartment in Paris, by rights they should have been shattered, but Darcie was far too wired to even think about sleep.

'I want to look at the book properly,' she said, plonking herself down on the sofa. She opened the sketchbook out in front of her and laid it on the coffee table. Matt brought them both a coffee over and sat down beside her.

He flicked to one of the designs and the corresponding page. 'So here are lots of numbers and workings-out which just look like measurements, calculations, how much fabric is needed et cetera.'

'On the face of it, they mean nothing,' said Darcie. 'But they must be the codes. We have no idea what we're looking at but these were written by Nathalie, giving names, details, information. It's amazing to think this is actually part of the war effort.'

'It's pretty crazy,' agreed Matt. 'So, we need an expert to look at those. In the meantime, we've got to find out if there's any other information hidden on the pages.'

'Maybe between the pages?' suggested Darcie, carefully looking at each page to see if two had been stuck together.

'I think that's too simplistic. It would be easily discovered,' said Matt. 'It's got to be something more sophisticated.'

They both pondered the conundrum for several minutes.

'It's nothing obvious. It can't be obvious,' mused Darcie. 'So it must be hidden and you'd only know to look for it if you knew it was there in the first place.' She peered closer at the page with the blue bow-dress design. 'I don't know why, but I feel it's here.'

'On this page? You think she's hidden it on what is potentially her most famous design?'

'Look, this may sound far-fetched and a bit spy thriller, but during the war, agents on both sides used invisible ink,' said Darcie. 'I went to a talk about it once when I was at a World War Two show. It was fascinating.'

'And you think the information is here, staring us right in the face?' said Matt. 'But how would we know?'

'It's a bit of a long shot but I think I know how.' Darcie put the book down. 'Do you have an iron?'

Matt gave her an odd look. 'Sure.'

'Go and get it. Plug it in.' Darcie could feel the excitement building in her stomach. 'There were several different types of ink and different ways of revealing the invisible ink. Sometimes it was a chemical and other times just good old-fashioned heat. I saw this at the show.'

Matt retrieved his iron from the cupboard and plugged it in. 'Imagine if it's that simple.'

'I know, right.' Darcie grinned. She took the book over to the worktop and picked up the iron. 'God, I hope I'm right and I'm not about to burn this design. That would be a catastrophe.' For a second, she hovered the iron over the page, before taking a deep breath and lowering it onto the sketchbook.

Gently Darcie pressed the iron onto the paper.

'Rub it around. Don't keep it in one place,' said Matt.

Holding her breath, Darcie slid the iron back and forth across the paper. 'I don't think anything's happening.'

'Keep doing it.'

The paper began to turn a yellowy-brown colour. Then, to Darcie's amazement and delight, the outlines of block capital letters began to form. 'It's working! Matt, it's working!'

A few minutes later, Darcie was looking at a whole page of writing. It was all in French and the handwriting was old-fashioned, but it was clearly names and a sentence or two underneath.

'I can't believe it,' said Matt. 'This is amazing.'

'What does it say? Can you understand any of it?' asked Darcie, as Matt studied the writing.

'It's mostly names with dates and times. Something here about troop movements. Something else about when . . . Göring . . . yes, definitely Göring is going to be at a meeting.' Matt paused to look up at Darcie. 'This is gold. Priceless.'

'Is there anything there about Padgett?'

Matt took another careful look at the paper. 'I can't see the name Padgett but like we said, if it's his maternal grandmother, then it would be a different name.'

'Are there any female names there.' She gripped his arm. 'Wait, that woman who came to England. The one who pushed Nathalie under the train. What was her name?'

'Damn, what did Odile say? Boch . . . Bochette. That's it.' He leaned over the page again, scanning the writing. 'Here! There's something here.'

Matt's usual laid-back attitude had been replaced by a sense of excitement.

'What does it say?'

'*Bochette. Collaborator. Spy*,' translated Matt.

'Nothing else?'

'I'm not sure. There's something else.' Matt studied the page for what seemed at eternity. 'It says: *Bochette, gold ring ruby stone, statue of angel, gold five-bar gate bracelet. From Kranz. Payment.*'

Darcie frowned as she computed the information. 'Kranz was paying Bochette for information. Jewellery being the currency.'

'Yeah and I bet that jewellery was stolen from Jewish people,' concluded Matt.

'And do you remember Padgett saying he was leaving the House of Chanel next year to go into politics?' said Darcie. 'Well, he wouldn't want any of this getting out, would he? Imagine the damage that would do to his political aspirations if it was even rumoured he knew the origins of the jewellery and had made no attempt to hand them back.'

'That would look pretty bad for him,' agreed Matt.

'We need to set up a meeting with Padgett,' said Darcie, thinking out loud as she arranged her thoughts into something of a plan.

The following morning they were once again inside the offices of the House of Chanel, with Christophe Padgett sat one side of the table and his two lawyers next to him.

'I'm going to assume you've asked for this meeting as you've finally come to your senses,' said Padgett. He leaned back in his chair, unfastening his jacket button.

'We've just been to see Odile Grandis,' said Darcie. She watched Padgett closely for any reaction. The only tell was a fast blink of his eyes.

'You'll have to enlighten me. What has this to do with the sketchbook?'

'Odile Grandis remembers you coming to see her several years ago, enquiring about the sketchbook,' Darcie continued.

'It's not something I recall,' said Padgett. 'Now can we get back to business? I'm very busy.'

'It seems the sketchbook is proving very popular,' said Darcie. She smiled sweetly at Padgett. 'The apartment I'm staying in was broken into.'

'I'm sorry to hear that.'

'I was followed by the same two men who broke into the apartment. They were looking for the sketchbook too.' Darcie paused and met Padgett's steely gaze. 'Odile Grandis tells me there were secrets in the sketchbook, which would explain why everyone is so interested in it. Anyway, to cut a long story short, Matt and I have discovered those secrets. The names, the codes, the information.'

This visibly jolted Padgett. He repositioned himself in the chair and adjusted the knot of his tie. 'I have no idea what information that might be.'

'I think you do,' said Darcie. 'There was one very interesting name, which I think you will be familiar with – Bochette.'

The colour drained from Padgett's face. He cleared his throat, before speaking. 'The name means nothing to me.'

Matt made a small scoffing noise.

Darcie let out a sigh. 'Bochette was your maternal grandmother and she was heavily involved with the Gestapo during the war. She worked with Nathalie Leroux.' She tapped the sketchbook. 'Nathalie Leroux was a secret agent, feeding information about the Germans in the Ritz to the Allied forces and the Resistance.'

'I think you will find a lot of Parisians worked with the Germans because they had to, just to survive,' said Padgett. 'It wasn't because they wanted to.'

'But your grandmother wanted to,' said Matt.

'What do you mean?' Padgett glared at his accusers.

'Your grandmother took payment from the Gestapo,' said Darcie. 'Nathalie Leroux documented several pieces of jewellery your grandmother was given by an officer named Kranz. Jewellery Kranz kept as currency. Jewellery that had been stolen from Jewish people.'

Darcie didn't miss Padgett subconsciously twiddle the gold ring on his finger. 'This is nonsense,' he said.

Darcie purposefully looked at the ring. 'I believe a gold ring with a ruby stone, such as that one, is recorded in the book,' she said.

Padgett's hands flew apart and he adjusted the knot on his tie once again. 'This ring, it's been in my family for a long time.'

'Can you prove its provenance?' asked Matt.

Darcie wanted to high-five Matt at that point and pushed on, sensing they had the Frenchman on the back foot.

'Your grandmother must have known Nathalie had information on her. And was scared that, at some point in the future, she'd be held accountable for not only being a spy but what essentially was theft. That's why she followed

Nathalie to England and murdered her and then met her own death.'

'And now you want your grandmother's name kept out of it because you would be held accountable for not returning the jewellery. Not a good political move, right?' finished Matt.

'This is nonsense,' said Padgett raising his voice. 'Fabrication. Stories. Lies.'

He got to his feet, pushing his chair away behind him.

At that moment, the door to the boardroom opened and in walked a suited gentleman. He was in his mid-fifties and waved his hand towards Padgett. 'Sit down, Padgett,' he said with an air of authority. Padgett did as he was told.

'Ah, Monsieur Auclair,' said Darcie. 'You've come at just the right time.' She smiled at the senior executive from the House of Chanel whom she and Matt had spoken with over a video call the previous afternoon. He had been most interested to hear what they had to say about Padgett.

'Monsieur,' began Padgett. 'I don't know what this young lady has told you, but . . .'

Auclair put his hand up to silence Padgett. 'What Mademoiselle Marchant has told me has been most disconcerting. I have been alarmed to hear the details. Purporting to be acting on behalf of the House of Chanel is a very serious accusation. One that I am not prepared to tolerate. And if the information I've heard about you knowingly possessing jewellery stolen from Jews during the war is correct, then you are not someone the House of Chanel wants any association with.'

He called out in French and immediately two police officers and two other men appeared in the room. Darcie assumed these were the House of Chanel solicitors that Auclair had said would be present.

Auclair pointed at the men sat either side of Padgett. 'If you are Monsieur Padgett's legal representatives, you should go with your client now. He's about to be arrested and taken in for questioning.'

'This is outrageous,' declared Padgett as the two police officers advanced towards him. 'You cannot believe what she said. What does she know?'

'She knows a great deal, as it happens,' said Auclair. He looked at the police officers. 'There's no need to handcuff him. He's not going to make a fuss, are you, Padgett?'

Padgett was breathing hard. The colour had returned to his face and he was practically red now with rage and indignation. 'You will regret this,' he ground out through his clenched jaw.

'I don't think so,' replied Auclair. 'Please be advised you are now officially dismissed from the services of the House of Chanel. We take these allegations and false representation of the company very seriously. *Au revoir*, Padgett.'

Darcie exchanged a look with Matt and then watched as Padgett was ushered out of the room, followed by his solicitors.

Auclair turned to Darcie. '*Mademoiselle*,' he began.

'Please, call me Darcie.'

Auclair smiled. 'Darcie, I would like to formally apologise on behalf of the House of Chanel for what has happened,' he said, taking a seat at the table. 'We have had concerns about Padgett's rather robust manner in the past, so while I am alarmed to hear how he has conducted himself, I am not entirely surprised.'

'What will happen to him now?' asked Darcie.

'Of course, the matter concerning the break-in and intimidation, possession of stolen Jewish belongings et cetera, is a police matter. We at the House of Chanel will have to go through our own process for dismissal and that is an internal matter, as I'm sure you will appreciate.'

'Of course,' said Darcie. 'We understand that. We're just glad he's going to be held to account for what he's done.'

'The House of Chanel is very sorry to hear what's happened,' said Auclair. 'We'd like to make an offer, without prejudice, as a gesture of goodwill.'

Darcie listened in amazement at Auclair's offer. It was beyond anything she had imagined.

He was talking about fashion scholarships and charitable donations to war veterans' societies and all in honour of Nathalie Leroux. 'Once all the finer details have been arranged, we will, of course, let you know,' said Auclair.

'That's amazing,' said Darcie. 'I'm so happy. It feels the right thing to do to honour Nathalie's memory and her part in the war effort and the ultimate sacrifice she paid.'

'Indeed,' said Auclair. There was a small silence and the Frenchman cleared his throat. '*Alors*, now the rather delicate matter of the dress and sketchbook.'

Darcie looked at Matt. They had discussed at length what she wanted to do with Nathalie's prized possessions. There was one thing she had been in agreement with Padgett about – she didn't want them locked away in a cupboard and forgotten about again.

'What did you have in mind?' asked Matt, taking the lead, knowing this was the hardest part for Darcie.

'As you bought them, you are the legal owner of the items,' said Auclair. 'It may be that you want to sell the items. They will be worth a lot of money, especially once they have been authenticated.'

Darcie looked up. 'It's not about the money,' she said.

Auclair eyed her for a moment. 'If you want to keep them, again as the legal owner, that is your prerogative.'

'I might be the legal owner,' said Darcie. 'But I don't feel I'm the rightful owner. I've asked Odile Grandis if she would like them back, as she is the closest surviving relative of Nathalie, but she was adamant I was to keep them. Having said that, I don't know what I should do with them now. I want people to know Nathalie's story.'

'What did you have in mind?' asked Auclair.

'My mother works for a fashion publication,' said Matt. 'We thought about writing an article about them.'

'I can see how that would work,' said Auclair. He put his

hands together and rested them on the table. 'What would you say to loaning the dress and the sketchbook to the House of Chanel?'

'Loaning?' Darcie wasn't sure what Auclair was proposing.

'Yes. We borrow them. At all times you remain the legal owner but the House of Chanel will be guardian. There is a UK exhibition in London next year and we would be honoured to display the dress, the sketchbook, and Nathalie Leroux's story.'

Darcie thought her eyes were going to pop out of her head. 'Oh, my goodness. That's amazing,' she gasped. 'Really?'

Auclair smiled warmly. '*Oui*, really.'

Tears of absolute joy filled Darcie's eyes. 'Thank you, so much,' she said, before starting to cry.

Matt put an arm around her. 'Happy tears, right?'

Darcie nodded. 'The happiest tears possible.'

Chapter 43

Darcie

After her adventures in Paris, Darcie had returned to England and had only told Lena, Chloe, and Hannah the details of what had happened and the outcome of her meeting with Padgett. She had, of course, told them about meeting Matt, but she had managed to avoid telling them about just how involved she'd become with him.

It had been difficult to say goodbye to him at the airport three weeks ago, but she hadn't wanted to come across as needy or having any expectations of their relationship. If she could call it a relationship – knowing someone for two weeks, wasn't exactly a relationship, more like a fling.

She was surprised at how much saying goodbye to Matt bothered her and how much she actually missed him. They had been keeping in touch with text messages every few days and they had FaceTimed but it wasn't the same as being with him. It felt disjointed, awkward, and distant.

It was a Friday morning, Darcie had just opened up the shop and was settling down in front of her laptop to check her emails.

Her heart jumped as she caught sight of a message from the House of Chanel in her inbox. Without hesitation, she opened the email, hoping it would be the confirmation she had been waiting for.

Dear Darcie

Following our meeting in Paris last month, our legal team have now been able to secure the annual charitable donation for the next ten years to the war veterans' charities both in the United Kingdom and in France as discussed and listed in our agreement. I am pleased to confirm the first payment has been made by bank transfer as per the attached receipt.

We are also delighted to confirm the Nathalie Leroux Scholarships for the Academy of Art & Design to support under-represented groups in both London and Paris have been established, with five scholarships available per institution. Again, further details are in the attached documents.

With all the necessary authentication certificates agreed both here at the House of Chanel and with the UK authorities, which I have no doubt will all be confirmed, we are honoured to be your nominated custodians of the Nathalie Leroux dress and sketchbook. These items will form part of the London 2023 Chanel exhibition and further exhibitions worldwide. As such, please find enclosed VIP tickets to attend the show at the Victoria & Albert Museum where you will be able to view the items on display.

We have also added the items to the official Chanel website, which you can see by following the link below.

Finally, we have reviewed the article prepared by Vivien Forbes-Langdon, editor of the *The History of Us* magazine, telling Nathalie Leroux's story and have approved the contents, which went to press last week.

I don't wish to sour the tone of this email, but I wanted to reassure you that Christophe Padgett has officially been dismissed from the employment of the House of Chanel for gross misconduct and misrepresentation. I understand that, unfortunately, the police have been unable to provide hard evidence connecting him to the break-in at your apartment and, for that, I would extend my sympathies. Please be assured that Padgett will never work in the fashion industry again.

On a personal note, I would like to extend my sincere gratitude for all your efforts to uncover Nathalie Leroux's story. I feel humbled by your determination.

Kindest regards

Daniel Auclair

Darcie closed the email. She should also thank Matt and his mother for backing her with this story. She forwarded a copy of the email to Matt.

Hi Matt

Take a look at this!

Thank you so much for everything you did for me when I was in Paris. I will never forget your kindness and blind faith. I'm not sure I'll ever be able to repay you but if you're ever in England I can treat you to a proper cup of English tea.

Catch up soon,

Darcie

X

She went through the rest of her emails and was about to close the laptop when Lena and Chloe appeared in the shop.

'Everything all right?' asked Darcie, suspicious at their presence. 'You both look very guilty.'

'Oh, we're fine,' said Lena.

Darcie eyed them speculatively. 'OK. If you say so. Anyway, look at this email I've received from the House of Chanel.' She reopened Auclair's email.

She stepped back while Lena and Chloe peered at the screen.

'Oh, Darcie, that's wonderful,' said Lena. 'I'm so glad something good came out of it.'

'And that it's for people who are under-represented or

experiencing hardships is just brilliant,' said Chloe. 'You have a good heart, my dear sister.'

'What I don't understand though,' said Lena, 'is why Padgett went to all that trouble. If he'd kept quiet, no one would have been any the wiser or even connected him to that collaborator, Bochette.'

'I know,' said Darcie. 'Padgett was ultimately a vain and greedy man. I believe he wanted the dress for his own personal collection or perhaps to sell to the House of Chanel, or a higher bidder, but he wanted to control the narrative, the backstory, and ensure his grandmother's name wasn't connected to his.'

A ping from the laptop broke their conversation.

'Aren't you going to open it?' asked Lena.

'Yes. It might be important,' said Chloe.

Now Darcie knew there was something going on, but she couldn't for the life of her figure out what it was. 'You two are up to something,' she said. 'And I'll find out.'

'Oh, just check your email,' said Lena. 'Before I crack under interrogation.'

'It's from Matt,' said Darcie, pretending she hadn't noticed the little flutter of excitement she got whenever he contacted her.

Hi Darcie
    That's awesome. I'm so happy for you. And for Odile and Nathalie.
    You know you don't have to repay me. You don't owe me anything. I was invested just as much as you were.
    Anyway, there's something I wanted to give you. Can you make time for a coffee or even an English cup of tea?
    I'm just across the square.
    Matt

Darcie had to steady herself on the counter as she reread the email. Just as she did, the bell tinkled above the door to the shop.

It was Hannah. 'Is this good timing?'

'It's perfect timing,' said Lena.

Darcie looked at her sister, her mother, and her friend. 'You all know?'

'Of course we do,' said Chloe with a laugh.

'But how?' It all felt so surreal, Darcie thought she was going to have to do that pinch-me thing.

'Oh, that's just detail, but if you must know, Matt got in touch with me on Facebook,' said Chloe. 'He didn't want to show up and put you on the spot.'

'But I never said anything to you about him, not in detail,' said Darcie.

'Oh, you didn't have to,' said Chloe, turning Darcie around. 'It was very clear how much you liked him.' She took Darcie's coat from the peg and slipped it onto her. 'Now, Hannah is here to look after the shop. I'm taking Mum to her physio appointment and you' – she bundled Darcie around the counter and towards the door – 'my dear sister, are going across the road to that coffee shop where a certain American is waiting for you.'

Darcie stepped out onto the pavement. She could see the coffee shop across the road and, yes, there was Matt, sitting in the window, looking right back at her.

Darcie's feet were taking her, in an almost trancelike state, across the square and into the coffee shop. She walked over to the table.

'Hi,' she said, suddenly feeling tongue-tied in front of him.

'Hey,' he replied, getting to his feet and kissing her on the cheek. 'You OK?'

'I think so,' said Darcie, not moving.

'Look, you never downloaded those pictures I took of you by Sacré-Cœur.' He took several photographs from his bag and held them out to her. 'I thought I'd drop by with them.'

'Drop by?' said Darcie, raising her eyebrows.

Her shock was wearing off and questions were queuing up in her head. Seeing Matt again, and those photographs of their first meeting, brought all her feelings of happiness that she associated with him rushing to the fore. He looked even more handsome than she remembered. Even more attractive.

An unexpected ball of emotion rolled up and lodged itself in her throat. She managed to force the words out. 'I didn't know if I'd see you again.'

'Did you think I was going to let you go that easily, Darcie Bytheway?' said Matt, moving closer still. 'I'm kinda tired of Paris. When you left, the magic of the city left with you.'

'Did it?' Her voice was only a whisper.

'I thought I'd relocate.'

'Where were you thinking of?'

'I hear there are some cool places in West Sussex to photograph,' said Matt. 'That's if it's OK with you.' Darcie took a moment to compute what he was saying. Matt reached out and took her hand. 'Is that OK?'

Darcie didn't care she was in the middle of the café, she flung her arms around Matt. 'It's more than OK. It's perfect.'

Epilogue

'It's arrived!'

Darcie looked up as Matt walked into her shop, holding a magazine aloft in his hand. He came up to the counter and leaned over to give Darcie a kiss, before dropping the latest publication of *The History of Us* onto the counter. 'Page five.'

'I can't wait to see it,' said Darcie, flicking straight to the article. She smiled as she began reading.

Lost Dressmaker of Paris Found

Identity of Chanel seamstress discovered after 80 years

When business owner Darcie Marchant purchased a suitcase from a left-luggage locker in a small English town in West Sussex, she never suspected what history she would find between the pages of a sketchbook.

'My mom has sent a copy to Odile,' said Matt. 'Special courier so she should receive hers today.'

'Oh good,' said Darcie. 'I spoke to Odile on the phone yesterday.'

'How was she?'

'You know, taking it all in her stride and only concerned that Nathalie is given full credit for everything she did and her ultimate sacrifice.'

'I think she'll be pleased,' said Matt with a smile.

Darcie turned back to the article and continued reading the abridged but detailed story of Nathalie Leroux and the Coco Chanel dress.

After a few minutes, she was nearly at the end of the double-spread article.

'It's making me emotional just reading it, even though I know all the details,' she said. 'Sometimes, it feels like it was all a dream.'

'I can assure you, it wasn't,' said Matt. He tapped the page. 'This is Odile's quote.'

Darcie took a deep breath before reading on.

Odile Grandis now lives quietly in a retirement home in Brittany but this week, together with her niece and great-niece, she visited Paris for a private viewing of the Chanel collection, which showcases Nathalie Leroux's story. Odile said, 'I have nothing but praise for the House of Chanel for everything they have done and cannot thank them enough for their understanding and generosity. If Nathalie were here, she would be ecstatic that her dressmaking skills have been displayed amid the Chanel collection. It was a dream of hers and I am so honoured to be here to witness her dream come true.'

Darcie swallowed hard at the words before her. 'I feel so humbled by everything Nathalie did,' she said. 'Not to mention everything Odile went through. I'm so glad everyone else knows now as well.'

Matt came around the counter and put his arm around her. 'You made that happen,' he said. 'I'm so proud of you.'

Darcie leaned into him. 'I couldn't have done this without you. Thank you.' She kissed Matt, before turning back to the article.

With tears in her eyes, Odile continued, 'And although it cannot be denied that this is a most wonderful dress and that my dear cousin was beyond talented, we must not forget her undeniable bravery and the ultimate sacrifice she made, not in the name of fashion but in the name of love for her fellow humans and loyalty to her country.'

When asked if she was happy Nathalie's story had finally been shared with the world, Odile replied, 'It is not Nathalie Leroux's story, it is . . . at long last . . . the truth.'

Acknowledgements

First of all, I want to extend a huge thank you to everyone at Embla Books for all their hard work and dedication in bringing this book to publication. Special thanks to my fantastic editor, Cara Chimirri, for her feedback and incredible insight into the story and how to make it truly shine.

Thanks, as always, to my wonderful agent, Hattie Grünewald, for all the encouragement and hard work that goes on behind the scenes.

I couldn't *not* mention my writing buddies, Mandy Baggot and Catherine Miller, who have always been there to listen to me ramble on about my book, offer their advice and thoughts, not to mention their expert cheerleading skills and endless encouragement (the latter also known as a good talking-to).

Finally, a huge thank you to my readers for all your wonderful support and messages – you are very much appreciated.

About the Author

Suzanne Fortin writes women's fiction with a dual timeline, often against the backdrop of France, and in particular Southern Brittany, which inspires the settings of her books. Despite having had a home in the region for over twenty years, Suzanne still wrestles with fluency in the Breton dialect!

Suzanne also writes mystery and suspense as Sue Fortin, and is a *USA Today* bestseller and Amazon UK #1 and Amazon US #3 bestseller. She has sold over a million copies of her books, which have been translated into multiple languages.

About Embla Books

Embla Books is a digital-first publisher of standout commercial adult fiction. Passionate about storytelling, the team at Embla publish books that will make you 'laugh, love, look over your shoulder and lose sleep'. Launched by Bonnier Books UK in 2021, the imprint is named after the first woman from the creation myth in Norse mythology, who was carved by the gods from a tree trunk found on the seashore – an image of the kind of creative work and crafting that writers do, and a symbol of how stories shape our lives.

Find out about some of our other books and stay in touch:

Twitter, Facebook, Instagram: @emblabooks
Newsletter: https://bit.ly/emblanewsletter